Elizabeth Waite was born in Tooting and lived there until she was thirty-four years old. During the war she worked as a bus conductress at Merton Garage. In 1956 she and her husband moved to Devon and bought their first guesthouse.

Now retired, they live in East Sussex.

Cockney Family

Elizabeth Waite

WARNER BOOKS

A *Warner* Book

First published in Great Britain
by Warner Books in 1994
Reprinted 1995, 1997, 1998, 2000

Copyright © Elizabeth Waite 1994

The moral right of the author has been asserted

A CIP catalogue record for this book
is available from the British Library.

ISBN 0 7515 0919 1

Photytypeset by Intype, London
Printed in England by Clays Ltd, St Ives plc

Warner Books
A Division of
Little, Brown and Company (UK)
Brettenham House
Lancaster Place
London WC2E 7EN

Chapter One

PATSY OWEN HAD been legally married for less than five years. That didn't alter the fact that she had two boys aged twelve and ten and twin daughters who would be seven years old in three months time. She herself was thirty-one. Certainly she hadn't led a dull life, and the hardships she had had to endure in the early stages hadn't done her any harm. She smiled to herself as she stood squeezing woollies in the kitchen sink on this brilliant Monday morning in July 1936.

Up to her elbows in soap-suds, she peered through the open window and tried to make out exactly what mischief her boys were involved in now. The noise and the laughter coming from the shed at the bottom of the garden had already aroused her curiosity. Alexander was the eldest but David, two years younger, never lagged behind in any scheme that they concocted. They had only broken up from school on Friday; now she faced six weeks of the summer holidays and Patsy knew full well that she would have her work cut out to keep tabs on the pair of them. They've got so much damned energy, she mused, pulling out the bung and turning on the cold tap.

Her smile widened. Her boys were nothing if not resourceful. One way and another they earned themselves quite a few pennies to add to their pocket money.

With the large tin bowl, piled high with well-rinsed jumpers and cardigans, resting on her hip, Patsy reached for the peg-bag, crossed the floor and flung open the back door. She took a deep breath as she walked towards the clothes-line. The sky was bright blue, not a cloud in sight, and the sun was already very warm. Standing on her toes she reached up, pulling each garment into shape before securing it with a dolly-peg. The sun caught the diamonds in the half circle of one of the rings that she wore on the third finger of her left hand and the glitter from it had her laughing out loud. She might only have been Eddie's legal wife for the past five years, but she had worn these rings for thirteen years. Of course she laughed. Anyone who knew the details of that September day in 1923 would have to be half-way round the twist if they didn't think the events that had taken place then were absolutely hilarious. She had promised herself time and time again that as soon as her children were old enough she was going to sit them all down and relate the full story to them.

When she was sixteen years old she had applied to the courts for permission to marry Johnny Jackson. It had been a disastrous marriage, and in a very short time Johnny and his gypsy family had told her in no uncertain terms to clear off. When Patsy met Eddie, Johnny had adopted a dog-in-the-manger attitude. Although he hadn't wanted her, he couldn't bear the fact that someone else loved her and wanted to marry her. He refused to even consider divorce.

Eddie Owen had changed her name to his by deed poll. As they had left the solicitor's office on that memorable day the skies had opened and the rain had lashed down. They had sheltered in the entrance hall of the Wimbledon branch of the Salvation Army, and it was there that Eddie had slipped a thick, plain gold ring and a second ring with a half-circle of diamonds on to her finger. Both rings had belonged to his mother.

Over the years there had been many a time when Patsy was plagued by the fact that she was not, in the eyes of the law, Mrs Edward Owen. To Eddie that had never been a problem. As far as he was concerned, he would repeatedly tell her, she had been his wife from the very first day that she agreed to live with him in rooms above his father's grocer's shop. Their feelings for each other had never dwindled. This great big man was still the very centre of her life. She had only to look straight into those huge dark brown eyes and, without words, the love that they had shared for so long spoke volumes.

Patsy's thoughts were interrupted now by the

slamming open of the back gate. 'Hey, steady on,' she called, but there was merriment in her tone as she turned and squinted her eyes against the bright sunshine and watched her twin daughters race across the grass towards her.

'Auntie Amy said if you've finished all your work shall we take our tea up on the Common this afternoon?'

'Did she now?' Patsy laughed at the serious expression on Ellen's face.

'Oh, go on, Mum, let's, and can we have a boat out on the pond as well?' The pleading note in Emma's voice was hard to resist.

Patsy gave in. 'All right, tell Auntie Amy we'll be ready by two o'clock, but I'm not sure that the boys will want to come.'

The twins made a grimace at each other and Emma called back over her shoulder as they ran, 'Good job if they don't come.'

Patsy's heart was filled with love as she watched them go. They were both so open and uncomplicated and each had a very lovable personality, always sunny and cheerful. Eddie maintained that the twins were a miniature replica of herself. They certainly had her colouring: clear green eyes, rich dark brown hair with the same chestnut glint, creamy skin and rosy cheeks. They were identical in looks, but there was a distinct difference in their attitude to life. Ellen, the eldest by about ten minutes, was a serious girl, easily saddened by other folks' problems. Emma was a tomboy. A girl with a mind of her own, a soft but sharp tongue, and already showing signs of having a strong set of her own opinions.

Using both hands, Patsy tugged hard on the rope until she had enough spare to wind around the pulley hook, then having made sure it was well and truly secure she stepped back and sighed with satisfaction. The woollens were now high in the air and would soon dry on a day like this. Turning round, she took a few steps to where the other clothes-line ran parallel. Feeling the sheets she muttered, 'I'm glad I got the copper on the go so early this morning and got this lot out. With any luck I'll be able to get them ironed and set to air before we take the kids out. Right now, though, I think I've earned myself a cuppa.' Picking up the empty bowl, she was walking towards the back door when something made her change her mind. 'I'd better see what the boys are up to first,' she murmured with a grin. She had to put her shoulder to the door and push hard before she was able to see inside the shed. The happy grin vanished, and Patsy's face dropped a mile. 'What on earth is going on in 'ere?' she asked crossly.

'Aw, Mum! You wasn't supposed to see it yet! Now you've gone and spoiled our surprise.'

'Surprise,' she almost yelled. 'Where did all this rubbish come from?'

'It's not rubbish, old Mr Draper will buy it all, and if you get out of the doorway, Mum, we'll show you what we've been making. It's taken us three days, but it's almost ready now.'

Patsy sighed with resignation. Both her sons were very dear to her, but there were times when she wondered just where they were heading. Alexander was tough, heavy in build, already as tall as she was, and he looked even more like Eddie now. He had the same good-looking features, thick mop of wavy hair and vivid dark brown eyes. Alex would never be contented with his lot: give him the stars and he would want the sky to go with them. One thing about this eldest son of hers, he would always be willing to go out on a limb and get for himself whatever he thought was his due; he didn't believe that the world owed him a living. David also resembled his father but he was slender, lighter in build. His temperament was nice, easy-going, asking nothing more of life than whatever came easily. The only thing that bothered Patsy about David was his admiration for Alex. If Alex told David to jump through a ring of fire she was sure that David would do it.

Patsy almost had to leap backwards from the doorway of the garden shed as her two boys came rumbling towards her. Bent nearly double, they were steering what she supposed was meant to be a cart. It was a ramshackle affair, really just a wooden orange-box mounted on a set of old pram wheels, with a length of thick rope threaded through the front panel of the box by which means they could control and direct the cart.

Alex straightened up and with a wave of his hand he indicated the contents of the shed. 'We'll shift all that this afternoon, won't we, David?'

Patsy shook her head in disbelief. Old newspapers tied with string were piled high on the work-bench, the floor was covered with dirty wooden boxes from which spilled beer bottles, jam jars and pickle jars. Propped against these were coarse sacks overflowing with filthy rags.

'Aw my Gawd! We'll be overrun with rats, and you two will have to be deloused,' their mother told them as they stood grinning cheekily at her. 'It's not more than a couple of days since I looked in here, how the hell could you have managed to gather up this lot in such a short time?' Giving the boys no time to think of an answer she rattled on. 'This would never have happened if your father had been home, or Grandfather come to that.'

'Oh, come on, Mum, you can't say that. Dad wouldn't create about us earning a bob or so, you know darn well he wouldn't.' Alex looked his mother straight in the eye, defying her to disagree.

'You can cut the cheek, young man, as quick as you like,' Patsy retorted sharply. 'It's not the earning of a few coppers that I'm objecting to, it's the handling of the filthy rubbish. God alone knows where it's been or who you got it from. But I'll tell you this much, the pair of you can start stacking that barrow right now, and I don't care how many trips you have to make up the alley to old Tom Draper's yard – I want this shed cleared and swept clean before the day is out.'

No sooner had she turned her back than she heard the pair of them snigger, and quickly she swung round. 'So you think it's funny, do you? Well, let's see what it takes to wipe the smile to the other side of your faces. First, you'll only get bread an' cheese out here for your lunch. Then when you have cleared everything up you will both get into the bath and have a good scrub down before you'll get any dinner tonight.'

There was a silence as Patsy picked up her bowl and headed for the house. She was grinning broadly herself now; little devils, she said to herself, but if the truth were known she was admiring the resourcefulness of her sons. They would never starve!

Patsy sat on the grass with her back against the thick tree-trunk, sucking a boiled sweet, smiling and nodding encouragingly as she watched her twin girls play at the edge of the pond. Dresses tucked into the waist-bands of their knickers, socks and shoes abandoned, they were bubbling with enthusiasm as they ran in and out of the water.

Amy Andrews was being her amusing self, relating to Patsy titbits of news and gossip about the neighbours in Clapham Manor Street, and, as usual Patsy found her stories — or at least the telling of them — very funny, and she felt more relaxed and happier than she had been for days.

Patsy had become friends with Amy Andrews when she and Eddie first moved to Clapham. Eddie had also hit it off straight away with Amy's husband Ted, and the two families had been almost inseparable ever since. Ted and Amy had three children: Laura, who was sixteen and had an office job in Balham; George, who had just left school, aged fourteen; and Tom who at twelve was just a few days younger than Patsy's son Alex.

Amy was two years older than Patsy, a shrewd and outspoken young woman. Taller and bigger-built than Patsy, she wore her fair hair short, probably because it was naturally a glorious mass of waves and curls.

When Amy stopped talking, Patsy reached into her basket and drew out two enamel mugs: releasing the wire stopper from a glass bottle, she poured home-made lemonade for each of them. As she passed a mug to Amy she let out a small sigh.

'Feeling sorry for yerself, are you?' There was nothing frivolous about Amy's question and Patsy gave a deeper sigh before she answered.

'I suppose I am really, Amy. It's bad enough when Ollie goes away for any length of time, but now that Eddie has gone with him I really do miss them both.'

'Didn't you say Ollie said this would be the last time he would have to go up to Liverpool?'

'Yes, I did,' Patsy agreed, 'but he also said he'd be able to wind everything up in about two weeks. It's three weeks since they left, and I'm still not sure why he had to take Eddie with him this time.'

'My Ted told me that Eddie asked him to keep an eye on you and the kids while he was away. As if he needed to ask! Eddie also told Ted that this journey would see the whole of Jack Berry's affairs wound up – at least as far as Ollie was concerned.'

Patsy shrugged her shoulders in resignation. 'Yeah, I know. He told me the same thing. Jack Berry must have been a very rich man, he seems to have had business interests in so many countries. Even Ollie, his own brother, had no idea that there would be so many legalities. Jack certainly left a mess to be sorted out when he died so suddenly.'

Patsy now got to her feet and, taking a small towel with her, went across to where her girls were.

'Mummy,' cried Emma, as she approached, 'that boy splashed me and he's made my dress all muddy.'

'Never mind, love, I saw what happened and I'll soon brush your dress down.'

'He didn't mean to do it, he slipped.' Ellen, ever the peace-maker, spoke quietly.

'Here, have a bar of chocolate each, and if you're thirsty come and have some lemonade.'

'Can we have a boat out? You did promise.' Emma had decided to press her point home.

Bending, Patsy hugged them both. 'Yes, later on, when we've eaten our tea we'll go on a boat. We'll make Auntie Amy row, shall we?'

They were giggling with delight as their mother walked the few yards to where Amy was stretched out on the grass. Before Patsy had even sat down, Amy asked, 'How old was Ollie when he last saw his brother?'

'I don't know. Only a lad at school, I think. Jack got into some trouble with the police and left home. Ollie never saw him again. Ollie said they used to get postcards from far-away places at first, then they stopped. He did try to trace Jack when their parents died but all he drew was blanks. It came as a bolt out of the blue to Ollie when that firm of solicitors contacted him. Do you realise, Amy, that was nearly six years ago?'

'Christ! I knew it was a long time, but not that

long. I hope for your sake things will be finally settled this time.'

'So do I,' Patsy murmured softly. 'So do I.'

A faint smile flickered around Patsy's lips as Amy got out her knitting and studied the pattern of the jersey she was making for Tom. Patsy settled back and thought about her beloved Ollie. She knew the story by heart, yet whenever her thoughts turned to those events of so long ago she never failed to feel a warm sense of being loved and cared for.

At the age of nineteen Patsy's mother, Ellen, was pregnant and before her young man could marry her he had been tragically killed. Her father had been cruel; his decision had given her no choice. The baby was to be put up for adoption the minute it was born or be sent to an institution. Ellen had not been prepared to abandon her child, so she had left the security of her well-to-do home, parents and the comfortable way of life that she had known. Alexander Berry had been the first person to befriend Ellen when she arrived in the south London district of Tooting. Bewildered and frightened by the noise and the crowds, Ellen had gratefully accepted Alexander's offer to take her to the street where he himself lived and where Mrs Holmes had rooms to let.

Just ten days after Ellen's arrival in Strathmore

Street, Patsy had been born in the upstairs back bedroom of number twenty-two, the house where Ellen had been fortunate to rent rooms from Florrie Holmes.

Naturally the rough and ready Cockney folk had been suspicious of Ellen at first. They had never had the likes of her living in their midst. Ladylike, beautiful, with deep expressive eyes that held such sadness, and a form of speech that was vastly different from their own. Suspicion had turned to admiration as Ellen proved her worth. Given a job by the Day family, Ellen had worked on their market stalls for the next thirteen years, but such was Ellen's acceptance in the community that when she died of consumption, leaving Patsy without kith or kin to care for her, the whole street had been up in arms when officials appeared on the scene with an order to commit her to the workhouse.

After a long period of indecision, which to this day was still vivid in her mind, Alexander Berry and Florence Holmes had been granted legal custody of Patsy. Ollie, as he had been known to her from the day she was born, had been a father to her in every sense of the word. Neither had she suffered for want of other relations. Florrie – fat, homely and lovable – had always been her second mother. Gran and Grandad Jack Day, who lived directly opposite number twenty-two Strathmore Street, had – despite their own vast family – opened up their hearts to include both Ellen and Patsy.

Not even the Days themselves could give the exact number of their relations who lived and worked in Tooting. Between them they owned ninety per cent of all the market stalls in the district. Gran presided over the entire brood with as much command as any queen, yet for all that she wielded a rod of iron, she was loved by her sons, her only daughter Queenie, grandchildren and in-laws. Patsy was no exception. 'Gran' had been one of the first words that Patsy was taught to say, and she had always considered herself lucky to be included in this love that knew no bounds.

To this day Patsy knew of no living person to whom her mother had been legally related, but she didn't feel deprived. Half the inhabitants of Strathmore Street would claim association with her. What mattered more was that she also had Eddie, and now they had their own family. All legal and above board, thanks to Ollie. Contemplating Ollie, a brilliant smile lit up her eyes. God had indeed evened things out when he sent Ollie into their lives. He was the only father she had ever known: always there when she needed him, loving, caring, loyal and protective. Most of her joys and triumphs had been provided by Ollie, and her mistakes, losses and defeats he had shared. Without him her life would have been a very different story. A tall broad-shouldered man, quite handsome with a mass of dark unruly hair, his quiet manners and mode of speech were in reality very deceptive, as many had found to their cost. None more so than the Jackson family! Ollie had sworn that vengeance would be his when Johnny and his family had abused her so cruelly, and he had lived to see the day! With almost the first sum of money that Ollie had received from his brother's estate, he had manipulated that family of gypsies so that Patsy had at last held the upper hand.

Money speaks all languages, and Patsy had used it to the full — ensuring, with the help of Mr Topple, their family solicitor, that she finally obtained her divorce. The day when she became Eddie's legal wife was a day that she would never forget if she lived to be a hundred. God knows, she had waited and prayed for it long enough.

Patsy twisted her body and gazed in surprise as she watched Amy walking towards her carrying ice-cream cones, with the girls, one on each side of her, licking away at their own dripping cornets.

'Here, eat this before it melts completely,' Amy insisted as she bent and handed an ice-cream to Patsy.

Nodding her thanks, Patsy quickly ran her tongue around the cornet licking up all the dribbles. 'I never even heard you go,' she said as soon as she had the ice-cream under control.

'Course you didn't, you were too busy day-dreaming to be bothered about me or your beautiful daughters. We could all 'ave been dragged away by some terrible ogre for all you cared about us.'

Ellen and Emma laughed aloud as their Aunt Amy winked at them. Patsy held up one hand and forced herself to frown. 'Forgive me,' she begged.

'Shall we make her pay a forefeit?' Amy asked the twins whose faces were flushed with excitement, which gave Patsy the clue that all of this had been rehearsed in advance.

'Yes, Yes!' the girls squealed.

'Very well. By a unanimous vote it has been decided that you, Mrs Owen, shall pay for the hire of a boat on that there pond.' She finished speaking on a laugh and the twins rushed at their mother, tugging and pulling her to her feet. 'Come on, you did promise,' they chorused.

It was still a brilliant day, hot and sunny, as they stood on the wooden platform watching the boatman pull in the boats by means of his long, curved pole. Another man stood further along on the wet boards, megaphone raised to his lips. 'Come in, number four, your time is up,' his voice boomed out across the water and the twins, their two heads bent close, were trying to smother their laughter. Were there ever two like them? Patsy silently asked herself. They made such a pretty picture, dressed in blue gingham dresses, their long hair tied well back with blue ribbons. They were such natural girls and laughter sprang so readily from their lips. Patsy prayed that it would always be so.

Amy did the rowing and with skill she steered the boat to the island which lay in the centre of the pond, where the overhanging trees provided a cool and sheltered spot. The girls had kicked off their shoes again and were busy trailing their hands over the side of the boat and screaming with delight whenever they saw a fish. Amy and Patsy settled back to bask in the sun; it was a rare treat for both of them to relax so completely. Presently Amy brought Patsy back to earth with a bump. 'Wonder what the boys are up to.' Her voice was lazy and warm but her words set off alarm bells in Patsy's head.

'George promised me he'd keep an eye on Tom; he said he was going round to help your pair with some job or other.'

There was a long pause before Patsy answered; it crossed her mind that she had been a fool to come out and leave the boys to their own devices, especially with the state that shed had been in.

'I told my pair that they had to get all the junk and rubbish out of the shed, and that I wanted the place properly cleared out by the time we got home.'

'Some hopes, eh!'

Amy laughed then, wishing she hadn't brought up

the subject of the boys. Like Patsy, she dreaded the six weeks holiday which stretched ahead of them. You certainly needed eyes in the back of your head to keep tabs on their boys. There wasn't much to choose between any of them. One way or another, whatever they turned their hands to seemed to be a bit dodgy these days.

'Bottom of our garden looks like a tip.' Amy spoke over her shoulder as she settled the oars securely in their ridges and Patsy told the girls to stop leaning over the side of the boat and to sit up straight in their seats. As the boat cut through the water and out into the dazzling sunshine once more, Patsy asked Amy, 'Have you any idea where the boys get all this rubbish from?'

'It's not all rubbish you know, Patsy. Old man Draper wouldn't give the boys cash for it if it were.'

'But do they go knocking house to house? They could hardly collect so much from doorways and dumps.'

'We'll 'ave to see if we can't find out a bit more. I always thought you needed a licence to go knocking on doors, not that a little thing like that would worry our kids. Tell you what, I'll get Ted to sort them out tonight; he'll maybe get more out of them than you and put me together.'

And with that Patsy had to be content, since it would be a sin to let the thought of what the boys

might or might not be up to spoil their lovely afternoon out.

As they walked home Patsy found herself rather
guiltily hoping that the boys had got rid of all the
stuff they'd collected, and that they'd made a nice few
coppers for themselves. The last thing she wanted was
a showdown with the boys while Eddie was away.
She was in for a very pleasant surprise!

The ramshackle cart was propped up against the
open door of the garden shed. It looked clean and
even the spikes of the old wheels were shining. Alex
and David were almost a shock to Patsy as the pair
of them, grinning like Cheshire cats, made a sweeping
movement with their right arms and gave a mocking
bow. They'd had a bath, their hair was still wet and
flattened down tidily above their well-scrubbed rosy
faces. 'All clear,' Alex said, indicating the empty
bench.

'Yeah, just as you ordered, Mum,' David piped up.

Pair of cheeky little sods, Patsy muttered beneath
her breath, and was immediately sorry as Alex held
out to her a penny bar of Nestlé's milk chocolate with
its splendid wrapper of red and gold. 'We finished up
getting eleven-pence out of old Mister Draper.' His
big brown eyes were sparkling with merriment as he
added, 'So we thought we'd treat the best Mum in
all the world.'

Patsy's first reaction was to swipe him one, she was

sure he was taking the mickey out of her. Then she saw the glance that David threw at Alex; silence lingered only for a moment, then it was hard to say which one of them burst out laughing first. The twins came racing down the garden path, not sure whether their mother was crying or laughing as she leant doubled up against the garden fence.

When at last Patsy stopped laughing and got her breath back she looked at her two sons and with a grin she said, 'Come on, you two villains, bring your sisters indoors and let's all go and have some dinner.' One thing's for sure, she told herself as she went towards the house, my life is never dull, nor never will be, not while those two boys of mine are around.

Chapter Two

PATSY WOKE VERY early on the following Wednesday morning, to find that the weather had completely changed. The sky was grey and heavy with rain and the trees were dripping with it, their lovely green leaves already sodden, while water was swirling away from the suddenly overflowing gutters. She loved this big bedroom that she shared with Eddie, with its large windows and views right out over the long garden. Now, lying between the sheets and gazing out through the open curtains at the rain streaming down the window-panes, Patsy was glad that Eddie's letter had told her that he and Ollie would be home before the end of the week. She missed Eddie dreadfully. Come to that, she mused, she missed Ollie just as much. She had been upset, even a bit angry when the pair of them had gone off together. Being without her husband was bad enough, but to have your father away at the same time meant that she was vulnerable. She had a right to think of Ollie as her father, there had been no one else to fill the gap. She adored him. Such a big man yet so kind and gentle, firm when he needed to be, fair always, patient with the children, and ever ready to be protective.

Turning on to her side in the bed now, Patsy became aware of the bedroom door opening and a few seconds later Eddie came into view, balancing a tray in one hand while doing his best to close the door quietly with his other hand. She sat up, then flew out of bed, her face one great beam of a smile. Fortunately, Eddie managed to set the tray down safely on top of the chest of drawers before she flung her arms around his neck and buried her face into his chest. Eddie grinned, then lifting her up until her feet were off the ground he hugged her close. Swinging her up now like a baby, he walked with her towards the bed, kissing her cheeks, her forehead, the lobes of her ears and finally the tip of her nose before setting her down in amongst the still warm bed-clothes.

'When did you get back? I never heard you come in. Is Ollie here or has he gone home?' The questions tumbled out.

'All the news can wait till later. Snuggle down in the bed, I've brought you a treat,' Eddie stated. He had, too.

The tray held enough breakfast for the two of them, also a slender glass vase with a single rosebud. As Patsy poured tea into the cups Eddie took his clothes off, folded them tidily and placed them in the

Lloyd Loom chair. She steadied the tray as he wriggled in beside her and then, like two school-kids having a forbidden feast, they ate their breakfast in bed. Some time later Eddie put his cup down and held out his arms. 'Cuddling time,' he said lazily. She had no worries now; Eddie was home and anything that needed to be done, or sorted out, she could safely leave to him. All too soon the kids would be clamouring for his attention, but for the moment he was all hers. Her cheeks were bright with happy anticipation as she slowly stretched her arms above her head and removed her nightdress. The action of extending her arms served to accentuate her slender figure, a fact that she was well aware of. It had the desired effect on Eddie, just as Patsy knew it would. Thirteen years, four children, and still their love-making had not grown stale. It was wonderful, and it was a reluctant pair who finally got out of bed and only went downstairs in time to get breakfast for the children.

Patsy was already busy at the stove, frying rashers of bacon and fried bread, when the kitchen door opened and Ellen and Emma appeared. They had washed and dressed themselves in their everyday gingham dresses and each had tied back the other's hair with clean white ribbons.

'How's my girls then, eh?' Eddie asked, smiling broadly at them as they flung themselves at him.

'I'm fine,' Emma said, while Ellen whispered, 'we missed you, Dad,' and smiling back at him they wriggled up on to his lap.

'Well, are you going to tell me what you've been up to while I was away?'

'Course we are,' they chorused. Within minutes the pair of them were quite breathless as they related the times that they had been up on to the Common, and most especially their boat ride.

'You'd better sit up to the table and eat this breakfast,' Patsy said, 'otherwise it will be stone cold.'

Eddie pulled a funny face, and the twins giggled. 'Oh, you, Dad!' they said, but before they slipped from his knee they stopped to kiss his cheeks over and over again.

As they scrambled on to their chairs, more than ready to eat the breakfast which had filled the room with such mouthwatering smells, their mother set down the big brown teapot at one end of the table and pulled the tea-cosy over it. 'Were the boys up when you came down?' she asked, quite crossly.

Ellen shook her head; Emma, reaching for a slice of bread and butter, looked up. 'Didn't see them. Were they supposed to be?'

'Supposed to be!' Patsy muttered, as she set down a large breakfast cup full of scalding hot tea in front of Eddie. 'You never know with them two. One day they're up and gone before you have time to look around, another day you can't shift them, they'd stay up there in bed all day long if I didn't go up and tip them out.' As she spoke, Patsy opened the door and walking along the passage she stood at the foot of the stairs and called loudly, 'Alex, David, if you're not down here within the next five minutes I'll be up to pour cold water on you.' Nothing but silence. Oh well, she sighed, I'd better see if the pair of them are still up there.

She needed no telling as she entered the room — they were there in the beds which stood side by side, tucked well down with the clothes drawn up over their heads. She could hear them both smothering their laughter and it made her so angry that she leaped forward, whipped the bedclothes off and flung them on the floor. 'You must have heard me calling you,' she almost choked on her words. 'I can't see why the pair of you think it's so funny, dragging me all the way up those stairs.'

'We didn't 'ear you, Mum, and—' David didn't get a chance to finish what he was about to say; his mother's arm came out, grabbing him by the shoulder, and her voice was fierce as she almost hissed at him, 'No lies. You know full well I won't stand for you telling me lies.' Shaking him roughly she added, 'So get yourself out of that bed, washed and dressed and down those stairs.' Swiftly she turned to face Alex who, having summed up the mood Patsy was in, was already sitting up on the edge of his bed. 'That goes for you too, my son!'

'We won't be long, Mum, we'll be down as soon as we've washed and cleaned our teeth,' Alex said, using a bit of tact for once in his life.

It wasn't until Patsy was across the room and going through the doorway that she turned her head and said, 'Your father and your grandfather's home.' With each step that she trod going down her smile became broader. That had put a spoke in their wheel! Oh, she knew right enough, their father being home wouldn't put a stop to all the ducking and diving that those two got up to, but at least it would curb them somewhat. Ollie often had a good laugh about the pair of them and their antics; he even went so far as to say that the boys showed initiative. Well, that was all very well, but she paused in her thinking and shook her head; it wasn't so much the ideas that they got, it was the methods they used to put them into practice. All she hoped was that one day they would not go too far. Pair of buggers, she murmured, but the smile was still on her face as she went back into the kitchen.

Eddie Owen felt that, as far as he was concerned, what was left of 1936 was going to be all right and if things continued as they were 1937 looked set to be an even better year. When Ollie had learnt the extent of the inheritance he was to receive because of his brother Jack's death, he had been overwhelmed. The Depression had been at its worst in England just then and Eddie's own job in Covent Garden had been cut to three days a week. The solicitors had told Ollie at the time that the web of financial dealings would take years to sort out, and they had been right. Even so, from the moment when money had started to trickle through, Ollie had resigned from his post at the Town Hall and insisted that Eddie also give up his job and join him in the quest for the truth about his brother's business affairs, which seemed to have taken him half-way around the world. As the original founder of J. & B. Enterprises, Jack Berry had at the time of his death still owned 100 per cent of this private company.

It was from a Peter Crawford, who had flown over to England from Australia, that they had eventually learnt the most. It appeared that, unlike Ollie, Jack Berry had been a wanderer. As a lad he'd got himself involved in some shady dealings, and rather than face the police he'd left England and been content to work and make his money wherever fortune sent him. Never satisfied to stay put in one place for too long, life was always beckoning Jack to a different challenge somewhere else. He also had business interests in New Zealand, which was where he had been staying when he'd suffered a fatal heart attack, but his main source of income was from various enterprises in Australia. The offices from which most of J. & B.'s dealings were conducted were sited in Melbourne. One of the main reasons why, as the only beneficiary, Alexander Berry's inheritance would be so great was that a gold mine, owned by Jack Berry and long since written off, had suddenly struck a rich seam. Jack had also been involved in sheep and cattle stations. Whether Ollie was going to sell every business that his brother had had his finger in, had not yet been decided. That the package would have to be broken down into various smaller enterprises seemed inevitable. After six years enough assets had been disposed of to ensure that Ollie could set up one or more businesses of his own choice here in England. Being the man that he was, and having regarded Patsy as his own flesh and blood from the day she was born, Ollie had already made known to Eddie that it was his intention to set up a company in which he intended to make both Patsy and himself equal shareholders.

Eddie sat back in his armchair in front of the open window, letting his mind consider what Patsy's reaction would be when Ollie arrived and told her exactly what the outcome of their long stay up in Liverpool had been. The weather was beautiful again now, the rain of yesterday had laid the dust and washed the foliage of the shrubs which were now a shiny green beneath the window-sill. Leaning over the side of his chair, he retrieved the morning newspaper and glanced again at the headlines. Things might be getting slightly better as far as unemployment went, but this news of their new King Edward VIII and his association with this American woman, Mrs Wallis Simpson, wasn't going to do the country much good. After all, his father King George V had only died in January. God knows what the old king would have made of it. It's not only that the woman is not British that folk won't like, Eddie said to himself, she's a married woman. You'd have thought there were enough beautiful single young ladies in the circles that Edward moved in for him to have had a wide choice.

Turning the pages, Eddie was still muttering away to himself. Bloody Civil War in Spain now, and God help us that fellow Hitler – whom the whole of Europe was up in arms about, the way he was carrying on in Germany – had declared that he personally would formally open the 11th Olympic Games next week on 1st August in Berlin. It seemed that less than twenty years since the Great War had come to an end and Germany had been defeated, this Adolf Hitler was making his own rules and spouting his theories for a 'Master Race'. Disgusted, Eddie folded the paper and placed it under his chair. Somebody should start thinking about putting a stop to that bloke, he mused as he got up and headed for the garden.

Eddie had to duck his head as he went between the clothes-line and the mangle. Patsy had been busy, there were at least six sheets flapping away in the breeze. She'd certainly picked her day, she was forever going on about how she liked to get the bedclothes dried outside. Can't say I blame her, was his immediate thought; it was horrible when she did the washing on a wet day, seemed as though they had them hanging around the kitchen for evermore. 'Damn!' he cursed aloud as he stubbed his toe against the tin bath that was full of wet clothes.

'What's up?' He heard Patsy's voice before he caught sight of her and when he did he laughed out loud. She was on her hands and knees in a far corner of the garden that hadn't been used for years, it was almost overgrown with tall grass and weeds. There had always been a pathway that led straight from the back door down to the shed and from there round into the long grass and on to this corner that none of them ever seemed to come to.

'Patsy! What the hell are you doing?' Eddie shook his head at the sight of her. She still had the sacking apron tied around her middle that she wore when doing the weekly wash, but her hands were covered with grease and there were smudges of oil on her face.

'Well you might ask.' Patsy gave an impatient jerk of her head. 'Early this morning I saw the boys from our bedroom window, down in this corner. Didn't think anything of it till I was pegging sheets on the line and then it came to me that they were down here a long time. I looked in the shed first, you go and look for yourself. You won't believe it any more than I did.'

'What won't he believe?'

Patsy's head jerked round and her eyes lit up at the sound of that voice. A lump came to her throat as she watched Ollie turn and close the back gate that he had just come through. She was up from her knees and pushing her way through the long grass and had her arms flung around him before he'd hardly had time to take a step. Having kissed him several times, she stood back and looked at him closely. Wearing a navy-blue suit and with his mop of dark hair greased and combed into place for once, he looked fit and healthy and full of self-confidence. 'Oh, I've missed you,' she exclaimed as she rubbed her greasy hands down the sides of her sacking apron.

'I'm sure you have.' Ollie grinned at Eddie as he wiped his handkerchief around his neck and chin. 'So much so that you had to mark me with your oil and grime!'

Patsy held her hands out in front of her and looked guilty, but before she could think of an answer Ollie asked. 'What were you doing anyway?'

'I haven't found that out yet,' said Eddie, walking towards the patch of ground where he had found Patsy on her knees.

'I was trying to sort this mess out and see if I couldn't find out where it all came from.' She dropped to her knees and grabbed up a handful of metal bits and pieces, holding them up for the two men to see.

Eddie was the first to bend down. 'Phew, what a mess!'

Ollie wrinkled his nose in disgust as he peered at the oil-stained patch of earth and the mound of twisted metal and discarded rubber tyres.

'That's not all. Look over there.' Patsy nodded her head towards two or three sheets of rusty corrugated iron which were propped up against the fence. Standing one on each side, Eddie and Ollie lifted first one and then a second sheet away from the fence. At first glance they were both of the same impression, that hidden there was a mound of dirty, shapeless wreckage. Closer inspection showed them that in the main it was several rusted, buckled bicycle frames.

'Oh, drat!' Ollie pulled his hand back from a frame that he had been examining; a nasty scratch down one finger was oozing blood.

'Come on, let's leave it for now. I want you to

see what's in the shed.' Patsy led the way round the overgrown path and opened the door to the shed wide, securing it back against the wall by fixing it with the hook. Eddie gave a gasp of surprise, but Ollie let out a great bellow of laughter.

Propped against the bench was a bicycle. Not new, but clean, even shiny in places, and complete right down to a bell on the upright handlebars.

Eddie bent down and ran his hands over the black-painted frame. 'Mudguards, even mudflaps, rear red reflector. If those boys of ours have made up this bike from scrap frames and bits and bobs that they've picked up, Christ, Patsy' – he paused and looked up at her – 'You've got to give 'em credit.'

'Oh, I might have known you'd side with them. Perhaps you'd better take some time and find out just where they're getting all this scrap from, and where they're getting the tools to build a bike like this.' She had to pause for breath and the fact that both Ollie and Eddie were trying to smother their amusement didn't make her feel any better-tempered. She shrugged her shoulders. 'If I tackle them they will only go at me on the defensive. A right sly pair of bounders those two boys are, when they choose.'

'Never mind, my love. Take that apron off and let's go and have a cup of tea. If Alex and David *weren't* up to something you'd be worried sick thinking they were ill. I've told you before, they'll go far, they use their initiative and if in doing so they make themselves a few coppers, well, what's wrong with that?' Turning now to Eddie, Ollie added with a laugh, 'Perhaps we ought to make them financial advisors in our new company.'

'Oh, and what new company is this?' Patsy asked eagerly.

'Now you've done it,' Eddie said. 'She'll not leave you be until she gets to know the ins and outs of a donkey's hind-leg.'

'All shall be revealed,' Ollie stated solemnly, 'just as soon as you place a large cup of tea on the table in front of me.' With that Patsy had to be satisfied as Ollie, with an arm around her shoulders, led her towards the house. 'Let's cut across the grass,' he said. 'I never seem to come here without you having at least one line of washing out.'

'She's happiest when she's up to her elbows in soapsuds,' Eddie retorted.

'Yeah, well, with our brood if I wasn't you'd soon notice the difference, but if you're going to be home now for a few days and fancy the job for yourself don't let me stop you. I'll even lend you me sacking apron.'

'No, no. Honestly, I was only joking.' Eddie walked backwards now facing her and held up his hands in mock horror. 'I'm sorry, truly I am.'

'Hmm. You're as mad as each other,' Patsy declared

as they reached the back door, but as she stood at the sink filling the kettle with water for the tea she was smiling quietly to herself. Everything would be fine now. Both her men were home.

Ollie had seated his massive frame in what he regarded as his own armchair and drawn it up to the table. Eddie sat next to Patsy, one elbow resting on the arm of his chair as he watched her lift the large brown teapot and fill two large cups and then a smaller cup for herself.

'Now then,' Ollie said after he had taken a few sips of his tea. 'We'd better let you in on all our business secrets, eh?'

Patsy gave him her full attention; her curiosity aroused, she couldn't resist saying, 'I wish you'd tell me what you're on about.'

'I'm on about us all becoming business partners,' Ollie said. 'We are forming a private limited company and the shares will be split three ways. We did think of including Florrie, didn't we, Eddie?' Eddie nodded his agreement but remained silent, his eyes fixed fully on Patsy's face.

'We decided against that. It isn't what she would want to be bothered with. Mr Topple is dealing with everything and suggests that I hold forty per cent of the shares and that you and Eddie each hold thirty per cent. Does that sound all right to you, my gal?'

Patsy didn't seem to understand what he was saying, she couldn't take it in. Dozens of questions were crowding her mind. 'I'll put some more water in the pot,' she said to the pair of them. There was on point in her asking, better wait for Ollie to explain further; she'd only make a fool of herself if she forced him to go into details now.

'Please, Patsy, don't worry so. I shouldn't have come right out with it like that,' said Ollie in a gentle voice. 'It's all very simple now. Really it is. After all this time a lot of my brother Jack's holdings have been sold off. Not all, mind you. I've still had to hold on to few of the shares, but I am only a minority shareholder now and the solicitors, between them, have arranged things so that I will not be involved in the running of the company.' He patted her arm and gave her a rueful smile. 'Ironic, isn't it? You and Eddie nearly went to Australia to make a new life for yourselves, and now because of my brother I own shares in a company which does most of its trading in Australia. Still, that's all settled for the time being.'

Ollie stood up now and reaching to the mantelshelf he took down his tobacco tin which he always kept there.

In the quietness that followed Patsy shifted about impatiently, realising that this was not as simple as

Ollie was trying to make out. Having packed the bowl of his pipe tightly, he picked a paper spill from the tin which stood in the hearth and walked with it to the gas stove. The light still burnt low beneath the big black kettle and he bent down, putting the spill into the naked flame. When the rolled paper flared he held it to his pipe and puffed away contentedly. As soon as he was sure that he had the pipe well and truly alight, he stood with his back against the door and said to Eddie, 'You tell her the next part.'

Before he began to speak Eddie flashed Patsy a loving smile, then he took a deep breath and began to explain. 'When Jack Berry's shares were sold, the money was eventually transferred to England, and it all belonged to Ollie. Believe me, Patsy, we argued about what happened next. Ollie decided he couldn't leave the bulk of his inheritance lying in the bank, neither did he want to invest it all and just live on the interest. We both know him better than that. He needs to work, to have an interest in life. So he decided to go into business for himself. At the same time he generously said there would always be a job for me, and that he was going to make a will with you as his main beneficiary. I won't go into all the details now, but it is on very good advice that he settled on forming this company. That's all there is to it, my darling. Once we've been up to town and

phone call to the owner of the premises and the estate agent had gladly accepted the deal on a very long lease. In the week that followed, several company meetings took place – or at least that was how Ollie and Eddie described them. As the majority of these 'meetings' were around her kitchen table and more often than not Florrie was present, Patsy could not bring herself to take the matter under discussion too seriously. Half the time Florrie's comments and her vivid imagination had Patsy in fits of laughter.

Ollie had it in his mind that to begin with they should get a footing in the transport business. 'What yer going to transport? Prisoners to the colonies? Bit late, ain't it! They've all had the King's pardon.' Florrie beamed at Patsy, having put her two pennyworth in. Patsy smothered her smiles behind her handkerchief while Ollie told Florrie to behave or go and find her herself something to do in another room.

Seriously now, Ollie put forward his views. 'Charabancs! That's what we should be thinking of setting ourselves up with.'

Patsy swallowed deeply and dared not look at Florrie or it would have been her that got the telling off. Charabancs indeed!

'Trams are nowhere near so popular today,' Ollie continued in a stern voice, though he was well aware that Patsy was beginning to think he had taken leave of his senses. 'They'll all be off the roads soon, you mark my words. Now that the London Passenger Transport Board has extended the Northern Underground line out to Morden, they've had to buy a whole fleet of single-decker buses and put them on the road to run feeder services from the housing estates to the Underground Station. Most of those buses take twenty-eight passengers and there's talk that Leyland are about to produce a revolutionary single-decker that will have a thirty-four-seat body.'

Eddie was nodding his head in total agreement – obviously he and Ollie had discussed all the details at great length. Patsy knew that she should behave and listen to what Ollie was saying with at least a show of interest, but for the life of her she couldn't imagine how all of this was going to affect her.

'Charabanc outings are the coming thing.' Ollie had started to speak again but Florrie quickly interrupted once more.

'Oh, yeah? Then why 'as that garage down at Ritherdon Road gone bust then? Tell me that. There's that coach firm on the corner of Blunts market down at Tooting – they ain't doing so good neither. Flossie Bagnell, she's the woman that runs our mothers' meeting on a Monday afternoon in Fairlight Hall – she was getting up an outing for us all to go to Southend but it never come off. Why? 'Cos the company are up the shoot, that's why, and now here's you wanting to spend good money getting yourselves into a business that ain't gonna last five minutes. Your trouble, Ollie Berry, is you got so much bloody money now you don't know what to do with it!' Having finished her tirade, Florrie heaved up her large bosoms and announced, 'I'm going to make us all some tea.'

As Florrie disappeared into the scullery they looked at each other and none of them could contain their mirth any longer. Wiping the tears of laughter from his eyes, Ollie said, 'The trouble is she is absolutely right – the only difference being that we would have the capital to sustain the company until such time as it became a profitable venture. There's no end to the work we could take on providing we find the right site and are able to purchase reliable vehicles. Trips to the coast could end up being only a small part of the work we could do.'

Two minutes later Florrie used her big bottom to push open the door. She ignored the pile of papers that were set out in front of Ollie, elbowing them out of the way, and taking no notice of his protests she set down a laden tray. 'Kettle won't be a minute. Settled everything, 'ave you?' she asked, tilting her nose towards Ollie as he straightened his papers into a neat pile.

'Enough for today,' he answered patiently.

'Hmm.' She sniffed as off she went back to the scullery. Florrie wasn't unintelligent – at least, not half as much as it suited her at times to make out that she was. While she waited for the kettle to come to the boil she studied herself in the small mirror that hung over the sink. She was under no illusions when it came to her looks. She was fat, fifty-eight years old, quite a good head of hair, and today she even looked smart in this yellow linen dress that hung loosely and hid most of her lumps and bumps. If only she didn't have these bloody awful legs she'd be able to get about a darn sight more easily. Count your blessings, gal, she chided herself. you could've ended up a very lonely widow, like a good many more women have 'cos of the Great War. Instead God had sent Ellen Kent to her door all those years ago, and then along had come Patsy. Couldn't be more me own if I'd given birth to 'er, she thought. The kettle lid began to bob up and down telling her the water had come to the boil, and as she filled the teapot she could hear the low tones of the three still seated round the kitchen table.

'Let's 'ope it all turns out right for 'em,' she mumbled beneath her breath. Patsy was as good a daughter to her as anyone in the land could wish for. And as for Eddie! Better than a son. Ollie, well, she had to laugh as she set out rock cakes on a fancy plate, a lifelong friend – suppose that's how you'd describe him. One thing she knew for sure; she'd never starve, not while Ollie Berry was still on this earth. Yes, one way and another she had a great deal to be thankful for.

'Where've you been?' Patsy asked, as Florrie set the pot down.

'Making the tea of course. You ain't done much I see, ain't even set the cups on their saucers.'

Eddie looked at Ollie, each raised their eyebrows heavenward and by mutual consent decided that the company meeting was over for today. Patsy didn't mind at all. She had her family round her, the children would be coming in soon for their tea. Everything in her world was fine.

As they drank their tea Florrie rattled on nineteen to the dozen, stating what in her opinion they should all be thinking about doing. Patsy's thoughts were on the dinner. Should she put some onions in the bottom of the pan with the sausages before she poured the batter-pudding mixture over them? Eight of them for dinner. Well, she'd have to make two toad-in-the-holes, one wouldn't be enough. I'll put onions in one and not in the other, she decided. The twins weren't that fond of onions.

Florrie was clearing the table and Patsy was at the sink peeling potatoes when Eddie came up behind her. He put his arms around her waist, bent his head and nuzzled his face into her neck.

'Oh, yeah. What's this in aid of?' she asked with a

smile as she put down the vegetable knife and, turning round, cupped his face in her wet hands.

He kissed her cheek before he spoke. 'You know, Patsy, you're going to have to take this business of being a company director a lot more seriously. We both owe Ollie that much. You can't go on treating the whole thing as a joke.' Although he sounded as if he was exasperated with her, there was a hint of amusement in his voice.

'I know. It's just that it's so damned hard to be serious when Florrie is around.'

'Never mind Florrie so much! You can't expect Ollie to put up with it. Will you try to take more interest in future?'

'Yes. Course I will,' Patsy promised happily. 'I'll pay attention to everything that both you and Ollie tell me.'

'Yes, well . . . I'll believe that when it happens.' He was looking straight at her now with those huge dark brown eyes of his, then half smiling he said, 'About time you got on with the dinner.'

'Oh, for heaven's sake!' said Patsy, flicking her hand into the bowl of dirty water and sending a spray up into Eddie's face.

'I'll get you for that later,' he promised, sounding just like a big kid as he left the kitchen. Patsy didn't mind his threat at all. Sometimes Eddie found very nice ways of getting his own back on her.

Chapter Three

THE SUMMER PASSED in a round of activity for Patsy. Eddie and Ollie were well set up. Having managed to buy a yard that was amply suitable for what he had in mind, Ollie had lost no time in setting out to find who owned the dilapidated warehouse next door which was an eyesore to the district of Vauxhall. Neither Patsy nor Eddie had been surprised when he announced that with the blessing of the borough council he had bought the warehouse and was moving builders in right away. Now her two men were often away for two or three days at a time as they toured the country seeking to buy any single-decker buses that would be suitable for renovation. Small operators of country service buses were being forced out of business as the larger area companies and national chains bought up exclusive rights to the main routes and employed men at union rates for the job.

Meanwhile, at home Patsy coped with the twins who had chicken-pox, and thanked the Lord that the boys had had it when they were quite small. She would never have been able to keep that pair indoors!

They were still the bane of her life! There were times when she would think that Alex and David were the brightest and kindest pair of boys that any mother could wish for; then they'd put the fear of Christ into her by getting themselves involved in some mess or another. Trouble was, they were so elusive. Hardly a day went by when she could have sworn where those two were or what they were doing. 'Keep an eye on the boys' was nearly always Eddie's parting shot as he went off on yet another trip with Ollie. All right for him; he wasn't lumbered with them. Keep an eye on them indeed! To coin a phrase of Florrie's, you'd need eyes in the back of your head to see what they got up to.

Yet the pair of them could charm the birds out of the trees when it suited them. Sometimes they would be very late home and although the evenings were still light and nice and warm, by seven o'clock Patsy would be sick with worry. Having given the girls their dinner and washed up the dinner things, she would tell herself to be sensible, but her anxiety grew by the minute, especially when she was in the house on her own. But eventually they would arrive at the open back door with their clothes covered in dust, socks down round their ankles and their hands and faces in need of a jolly good wash. Broad smiles on their faces, totally unaware that she'd been worried, they would turn those beautiful big eyes of theirs on to her and chorus, 'What's for dinner, Mum? I'm starving.'

Come the middle of August David had his tenth birthday coming up. His father had long promised to buy him a bicycle. 'Much safer than having him ride around the streets on those contraptions that the two of them put together from old scrap,' Eddie had stated in answer to Patsy's protest.

'That's not fair,' Alex shouted crossly. 'I'm older than he is. If you're getting 'im a bike you should buy me one too.'

'I will, when it's your birthday,' his father promised.

That wasn't good enough for Alex. Wait till next April! Patsy summed up her son's mood with motherly accuracy. It was natural for him to be jealous and angry, the injustice of it all was boiling inside Alex and she wasn't about to sit by and see this argument turn into a nasty ugly row which in turn could well cause a rift between the two boys.

'Buy them both a bike, if you're going to get any at all,' Patsy said with unusual determination. Then, before Eddie had time to answer, she added, 'It can count as an early birthday present for Alex.'

The way Alex's eyes lit up and the look of appreciation that he shot at his mother didn't go unnoticed. 'So, you've got yourself an ally, my son,' his father said, doing his best to sound stern but without having much success. David, who had been hovering behind his mother while she cut thick slices of bread ready to toast for their tea, heaved a sigh of relief. He hadn't thought it was exactly fair that he should be getting a bike and not Alex, but he'd been afraid that if Alex complained too much his father might have said, 'Right, neither of you will get one now.' Oh, their mum was a gem! She could wheedle anything out of their dad and their grandad as well if she put her mind to it.

'There you are then, the two of you are getting a bike now,' Patsy said softly. 'How about saying thank you to your father?'

'Thanks, Dad,' they both said in agreement, and Eddie stood smiling proudly as his two boys went to their mother and gave her a hug.

Before they'd even got their bikes from the shop Alex had a job lined up for each of them. Patsy didn't know whether to laugh or cry as she stood at the front door at six o'clock in the morning watching both her sons come from the paper-shop to start their first delivery. Perched on their shiny new bicycles, with a heavy newspaper sack slung round their shoulders, their faces were half hidden by the enormous flat caps they had on their heads.

'It's as I've always said, those two could find a way of earning a few coppers even if they were marooned on a desert island,' she muttered to herself as she turned and went indoors, yet there was a touch of pride to the way she shook her head.

Suddenly it was almost time for the children to go back to school. 'Will you come over tomorrow and give the kids their tea for me, Florrie?' Patsy asked as she handed down the great meat dishes from the top shelves of the dresser. At least once a week Patsy did her best to come down to Tooting and spend the day with Florrie. Gran, who lived opposite in Strathmore Street, nearly always managed to waddle over to Flo's while she was there, so she could kill two birds with one stone by seeing that they were both all right. Gran's daughter Queenie lived two doors along, and she saw to her mother's needs and indeed to Florrie's as well. Still, when she was here Patsy liked to do a few jobs, and cleaning down the dresser was one task that was utterly impossible for Florrie to attempt with her bad legs.

'Right, that's all the china down, I'll make a start on washing it,' Patsy said as she rolled up her sleeves and carried some of the matching china jugs through to the scullery. From the smallest cream jug they ranged through six sizes up to the largest one, and had hung from their brass hooks for as long as Patsy could remember. Lowering each one into the sink which she filled with hot soapy water, Patsy recalled with a grin how many times Florrie had sent her off with the largest, orange-coloured jug that had a picture of a brown Alsatian on the front.

'Pennyworth of eel liquor, please,' she had stood and called, raising the jug high in the air because she was never tall enough to reach the marble-topped counter in the 'Pie an' Mash' shop. Life hadn't been all bad when she'd been growing up in this street amongst these working-class folk who had taken her to their hearts and seen that she had never gone hungry.

'Where you off to tomorrow?' Florrie asked as she leant against the draining-board.

'We're going to Brixton, to get the kids' school uniforms.'

'What, you an' Amy?'

'Yeah. Don't suppose we'll be late back but you never can tell.'

''Ave you settled whether David's to have long trousers, or not?'

Patsy laughed and Florrie joined in with her. 'Might just as well give in gracefully,' she told Patsy. ''Sides, with the dark nights coming and him riding a bike, poor little sod will freeze to death if you make 'im wear short trousers.'

'You're right as always, you wise old bird. Amy says that Bon Marché is stocking all the uniform for the girls, but we'll probably have to traipse all the way up to Morleys fer the boys' things.'

In some ways Patsy felt that the coming of the dark evenings was not entirely a bad thing – though she didn't like the cold, and especially not the fog and the dreary streets lit only by gaslight. Even standing beneath a lamp-post, the yellowish glare that the gas-jets gave off was always a bit eerie.

One thing, though, she *could* keep better tabs on the two boys. They'd be going back to Boys Brigade on Thursday evenings and the Youth Club on Mondays. Both were held in St Peter's Church Hall in Clapham Manor Street, which was only a matter of yards from where they lived. Ellen and Emma went to the Brownies and the Club on the same two nights, so at least for a couple of hours she knew where all her children were.

The whole of the Willow-patterned dinner service was now washed and dried, so were the jugs and the meat platters laid out on the kitchen table ready to go back up on to the dresser and be displayed in all their glory. Patsy was just about to complain about how long the twins had been when the kitchen door burst open with such a rush that the brass door-handle hit the wall behind.

'Here, steady on!' Patsy called to her girls. 'You're suddenly in a rush, aren't you, where have you been? It can't have taken all this time to choose the pattern of a penny packet of shelf paper.'

'Not really,' Ellen explained, 'but we did have a

job deciding between yellow with a green border or pink with pretty roses. We bought you the pink one, Auntie Florrie. Is that all right?'

'Course it is, my luvvie. But like your mum says, you have bin a long time. Not bin getting yourselves tied up with that daft old Mister Gosling, 'ave you?'

The colour in the twins' cheeks flared up and they giggled nervously as they glanced towards their mother.

'I can see you 'ave,' Florrie cried. 'Ought to be locked away, that daft old sod should be. Don't know whether he's coming or going half the time.'

'He's nice,' Emma cut in. 'He gave us a glass of his home-made lemonade. It was lovely, wasn't it, Ellen?'

'And I suppose he asked you to sing with him,' Patsy asked, well remembering Gosling at the corner shop from her own school days.

The twins drew closer together, then seeing that they weren't going to get a telling-off they gave Florrie a cheeky grin and began to sing: 'Jesus loves us, this we know, 'cos the bible tell us so.'

Patsy turned her head away so that the twins should not see her shaking with laughter, and Florrie did the same.

How many times had Patsy herself come back from Gosling's shop singing and got into hot water from her own mother? 'Jesus wants me for a sunbeam, and a bloody fine sunbeam I'll be' – this was the rendering she and her school-mates used to give. Mrs Gosling had been alive then and even as a young married couple, the Goslings had professed to being Four Square Gospel Workers.

'Oh, you're both very naughty, singing for the old man just so's he'll give you a free glass of lemonade,' their mother said, pretending to scold, but the hoots of laughter coming from Florrie were making the twins smile too much for them to take her seriously.

With the aid of many drawing-pins they got the shelf paper in place and the china back on the shelves. As they worked, with the twins helping, Patsy didn't dare glance at Florrie. Both of them were curled up inside at the memories that the twins had invoked.

The hot summer was over and the children had started their new terms at school. Ellen and Emma were still attending Parochial School in Clapham Old Town, which was handy because it was within walking distance. Patsy had had to turn away quickly when she left them at the school gates. Making a fool of yourself like that! But she couldn't help herself. They were still her babies, even if they were seven years old. So neat and pretty they looked, almost angelic. Navy skirts and cardigans, white blouses, white socks and black ankle-strapped shoes. A touch of colour was the red ribbons which held back their long glossy hair. Oh, they were lovely girls.

The boys had looked smart as they set off to catch the bus that would drop them off at Burnwood Lane. Of course there had had to be an argument over whether or not the pair of them were going to wear their school caps. All Patsy could vouch for was that when they left the house the caps were on their heads, and that the leather satchels that Ollie had bought for them – which not only smelt lovely but looked good – were slung across their backs. How long the caps would be worn and the satchels would remain ink-free, only God in heaven knew.

Now the biggest and last fair of the year was setting up on the Common, a sure sign that autumn had arrived. The nights were drawing in, the leaves on the trees had turned their rich red and golden colours, nature giving them one last chance to show how beautiful they were before dropping to the ground and leaving the branches bare. The road-sweepers cursed as the gutters became clogged with deep layers of dried leaves, while the council workers from the Parks Department used wide rakes to gather the leaves into heaps.

The air became full of nice-smelling smoke as bonfires were lit by the council workers to save them the trouble of carting away all the dead leaves. Wonderful! Patsy sniffed as she skirted the Common on the way home with her shopping. Not at all like the foggy-smelling smoke which Londoners had to put up with during the winter months. Living so near the Common was grand really. You got to see all the seasons of the year, and there was always something going on. It was good for lonely people too. Sit on any one of the benches and you could bet your bottom dollar someone would come along and strike up a conversation. Yes, the Common was a lovely place and so near to London, it was a bonus, a bit of the countryside to the folk who were lucky enough to live there.

Saturday night and they were going to have a proper treat. Ollie was away on business again, this time on his own. Florrie was staying with them in Navy Street for the week-end and Kitty from upstairs was coming down to keep her company, because the Owen family were going to the fair.

The roads and pavements were so crowded that they couldn't all walk together so Eddie went on ahead, holding tightly to the girls' hands as they walked one on each side of him. The boys looped their hands through their mother's arms and made sure that the way was clear before they stepped off the kerb. Every inch of the grass on the north side of the Common was covered by the fair. Sideshows,

'Try Your Luck' stalls, open-sided caravans selling hot dogs and chips with meat pies, 'Gypsy Rose Lee' offering to tell your fortune, home-made humbugs and toffee apples and toffee pears, sticks of rock, jellied eels and cockles and whelks, bags of winkles with a free pin thrown in. All these and more were set up around the perimeter of the Common. You paid your money and you took your choice.

The whole centre area was a mass of rides and swings, each one they came to more frightening than the last. The noise was deafening. Hurdy-gurdy music blared out from every corner, brilliant-coloured electric lights flashed on and off as folk rushed to get their children aboard a roundabout the minute a ride came to a stop. Teenagers queued to buy tickets to see riders on the 'Wall of Death' or to get the fright of their lives by riding chairplanes on chains which flung out in a wide circle high up in the air. Trying to stay close to Eddie for fear of being crushed, Patsy thought that the whole of London must have come to Clapham to see the fair this Saturday night.

'Can we go on the moving horses?' Emma asked, tugging at her father's sleeve.

'Oh, we ain't got to stand here and watch you and Dad wave at Ellen and Emma as they go round and round on those things, have we?' Alex was quick to ask.

'We could go on the cake-walk?' David offered.

'I'd rather go home if we've got to stay with you all the time.' Alex was being Alex!

'Can they go off on their own?' asked Patsy.

'Yes, well.' Their father appeared to be considering the matter.

'It's no good saying we'll meet you later 'cos we'll never find you in this throng.' Eddie was having to lower his head and shout at the top of his voice to make himself heard above the din.

'Here.' He handed over half-a-crown to each of the boys. 'That ought to last you a while, but now listen to me, I want you both home by ten o'clock. You've got your wrist-watch on, Alex, so I'm relying on you to keep an eye on the time.'

'Aw, Dad. It's gone nine now. We won't 'ave time to see half the fair.'

Eddie sighed, then grinned. 'All right. Half-past ten, then. Go on, off you go and 'ave a good time the pair of you.'

Patsy threw wooden balls at coconuts and won nothing. Eddie protested that he could do better; he paid his tanner for three balls and to the delight of all three female members of his family didn't manage to dislodge one coconut from its stand, so he won nothing. He did better at the dart stall. Three hundred and one with six darts won a long-eared pink rabbit, much to the delight of the twins who promptly named it Wilfred and took it in turns to carry it.

Tired out, their feet aching and their shoes filthy from the dry dust that was being churned up by hundreds of people walking to and fro, they held hands and once clear of the Common walked four abreast and made for home. The twins' faces were still glowing with excitement as they ran up the garden path and into the house, yelling to Auntie Florrie to see what their father had won for them.

Florrie was seated at one side of the fireplace and Kitty on the other.

'I put a match to the fire,' Florrie said, as Patsy and Eddie took their coats off and sank down on to the sofa. 'Thought it was getting a bit chilly in 'ere.'

'You did right an' all,' Eddie smiled at her. 'Makes a nice change to see a bright fire.' He rubbed his leg, the one that had given him trouble from the day he was born. Since the operation that he'd been lucky enough to have, the leg didn't play him up much, but tonight it was aching like billy-o. Seeing Patsy watching him he grinned. 'Getting too old for this fair lark.'

'Oh, poor you,' Patsy mimicked.

'What's 'appened to the boys?' The front-door bell rang as Kitty asked the question.

'That'll be them now,' Patsy said with a sigh of relief.

'I'll go,' said Ellen, and came back a few moments later followed by her brother David.

'Where's Alex?' Eddie and Patsy both spoke at the same time.

'Don't know,' David admitted.

'What d'you mean, you don't know? Don't try to be clever, son.' Eddie had raised his voice, more in fear than anger.

'I'm not, Dad. I honestly don't know. He was talking to a bloke that was taking the money on the dodgem cars the last time I saw him. Then I couldn't find him. I did look. Honest. Then I thought I'd better come home.'

'Was he paying to go on the dodgems?' Patsy quietly asked.

'No, Mum. We didn't 'ave no money left. We'd spent it all.'

Eddie took a deep breath and tried to control his fear as he gently pulled David towards him and, looking straight into his face, said, 'Tell me what this fellow looked like, son. Was he a fairground worker, d'you think?'

'Well,' David thought for a minute, 'he could 'ave been. He had a funny-shaped head, a big head really.' He smiled at his own words, not yet fully realizing just how worried his parents were becoming. 'He was ever so broad, like he had big muscles. And oh yeah, I remember his 'air was all short and spiky-like.'

'Good boy, David,' his mother said.

Florrie had listened to it all and now as she threw a glance at Kitty the colour had drained from her face. 'Are you hungry, lad?' she asked.

'A bit, Auntie Florrie, not much, but I'm ever so thirsty.'

'I'll make the tea,' volunteered Kitty.

'Well, you and Emma hand the plates round.' Florrie said to Ellen, giving her a reassuring pat on the back. 'I've made three platefuls of sandwiches; just lift that damp cloth off them, I covered 'em over to keep 'em moist. There's corned beef and mustard pickle, or cheese and chutney.'

Dear old Florrie! I do love her. She's doing all this to take our minds off Alex being so late, thought Patsy as she got up and went to help Kitty with the tea. As she passed Florrie she bent and kissed the top of her head. 'Thanks,' she murmured.

'Ten minutes. That's all we'll give him,' Eddie said as he looked up at the clock on the mantelshelf. 'It's five past eleven; we'll wait until a quarter past, then we'll go back up the Common and start looking for him.'

The cup rattled in its saucer as Patsy handed Florrie her tea. 'Steady yerself, love,' Florrie whispered, giving Patsy a look of understanding that said they both knew exactly what fear was in Patsy's mind.

It was true. The minute David had stepped into

the room without Alex her heart had missed a beat.
She'd thought that never again would she have to
even think that the Jacksons might do her or her
family any harm. That terrible period of her life was
behind her . . . or it should be. Fairs and the Jacksons
went together. Oh, dear God, please let me be wrong.
But wasn't that how she'd first met Johnny — at a fair?
And by Christ, she'd lived to rue the day. From that
meeting had stemmed a disastrous marriage and life
hadn't been worth living — not until she'd met Eddie.
He was my friend right from the first time we met.
In spite of the fact that her heart was still thumping
away far too quickly, a sweet smile came to her lips.
Eddie. Lover, partner, eventually husband, but still to
this day my best friend. She nearly jumped out of
her skin as a rat-a-tat-tat from the street door-knocker
broke the silence that had settled over them all. Patsy
reached out, clutched at Florrie's work-worn hand
and hung on to it tightly as Eddie strode towards the
door.

The twins looked up at their mother and their
auntie, their little faces showing how frightened they
were. David had followed his father up the passage.
Loud knocks at the door like that didn't mean good
news — not at this time of night they didn't.

'Evening, Missus.' The policeman directed his
words towards Florrie, then nodded first at Kitty and
finally at Patsy.

'It's our boy, isn't it?' White-faced and shaking, Patsy managed to stammer out the question.

'He's had a bit of an accident,' the bobby said, taking off his helmet and tucking it under his arm. 'Seems he came off the back of a motor-bike. Sorry I don't know the details. Only that you and his father ought to get up to the hospital right away.'

'Oh, Alex!' Patsy moaned, sinking down on to the sofa and burying her face in her hands.

'What the hell was our boy doing on the back of a bloody motor-bike?' Eddie shouted, as if he was blaming the policeman.

'Come on, son, pull yerself together, see to Patsy an' the pair of you get going,' Florrie said sensibly. 'And don't worry about the kids, we'll see to them all right, won't we, Kitty.'

'That would be best,' the policeman said doggedly. 'I'll be off meself now. Let's hope you find things are not so bad when you get there.'

'Thank you, officer,' Kitty said, struggling to her feet. 'I'll come to the door with you.' At the front door she stepped outside, 'What a dreadful thing! Don't you really know how badly the boy is hurt?'

The policeman hesitated; situations such as this were always tense. Naturally the parents were worried sick, but on the whole this case had not been too bad. He hadn't minded that the father had had a go at him. He'd got kids of his own. Best that they cut along and see the boy for themselves. All he wanted to do now was get back on his beat, and he was trying to think of a way of saying goodnight and not having to answer the old lady's question. Placing his helmet back on his head, he fiddled with the chin-strap and then suddenly let out a gasp. 'Bloody fool! Sorry, Missus, you know I ain't even told them what hospital their boy's been taken to.'

'That's all right,' Kitty told him. 'Which one is it?'

'St Thomas's, on the Embankment. I'll pop in tomorrow, see how they've got on.'

'Thanks,' she muttered as she went back inside the house.

It was turned midnight by the time they arrived at St Thomas's, yet the place was all hustle and bustle. 'Typical for a Saturday night,' a porter told them as he directed them down a long corridor. Patsy clung to Eddie's arm as they walked, afraid of the noise their footsteps were making on the stone floor, and feeling sick as she tried not to let that horrible hospi-tal smell of disinfectant get to her. They found a nurse in a different uniform sitting in a small box-like office. Her dress was navy blue, not white, and her cap was a large, flowing affair. Eddie assumed she was the ward Sister and he was right, as he soon found out when she asserted her authority. 'You're the parents, are you?' she asked in what to Patsy was a well-educated voice. 'Yes, Mr and Mrs Owen,' Eddie confirmed. 'May we see Alex, please?'

'Not yet, the doctor is still with him. Waiting-room is two doors down on your left. I'll have a nurse fetch you when it's convenient.'

Patsy saw Eddie's great fists clench at his sides and she too felt utterly frustrated. 'I want to see my son!' – she felt like yelling at this nursing Sister who didn't seem to have an ounce of compassion in her whole body. When she glanced up at Eddie he looked so awful that the sight of him gave her a shock. He's blaming himself. The realisation came to her and she had to struggle to stay calm. We shouldn't have let the boys go off on their own; we should have insisted that they stayed with us.

'Come on, love, I'm sure it won't be long.' It was Patsy who was being the comforter now.

My God! The poor nurses. The waiting-room looked like a public bar in a pub . . . a rough pub at that. The walls were painted a dark green, there was worn linoleum on the floor which was littered with stamped-out dog-ends of cigarettes. The air was foul and the smell was worse than that of the disinfectant. But it was the occupants who shocked them the most. Men and women lay sprawled out in the chairs. All forms of decency seemed to have been discarded. Two or three looked as if a wash would do them good: one man, slumped on the floor in the corner, was snoring and the man next to him had dew-drops hanging from his nose and a patch of dried blood above his eye.

'We'll wait in the corridor,' Eddie said as he took Patsy firmly by the elbow.

'Who are they?' Patsy asked as they each took a deep breath.

'Drunks, I expect. Overflow from pub brawls, more than likely,' he answered.

'No wonder the Sister wasn't in a very good mood.' Patsy spoke in a whisper as though they were in a church.

'Come over this side,' Eddie beckoned her from across the corridor, 'Tisn't often you get to see a sight like this.'

Rising up into the night sky, and so near to the window that you could almost touch it was Big Ben, its faces brightly lit. 'Oh, isn't that wonderful!' Patsy couldn't help exclaiming. Big Ben belonged to all Londoners. Many a time she had sat with the kiddies on her knee and let them hear the chimes ring out before the news on the wireless. She'd even taught them the words the bells said: I AM BIG BEN, AND HERE I GO, LET ALL THE PEOPLE, KNOW THE TIME.

Suddenly she wanted to cry but knew that she mustn't. Surely they'd let them see Alex in a minute?

It couldn't be much longer – not unless something was seriously wrong. Don't even think it, she chided herself.

'Hold on, won't be long now.' Eddie had read her thoughts. Then giving her arm a shake he added, 'Look down.' She did, and stood there staring into the deep water of the Thames. She hadn't realised that they were in the very heart of London. 'Suppose a lot of those in the waiting-room are people who doss down on the Embankment,' Eddie remarked. 'It's warmer in here for them. The doctors and nurses must have a helluva lot to put up with one way and another.'

Footsteps sounded loudly in the empty corridor and they both turned quickly to face the young nurse who was approaching them.

'Hallo,' she said brightly. 'Sorry to have kept you waiting around so long.' They were both pleased to hear how cheerful her voice sounded. Alex couldn't be hurt that much. Thank God!

'First bed on your right,' the rosy-cheeked nurse smiled at them as she held open the ward door. A whimper escaped from Patsy's lips when she saw that screens were drawn around his bed.

'Ssh!' Eddie hissed at her. 'Put a smile on your face, whatever you do don't cry and don't start asking him questions neither.' There was no need for the instructions, for Alex was unconscious.

Patsy sat on one side of the bed while Eddie placed himself at the foot. There was an arch-shaped cradle holding the bedclothes off his legs, one side of his face was badly bruised, his arms lying out straight on top of the bedclothes bore scratches, and both of his hands were heavily bandaged. Gently Patsy stroked the bandage that covered one hand, and as she did so tears welled up in her eyes and her whole body began to tremble. After what seemed only a few minutes the curtains around the bed parted and the stern face of the Sister appeared; she signalled for them to leave.

Eddie stood guard while Patsy bent low and pressed her lips to Alex's forehead. 'You'll be fine, Alex. We'll be back in the morning,' she promised her sleeping son.

'Goodnight, God bless,' Eddie whispered.

'He doesn't even know we were there,' Patsy said sadly.

'Don't worry about that, he'll know you both well enough in the morning and have plenty to say, I'll be bound.' The words of the Sister were this time said quite kindly as she stopped outside her office and with a nod of her head bade them enter. 'Doctor can spare you a few moments now,' she said before she bustled off, her starched apron making a rustling sound as she went.

'I doubt that he'll remember very much,' the doctor – who looked no more than a boy – told them. 'It's the drugs we've given him that have sent him off to sleep. We can be thankful that his head wasn't smashed. There is a bad lump and bruising just beyond the hair-line, but no bad damage as far as we can tell, though we'll have to wait and see if there is any concussion.'

'His legs and hands?' Eddie ventured to ask.

'What?' The doctor pulled his white coat tightly around him and seemed to make an effort to collect his thoughts. At this time in the morning he's bound to be feeling dead on his feet, was Eddie's first thought. 'Oh, yes. No bones broken. Legs pretty rough, where he was dragged along, hands actually saved him from a worse fate. Do you know what he was doing on the pillion seat of a motor-bike?'

Eddie shook his head.

'The police will want to know the answer to that question. Still, time enough for all that in the morning. Better take your wife home now and both of you try to get some sleep.' The doctor got to his feet, held out his arm and shook hands with Eddie.

By the time they got home Eddie was in a blazing temper. Now that he knew that Alex wasn't going to die he was certainly relieved, but that didn't stop him wanting a damned lot of answers to a damned lot of questions himself. The main one being, what bleeding idiot had put his twelve-year-old son up on the back of a motor-bike?

★

This was going to be no ordinary Sunday morning; everyone in the house knew that by now. Down in the kitchen Florrie was cooking breakfast for David and the twins. Bacon and sausage with bread that had been dipped in beaten egg and fried. That kind of fried bread was Mum's special treat; she would tell them how her own mother had invented it because sometimes they had only been able to afford cracked eggs. It was lovely, all crispy on the outside and soft inside.

'Could you eat another piece?' Florrie held out the frying-pan and smiled at the children seated around the table. All three shook their heads. Nothing could make them smile this morning. It wasn't that they minded that their Auntie Florrie was seeing to them instead of their mother. It was that Alex had been hurt and was in hospital, and that Dad and Mum were up in the front room with Uncle Ted and they all sounded ever so cross as they shouted at each other. Auntie Florrie was a dear really. Her hair was never very tidy, except when Mum did it for her, it had an awful lot of grey mixed in with the brown, and the skin of her face was red and wrinkled. Still, none of that mattered. Her eyes were the brightest blue you ever saw, and you could always tell when she was having a joke on anyone because those bright eyes of hers would twinkle. Besides, Auntie Florrie had a way of making everything turn out all right.

Mum was always telling them that. She was always ready to give any one of them a hug and a cuddle and if you weren't feeling well, Florrie had some wonderful drinks that she mixed up that tasted all warm and sweet, like, and were sure to make you feel better.

'Auntie Florrie.'

Florrie was half-way across the kitchen but she stopped abruptly, swinging her body round to face Ellen.

'If you go with Mum and Dad to see Alex today, couldn't you take him one of your special mixtures?'

Oh, the faith of the child! Tears stung at the back of Florrie's eyes as she tried to think what to say. Sweet little Ellen, so serious now and yet doing her best to smile.

'Don't be daft. The doctors won't let you take him any medicine. Hospitals are funny places.' David explained patiently. The colour in his cheeks was high and Florrie felt so sorry for him. Got a lot of sense, that boy has. Taking it hard about his brother. Term time or holiday time didn't make no difference, wherever Alex was you'd be sure to find David. Rarely were the two ever parted.

'I don't see why Auntie couldn't sneak something in for Alex. Don't suppose they search you, do they?' There was annoyance rather than fear in Emma's voice, but then she was always the practical one.

'Well, my loves, I'll do me best. I might not be able to go with your mum and dad today. They probably wouldn't let me in. We'll just 'ave to wait till they've been, and then they'll tell us how Alex is getting on.' As she cleared the table and stacked the dirty plates in the sink, Florrie was crying. She'd rubbed at her eyes with her fist so hard that her eyes ached. Christ! I love those kids, she mumbled to herself. If only I were half as clever as they seem to think I am, I'd be able to perform bloody miracles.

'Any chance of a cuppa tea?'

Florrie had been so moved by the fact that the children thought it was quite possible that she would be able to make Alex fit and well that she hadn't noticed that Patsy had come into the kitchen.

'I was just going to bring a tray up for all of you,' she said, keeping her head down.

She didn't fool Patsy, who knew her too well. 'What's up? Come on, tell me.'

It was too much and Florrie started to blubber. 'Ellen said I should mix a potion for Alex. Emma seems to think I should storm the 'ospital and David, well, Gawd above knows what *he* wants me to be doing.'

In spite of everything Patsy had to laugh, but she smothered it well. So that's what it was about. No different to when I was a kid. I always ran to Florrie – cut knees, bad cough, big bullies out in the street, she'd even seen off the officials that were hell-bent on sending me to the workhouse. Fancy my kids having exactly the same faith.

'Are you going to make me that cuppa or not?' Patsy asked as she took the teacloth out of Florrie's hand and gave her a peck on her cheek.

'Might as well, kettle's boiling,' Florrie agreed. 'Someone's got to take a cup to them two in the front room. Gone quiet, ain't it? It was all the shouting and hollering that upset the kids.'

'Only tea for just us two,' Patsy said, rubbing at a cup with the teacloth much harder than was necessary.

Florrie surveyed Patsy guardedly and waited for her to explain.

'Eddie's gone up the Common. Said he was going to find out exactly what did happen last night.'

'Aw, Gawd Almighty!'

'Now don't you start. I've argued with him till I'm blue in the face, it makes no difference. We both ought to know by now that when Eddie says he's going to do a thing, he does it. Ted's gone with him.'

'Ah well. Can't say I blame 'im. Better to find out from the horse's mouth, what's what,' said Florrie, bending down to pick up the teapot from the hearth.

★

The sun had come out, not a bad morning at all taking into account that there were only about two and a half months left of this year. Strange really how summer had dragged on. The Common looked very different in the light of the pale sunshine. 'Bit of a mess!' Ted Andrews remarked, as he and Eddie strode across the grass. Litter was scattered everywhere and the grass was no longer a bright green. The dust from last night's activities had settled, giving a grey look to everything.

It was as if the fairground workers were expecting them; there were quite a few men standing in a group beneath the shade of a big tree. The people standing at the doorway of the caravans were mostly young couples, Eddie saw, and in the spaces between the vans older women seemed to have charge of the young children.

The caravans didn't look nearly so gay this morning, no bright lights and no music blaring out; even the people themselves looked different, more normal like. Probably because the women weren't heavily made-up, their heads were not covered with gaily coloured scarves, and long gold earrings weren't dangling from their ear-lobes.

A burly-looking man stepped to the front of the group as Eddie and Ted approached. He was clean-shaven with fair hair and almost as broad as he was tall.

'I'm Jack Norman,' he said, offering his hand to Eddie.

'Eddie Owen, and this is Ted Andrews.'

'Was it your boy that got took to the 'ospital?' Jack Norman asked Eddie, as he indicated that they should all move over a few yards to where the woman was setting out an assortment of chairs.

'Yes, it was,' Eddie answered, trying to control his impatience. He'd come up here to learn the facts of what had happened, not to have a pow-wow.

''Ere.' A man who was reasonably well dressed pushed a glass of dark brown beer towards Eddie, while another older man offered the same to Ted.

'Thanks' they said in unison, as they took the glasses and sat themselves down.

''Ow is the boy?' Jack Norman asked, with sincere concern in his voice, which gave Eddie the opening he had been waiting for.

'We won't know much till he comes round. He was out for the count when we left him last night. Drugged, the doctor told us. Didn't seem too badly hurt – not as much as we'd feared – but it's concussion that might be the trouble. What I'd like you to do, Mister Norman, if you would, is tell me exactly what happened and what bastard was responsible.' Eddie paused for breath and took a long drink of the warm beer from the glass he'd been given.

'The name's Jack, and before we go any further let's get one thing straight: we none of us here had

anything to do with what happened last night.' He
held up a finger in protest as Ted was about to interrupt. 'Hear me out, the pair of you. Please. Then
you can have your say.'

Ted looked across at Eddie; when he gave a slight
nod he turned to face the ring of men, and said, 'All
right, we're listening.'

'Right,' Jack Norman began, turning his body so
that he was facing Eddie eye to eye. 'Fact number
one, we're not thieves out to rob the public, we're not
gyppos either, we're fairground workers, and there's a
bloody lot of difference, believe you me. The bloke
that put your kid in the hospital is not kosher, he's
not one of ours. Goes by the name of Bill Whitly.
He hangs around fairs and gets a job here and there
when someone is short-handed. Turned up last
Thursday on a three-fifty B.S.A., says he wants to
ride the Wall of Death. Course, Tom over there sends
'im packing with a flea in 'is ear. It's professionals
only what can tackle that ride. 'Stead of clearing off,
Les – him that just give you the beer – lets him doss
down in the back of his van an' gives him a couple
of bob to help 'im on the dodgems.'

''Twasn't my fault,' protested the fellow Jack had
pointed to as being Les. 'I'd never come across 'im
before.'

Jack had used the interruption to raise his own
glass of beer and drain it. Setting down the empty

glass on the grass at his feet, he said, 'Well, you have now, Les – more's the bleedin' pity.'

What had all of this got to do with Alex? Eddie was growing more impatient by the minute.

'He was showing off to your boy, that's what the sod was doing,' Jack said, as he took up the story again. 'Saw the youngster at the dodgems, told him he could give 'im a better thrill than them an' it wouldn't cost him nothing. Course, we found out the boy hesitated but the bastard dared him. I ask you! Daring a kid of that age to to get on the back of his bike! Course the kid took the dare. Most boys would, didn't want to lose face with mates standing watching an' all.'

Eddie groaned and Ted asked a question. 'How come Alex came off? Must have been speeding, was he on the road?'

'He was at first apparently. Round an' round the north side of the Common. Never got enough notice taken of 'im if you ask my opinion; we was all too busy that time of night, especially it being a Saturday. So, the bugger cut across the grass. Thrilled to bits when women screamed and folk 'ad to dash to get out of his way. Weaving in and out around the trees, zigzagging amongst the crowds, so I'm told. Swerved to avoid a little girl, skidded an' hit a tree. Pity is that it was your boy that came off worse. About all Whitly's got is a broken finger, squashed it between the clutch lever on his handlebars and the tree. Could 'ave killed the little girl; she never stopped screaming for ages, poor little mite. He certainly put the fear of Christ into her.'

Eddie had heard enough. His face was white with anger as he got to his feet. Ted, recognising the signs, stood up at the same time. Eddie was one of the easiest blokes going – hardly ever lost his temper – but this was different. His eldest boy had been hurt, and God help the fellow when Eddie got hold of him!

'Big-headed slimy bugger! I'll give him show-off when I get my hands on him! I'll make the bastard wish he'd never seen a bloody motor-bike, let alone rode one with my son on the back.'

''Ang on there a minute,' Jack Norman yelled, as Eddie made to stride off. 'He's not on the site. Believe me he's not. Don't you think we'd have 'ad the geezer by now if he was? He thinks he's solid, got it up top, stays one jump ahead of the police so he thinks he can piss on all of us an' get away wiv it. Well, this time *we're* going teach him a lesson.'

'Yeah,' the group of men agreed. 'One he ain't likely to forget in an hurry. Should have bin banged up years ago.'

Ted Andrews, who still had a restraining hand on Eddie's arm, quickly asked, 'And how're you going to set about getting this sod if you don't know where he is?'

'We never said we don't know the bastard's whereabouts, only that he ain't on the site no more.'

'Christ Almighty!' Eddie took a step towards Jack Norman, his face flushed with anger. 'A bloke puts my kid in hospital. He don't give a toss, and you don't want to tell me where he is.'

Jack Norman turned away and took in a great gulp of air. 'It ain't like that at all. All right, suppose we tell you where to find the bugger, you dash off, give 'im a right old kicking and what'll happen to you? I'll tell you. You'll end up seeing the inside walls of the Scrubbs.' Then to Ted he pleaded, 'Take 'im home. You have me word that Bill Whitly will be sorted afore the day's out.'

Much as a great shaggy dog would shake itself, so did Eddie, and with that all the pent-up anger seemed to leave him.

'Come on, mate, leave it to this lot,' Ted said quietly. 'Time you were thinking about going back up the hospital.'

Eddie went from one man to another, shaking hands with each of them in turn and when he came to Jack Norman it was with a great deal of earnestness that he said, 'Thanks, mate,' for which he was rewarded by a slap on the back and a gripping handshake.

★

It seemed ages to Patsy since Eddie and Ted had set off to see if they could discover the ins and outs of just what had gone on at the fair and how Alex had come to be hurt so badly. She had tried to settle down and catch up on some darning but it was no good – she hoped to God that Eddie hadn't lost his temper and made things a whole lot worse than they already were. She bit hard on her lip as she stood staring out of the window. Were the Jacksons involved? Would they stoop so low as to harm one of her children? Surely they didn't still bear a grudge against her for blackmailing Johnny into agreeing to give her a divorce? After all, they hadn't done so badly for themselves out of it. But if it was a case of revenge, then she would stake her life that Johnny would be the instigator.

She sighed heavily. Was she never to be free of the threat of him? Johnny Jackson, who had played such a fateful role in the Owens' lives over the years. Pig-headed sod! He'd married her when she was sixteen, discarded her before she was seventeen and yet kept her legally tied to him for years. There was a time when she had almost given up hoping that she would ever legally be Mrs Owen.

Eddie was the only man she had really loved, from the very first moment she had set eyes on him. She loved him still and he loved her, but now their love was different. There were no more skeletons in the cupboard, no fears that friends or neighbours might find out that she used the name of Owen merely because Eddie had changed her surname by deed poll. No more embarrassing questions to answer, such as how long had they been married, or what kind of a wedding did they have. No more sleepless nights pondering over the fact that all four of her children were illegitimate.

A knock on the front door made Patsy jump; it couldn't be Eddie back, he'd use his key. Flinging the door open wide she stared at the shabbily dressed woman for a few seconds before recognition dawned on her. Daisy Jackson! Her heart was beating like a hammer inside her chest as she made to slam the door shut.

'Patsy, half a mo. Please. Just listen to me for a couple of minutes.'

Patsy's mind went back to things she had tried so hard to forget. Daisy, Fred Jackson's wife and Johnny's sister-in-law. Be fair, she chided herself: of all the Jackson clan Daisy was the only one who had never done her any harm. Come to that, she had been kind to her, especially when she had been so young and daft enough to go hop picking and almost every member of the Jackson family had turned on her.

She stepped back. 'You'd better come in.'

'Thanks, Patsy,' Daisy murmured as she walked down the passage.

'Well, what can I do for you, Daisy?' asked Patsy as soon as they were both in the kitchen.

'It's about your boy – and before you go off the deep end at me, I promised the family I'd come and explain. I bet you've been thinking it was Johnny having a go at you through your kid but, 'onest, it's nothing like that at all, not that I can blame you if you are of that mind. But please, I'm asking you again, take that sneer off your face and give me a chance to say what I came to say, will you?'

Patsy cottoned on to the fact that Daisy no more wanted to be here than she wanted her here. Trust the Jacksons to send someone like Daisy, who was only a Jackson by marriage . . . if any one of them had turned up on her doorstep she really would have slammed the door in their face, so she relented somewhat. 'All right, I'm sorry, Daisy. There's never been bad blood between you and me, so sit down and tell me just what you are doing here.'

'Well, to start off with, I expect you know by now that it was Bill Whitly who was riding the motor-bike with your boy on the back?'

'Here, hang on, I don't know anything of the sort,' Patsy interrupted. 'My Eddie and his mate Ted have gone up the Common to see if they can get to the truth of the matter.'

'Sorry, love, I just sort of thought you'd know by now.' Daisy Jackson had been a slim, pretty-looking girl when Patsy had ridden on the flat cart with her, drawn by horses, all the way down to the hop fields in Kent. Now she looked old beyond her years, quite fat and with none of the red colour left in her short hair, only grey. Her eyes no longer sparkled, rather they were beady-looking, and Patsy realised she was feeling sorry for her. Life hadn't been easy for Daisy, that was a dead certainty.

'Do you remember Johnny's sisters?' Daisy asked, and without waiting for a reply carried on talking. 'Bill Whitly is Annie Jackson's eldest boy – Whitly is Annie's married name. Over the years, Johnny has often boasted about how you and 'im got wed: you know, Patsy, he was ever so proud of you in his own way.'

'He had a funny way of showing it, is all I can say,' said Patsy with bitterness in her voice. 'Anyhow, how did you know where to find me?'

'Come off it, Patsy, Clapham ain't a million miles from Mitcham. We've all known ever since you decided not to emigrate, and your exact address was on the divorce papers. Johnny and his brothers were at the fair, I think it was my Fred that recognised you and pointed you out to Billy. Always has been a thorn in Annie's side, has that one. Even as a kid he was in and out of Borstal like a yo-yo. Saw your boys with you and when the biggest one got separated from the rest of you, thought he'd chance 'is arm and do a bit of showing-off. Wasn't nothing to do with the family, you must believe me, Patsy. Course they were mad, especially Ma, when you turned up telling them you were the owner of the houses we all lived in, and they realised they'd 'ave to start paying rent . . . but that was all a long time ago, no grudges now. Live and let live it's been since then, so please, Patsy, don't go getting worked up into a state and start thinking about throwing us all out on the streets again. None of us would think about getting at you through your kids.'

Wouldn't you? Patsy almost said aloud. She hadn't been much more than a kid herself when the whole blooming clan of Jacksons had made her life hell.

'I'll make us a cup of tea,' she said to Daisy without making any comment on what she had been saying. Going through to the scullery, she filled the kettle and put it on to boil. While she set out cups on the tray Patsy gritted her teeth as she recalled the terrible taunts – yes, and blows – that she had suffered at the hands of the Jacksons. Her first baby! Ma Jackson had screamed at her, denying that Johnny was the father. Vile suggestions made not only about her but about her mother. According to Ma Jackson, she was a woman from a brothel and Patsy was a brothel-bred git! Oh, never would she forget those spiteful words. Vividly she remembered the tight pain in her chest as fear made her short of breath when the whole load of Jacksons had surrounded her and threatened to set their dogs on to her. She had come home to Florrie with agonising pains in her stomach from the kick that Johnny had aimed at her, and that same night she had miscarried her baby. Thanks to Ollie, his foresight and generosity, she did later come to own all three houses in which the Jacksons now lived, and yes, she had threatened to have them all evicted unless Johnny agreed, after all those years, to a divorce so that she could be free to marry Eddie and become Mrs Owen legally.

Reluctantly Johnny had appeared in court, given evidence that he had lived with Mary Best for seven years and that they had five children. A barrister, paid for by Ollie, had asked the court's discretion on Patsy's behalf and the judge had granted a decree nisi. Finally the divorce had been made absolute, and to her dying day Patsy would remember the joy she had felt when she had become Mrs Owen in the eyes of the law. She had kept her part of the bargain, never pestering the Jacksons for payment of their rent although more often than not each and every one of them were in arrears.

The kettle came to the boil. Patsy poured the water on to the tea-leaves in the pot and carried the loaded tray back into the kitchen where Daisy sat staring at her feet, not yet daring to raise her eyes. Still without saying a word, Patsy poured out the tea and handed a cup to Daisy, who eventually broke the silence.

'Things haven't gone well for the Jacksons you know, Patsy.'

'And I'm supposed to feel sorry for them, is that what you're saying?'

'No. Course not. I'm just saying there hasn't been the work about, hard winters and not such good summers. To top the lot, Ma lost her youngest girl. Remember Maisie? So small she got nicknamed "Half-pint".'

Patsy nodded.

'She caught the fever, diphtheria the doctor at the hospital said it was. She was dead within five days.'

'I'm sorry,' Patsy whispered. And she was. No one likes to hear of a child dying, and diphtheria was a horrible death so she had been told.

'So,' Patsy sighed as she set her empty cup down on its saucer. 'What's going to happen now? Because if you or any others of the family think they can get away with hurting one of my children, they've got another think coming. I mean it, Daisy! I'll do more than threaten them this time, and God knows what Eddie will want to do when he finds out it was one of your lot that enticed our boy on to the back of that great motor-bike.'

'Billy will be dealt with. It won't 'appen again.' Daisy was already getting to her feet and buttoning her coat, relief spreading over her face. In silence the pair of them walked to the front door which Patsy opened.

Daisy hesitated. 'You're not going to take it out on us, are you, Patsy?' she asked in a miserable quiet voice.

'We'll see,' was all that Patsy was prepared to say until she had talked to Eddie. 'But thanks for coming, Daisy. It can't have been easy for you.'

In a hushed tone Daisy had the last word before she set off down the front garden path. 'God pays his debts without any money, Patsy. You've prospered . . . the Jacksons haven't.'

Half an hour later Patsy jumped up quickly, startled by Eddie's voice, and saw him striding down the hall-way. She almost ran to him and he drew her into his strong arms. Minutes passed before he eased her away gently and looked down into her anxious face. 'Let's get ourselves a stiff drink, take it into the front room, and I'll tell you all that I've learnt from the men working up on the Common, and you can tell me all that your visitor had to say.'

Patsy gasped in surprise. 'How do you know I've had a visitor?'

Eddie laughed. 'How does anyone know anything

that goes on around here. Neighbours watch, neighbours gossip.'

'Bet you don't know who she was.'

'You're right there, but I'll bet you a pound note to a penny she was one of the Jackson clan.'

'Blooming old know-all, that's what you are,' she told him as he handed her a good measure of whisky that had only a dash of soda water in it.

Much later, all details having been told item by item until each was sure they had all the facts right, Patsy pleaded, 'You don't believe it was Johnny, trying to get back at me through Alex, do you?'

Eddie smiled at her, knowing he had to reassure her. Patsy was the most precious thing in his life, and he doted on all four of his children.

'No, I don't. I'm sure we have been told the truth. It worried me though because it crossed my mind straight away that as it happened at a fairground you would jump to the conclusion that Johnny Jackson was behind this. Now I'm convinced that he wasn't, so stop worrying.' Then to himself he said, 'But God help him if I find out that he was.'

Alex had been in hospital for a week now. Being Sunday, visitors were allowed in the afternoon and again from seven to eight in the evening. Young Tom Andrews had offered to go in the afternoon and had come back home full of the joys of spring. 'He's all right, Auntie Patsy, really he is,' he was telling her, even though he knew that she hadn't missed a day yet from going up to the hospital. 'The nurse gave us a pack of cards, an' I sat on the bed and we played all the time I was there, an' when they brought the tea round they gave me a cup as well. Wasn't much cop, bit cold really, but it was nice of them, wasn't it? Alex said "two" when they asked how much bread an' jam he wanted, then when they'd gone he gave me a piece.'

Alex was doing well, thank God. He had all the nurses running around for him, even the frosty-faced Sister they'd met on the night he'd been admitted couldn't help grinning when they spoke to her about his progress. My God, that lad had been lucky. No serious damage to his head, his legs were the worst: lacerations to the left one, but the knee of his right leg had been gashed when he was thrown off the bike.

'What a long time they are taking the screen away and opening the door,' Patsy whispered to Eddie as they stood waiting to be allowed in the ward. Ollie had arrived home last night and he and Florrie were seated on a bench a little way down the corridor. Only two visitors at a time were permitted around the bed, so his parents were going in first and then it would be a smashing surprise for Alex when his grandad and his aunt followed them.

Eddie and Patsy stood at the back of the crowd dressed in their Sunday best, clutching bunches of flowers and paper bags that held grapes. It was awfully quiet until Florrie loudly exclaimed, 'Would you look at this. Who'd believe the carryings-on?'

Patsy let go of Eddie's arm and hurried the few steps to where Flo was sitting. 'Be quiet, Flo,' she ordered. 'You'll have Sister come out to you.'

'Why? Ain't you allowed to talk up here? I thought it was an hospital, not a funeral parlour.'

Patsy plonked herself down on the bench beside Florrie, looked at Ollie, raised her eyebrows and they both laughed.

'What was it that you were all steamed-up about?' Patsy asked her.

'Read this.' Florrie folded her *News of the World* until it was a small square and then tapped the page with her forefinger. 'See, that American woman has divorced her 'usband. Look, it says Mrs Wallace Simpson divorces her husband Ernest. Perhaps our King will marry her, who knows, but I'll tell you one thing, and you mark my words, our old Queen Mary – Gawd bless her – will 'ave something to say before her son makes that woman Queen of England. And she won't be the only one, Baldwin will soon put a spanner in the works an' all.'

People were tittering, Ollie had his handkerchief out and was covering his mouth, Eddie had turned his back and Patsy was greatly relieved when then bell rang and a nurse removed the screens and opened the door to the ward. Everyone rushed forward and both Eddie and Patsy were pleased to see that Alex's bed had been moved further down the ward. That meant, so the nurse said, that he didn't need such constant attention.

'You look a lot better,' Patsy said as soon as she had hugged and kissed him.

'Yeah,' he said. 'Feel great now.'

'I've got a lot of things for you. The twins bought you some toffees and David sent you these three comics. Ellen is going to write to you and Emma is making you a card.'

'How's the knee, son?' Eddie asked when he could get a word in edgeways.

'I'll be able to come home soon, Dad. Doctor said I got to keep these tight bandages on for a while, but I can get about all right, I've been up to the toilet.'

Patsy was a bit anxious as she and Eddie went outside in order to let Florrie and Ollie have their turn. She had a right to be, for Florrie soon had all the ward laughing and Alex blushing to the roots of his hair as she told the nurses what a darling boy he was! Grandad, as usual, promised to buy him any present he chose as long as he got well and came home quickly. Ten minutes before the hour was up, they changed places again to give his parents the chance to say goodnight to him.

Grandad must have had something else to say to Alex, because just as Patsy was about to leave he clutched at her hand and said, 'Sorry, Mum. I won't go doing no more daft things when I get home.'

She choked back the lump that had come up in her throat and kissed him again. He meant the words *now*, course he did. But being Alex she didn't for a moment believe that he'd be able to keep his promise, though being a mother she pretended that she did.

'Are we all ready?' Alex asked impatiently as he came bursting in through the back door.

'I won't be a minute,' his mother called from up the passage as she wrestled with a hat-pin. 'You go on. Take David with you, wait for us at the bus stop.'

'All right, but don't be all day,' he yelled back.

Satisfied at last that her hat was straight and securely fixed to her head, Patsy opened the door to the front room and popped her head in, 'You awake, Florrie?' she asked in a whisper.

'Awake! The noise you've all been making? It's enough to wake the dead.'

'Good! I can see you're in fine fettle on this mucky

morning,' Patsy said, a broad grin on her face as she reached up and pulled the curtains open. 'I've set the table for your breakfast and the kettle has boiled.'

'I'm not a bloody invalid! Just 'cause I've had a bit of a lie in this morning.'

'Why don't you tell the truth?' Patsy smirked at her. 'You had too much to drink last night and now you've got a thick head.'

'Nothing of the kind, you cheeky little madam.' Florrie raised herself up against the pillows and laughed at Patsy. 'Was a good night, wasn't it? Best pay-out the club's had for years. Must have 'ad a lot of loans, the interest at a bob in the pound soon mounts up, don't it?'

'Yes, it certainly does. Twenty-eight shillings a share. Damn good when you think we all of us only paid in a tanner a share for fifty weeks, twenty-five bob. Kids are thrilled with theirs, can't wait to get to the shops. They've been making their Christmas present lists ever since they opened their eyes this morning.'

Patsy took Florrie's dressing-gown down off the hook behind the door and laid it on the bed; her slippers she set near, ready for Florrie to put her feet into.

'Aw, stop fussing. I heard you tell Alex to wait at the bus stop. Where's the girls?'

'Over at Amy's. We're all going to meet up the

High Street. Have you made a list of what you want me to get you?'

'No. You'd better get going. I'd rather you took me out on our own one morning. Plenty of time. Couldn't think what I was up to if I came with all you tribe. End up buying a load of old rubbish.'

'Well, if you're sure you'll be all right?'

'Glad of the peace an' quiet, to tell you the truth.'

Patsy bent over the bed and brushed the hair away from Florrie's face, then she kissed her on both cheeks. At the doorway she stopped and looked back and they smiled at each other.

It was quite a gang of them who trooped up the stairs of the bus, hell bent on spending their club money. But then the first week-end in December was quite an event all over London. First Friday was pay-out day. First Saturday was spend-up day. Every Friday, for fifty weeks, pubs, shops and offices had collected the payments. Everywhere was the same, a tanner a share. You wanted a loan, any time from January to November, you paid back to the club twenty-one shillings for every pound borrowed. More borrowers, more the share-out. All the Owen children had two shares each, had done from the day they were born. Grandad gave them each three pennies to spend every week and paid a shilling into the club for each of them. Ted Andrews' father did the same for his three children.

'I'm really looking forward to Christmas, aren't you, Patsy?' Amy asked, but Patsy didn't get a chance to answer.

'Fares, please,' the conductor bellowed as he came down the gangway.

'Three and six halves to Bon Marché, please,' said Patsy holding up a two-shilling piece.

Ding, ding, ding, the bell pinged away as the conductor punched a hole in three twopenny tickets and six penny ones. 'Pity they weren't all boys,' the conductor joked as he handed Patsy the tickets and her shilling change. 'You'd nearly 'ave had a football team between you.'

'Cheeky sod,' Amy said, nudging Patsy and laughing.

Remembering what Amy had asked her, Patsy suddenly said, 'Course I'm longing for it to be Christmas, but I wish Ollie wasn't such an old pessimist, and Florrie's not much better when it comes to it.'

'Why? They both like Christmas, don't they?'

'Oh yeah. It's not that, it's just that Ollie will keep on telling us that war is inevitable. He's got Eddie agreeing with him now.'

Amy sighed. 'I know what you mean. All Ted

keeps on about is the Nazis in Germany. You don't think it will come to war, do you?'

'Don't know, love. Not often that Ollie is wrong about anything, and he says that if we don't put a stop to this Hitler it will only be a question of time.'

'Depressing, ain't it? One way and another the news is not worth listening to.'

'Come on, Mum, we're there.' David was tugging at her arm.

'Alex!' The shout from his mother stopped him short. He was already at the top of the stairs, one hand looped round each side of the hand-rail, ready to slide down to the platform. 'Behave yourself and see to your sisters.'

'Right,' he said cheekily, giving her a cheerful grin. Now all the kids were scrambling on to the stairs, Alex pushing the twins ahead of him.

'We don't want none of your racing off,' said Amy, as they stood in a group on the pavement. 'If you bigger ones do shoot off, we'll be at the café next door to Woolworth's at one o'clock. We're bound to be thirsty by then.'

'Where're you going first, Mum?' George asked.

Amy didn't have to answer. A chorus of young voices stated, 'Woolworth's!'

'Might as well,' the two women agreed. 'Got to start somewhere.'

★

The only one missing when they all met up later was George. 'Ah well, he is fourteen,' his mother said. 'Can't really expect him to tag along with us all the time.'

'Our George has gone with a girl,' Laura told them as if she was letting out an important secret.

'Has he now!' Laura looked up to see her mother's eyes fixed doubtfully on her. 'Well, good luck to him. I for one am not going to stand out 'ere and freeze to death. Come on, you lot.'

The warmth of the steamy café hit them as soon as they were inside. 'Just goes to show how cold it is outside,' Patsy said, pulling two tables near to each other so that they could all sit as one party.

'Yeah, didn't notice it when we were in the shops, but I saw a few flakes of snow when we were waiting outside. Don't think we're in for a white Christmas, do you?'

Beans on toast for the kids, toasted teacakes for the mothers, with two large teas each to wash them down. An argument over which flavour milk-shake each of the tribe was going to have, then at last they were ready to set off again. George came in just as they were about to leave. 'You're a bit late,' his mother started to say. He merely gave her a look like that of a cat that has got at the cream, and told her, 'It's all right, Mum, I've eaten.'

Patsy was wrapping a scarf around Emma's neck.

'You do the same with yours, Ellen. If we're going to have a look at the stalls up the Market, it'll be bitter, most of them are out in the open.'

'Kids!' Amy exclaimed as they walked together, the tribe already yards ahead. 'There was me thinking thank God none of mine would be old enough to have to go an' fight if it does come to war, then I find out George is off somewhere with a girl. Don't realise, do you? All of a sudden they're growing up.'

'Stop trying to be a wise old philosopher and let's get this shopping done and get home before it does start to snow. Christ, George is fourteen, not twenty.'

The afternoon was a happy one, Amy and Patsy agreed, even if they were both dog-tired. The kids had rushed from stall to stall, consulting their lists from time to time, the twins deciding to go halves with their cards, so as to leave enough money for all the presents that they'd planned to buy.

It was nearing six o'clock when they got off the bus outside the Underground station, and most of the barrow-boys were packing up. Amy wrinkled her nose at the smell as an old man swept the gutter, pushing rotting vegetables into a heap. They turned off the main road, all of them walking quickly as they skirted the edge of the Common. It was bitter cold and the pavement was already slippery beneath their feet as the frost set in. There was no moon tonight, but their eyes soon became accustomed to the darkness. Once they'd turned into Clapham Manor Street, there was the ghostly yellow light from the gas-mantles shaded in their glass boxes high up on the lamp-posts.

'Are you coming in for a cuppa?' Patsy asked as they came almost level with Navy Street.

'No, I'd best get home, see to the tea. Expect Ted's in by now. I'll see you tomorrow.'

Laura held up her face for Patsy to kiss, as did the twins to Amy, but the boys walked on; even young Tom considered himself too big now to be kissed, especially in the street.

'Look, Mum! Wonder what's going on over there?' Both George and Alex had stopped dead in their tracks and were pointing to the big house that fronted Clapham Manor Street yet was sideways on to the corner of Navy Street.

Flock mattresses with grey and white tick covers were propped up against the coping, two iron bed-springs and wooden head-boards lay at the top of the steps that led down to the basement, a table and chairs stood on the pavement, and a hand-cart loaded high with boxes was leaning against the kerb. It was a big house, let off into flats, but the basement flat had been boarded up for as long as Patsy could remember. She saw very little of her neighbours, except to pass the time of day when they met in the street. Her days were too full to allow her to pop in and out of other folks' houses. What gossip and news there was going the rounds, she usually got from the children. She hadn't heard that this bottom flat had been let, but obviously it had been. A short flight of stone steps led down from the street to a door which was now propped wide open and light from a gas-jet fixed to the wall poured out into the darkness.

'Funny time of night fer a family to be moving in,' said Amy, as she stood shaking her head in disbelief. 'The place can't be fit to live in. Must be damp. The walls will be running with water, it's been boarded up fer months.'

'Most likely they've done a moonlight,' Patsy answered evenly. 'In which case the poor beggars would have been glad of anything they could get. Oh well, our pitying them's not going to help. Come on, kids, let's get going.'

Patsy gave the twins a gentle push, but they had barely moved when there was a clatter of tins being dropped and metal objects hitting the pavement. Give the boys their due, they thrust the parcels they were carrying at Amy and Patsy and ran off up to where two small boys were standing silently looking at what must have seemed to them a total disaster.

Pots and pans, baking tins, a big tin kettle and cooking utensils of every shape and kind were scattered across the pavement; some pieces of cutlery lay in the gutter.

'Bottom fell out your box, did it?' Alex said firmly. 'Well, don't matter, won't take us long to pick up this lot.'

Amy took young Tom by the hand and, giving some of the bags of shopping to Laura to carry, she walked across the road. She paused at her doorway and waved to Patsy.

Patsy put her key into the lock and pushed with her knee at her own front door. Two steps down the passage and she let out a cry, 'Cor, what a lovely smell.' Emma and Ellen sniffed appreciatively. 'Bet Aunty's got the dinner ready.'

Moving awkwardly, because she was loaded down with parcels, Patsy shoved past the twins who had stopped to hang their hats and coats on the wall rack, and entered the kitchen. Her first thought was how lovely and warm the room was, and how lucky she was to have Florrie, not because she was clever but because she took time to do things and always cared for them all. Heavy curtains were drawn across the small bay-window, the glow from the fire was bright, the top of the hob almost red, and to one side of it three large black saucepans were grouped. Florrie was on her knees in front of the hearth just about to shovel more coal on the fire.

Eddie was settled in his armchair with his feet up

on the fender. Both gave her a lovely smile which said, far clearer than any words, welcome home. With the picture of what she had just seen up on the corner still vivid in her mind, she felt guilty. The thought that anything as bad should ever happen to her family put the fear of God into her.

'You should see what we bought Dad, got something lovely for Grandad.' Emma, full of excitement, wanted her father's full attention.

'Should we show you now?' Ellen asked cautiously.

He didn't reply. The boys came barging in and suddenly everyone was talking at once.

'Moving in to that basement!' Florrie didn't believe it.

'It 'ain't half cold in there, Dad. They ain't got no fire. Don't you believe me?' David asked, misunderstanding the expression on his father's face.

Anger flickered on to Florrie's face. 'Got kiddies, did you say?'

'Yes, two,' Patsy told her in a gentle voice. 'Doesn't bear thinking about, does it?'

'No, it doesn't.' Eddie's voice rose in anger. 'Alex, get some wood from the shed.' Next minute they heard the sound of Eddie at the coal-hole. Swiftly, shovels-full of coals were being shot into a galvanised bucket.

'Shan't be long,' Eddie told Patsy as he took the bundle of wood from Alex and tucked it under his arm. 'No one should have to be without a fire on a night like this.'

'Pop the cloth on and lay the table for me, luvvie,' Florrie said to Ellen as the door closed behind their father. 'And you can get the bread out of the pantry,' she instructed Emma.

'Smells good,' Patsy muttered, raising the lid of the largest of the saucepans on the hob. Dipping in the long-handled spoon she found she had a job to stir the contents. 'What have yer put in here? It's thick enough for the spoon to stand up on its own.'

Florrie chuckled. 'Stick to your ribs, that will. Eddie got me a couple of oxtails, beauties they were. What did I put in with them? That's a daft question. Onions, carrots, turnips, lentils and a coupla handfuls of pearl-barley, broth's never no good without a bit of barley. Oh yeah, and I added a few split peas an' some butter-beans and anything else that I found in the cupboard. That's a pot of spuds there, and in that other pan is extra gravy and a load of dumplings. Got a rice pudding in the oven. Thought I might as well; daft to 'ave a great fire going and the oven at the side sitting there with nothing in it.'

'You're a marvel, Florrie. Sometimes you surprise even me,' Patsy told her. Florrie didn't answer, she just stood there looking as if she was miles away. Patsy touched her arm. 'Thinking about the kids up the road, aren't you?'

'My God, yes.' She hitched her bosoms up. 'Do you know something, Patsy? That food will stick in me throat if we don't do something, for them kids at least.'

'Well, we will then, eh?'

'Yeah, get that enamel mixing bowl out from under the dresser, we've enough to feed an army so we won't miss a bit.'

Steam rose up, misting the mirror that hung over the mantelshelf, as Florrie spooned potatoes into the bottom of the bowl and Patsy ladled out pieces of meat and the thick soup to cover them. Alex carried the third saucepan to the draining-board and dumplings were added. Lastly, to the cheers of the twins and great belly laughs from the boys, Florrie raised the pan high and tipped out extra gravy until the bowl was full almost to the brim.

Ellen was allowed to break the top off the cottage loaf, and Emma was just wrapping it in a cloth when their father came in. His face was white and pinched with the cold, but his expression brightened as he said, 'I'll take it over.' He pushed his arms back into the sleeves of his jacket and wound his muffler tightly round his neck. 'God knows they can do with this,' he murmured, picking up the heavy tray.

What a day! A last look to see that the window was securely fastened and the fire banked down safely, then picking up her book and the evening paper for Eddie to read, Patsy was ready for bed.

Eddie was still sitting in his chair, gazing into the glowing embers, lost in thought. Finally he turned to her, with a look on his face so sad that it tore at her heart.

'Reckon we've got a lot to be grateful for.'

'Reckon we have.' They stayed quiet a few minutes more, then went up to bed together.

Sunday afternoon and the house was quiet. The twins had gone to Sunday school, the boys should have gone as well but Patsy wouldn't vouch for the fact that they had. Eddie had taken Florrie home to Tooting; he'd be a while yet, seeing her fire was lit and making sure she was safe and warm. Patsy felt thoroughly relaxed as she snuggled back against the cushions of the settee. It was lovely up here in the front room with logs burning in the wide open-hearth fireplace. In the winter Eddie always lit a fire in the front room on Sundays. Her eyelids began to drop and the *News of the World* slipped from her hands down on to the floor. 'Mmm,' she muttered lazily, 'let it stay, can't be bothered to read.' But a single knock on the front door shattered any hope that she might have drifted off and had forty winks. Better answer it, she sighed – never know, it could be the boys, but she knew it wasn't. Too quiet for them.

On the step stood a tall, thin lady, dressed neatly in grey. Light brown hair, twisted into a bun at the nape of her neck, peeped out from a grey hat. Her long straight coat was grey in colour, so too were the hand-knitted woollen gloves that she wore. On her feet were black high-buttoned boots, the toe-caps of which were so highly polished that Patsy was sure that if she knelt down she would be able to see her face in them.

'I've brought your bowl and cloths back,' she said in a half-whisper as she held out her shopping bag.

Realisation dawned on Patsy and she stood aside and held the door open wide. 'Please, come in. I'm sorry I don't know your name,' she ventured, once they were inside the front room. 'Won't you take your coat off and sit down?'

The woman tried to answer but seemed afraid to speak and Patsy was worried that she was going to cry. Gently she pushed her into a chair that was placed near to the fire. 'I'll make us a cuppa tea, won't take me a tick.'

But before she had a chance to move the woman put out her arm, blocking the way. 'Mary Briggs. Me and me husband Stan will never be able to repay you.' The words came out in a rush. 'What you and your man did for us was a life-saver.'

Patsy felt she should say something, but she didn't know what. She bent over and at once saw that the eyes of this Mary Briggs were quite lovely: a deep blue that was almost violet, and now brimming with tears. Placing her hand on to Mary's shoulder, Patsy told her, 'We all of us need help at some time in our lives.'

Mary took a clean handkerchief from her coat pocket and wiped her eyes. 'That's as maybe, but one good turn deserves another and I won't rest till I've been able to repay you in some way or another.'

Patsy felt choked up as she went down the passage to the kitchen. Returning some ten minutes later with tea and scones for each of them, she was relieved to see that Mary had at least loosened her coat and now seemed to be more at ease, even eager to talk.

'My Stan's got a job. Starts tomorrow,' she blurted out with a note of pride in her voice.

'Oh, I am pleased,' Patsy exclaimed as she set a small table at Mary's elbow.

'Stan was in the Army, you know. Done seven years. Not been able to get a job since he came out. Not till now, that is.'

'Do you take sugar?' Patsy asked.

'One spoonful, please.'

'Going to be an attendant, up at the swimming-baths. Smashing swimmer, my Stan is – used to swim for the Army. Both our boys can swim.'

Patsy's heart was aching for this poor woman. They'd obviously known better times.

A sudden thought seemed to hit Mary, and her whole face brightened as she asked, 'Do your children go swimming?'

'Alex and David do – that's the two who were with George last night. We've also got twin girls, Ellen an' Emma, they're seven years old. They've never learnt to swim.'

'Well.' For the first time a smile spread across Mary's face. 'When we get on our feet a bit, perhaps we could all go to the baths together? I'm sure my Stan would soon be able to teach your little girls to swim.'

It was a very much happier woman that Patsy later showed to the door. She had made some friends and been shown kindness, so much so that her troubles no longer appeared to be gigantic.

Before closing the front door Patsy walked to the gate and stood looking towards Clapham Manor Street. It was a wonderful street really. It had everything: a school, two pubs and a church with a church hall where some activity was always taking place. Bassett's, the corner shop, where the kids got good value for their pennies. A dairy, owned by Ebdon who delivered milk round the streets on a push-cart. An off-licence, open all hours of the day and night. Old Tom Draper's yard; you could buy and sell almost anything there if you'd a mind to. Last but by no means least, the swimming-baths. Thank you, God. Patsy offered up her silent prayer. Make things go right for this new family in the street. Let his new job work out well. What if that woman had come to return her things, seen her lovely home and warm fire and hadn't had any hope for the future for herself?

Stop it, you daft thing. She *has* got hope. Her man's got a job, they'll soon get themselves sorted out now. All the same, as she settled herself back again on the settee she wondered if there wasn't someone up there who watched out for her and her family.

Just fourteen days to go to Christmas. The kitchen had an air of contentment about it this evening. Eddie had set a gate-legged table in front of the dresser and the twins sat one at each side of it, writing their Christmas cards. Patsy hadn't bothered to put the chenille cloth over the table when they'd finished dinner. Alex and David were wrapping up their presents. The wooden table-top was covered in coloured paper, bright string, scissors and glue. A lot of laughing was going on. Pink bedsocks for Auntie Florrie: David held them high. Alex produced from his bag Yardley 4711 eau-de-cologne: 'if her poor old feet get hot and sweaty in your socks, she can sprinkle

them with this.' They both had a fit of the giggles.
'Stop mucking about an' put your finger on this knot,'
Alex ordered. David did as he was bid, pulling back
his hand as Alex was about to tie the gold-coloured
string. Alex went to swipe him around the head,
David ducked and they both fell forward which made
them chuckle even more.

'Hold on, boys.' Their father's voice was firm and
they both looked at him in surprise. He didn't normally mind if they were making a bit of a racket.
'The King's going to speak in a minute. Just be quiet
while I listen.'

Patsy looked up from her sewing. She'd forgotten
all about this. It had been announced by the Prime
Minister in the House of Commons yesterday that
King Edward VIII was intending to abdicate. The
boys did keep quiet, and you could have heard a pin
drop in the kitchen as they heard the King say that
he was speaking to the nation from Windsor Castle.
He couldn't carry on being King of England: '. . . not
without the help and support of the woman I love.'
How sad his voice sounded.

'Readallaboutit!' Alex and David were out early next
morning, shouting, as were hundreds more paper-
boys. This kind of news sold papers.

The Duke of York had succeeded his brother and

was now King. The reporters had soon got the news. The first act that King George VI had done was to create the ex-King Duke of Windsor.

'Wonder what kind of Christmas he'll have,' Patsy remarked to Eddie as she placed his breakfast on the table in front of him.

'God only knows,' was the only answer he could give her.

Chapter Four

IT WAS SPRING-TIME again: the spring of 1939. So much had altered in the routine of Patsy's life over the past two years. This was the third season that Ollie, Eddie and herself had been involved in the motor-coach business. It's hard to believe that we have done so well, Patsy thought as she settled back in her swivel chair, and through the open window surveyed the Saturday morning activity going on in the street below. Typical, busy old London. She loved the noise and the sights of the city clattering about its business.

Barrow-boys with their carts placed out along the kerbs, tall old-fashioned pub on the corner with a shellfish stall on its forecourt. Paper-boy outside Stockwell tube station, trams rattling to a stop in the centre of the road. A queue of men and women waiting for an 88 bus. Now that was a fascinating bus route, with all kinds of history mingled in one journey — a journey that she loved to take whenever she had any spare time. Up past the Tate library and the Guinness tenements whose outside walls were blackened by dirt, soot and grime. Over Vauxhall Bridge and on to the Embankment. Who wouldn't stop and stare at the Thames? Busy old thoroughfare, was London's River Thames. The bus would turn left at the Tate Gallery, passing Millbank Military Hospital where, on a day like this, patients would be sitting in the grounds. Then you *would* be in London. From the top deck of the bus and with a few pennies for a ticket you could have a bird's-eye view of Parliament Square, the Cenotaph, Downing Street and Scotland Yard, Admiralty Arch, Nelson on his Column in Trafalgar Square. Who could be bored with all that on the doorstep? There couldn't be another place like London, not in the whole of the world.

A smile played around Patsy's lips and she relaxed in her chair. That bit of day-dreaming had done her the world of good. Now she could tackle the busy working morning stretching ahead of her; being Saturday, the office closed at half-past twelve. A lot of her time was spent in this office, high above the main street in Stockwell. There had been a time when she cursed Ollie and this job: she hadn't been cut out for book-keeping and suchlike, or so she'd thought. But Ollie had taken a different view. 'You'll take to it like a duck to water,' he had assured her. Now she liked to think he had been right; she certainly did enjoy most days.

Ollie now had seven motor-coaches operating on the roads. Besides the place at Vauxhall, which was now a busy yard, he had bought up two adjoining premises in Garratt Lane, half-way between Tooting and Earls-field. It had taken more than six months before he had been entirely satisfied with the modernisation of these properties, but in the end all the financial outlay had paid off and they were all extremely proud of that coach station. Not that it had been easy at first. Work hadn't just dropped from the skies, and for the first twelve months expenses had tended to exceed the takings. Not so any more; now they had enough work to keep all the coaches on the road, at least until the autumn. Ollie hadn't penny-pinched. The interior of all the coaches had been renovated; there were curtains at the windows and antimacassars on the backs of the seats, all of which had been re-upholstered. The men were proud of their job and of the vehicles they drove. Ollie provided them with a 'uniform' of long white coats and caps with shiny peaks. Slogans painted on the sides of the coaches read: 'Tour Britain with Ace'.

The era of excursions to England's beauty spots and seaside resorts had dawned, bringing considerable competition to the railways. A lot of thanks was due to the four men employed between the two yards. Geniuses – that's how Ollie described them. 'Good blokes,' said Eddie, 'never happy unless they have a spanner in their hands and blobs of grease up their arms.' A happy bunch, Patsy would think every Friday morning as she made up the wage-packets.

She wished Alex would work for Ollie, but Alex had other ideas. Both her boys were independent, determined to make their own way in this world. A year now since Alex had left school – not that he was a layabout, oh no, quite the reverse. Tough, and still heavy in build, Alex at fifteen was taller than Patsy by at least six inches; he looked older than he was, and now that he no longer went to school he liked to think that he was grown up. He'd always been a handsome child and was now undoubtedly growing into a handsome man. Four newspaper stands – Clapham Common, Clapham South, Balham Station and Tooting Bec – were all under his control. Up and out at the crack of dawn, he no longer delivered papers for the local shop but rode on the back of the printers' vans, throwing off the bundles of dailies at street corners and news-stands. He had acquired those four main sites, subletting them off to young men and raking off a percentage of their takings for himself.

To the astonishment of both his parents, Alex also had another lucrative business on the go: he sold flowers. Patsy could never recall how she had come to find this out without having to smile to herself. She had watched him make a mobile stand, paint it dark green and fix wheels to the bottom. No good asking what it was for, since Alex was a master when it came to evading answers. One Friday evening she had come home from visiting Florrie in Tooting – funny really what made her decide to take the tube, she nearly always used the trams. Coming out of the Underground station entrance she had paused to admire the flowers which were being offered for sale to passers-by. It really was a lovely show the street-corner vendor had set out: masses of chrysanths, long-stemmed roses, heavily scented carnations and early spring flowers stacked in tin vases one above the other, with pot-plants and green ferns displayed on the ground at the base of the stand.

'All fresh cut,' Alex was shouting. 'Treat the old woman – works wonders, does a bunch of flowers.' Trade was brisk as he kept up his patter, and David was there too – running round, tearing off sheets of wrapping paper from a huge roll, opening fresh boxes to display the contents, taking the money from the customers. Her two boys certainly made a great team, and within two weeks Alex had expanded. On Saturdays and Sundays he and David now pushed their mobile stand to the steps outside the Women's Hospital at Clapham South, where by all accounts they did a roaring trade with folk visiting their sick relatives. On the quiet Patsy had a great deal of admiration for the pair of them. It was a long slog down to the hospital, especially pushing that great flower stand in front of them.

When Alex realised that Patsy had found out about his flower selling, he had come in through the back door one evening and – with a mock bow and his huge dark eyes twinkling with silent laughter – he had presented her with the sweetest-scented bouquet of flowers any mother could wish for. Yes, this eldest lad of hers had his sights fixed firmly on making his fortune, totally oblivious to the rumours that England was preparing for war.

'Ready for a cup of tea, Mrs Owen?' Patsy started, brought back from her musings with a bump. She hadn't heard the door to her office open.

'Oh, yes please, Vicky,' she answered quickly.

'Right. I'll bring it through in just a tick.'

Vicky Baldwin! There's a girl who's had it rough if ever there was one. Patsy screwed the top on to her fountain pen and moved a few papers out of the way, ready for Vicky to set down the tray. That girl had worked for them almost from the start. Brought up in an orphanage, without a single clue as to who her parents might have been, she had been turfed out to earn her own living as soon as she had reached the age of sixteen. First of all she had lived in a women's hostel, but that hadn't worked out; then a Salvation Army officer had used her influence and Vicky had moved into a home that was owned and run by the Salvation Army. This was in Vauxhall, where she and Ollie had first met, sharing a table in a local café. He had offered her a job and all the family had taken her to their hearts. Such a happy person was Vicky, never bemoaning the fact that she had no family of her own. Fairly tall, with light brown hair and a freckly face, her pale blue eyes sparkled with merriment whenever she showed off her cheeky grin. Most of the fun that went on in the office stemmed in one way or another from Vicky. Out on the road she was excellent company, poking fun at the coach drivers, imitating the Cockney slang of the passengers, making everyone laugh.

Funny how life turns out, Patsy thought. Her own childhood had been made better by the folk of Strathmore Street and the loving care they had freely given. Time and things had changed and now she and Eddie were set up nicely, thanks to Ollie, but who would have thought that a lonely young girl like Vicky would have been sent into their lives?

'There's a good girl,' Patsy said, as she took a cup of tea from Vicky's hand, then watched as she sat down in the chair which stood in front of the desk opposite.

'How's the work going?' Patsy asked, when she'd drained her cup.

'Fine. I've a couple more letters to type, but I'll finished well before eleven. Anything I can do for you?'

'No,' Patsy answered, then quickly changed her

mind, 'unless you'd like to help sort out Monday's work-load? That way I could get off a bit early as well.'

'Course I will. Got a double going from the Leather Bottle Monday morning, haven't we?'

'Yes. And that reminds me, don't come to the office first but meet me there will you? About quarter-past eight will do. Coaches are booked to be leaving at nine.'

Vicky set her cup down on the tray and with a laugh said, 'Wouldn't miss it for the world. If it's anything like the send-off they gave the women on the outing from the Fountain . . .' She gave another laugh and the sound was infectious.

Patsy was grinning as she said, 'So I've been told. Largely due to you, wasn't it? You little monkey.'

Vicky was still chuckling as the door opened. 'Here's the guv'nor,' she whispered as she picked up the tea-tray, walked towards Eddie and made to sidle past him.

'Don't go on my account, just 'cause I caught the pair of you wasting time and guzzling tea.' The amusement in his voice set Vicky off again, and with a tinkling laugh and cheeky grin she said, 'Suppose you want a cup, do you?'

'Are you coming to us for your dinner tomorrow?' he asked with mock severity, ''cause, if you are, young lady, then I think I'm entitled to a cuppa in this office, don't you?'

'Yes, Sir! Right away, sir! On the double, it's coming up!'

As the door closed behind Vicky, Patsy looked up into Eddie's eyes. 'Marvellous kid, isn't she?'

'Yes, she is,' he agreed. And not for the first time he told himself, she's very much like you were, my love, when I first met you. Takes all the knocks life throws at her and still comes up smiling.

This Sunday dinner-time was turning into a riotous affair; with everyone wanting to put their point of view, the chatter was becoming deafening. On to the end of the large kitchen table Patsy had added the small oblong table which usually stood out in the scullery, covering the two of them with a heavy damask cloth which had belonged to Eddie's mother. There were ten of them there for their dinner. Ollie and Florrie came every Sunday, and added to the tribe today were Kitty from upstairs and Vicky from the office.

'Have you all had enough?' Patsy cried. 'I'm waiting to clear these vegetable dishes and dish up the pudding.'

Everyone went quiet for a moment at the sound

of Patsy's raised voice. Then heads nodded and voices said, 'Yes, more than enough.'

Vicky got to her feet and began to help Patsy. Out in the scullery Patsy stood the largest of the vegetable dishes on the draining-board and began to scrape all the left-over vegetables into the one dish.

'I think it's lovely to have Sunday dinner with the veg all in separate dishes, but it makes a helluva lot more washing up,' murmured Vicky as she stacked the plates in the sink and stood the cutlery in the stone jar that she'd filled with hot water from the kettle.

'Yeah, I know,' Patsy told her, 'but there's method in my madness. Couldn't use left-overs from the plates, but that lot that's been in dishes will make lovely bubble and squeak tomorrow.'

'Do you want this bowl of trifle put on the table?' Vicky called from inside the larder.

'No, that's for tea-time, but on the lower shelf you'll find a jug of custard – bring that, will you? Mind, it should still be hot; I only made it just before we sat down.'

Vicky walked backwards out of the larder to be met by a cloud of steam as Patsy took the lid off the huge black saucepan. 'Horrible job, this,' she muttered under her breath as she struggled to unwind the hot cloths from the two long suet puddings.

'Spotted Dick or Treacle Roly-poly?' Patsy asked

each in turn, beginning with the twins as they were the youngest. Florrie took the plates from her hand and poured custard over everyone's choice. At last they were all served and silence reigned, but not for long.

Kitty nudged Ollie's arm, 'Did you know the Town Hall is offering Anderson air-raid shelters for folk to put in their back gardens?'

'Yes. I was saying to Eddie, we should think about applying for one: have to dig deep for it to be of any use, though.

'Oh, we're not getting off on that subject again, are we?' Florrie remembered the First War too vividly to be excited about another.

'Afraid it's a certainty,' Ollie told her. 'Not many that won't admit it now.'

'Seems like it, Flo,' Kitty added. 'What I'd like to know is what the hell Chamberlain thought he was up to. Came back here from meeting with that Hitler, waving a bit of paper saying it would guarantee us peace. Always did say you never could believe a guarantee. Only a bit of paper after all's said and done. Never should 'ave trusted 'im.'

'It wasn't only the ordinary man in the street who had faith in Chamberlain.' David, quiet as a mouse but not missing a single word, now spoke up. 'The Royal Family trusted him, as did many politicians. You know, Auntie Kitty, when Chamberlain landed at Heston Aerodrome the Lord Mayer of London was there to meet him. Yes, he was.' David emphasised his point. 'Then they went to Buckingham Palace and the King and Queen must 'ave thought he'd done a wonderful job because they came out on the balcony with Mister Chamberlain and the Mall was packed with crowds of people who all cheered him.'

Eddie was proud of the way David had followed the news, by far the more serious of his two sons. Now Eddie sadly shook his head. 'Right farce, that's what that turned out to be, son. Five days after the Royal Family had stood there thanking our Prime Minister for his peace-making effort, Hitler led his troops into Czechoslovakia.'

Florrie was feeling properly morbid by now. 'We didn't get offered no shelters when the Zeppelins come over in the last War. And in 1916, not thousands but tens of thousands of young men – most of them mere boys not much older than you, Alec – died, swamped in the rotten mud of the Somme in Northern France. And what for, eh? You tell me. War to end all wars! Huh! Will be the same as last time; the big-nobs will make a fortune and the country will be left with loads of young widows, kids that 'ave never known their fathers and fine boys who've lost 'alf their limbs. And what if the bleeding Germans use gas again? You'll have the hospitals full of blokes coughing their 'earts up, dying a slow death.'

You could have heard a pin drop when Florrie stopped talking and the quiet was only broken by Ollie tapping on the side of the teapot. 'That tea will be well and truly stewed,' he told Patsy.

She poured tea from the large brown teapot into the best gold-edged cups that she only used on Sundays and bank holidays, and Eddie handed them round. 'Come on now, girls, get ready, or you'll be late for Sunday school,' Patsy urged the twins.

'I'll go with you,' Vicky offered, 'and we'll have a walk round the pond on the Common when we come out.'

'We've got to get going an' all,' Alex told David. 'Visitors start arriving well before three, and we've a lot of flowers I want to shift today.'

All five adults breathed a sigh of contentment as they settled themselves down in the comfort of the front room. Eddie was reading the *News of the World*, Ollie was packing his pipe with tobacco, Florrie was fishing her knitting out of her canvas bag and Patsy was already dozing, when Kitty tapped the page of the magazine that she was looking at.

'Well, I never!' she declared. 'I didn't believe Old Mother Beasely when she was spouting off in the corner shop the other day. Bloody wicked, it is.' Her voice was deep with feeling as she went on, 'Ma

Beasely said she saw on the news at the pictures that old Jewish men and women were made to go down on their hands and knees and scrub the streets in Vienna, while Hitler's Nazi Stormtroopers stood laughing at them. What can't speak can't lie. There's a picture of them here in this book. I'll 'ave to tell Ma Beasely I'm sorry when I see her 'cause I let her know I didn't believe a word of it. Bloody awful, ain't it? Beats me how a human being could torment old people like that. Still those Nazis, as they call themselves, ain't human – bloody monsters, they must be.' Kitty was very quiet for the rest of the afternoon.

Patsy and Vicky arrived at Bendon Valley at almost the same time on this beautiful sunny Monday morning. The sky was blue, not a cloud in sight. 'They should have a good day,' Eddie said as he got back into his car. 'I'll see you both back at the office.'

Six months ago Ollie had decided that both he and Eddie needed a car. Ollie had a beauty: an Austin Saloon, sixteen horse-power. Eddie had settled for a Morris Cowley Family Saloon; it was big and roomy for them all to ride in, and gave space enough for him to manoeuvre his gammy leg. Mr Quinton, landlord of the Leather Bottle, was smiling at them from the doorway of his pub as Patsy and Vicky approached. 'Morning, Mrs Owen,' he called in a loud hearty voice. 'D'you fancy a snorter?'

Patsy pulled a horrible face.

'Well, how about a cuppa before the riff-raff start arriving?'

'Now you're talking,' she smiled. 'We've never been known to refuse a cup of tea, have we, Vicky?'

Vicky nodded enthusiastically. She couldn't voice an answer because she had a pencil stuck in her mouth and was busy totting up the number of passengers booked to travel on the coach she was responsible for.

The courtyard of the Leather Bottle was packed by half-past eight. Women of all shapes and sizes, dressed in their best, showing off straw hats that had been retrimmed with flowers and artificial cherries and were secured to their heads with long hat-pins. 'All aboard!' the driver shouted as Patsy did her best to count the heads. 'No crates of beer to be loaded,' he whispered. 'Not like the men, but I'll bet you a bob to a tanner they've a few bottles tucked away in those bags of theirs.'

Patsy laughed. 'Get on with you, Bert, you love them. Day away from your Missus, surrounded by women, you ought to pay us for the job, not the other way round.'

'If you were coming, Mrs Owen, I'd be inclined to agree.'

'Forget the flattery, you old charmer, and see about getting this bus on the road. I suppose you do know it's Hastings you're supposed to be making for?'

'Really? I thought it was Timbuctoo today.'

'Bring us back a rock, Mum.'

'You didn't give us a penny like you promised.'

'Can we 'ave fish and chips when you get back tonight?'

Patsy got elbowed out of the way as the children stood on the step, jumped up at the windows and ran alongside the coach, yelling at the tops of their voices to attract the attention of their mothers.

'What's tickling you, love?' Patsy asked Vicky as they stood amongst the kiddies waving until the coach turned the corner. Whatever it was, it had to be wildly funny, because it was a good few minutes before Vicky was able to tell her.

'Yours was supposed to be the rough outing, street collections and all that; mine was the hoity-toity one. Ladies' sewing circle from the church – right?'

'Right,' agreed Patsy.

'Load of old cods-wallop! They might give themselves airs and graces and act as if they were royalty: 'Seats at the back of the coach are reserved for us, young lady.' 'Do take Miss Saxton's bag, the steps of this bus are rather high.' Then when I was in the gangway, counting the passengers, what do I see? Both of 'em swigging from a gin bottle! Wouldn't mind, but the bus hadn't even moved off! They'll be pissed as parrots time they get to Hastings. And where d'you think they were hiding their bottles? Up their long skirts! Must have a bag tied round their waist, or perhaps they shove 'em up their knicker-leg.'

Patsy's sides were splitting; Vicky's mimicking of the two old maids had been so exactly right.

'Knock it off, love,' she pleaded between her own giggles. 'Good luck to them, I say. Probably the only bit of joy they get out of life.'

'Yeah, more than likely, but all the same old Cecil wants to watch his step today.'

The thought of Cecil Woodman, one of their best drivers but a reserved man at the best of times, being propositioned by two ladies from the church was too much. As they went across the road to the bus stop arm in arm, it would have been hard to say who was laughing the most, Patsy or Vicky.

The summer was one of the best, weather-wise, that Patsy could remember. Business was very good and they could have done with more buses, as they were turning bookings away. Charabanc rides didn't cost the earth and were extremely popular. Often Patsy had the feeling that if folk did know that war was inevitable, they were pushing the fact to the backs of their minds. The weather was simply glorious and families were determined to get out and about and enjoy it while they still had the chance. Picnics in the parks and on the Common were only an everyday treat, it seemed; what most regarded as a marvellous idea was to get to the seaside and see the sea. So neighbours in the back streets, customers in the pubs and men and women in factory canteens all clubbed together and arranged outings. Margate, Ramsgate, dear old Brighton known as 'London by the sea', all these resorts became packed at week-ends and on bank holidays. By far the most popular, at least with Ace Coaches, was Southend. It had been a unanimous decision between Ollie and Eddie to lay on an evening coach to see the lights at Southend. The fare was set at three and sixpence return, and there were never any vacant seats.

'Maybe the women and children go to see the illuminations, and have rides in the fun park,' Ollie commented one evening as they were all having dinner, 'but I'd like to bet the men never get to see the sea. Half cut, time they get there, with the number of crates of beer they load the bus up with, and then make straight for the pubs the minute they reach the coast. Doesn't make sense, does it?'

'Don't knock it,' Eddie had a wide grin on his face. 'It's good for trade, whether they bathe or booze when they get there.'

★

Another Sunday, with dinner well on the way to being ready. Roast ribs of beef today, with baked parsnips and Brussels tops, not forgetting the Yorkshire puds. This must be the best time of my life, Patsy told herself, though I'm frightened it's all too good to be true. The twins were doing well at school and Ollie had suggested that they go on to secretarial college when they were old enough. We can certainly afford it, she mused; even cash seemed plentiful at the moment. She'd almost given up worrying about the boys. David only had one more year at school, and it was still a case of where Alex led David was sure to follow. Alex was still up to his tricks, though to be fair – as Eddie pointed out often enough – Alex had never been in trouble with the police. There were a great many pies that he had his fingers in and he seemed to be always one jump ahead of his associates; fancy, only fifteen years old and he had men working for him! She begrudged him nothing though. Up at the crack of dawn, never asking anyone to call him, Covent Garden was his favourite territory. Fruit, flowers and vegetables, anything that was in season, you could be sure that he came away having struck a good bargain.

'Born with an old head on his shoulders,' was Florrie's opinion, 'but a damn clever one at that,' she would state, when Alex buttered her up by bringing her a bag of her favourite boiled sweets, or a sweet-scented bowl of plants. Always could charm the birds out of the trees, could Alex.

'Join up now,' the posters were urging. Surely if war did come it wouldn't last that long? Not long enough for her boys to be old enough to be called up. The Prime Minister was clinging to his policy of appeasement despite Hitler's increasingly blatant tactics. Tension was growing by the day.

'Dig for Victory' was another slogan appearing on the hoardings. 'Not a bad idea,' Eddie told the whole family. 'We may as well have a few chickens whilst we're about it. Might end up being glad to eat anything.'

No sooner the word than the deed. Hard to say who were the biggest kids, Ollie, Eddie or the two boys. Stripped to the waist – the sun was beating down and it was almost unbearably hot – the four of them set to with shovels, spades and garden forks. Fervent hammering began, nails were handed up at the double, planks of wood started to form a shape, and before darkness fell a hen-house had been built, with a long run made secure by the use of small-mesh wire netting. A quart milk-bottle filled with water and wired to a block of wood had been upturned over a bowl of water on the ground. 'Simple but clever,' declared Patsy when the boys explained that as the chicks drank and the level of the water went down it would fill from the milk-bottle. Nest-boxes in the hen-house were filled with clean straw. Kitty said she would bake her stale crusts of bread in the range oven and then grind them down with the rolling-pin. Ellen tied a cabbage to the top wire for the hens to peck at, and Emma declared she was going to be the first to throw corn to them.

All that remained was to buy the chickens. Come Saturday afternoon the whole tribe set out in the two cars. Following the advice given in the local paper, they were off to Finch's Farm at Mickleham in Surrey.

'It'll pay to buy the best,' the young man with the ruddy complexion told Eddie, as he took the cap off his head and used his forearm to wipe the sweat from his forehead. 'How much space 'ave you allowed?'

Eddie took a drawing from his pocket and passed it over.

'Hm. I'm impressed,' the lad was honest enough to admit. 'Most townies ain't got a clue as to how to go about setting up poultry. Coupla dozen, I'd say, to start you off. Best egg-producing breed is Rhode Island Reds, without a doubt.'

The choice was settled. Only a matter now of going to the office, making the payment and waiting for the hens to be packed into special boxes.

'Look, Ellen.' Emma tugged at her twin's sleeve. 'See what the notice says: "Inspection of Farm cordially invited".'

'Oh yeah. It's a bit boring standing around just waiting, and I'm boiling hot.'

Gingerly the two girls looked around to see if anyone was going to forbid them to wander off. Florrie was still in the car. 'Snoozing, I expect,' said Ellen.

'More like snoring,' giggled Emma. Their mother had gone off with the boys to the packing shed, and Dad and Grandad were nowhere to be seen.

'Let's go!' they said in unison.

Across the yard they scampered, round the side of an enormous barn, and were met with a lovely sight. 'Ducks, aren't they beautiful?' Ellen cried, kneeling down to trail her hand in the pond. A sudden commotion made them both jump and they turned to see some baby ducklings waddling towards them across the grass. Creamy-coloured, with downy feathers and bright yellow beaks – making a right old racket, they were.

'Them's early-hatched ducks, they are.' They got up from their knees to see a young girl smiling at them. 'Have you come to buy some?'

'No. Wish we had; we ain't got a pond, but we're going to have some chickens,' Emma told her firmly.

'What did you mean by early-hatched ducks?' Ellen asked cautiously. 'Is there a difference?'

''Course there is,' the girl said, giving Ellen a smug little smile. 'These will produce early eggs. Others that we have don't care where they lay their eggs. It's fun searching for them though: sometimes it's only in the yard or on the grass, but others lay them in the pond and we have to use a net to get at them.'

'Cor, you are lucky, living here on a farm.'

'Well, you two won't be so lucky if you don't soon come on.' Alex sounded properly annoyed. 'Dad's ready to go and I've been sent to look for you.'

The twins looked at their new-found friend and they all laughed. 'Hope we can come back and see you another day,' they told her wistfully.

Let free from their boxes, the young hens soon found their legs, making squeaking noises as they picked at the food trough.

'Ain't you got enough to do, Patsy? You'll have to feed them, clean them out – and in the winter you'll 'ave to cook hot mash for them.' There was pride in Florrie's voice as well as exasperation.

'I know all that,' Patsy agreed happily. 'Think of the eggs, fresh and warm – you shall have the very first one.'

'Oh go on with you.' Florrie pretended she wasn't interested but really she was delighted.

It was strange how the summer continued to be so marvellous, almost as though the weather was urging them to get about and see the countryside before war was declared. 'There is going to be a war, isn't there?' Patsy said to Eddie as she lay snuggled up to him in bed.

''Fraid so. Makes me feel so helpless. I'd have joined up by now, if I thought they'd have me.'

She pondered on that for a while, then said, 'I'm sorry, my darling, but I've got to admit that I'm glad about your leg. I don't want you to go in the Forces. Must be something else you can do, not everyone will go off and fight.'

'Yes, have to wait and see. I'll volunteer my services and do the best I can.'

Patsy felt helpless all of a sudden, seeing it from Eddie's point of view, and she comforted him in the best way she knew how. Tucking her head in underneath his arm to rest in the hollow of his shoulder, she began to gently stroke his bare chest. Despite the rumours and the depressing news that came over the wireless, they had each other and their love-making was still something to enjoy. This was their time: no children, no business, no wondering what meals to prepare, just the wonderment of each other. 'Oh, Eddie, I knew our life was too good to be true,' she said, as he lay on his back now with his arm flung out across her. How could grown men talk about bombing and killing each other? While she was tucked up safely in this bedroom with Eddie beside her everything felt so right, normal and lovely. The very thought of England having to fight another war seemed absurd. 'I wish we could stay like this for ever.'

'You'd probably end up complaining you'd got cramp.'

'Daft thing,' she said lovingly as she cuddled up to him once more.

Chapter Five

NO MATTER HOW grave the news had been, nothing seemed to have prepared folk for the reality. One thing was certain, there wasn't an adult alive who would forget this Sunday morning: 3rd September, 1939, and Neville Chamberlain had just told the nation on the wireless that a state of war now existed between England and Germany. It would be one of those incredible memories which people would shake their heads over for the rest of their lives. Within minutes the air-raid sirens sounded all over London, and from that moment the camaraderie flowed. As women sobbed and men cursed, old folk remembered the First War and young ones dreaded the outcome of this one, friendships were formed that would last through the war.

'You haven't got a shelter yet, 'ave you, Missus? You're welcome to come down in ours.'

A woman from across the street to whom Patsy had hardly done more than nod good morning up to now, was crossing the road as she spoke. 'My name's Ada Nicholls, about time we got to know each other. Bloody awful, ain't it!'

'Patsy. Patsy Owen,' she managed to stutter. 'Thanks for the offer, my lot seem to have gone indoors. Better see what they're up to.'

A moaning wail rent the air. 'That's the all-clear,' Ollie told the people still gathered at their gateways. 'It was a false alarm.'

False alarm or not, it was a grim reminder to all Londoners that in this war they were likely to be in the front line of it all from the very word go.

Things moved quickly. Air-Raid Wardens saw to it that everyone had an adequate blackout system.

'We ain't got enough thick stuff to cover every blasted window in the 'ouse,' moaned the old couple who lived in the top flat of the corner house. Stan Briggs was altogether a different kettle of fish from his timid wife. He'd proved to be a very good friend to the Owens since taking up his job at the swimming-baths. He was standing for no nonsense now that he was also the area Warden.

'Well, you'd better set to and find some,' he bawled in a voice that would wake the dead. 'Just let me see so much as a hint of a light showing and you won't be facing no fine, you'll be going to prison. We're having no signalling to German bombers from round here.' Thick-set, clean-shaven, meant what he said, a real Army man was Stan Briggs.

Rolls of sticky tape were sold by the hundred. 'You needn't buy any, Mum,' David told Patsy. 'I'll bring some home tonight. Alex's got a load of it.' That figures, Patsy smiled to herself, trust Alex to have for sale what everyone needed. Every glass window had to be heavily taped, to prevent flying glass; not only windows in houses but on trams, buses, railway carriages and even taxis.

Ollie and Eddie took the two boys with them and together with Ted Andrews and his sons, George and Tom, set off to the Civil Defence centre to be given instructions on how to handle a stirrup-pump. Although they couldn't possibly have know it then, there would be many a day in the months ahead when one or another of them would bless the fact that they had been taught how to deal with incendiary bombs.

Before September was out, an Anderson shelter had been erected in the Owens' garden and vegetable seeds had been sown behind the hen-house. Trees, kerbs, lamp-posts and all steps leading up to buildings had been painted white in order that they might be seen more clearly in the blackout. The few lights that were allowed on public transport were hooded with black tin shades and only small slits masked by dark blue paper allowed faint pencils of light to show through.

Ration books were issued, special green ones for children under five; identity cards; and gas masks in cardboard boxes with a long string attached because you were supposed to have them hanging round your neck at all times. A man from the Council came to the door armed with a huge respirator. 'Any new-born babies in this house?' he enquired politely.

'No there ain't, and we wouldn't be so daft as to put it in one of them things if there was. Suffocate whether there was gas or not, poor little mites! Whoever dreamed those contraptions up wants 'is head read.' Having had her say Florrie closed the door, still muttering to herself, 'If the Germans don't get us, the bloody daft officials will; what mother in her right mind would strap a baby in one of those bloody things?'

Nevertheless, on the home front Britain went to war in good heart. Corner shops, small garages and stalls in the market were boarded up. Slogans painted on the shutters announced: 'Gone to do the Germans for the second time. Back as soon as we beat Hitler!'

The signs of war were everywhere. Even the local policeman's familiar helmet was replaced by a tin hat. Yet as to the actual conflict nothing happened. No German planes flew overhead, there was no bombing, no landing of enemy troops on British soil. There was, of course, the total blackout to contend with, and life as regards business came to an abrupt halt.

Petrol rationing was brought in immediately; so restricted was the allowance that most private cars were taken off the road. Garages advised removing

the wheels and propping up the axles on bricks for
the duration of the war. 'And God knows how long
that will be,' Ollie said, as he looked sadly at his
beloved Austin.

'Without headlights and with the winter coming
on, it'd be a bit hazardous anyway,' Eddie was moved
to say.

'Who for?' Alex winked at David as he asked, 'You,
or the poor old pedestrians?'

'Saucy sod,' said Florrie. 'Buggered if I know what's
going to become of you.'

'I'll make a million one of these days,' he told her,
'and when I do, I'll deck you out in diamonds 'cause
you're my favourite lady.' Then impulsively he bent
and kissed her on both cheeks.

'Oh, Gawd 'elp us,' bawled Florrie, and went out
into the scullery so that they wouldn't see that she
was laughing fit to bust.

The war might not have come to London, but
food shortages had.

'How can everything have disappeared so quickly?'
asked Patsy as she dished up what was virtually a feast
for their Sunday dinner.

'Most of the food you're grumbling about like
sugar and tea has to be imported into the country by
sea, and already it's dangerous out there,' Ollie stated
rather sharply.

'How is it then that there seems to be no shortage

in some quarters?' Patsy cried, as she scraped the bottom of the roasting pan ready to make the gravy.

'There'll always be a black market flourishing where there's folk that are willing to pay over the odds. Stands to reason.' Eddie was nodding wisely. 'Old Fred in the Bowery the other night had two chickens, killed them off 'cause they weren't laying. Sold 'em to the highest bidder. Don't blame him, do you? Supply and demand.'

'Yes,' Ollie agreed. 'And we'll see a hell of a lot more of it before this war is over.'

'I ain't noticed you're short of anything yet, Mum,' said Alex as he sat up to the table.

'Well, you wouldn't, would you?' said Florrie, putting her spoke in as usual. 'Your mum will go short herself before she lets us lot suffer.'

'Know something, Auntie Florrie?' asked Alex, his huge eyes twinkling with merriment. 'We've no need to go short of nothing, and I won't be paying through the nose for goods neither. Barter, that'll be the game. Find out what one person's got too much of, who needs it, and what he's got to offer in return – and then do a deal. Simple!'

Patsy raised her eyes heavenward. 'You really are a shocker, I don't know where we got him from, do you?' she turned to his father and asked, but Eddie was no help, nor was anyone else seated around the table: there was nothing but boisterous laughter. 'Oh, you lot encourage him,' Patsy claimed in a loud voice, while Florrie heaved her bulk forward, wrapped Alex in a great bear hug and declared, 'You'll do, me boy! You'll do!'

Taking all in all, Patsy decided as she gazed at her family – which regularly now included Vicky Baldwin at week-ends – she was a very privileged person despite the war. Her biggest worry was the twins. She had stood in the main hall of their school and listened to every word the headmaster had to say on evacuation: it was in the children's best interest that they be sent away to safety. But was it? She had lain awake for nights on end, asking herself the same question. Suppose she let them go and they got parted? They were such dear little girls, and so pretty with their long, reddish, curly hair. Ellen was a little shy, but Emma was never far away with her bubbling laughter and down-to-earth common sense. They'd be lost without their brothers. Without each other they'd be worse. Suppose the people they were billeted with were unkind to them? I'd end up killing them, she vowed. Suppose she and Eddie were killed, then they'd be orphans.

Eddie had sensed her restlessness and, turning in bed, he had taken her into his arms. 'Do you think they should go?' she whispered.

'God help me, I really don't know,' he had muttered, sighing heavily at the same time. The thing he couldn't get out of his mind was the look of fear in those two pairs of green eyes, so exactly like their mother's, when the subject had first been brought up – which was before war had even been declared. Not fear of being bombed but fear of being parted from their parents and their brothers, not to mention Grandad and Auntie Florrie who spoilt them rotten.

'Please, Daddy, don't let us be evacuated,' Ellen had pleaded, while tomboy Emma had stated, 'We *won't* go anyway. We'll stay here with you and Mummy.'

The words had been brave, but Eddie loved his two daughters too well not to have heard the sob in their voices. Both he and Patsy knew the value of having folk around you who loved you. Life for him had never really begun until he met Patsy. She had had a rough time of it too. Ollie had shielded her against a lot of the knocks that life had dealt, a father to her in every sense of the word. Unbeknown to Patsy, Eddie had asked Ollie's advice.

'Don't. Please Eddie,' Ollie had beseeched. 'I just can't answer that one. Send them – and Patsy will worry herself sick. Keep them in London – and if anything happens to them you'll never forgive yourself.'

What a problem! It had been Gran and Grandad Jack who finally settled it for Patsy.

'Mind you, love, I'm not giving you no advice. I'll merely say to you what I've said to Queenie and the rest of our tribe.' Gran was staring Patsy in the face, teapot dangling dangerously in midair from one hand while with the other she poured milk from the bottle into their cups. 'Whoever they got billeted with – they're not going to look after 'em as if they were their own. Let's say they've got hold of a few sweets; got kids of their own, and not enough to go around. Who do you think will get them? Not our Emma and Ellen, that's for sure. No, my luvvie, we've been through some hard times, none knows that more than you, but you was never sent away – though I'll grant you it nearly came to it the day the old cruelty man came round 'ere.' Gran paused for breath and let out a shriek of laughter at the memory. 'Toss-up it were – whether Flo or me landed him one. Even Ollie was all set to punch his face in if he laid a finger on you. You've asked me, and I've told you. Kids' place is with their mothers and fathers; stands to reason you shouldn't be asking other folk to see to your kids. War might be war, and they're still telling us that this Hitler will be sending 'is bombers over, but that's still no reason why proper folk should send their kids miles away to a place they don't know, and people you've never set eyes on.'

'You make it sound real wicked,' murmured Patsy.

'Well, I've had my say – now get up off your backside, Patsy Owen, and see about making us something to eat.'

'Gran, you take the biscuit! I do love you.'

'Now she's going to go all soppy-like on me. Get on with you, the bread's in the bin on the draining-board.' Patsy took herself off, but she was well aware that Gran was wiping tears away from her eyes.

'Bloody war,' she declared, banging her head in the process of bending down to search for the bread-board. She'd known in her heart all along that she didn't want to let the twins out of her sight. What she had really wanted was for Eddie to say that they weren't to be evacuated. Each of them was afraid of the outcome, whatever decision they came to. Best wait and see, she'd decided – happy that for the moment, at least, her beloved daughters were staying put where they belonged.

Register for food. There were dockets and permits for anything that was in short supply, and already that meant nearly everything.

You had to decide which shop you wanted to be registered with. No more looking in shop windows and comparing the prices: each retailer was only getting supplies according to the number of customers who had lodged their ration books with them. Patsy took seven books up to David Gregg's: for her and Eddie, the four children and Kitty. Kitty's legs wouldn't stand queueing, so Patsy would see to it that she got all that was going. Queenie Day had registered Florrie and Ollie together with her own tribe at Gunn's in Tooting High Street.

Eight ounces of butter, eight ounces of margarine and lard, and half a pound of tea. A jar of jam or a two-pound packet of sugar. *Not both*. That was the allowance per person per *month*!

'How the bloody 'ell they expect one person on their own to manage beats me,' was Kitty's reaction.

Coffee was not rationed, but just try and find some; a bottle of Camp coffee became worth three times its normal price overnight. Soap was rationed. Fruit and vegetables were not rationed, but they disappeared from the shops and stalls almost overnight. Meat, 2/3d worth each per week; part has to be taken in corned beef, Bert Langford, the manager at Beale's, warned Patsy. Offal was off the ration, but suddenly animals didn't seem to have any liver or kidneys. Fish wasn't rationed either, but folk knew only too well the hazards that faced the fishermen if they put to sea. There was one egg weekly per book, if and when supplies came through.

Thank God for our vegetable patch and for Eddie's foresight in getting us set up with chickens – the thought reminded Patsy that she must ask him to lay in a supply of feed and corn for the hens. That turned out to be a laugh!

'You can't have any more chicken-feed unless you

have people registered with you,' Eddie told Patsy when he came back empty-handed from the corn-chandlers.

'What the hell are you talking about?' Patsy peered suspiciously at him, thinking he looked so smart today all dressed up in his best suit, blue shirt and striped tie, which made him look taller than ever. 'Where have you been? You've not been drinking, have you?'

'No. I've been up before the selection board to see what war work they'll want me to be doing.'

'And?'

'Nothing for now – got to wait till I hear from them. I called in to get the chicken-feed on the way home, and that's what the bloke told me. We won't be allowed eggs on our ration books, and we'll also have to let other people have some of our eggs. That's how you'll get the feed, according to the number of people who register their books with you. You've got to go to the Food office and take all the books with you and they'll register you with the Ministry of Agriculture and Fisheries.'

'Christ Almighty! What a rigmarole! Makes you wonder if it's all worth it.'

Patsy climbed the steps to her office in Stockwell with dragging feet. Like she'd said all along – too good to be true! Today she and Vicky had the job of closing down the business for the duration.

The weather didn't match her melancholy mood. It was a bright, cold day, the sky had only fluffy clouds and the sun was doing its best to shine even if only weakly. She had taken pains with her dressing, she really couldn't have said why, except that it seemed to her that the occasion warranted it. Face made up, hair brushed until it shone and now swept up into a French pleat with pin-curls on top, which she liked to think gave her a little bit of added height. She wore a costume of dark navy, a pale blue blouse fastened at the neck with a tiny cameo brooch, a present from Eddie, and she carried her winter coat over her arm.

The outer door was ajar, indicating that Vicky had arrived ahead of her.

'Hallo, love,' she called.

'Morning, Patsy,' Vicky called back, long since having been told to stop calling Patsy 'Mrs Owen'.

'First we'll deal with the one contract that Ollie has managed to secure,' Patsy said, as she hung her coat, gas mask and handbag on the hat-stand.

'I've typed out all the details, they're lying on your desk. Suppose I might as well cover up both type-writers; be a long time before we get to use them again.'

'Oh, don't say that!' cried Patsy, knowing in her

heart that it was probably true. All but two of their buses were gone. Patsy had seen three of them converted into ambulances with red crosses painted on the side. Ready for use at the railway stations, Ollie had said, ferrying the wounded from the trains to the hospitals. She hoped it wouldn't come to that, but she knew it would.

At the age of fifty-five Ollie was still a good-looking, upright figure of a man, with more than a little grey in his mop of hair which only served to make him more distinguished in Patsy's eyes. The contract that he'd obtained was for driving shift-workers to and from a factory that had turned over to munitions, at the back of Vauxhall station. He also had another job – 'something in Whitehall' was all that they had got out of him. All very hush-hush. Volunteered to drive the big-nobs around, I shouldn't wonder, had been Eddie's only observation.

Eddie himself had been offered a choice. Munitions, or shift-work for the Post Office, on the London Telephone Exchange, after training. He'd plumped for the Post Office, and at the same time volunteered his services, part-time, as unpaid Air-Raid Warden. Stan Briggs had been recalled to his Army unit and the paid Wardens at the post in Clapham Manor Street now consisted of two women and only one older man. Mary Briggs was well installed in her wartime job on munitions; already her skin had a yellow pallor to it, and Patsy sometimes wondered how long she would be able to stand it. Very lonely was Mary now, with her husband back with his regiment – still in England, but who knew for how long? – and her two little boys evacuated down to Wales. Both Patsy and Amy Andrews did their best to offer their company to Mary, but she was a woman who seemed to like to keep herself to herself.

Patsy, Amy and Vicky were all to start their new jobs in three days' time, which would be a Thursday. Funny day to start a job, but theirs was not to reason why – not while there was a war on. The review board in their wisdom had sent all three of them to the Civic Canteen, set up in Old Town on the north side of the Common. Seeing there were barrage-balloons and anti-aircraft guns being set up on the Common, it seemed more than likely that it would turn out to be a soldier's canteen.

Stout, rosy-faced Mrs Morley, the canteen manageress, was delighted to have two willing volunteers. 'We have to have quite a few volunteers on the staff, because it isn't always possible for them to turn up,' she explained to Amy and Patsy. Then she turned to Vicky, smiled and said, 'That's why we're allowed to have two full-time paid staff on each shift. Most of them are young girls like yourself.'

Amy and Patsy were exempt from being called up

because they both had children under fourteen years of age at home. Amy had been of the same mind as Patsy over the evacuation business, though it wasn't quite the same in her case. Tom, her youngest, who at fifteen was the same age as Alex, considered himself far too old to be sent off with a 'load of little children'. Ted Andrews, forty-four years old – too old for call-up, at the moment anyway – had gone into a reserved occupation: the Fire Brigade. With everybody's life rearranged, they settled into their given grooves and tried to look forward to Christmas.

What a farce that was, for shopping was a nightmare. A few oranges appeared in the shops and anxious mothers joined the end of the queue. There was one orange only, and a green ration book belonging to a child under five had to be produced in order to get that. No nuts, no fruit, what a Christmas! Still, nothing much happening on the home front until a few days before Christmas when the papers had a field day. A powerful German battleship, the *Graf Spee*, had been cornered by three British cruisers at Montevideo; the Uruguayan government, anxious not to be involved in the war, refused to give her sanctuary.

Ollie got out the maps and showed the boys where Uruguay was. 'Montevideo, God bless 'em.' Florrie and Kitty were in complete agreement as they listened to the news on the wireless. 'Our boys of the Senior Service will get their first strike now,' declared Kitty with unshakeable conviction. But she was wrong. Rather than surrender to the Royal Navy, Hitler ordered her captain and crew to scuttle the ship.

However, as regards company the Owen family had a good Christmas. Stan Briggs got a five-day leave from where he was stationed on the South Coast, and he and his wife Mary were persuaded to join Ollie, Florrie, Kitty, Eddie, Patsy and their four children. Although both Eddie and Ollie had to work on Boxing Day it was a happy crowd of eleven that sat around the dinner-table and marvelled at what Patsy had been able to produce. She didn't tell them of the arguments she had had with Alex as to where exactly several of the surprise presents had come from. Oh, that boy was a marvel!

With Christmas over, the weather changed. 'It's enough to freeze the brass balls off the pawnshop.' Florrie cried as Patsy opened the door to number twenty-two Strathmore Street.

'Haven't you got a fire going in the front room?' asked Patsy, removing layers of clothing and piling them up at the foot of the stairs.

''Course not, hasn't anyone told you coal's rationed? Don't mean a thing whether you've got the money or not; if you've 'ad your ration, then that's it. Remember, it's the transport that's the trouble now, and we ain't got no coal-mines in London.'

'You're not short of money, are you, Florrie?' Patsy

was deeply concerned, but before she could ask any more questions Florrie waved her hand in the air.

'Now don't start worrying. You give me more than enough. I keep telling you that; so does Ollie. Between the lot of you, and that includes Eddie, I could go round the world on a cruise if I'd a mind to.'

'No, you couldn't,' Patsy said, laughing at her. 'There's a war on.'

'That's what I'm saying. Bloody war! Won't need to come and kill us all with bombs, we'll freeze to bleedin' death if this weather don't soon let up. Nice and warm out in the kitchen though,' she added; 'don't know what we're standing in this draughty passage for.'

Patsy made a mental note to tell Alex that Florrie was short of coal. She'd worry about the rights and wrongs of her son's dealings after the war: if it was going to be a case of the survival of the fittest, then so be it. She wouldn't stand by and see Florrie suffer from the cold.

With February came the snow. By now, all entrances to buildings were heavily banked with sandbags and that included the Warden's posts; supposed to keep out the draught as well as take the blast from falling bombs, they did little to prevent icicles forming on the walls both inside and out. Eddie took hot soup in a Thermos when going on duty, and came home complaining of the long wasted hours and how the wind whistled relentlessly around the post. 'Doris Thompson always knits to pass the time. She's a Granny, nice jolly woman as a rule, but she couldn't knit tonight; her fingers are so bad with chilblains she never took her woolly gloves off, not even when she made a brew-up.' Eddie told Patsy all this without moving an inch from the fire which she had purposely kept well banked-up.

The soldiers on the Common were browned-off. What with the 'phoney war' and this bloody awful weather, they, like a good many more would like to have packed up and gone home.

Conditions in the Canteen were not much better, but at least it was warm. Patsy was grateful that she didn't have to sit in a Wardens' post waiting and watching for God knows what.

Tonight when she entered the Canteen through the front door the steamy atmosphere and tobacco smoke were welcome. Already her nose felt red and horrible and her ears, even beneath the thick woolly balaclava that Florrie had made for her, were freezing enough to drop off, though it was not much more than ten minutes since she'd left home.

She greeted Vicky, who still had another two hours

of her shift to do, and turned to see Amy struggling to wind a long knitted scarf round her neck.

'Here, let me do that,' she sniffed, pulling off her own outdoor trappings and tying the ends of Amy's scarf in a knot for her. 'Been busy?' she asked.

Amy chuckled, 'On and off. Few of the soldiers sneaked in for a cuppa, more likely for a warm, poor sods. Highlight of the evening, though, you'd never guess!'

Patsy was now ready to start work: her dark green cross-over overall covered in front by a white bib apron made her look very efficient.

'I could do with some more chips, please, Patsy,' the ladylike voice of another volunteer called.

'Shan't be a moment,' Patsy called back. 'Come on, tell me quickly if you're going to,' she urged Amy.

'It was my Ted. Been on a call-out, nothing serious, drew up here and brought five other firemen in with him. The lot of 'em sat there eating fried bacon sandwiches with large mugs of tea. Engine was parked right outside. Thought Mrs Oliver – you know, the posh one – would have said something, but she didn't. The customers had a right old laugh with them.'

'I bet they did,' said Patsy, as she held up the blanket that covered the back door. 'Say when, and I'll switch off the light.'

'Good-night, love, say good-night to the others for me,' said Amy, ducking out into the blackout.

'By the way,' Patsy called after her, 'have we got bacon on the menu tonight?'

'Not any more we ain't!' the answer came back, and Patsy could hear Amy chuckling away as she made for home.

'Omelette? With chips?' her first customer of the evening asked. The man was a railway worker and he looked fit to drop, eyes red-rimmed and his face smudged with sooty smears. Must be awful for them, this blackout lark, Patsy thought.

'Only got dried egg' she told him, 'but I can put a bit of tomato in it – don't make a bad omelette actually.'

'I'll take your word for it, luvvie, if you'll give me a large tea and two slices of toast to be going on with. I'm that hungry my stomach thinks my throat's been cut.'

'Right. You're on. Dripping or marge on the toast?'

'So long as it's spread by your fair 'ands, I don't give a monkey's what it is!'

Patsy laughed. Work at the Canteen was far more fun than staying at home while Eddie was out doing his bit for the war effort.

Chapter Six

WITH THE COMING of spring and the lovely pink and white blossom covering the trees, not only on the Common but in the side streets as well, hopes were being raised. Neville Chamberlain resigned and Winston Churchill replaced him as Prime Minister. 'Now we'll get things moving!' was the general opinion; 'Churchill will soon teach Hitler a lesson.'

That was at the beginning of May, and before the month was out the German Army had swept through Northern France. British troops were forced to retreat until they were cut off on the beaches of Dunkirk, near the Belgian frontier.

The Royal Navy, together with hundreds of owners of small vessels, went to the rescue. Churchill later described the evacuation of Dunkirk as a miracle of deliverance. Thousands had been saved, clutched out of the water and from off the beach. Many, many had died. Boats had been sunk and set on fire, and men had been killed as German planes swooped down attacking with machine-gun fire and dropping their bombs on troops who were entirely at their mercy.

Arms linked, Patsy and Amy stood on the kerb and

watched the Army lorries drive in convoy down the High Street.

France was finished. Occupied by the Germans.

'We're not done for yet,' the boys in khaki yelled defiantly. The bitter humour of these soldiers was something they would remember for a long time.

'Wonder what will happen next,' sighed Patsy, as she tried to imagine what those young lads had gone through.

A woman behind them started to sob – maybe she had already lost a son or a brother – but another group of women were unnaturally cheerful. 'We don't need the French, bugger 'em.' More and more Cockney voices were boldly doing their best to give encouragement to these young boys whose faces were gaunt from the nightmare they had been through.

'Come on, Patsy,' Amy said to her. 'The sooner we get home now the better; we're not doing much good standing here.'

'One thing's for sure,' Ollie stated that evening as he laid the evening paper aside, 'the RAF will have to get a move on now. Hitler's well and truly in Europe, now his aim will be the invasion of England.'

'Lord above, Ollie!' cried Patsy, 'For Christ's sake let's have our cuppa tea in peace. Germans invading us! Next you'll be telling me that they'll be landing on the Common.'

Ollie grinned at her and passed his cup for a refill. He didn't dare say that that was a probability.

Patsy got off the tram at the corner of Chestnut Grove and looked across to where Alex still had a flower stall. Bert Chandler, a man turned sixty-five, managed that one now – very glad of the job, I shouldn't wonder, thought Patsy to herself. Alex was still managing to get a small supply of flowers, even with the restriction on transport. Refusing to be outdone, he travelled out as far as Sutton and Surrey and bought straight from the growers. He'd bought himself an open-sided truck; seeing he was only sixteen, he couldn't get a provisional driving licence for another year yet. He'd told his parents that he employed a man to drive the truck; whether or not that was true, and from what source he got the petrol, both Patsy and Eddie had long since given up asking.

David was another matter. A nice, easygoing young lad, fourteen three days ago on the 20th August, he'd left school when they broke up for the summer holidays. Not that he'd attended school much in the last year; what with half the teachers being evacuated and more than half the children returning to London, the schooling system seemed to have gone to pot. More than likely David would get himself involved in Alex's wheeling and dealing.

A pity, really, Patsy thought. If it weren't for this ruddy war David might have continued with his education. All she could hope for now was that the war would soon be over.

Schooling was the reason for her being here in Balham this afternoon. The twins would be eleven years old come October, too old to go back to their elementary school, and Patsy had been worrying herself sick about them having to travel too far afield. Eddie had been very fortunate to hear about a husband and wife, both teachers, and the wife's brother who had also taught at a girls' school. The three of them had set up classes for children between the ages of ten and sixteen, within their own large house.

Patsy climbed the front steps and rang the bell, realising that she did not know what to expect. She certainly wasn't prepared for the man who opened the door and greeted her so warmly. 'Henry Burgess,' he said, holding out his hand. 'My pupils call me Mr Henry.'

Being a very hot August day, Patsy wore no coat. He took her white net gloves and laid them on the hall table, then drew her into a very large sitting-room. 'My wife Paula, and my brother-in-law Edward.'

The lady introduced as Paula took hold of Patsy's hand as she said, 'I'm so pleased you were able to come and visit us. Your husband's letter told us you have twin daughters – how lovely, we've never had twins as pupils before.'

She was wearing a beige silk dress with a full skirt, short sleeves and a pretty lace collar. Her features were delicate, her high-piled hair a light honey colour. But it was the way she spoke and her movements that attracted Patsy most. Good breeding tells, she told herself. The two gentlemen were entirely different. No mistaking that 'Mr Edward' was Paula's brother – tall, slim and immaculate – while 'Mr Henry' was more the jolly type with rosy cheeks and eyes that twinkled at you.

While Miss Paula excused herself to fetch the tea-tray, Patsy took the time to look around the room. Although large it was not over-furnished, but she knew that the mahogany furniture was extremely valuable and that the figurines on the sideboard were the same kind as those she had inherited from Eddie's mother: Dresden. From where she sat near to the great marble fireplace, Patsy could see through the criss-crossed tape on the long windows the well-kept lawns of the garden and the tennis court beyond. This was a truly beautiful house, and the occupants were well-educated people who were quite comfortably off.

With tea and polite conversation dispensed with, Henry Burgess took the lead in a business discussion. Quotes of the school's fees and courses were outlined and agreed upon. Paula Burgess told of her preference for her young pupils to wear a uniform. 'Though naturally, we don't insist in these difficult times,' she smiled at Patsy. 'Clothing coupons must be a nightmare for mothers with growing children.'

'Yes, they are,' Patsy agreed as she rose to say her good-byes.

'I want you to promise that you will come to see us at any time you feel like it, and that if the twins aren't happy or if there is anything at all that is worrying them, you will tell us,' Miss Paula said later as she stood at the door holding Patsy's hand.

'Oh, that is kind of you. I promise I will. Thank you for the tea.'

A few steps along the road and Patsy turned. Miss Paula was still watching and they waved at each other in the most friendly manner. Aren't we lucky! Patsy felt like hugging herself. It couldn't be better. War or no war, come September her two girls would start having lessons with those nice people. Wouldn't it be wonderful if Ellen and Emma ended up speaking really ladylike and acting a bit more dignified, especially Emma!

The long-drawn-out wail of the siren made Patsy jump like a scalded cat. This was what everyone had been dreading, half expecting, yet now it had finally come it was a complete and utter shock. I must get home, was her only thought as she ran for the tram.

'How far you going, love?' the conductor asked, as he placed his hand under Patsy's elbow and helped her aboard.

'Clapham Common,' she managed to gasp.

'That's all right then, 'cause we're running into the depot. Better make for a shelter when you get off; don't know what the perishers 'ave in store for us, do we?'

The very word 'shelter' made Patsy shudder. Grim, cold places at the best of times, but seeing it had become what most folk were calling a 'phoney war' until now, the brick-reinforced shelters that had been built above ground had become a sanctuary for down-and-outs and even drunks. The one near the Canteen smelt horrible, a place which the drop-outs used when they needed to urinate. If I'm going to be killed I'd rather be with my family in my own home, she decided, clutching the hand-rail beside her seat so hard that her knuckles showed white. I'll run like mad as soon as I get off this tram, she thought, trying to steel herself for the ordeal ahead.

But she didn't need to, for she wasn't on her own. Ollie was pacing the pavement and as he spied Patsy standing on the platform, his long legs needed only a couple of strides to take him out into the middle of the road and be there to almost lift her down as soon as the tram shuddered to a halt. Relief flooded through her as she clung to him, and he gave her a reassuring pat on the back before releasing her from his hug.

The great silver barrage-balloons bobbed above the Common, straining on their steel wires like beached whales, but apart from them there was nothing: no sound of gun-fire, no planes to be seen in the sky, everything looked normal in the late afternoon sunshine.

When they reached the pavement Patsy found she was trembling. She hadn't known how she would manage to reach home safely. Thank God for Ollie!

'How did you know where to meet me?' she asked, her eyes expressing her gratitude and love.

'Eddie told me you were going to see the Burgesses this afternoon, and Kitty told me what time you left. Figured you must be on your way back when the sirens went, so I walked up to the tram stop.'

No one knew how deep was his love for Patsy, nor the extent of his pride in her . . . except perhaps Florrie. To Ollie, Patsy was the daughter he never had, and like her mother she was beautiful to him in every way. As a youngster she had been through so much and had come through with flying colours; he loved her dearly.

'Mum, Mum!' Emma yelled at her as they turned

the corner. 'There's only me and Ellen in, and we didn't like it down the shelter.'

Ellen was crouching in the porchway with her hands over her mouth. 'I feel sick,' she murmured as soon as she set eyes on Patsy.

'No, you don't,' Patsy said calmly, putting her arm around her shoulders, 'because we're all here now, and I've got some wonderful news to tell you about your new school.'

When the all-clear sounded later, it was a marvellous feeling Patsy had as she gazed at the whole of her family now seated around the table waiting for their dinner. Full of relief and happiness, she added a knob of margarine to the saucepan full of hot potatoes, then poured in milk from the quart bottle, whisking vigorously with a fork until the potatoes were creamy and fluffy.

When they were all served with sausages, fried onions, carrots, greens and mashed potatoes – all the vegetables having come from the patch down at the bottom of the garden – Patsy asked Alex a question.

'What have you got in that truck of yours? It smells a bit – and why is it covered over with a tarpaulin? A tarpaulin which incidentally, my lad, has Army markings on it.'

David grinned. 'Get out of that one.'

'Pig bins,' said Alex. 'It's war work – can you believe that?'

'Mind what you're saying, you're getting too big for your boots, me lad,' said Patsy, bristling as he smiled at her.

'It's honest, Mum, truly it is. I've got a contract to prove it. Out where I get the flowers there's this pig-farm, and I got talking to the bloke. I'm collecting swill from hotels, cafés, even hospitals. It's my war effort – feeding pigs will help the country.'

'Is he telling me the truth?' Patsy asked David.

'Course he is,' he answered, still with that lazy, cheeky grin on his face. Their father and grandfather were both having a job to contain their laughter as they listened to this exchange.

'Ugh,' said Emma as she made a grimace. 'Fancy having to collect slops for pigs!'

'Well, pigs have to be fed just like other animals,' Ellen stated kindly.

'I'll take all our left-overs, if you like,' said Alex through a mouthful of fried sausage. 'I'll even put Emma in one of the bins if you want to get rid of her!'

'With you lot we don't get any left-overs, and don't talk like that about your sister or I'll box your ears. You're not too big, you know,' Patsy added as she saw that he was smirking at her.

'No, Mum,' Alex answered with exaggerated politeness.

'Clear the plates for me, please,' Patsy said to Eddie, 'and don't encourage the boys so much. Alex will end up in trouble with the police for sure, and it's beginning to look more likely every day that David won't be far behind him.'

Secretly, of course, she was proud of her two boys. They got out and about, and got themselves work of one kind or another. Still, she hoped and prayed they would not stray too far beyond what was right and proper.

In the scullery she bent down to lift the enamel pie-dish from the oven, using the thick oven-gloves that Florrie made so well from old pieces of cloth that she collected. Bread and butter pudding – not very appetising seeing it was only marge on the bread and only a very few sultanas; still she had put two eggs in the custard – that was something to be grateful for, that they had their own chickens. Which reminded her that the hens were laying well, so she'd be able to give Florrie, Kitty and Ollie at least half a dozen eggs each this week, which was a darn sight more than they'd get if they were registered at the shop instead of with her. Must give Ollie a few eggs to drop in to Gran when he goes home tonight, she told herself as she carried the pudding into the kitchen.

When they had finished eating the twins said, 'Make a nice cup of tea, shall we, Mum?'

'Oh, that would be lovely. Be careful with that kettle,' Patsy called after them. 'The handle gets very hot, so use the pot-holder.'

Ellen was setting down the tray, laden with cups, saucers, sugar-bowl and jug of milk, in front of Patsy when the wail of the siren sounded again. It was past eight now, the sun had set some time ago, though it wasn't dark yet, but because of the evening light the wailing sounded more eerie. Several things happened at once. Emma came dashing in from the scullery; Alex and David flew to the back door; Eddie went out into the passage calling to Kitty to come down; Ollie flung the window up as high as it would go and put his head and shoulders out in order to look up the sky. Already they could hear the anti-aircraft guns firing, and the droning sound of engines told them that planes were overhead.

This was no false alarm. The Blitz on London had begun.

Day and night raids by heavy German bombers now became commonplace. With France occupied, the Germans were able to mass large numbers of troops on the coast opposite Britain, and invasion began to seem very probable. German air attacks had until now concentrated on shipping in the Channel, then on airfields in the south-east. Now the Luftwaffe switched to the easier target of London. Such were the direct hits on buildings, places of work, even air-raid shelters, that thousands of Londoners regularly slept on the Underground station platforms to get away from all sight and sound of London being destroyed.

If I had to live like that I'd give up the ghost, Patsy told herself as she came back from Tooting by tube one afternoon. Only just four o'clock and the plat-form was swamped with human beings anxious to secure their places, their pathetic collection of belongings stuffed into suitcases and carrier bags. Old folk who should be enjoying what remained of their lives, young babies who hardly ever saw the sun or heard the birds sing, teenagers robbed of the fun of going to a dance kissing and cuddling in amongst the trees on the Common with young men who were now far away fighting a war they had never wanted. All this mass of humanity was sleeping on the hard cold platforms hundreds of feet below the ground. What did they do to keep their minds occupied? Surely they weren't able to read, not with the din of the crowds and the roar of the trains passing through the station. Never! Not for me, Patsy decided, I'll take my chances up top where there's fresh air, not down here with the stench of sweating bodies and foul-smelling stale air.

She suddenly felt dog-tired later that evening as she made her way to the Canteen to do her shift. She'd seen Ellen and Emma tucked up in their bunks down in the air-raid shelter; it was cosy enough, for Eddie had fixed two miner's lamps to the roof – well shaded for the blackout, but it was still possible to read by them. Kitty was sitting in the Lloyd-Loom armchair that they'd taken down for her, well padded with cushions, reading to the girls when she'd popped her head in to say good-night. Eddie was on duty at the Wardens' post but would look in home at regular intervals. The two boys were on fire-watch duty. Give them their due, they could be responsible young men when it came to the crunch. Patsy now did only three mornings and two evenings at the Canteen, and tonight she would finish at ten.

When the raids had first started they'd closed the Canteen and all staff had gone to the shelter as soon as the siren sounded. Familiarity breeds contempt, however. With the raids now so regular, there were plenty of reasons why they took their chances and stayed at their posts. The forced enclosures of being underground frightened the life out of Patsy, and a good many more folk felt exactly the same. On the other hand, some people were scared that every bomb that fell was meant for them. Each to their own, Patsy sighed, wishing that something good would happen for a change, something that would give people hope, even bring a little joy into what was now a very humdrum existence.

Amy looked up from the slices of bread she was scraping with dripping, and greeted Patsy as she ducked under the blackout curtain.

'Just in time,' she said. 'Will you dip those slices of corned beef into that batter and fry them? It's for those four over there.'

Patsy looked across to where Amy had indicated and saw four men slumped in their chairs, chins resting on their elbows, faces gaunt, eyes red-rimmed with fatigue. For nights on end now they'd had the planes over, it didn't seem as if there was going to be any end to it. No one and no building was safe from the incessant bombs that rained down from the sky.

St Paul's, London's most famous landmark, the Houses of Parliament, even Buckingham Palace – all these and many more famous buildings had been damaged.

Patsy lowered a basket full of chips into the boiling fat and stepped quickly back as they hissed and bubbled, causing the oil to rise to the top of the chip-pan. As she waited for them to cook she idly turned the battered slices of corned beef in the huge frying pan. At least they were turning a nice golden brown, which made them look much more succulent than just cold slices of the wretched stuff served up on the plate.

Another deafening detonation made the old building shudder and sent bits of plaster flying from the ceiling to settle on the scrubbed table-top. Patsy flicked two white flakes from the dinner-plates, lifted the lid of the chip-pan, gave the wire basket a good shake and put a generous amount of chips on to each of the four plates.

'Thanks, love,' the first man said as she placed his food in front of him.

'Fit for a king and served by a queen,' said another, patting her bottom with more liberty than Eddie would have permitted.

'Get on with your dinner,' she told him, pretending to sound severe. Back behind the counter with Amy, she said, 'They're absolutely whacked out and still they can joke and muck about. Hitler ought to be able to listen to these Londoners some time; he might be shaking them but he'll never break them, that's for sure.'

'Nor British people anywhere,' Amy reminded her. 'Christ knows London's not the only place that's getting it. Liverpool, Manchester, Bristol, the whole bloody country is getting a hammering. Want a cuppa?'

Filling two mugs with the steaming liquid from the giant enamel pot, Amy passed one to Patsy and said,

'I've got two bits of news. Which d'you want first, the good bit or the bad bit?'

'Oh, the good news, please, spare me the gloom and doom!'

'Right,' Amy began, and Patsy thought how lively she was tonight; when she smiled, everything that was nice about her came shining through. And there was plenty that was nice about Amy – unselfish, kind, a loving mother and a damned good friend.

'Mary Briggs popped in on her way home from work. Poor cow! I felt so sorry for her even though she was full of the joys of spring.'

'If she was so jolly, why the hell did you feel sorry for her?'

''Cos she looked dead-beat, and lonely, and her skin still has that awful yellow look to it. Wouldn't catch me working in munitions, not for all the tea in China.'

'So, go on. What did she come in to tell you?'

'Her Stan's coming home, got seven days' leave. I told her I'd invite them over for a meal one night, with you and Eddie. Be a bit of company for them, though God knows what I can give them to eat!'

'That's lovely,' Patsy declared, sipping gratefully at her mug of strong tea. 'We'll manage something between us for the meal.'

'The bad news is Vicky!'

Patsy felt fear swell up inside her. Vicky had

become very dear to her, indeed to the family as a whole. The poor kid had no family of her own.

'She hasn't been hurt, has she? It's only three days since I did a shift with her.'

'No, no.' Amy was sorry that she had alarmed Patsy. 'She's all right in herself, just down in the dumps. Seems she had a row with that bloke she's been seeing. Air gunner, isn't he?'

'Oh!' Patsy breathed a sigh of relief. 'Can't say I'm sorry, though I wouldn't want Vicky to hear me say that. Arthur something or other, she brought him to our house for his tea a few weeks back. You should have heard Florrie going on about him.' Patsy paused and laughed at the recollection.

A draught caught the curtain as men struggled to come into the Canteen, bringing with them a smell of burning, their clothes reeking of smoke, their faces bearing the tell-tale smudges of blackened soot.

'Five,' counted Amy, all concern for these men now uppermost in her mind. Five large mugs were placed in a row on the counter by Patsy as Amy emptied the pot and measured several spoons of fresh tea into it. Holding the pot beneath the hissing jet of the urn, Amy yelled across to the men, now seated at a table, 'Won't be a minute, just making you fresh tea.'

'Thanks,' they murmured as Patsy went over to see what they would like to eat. Doing her best to be jovial, she faced them and said, 'I know. You'd all like steak, onions, chips and peas.'

'And a slice of Hitler's backside for our pudden,' one man grinned at her, showing his appreciation of her wit.

'About the best we can do is cheese omelettes, corned-beef fritters or rissoles.'

'Crikey! Ain't you got no chips?'

Patsy threw back her head and laughed. These men would suffer most things, but take away their chips and there would be ructions to pay.

'Course we got chips, didn't I go down on my hands and knees and dig the spuds from the earth before it was daylight this morning?' She was grinning from ear to ear as she set a knife and fork in front of each of them.

One of the men, quiet until now, gave Patsy a weary smile. 'What's in the rissoles, love?' he asked.

Patsy just managed to stop herself from sighing; a little white lie was in order here. 'They're not bad at all, really, ever so tasty; my mate Amy – that's her bringing the tea now – she made them. Onions from my own garden, nice lot of herbs and a bit of minced-up pork.'

'Sounds good to me, lass. Yes, please, that'll do me fine.'

They all settled for the same, two each plus baked

beans and two thick slices of bread and dripping, and of course a great helping of chips.

Whilst Patsy set about the cooking, Amy stood near the table and talked to the men. 'Don't seem quite so noisy tonight,' she ventured.

'Not round here it's not. East End's getting it. Bad do a couple of hours ago though. Pub it was, along Vauxhall Bridge Road, direct hit. We've been trying to shift the debris, there's tons of it.' The man raised his mug to his lips and drank as if his throat was parched.

Another of the men took up the telling. 'Waiting now for the firemen to arrive. Foreman Warden told us to take a break. If there is anyone trapped alive under that lot, we can't get at them till we have some lifting gear.'

'Doubt we'll find anything other than bodies,' was the sad remark from the quiet man. Then he looked up into Amy's face and said, 'No rhyme nor reason to life while this bloody war goes on, is there, love?'

Amy shook her head, unable to think of a reply.

'Do you know,' the man continued, 'the publican and his missus is buried under that lot, yet his son has survived. How come? 'Cause he went up the street to see if the fish-and-chip shop was open. It was a million to one chance that the first shop wouldn't be frying, it's not been for weeks. Lad must have been feeling hungry, and that saved his life!'

Patsy came through from the kitchen carrying three plates and Amy went to fetch the other two wiping away a tear as she went.

'What were you saying about Florrie, and Vicky's boyfriend Arthur?' Amy reminded Patsy, as they set about clearing the tables and wiping down the oil-cloth tops ready to close up for the night.

'That's just it,' Patsy told her. 'He ain't no boy. "Old enough to be her bleeding farther", is how Florrie put it.'

'What about the rest of you? Didn't any of you like him?'

'Truth is, no. A bit slimy, I thought. Eddie didn't pass any comment, nor did Ollie come to that, but I could tell. Thought he was the cat's whiskers because he was in the RAF Reserve before the War. Lived with his mother up in Peckham, never been married, must be about forty; a bit too frightfully-frightfully for me.'

Amy chuckled. 'Vicky thinks her world has come to an end. Love's young dream, eh? Though I suppose we're too old to remember all that.'

'Cheeky cow!' Patsy threw the dishcloth she was using and Amy ducked.

'You speak for yourself. I can still remember lying

awake all night because I thought that Eddie's good-night kiss hadn't been very passionate.'

'Now I bet you pray he goes straight to sleep most nights!'

'Don't be so saucy. I don't think you can have gone off your Ted, not the way you two were behaving in the Bowery the other night.'

'One port and lemon, that's what did that. Made a change from the usual half of shandy.'

They were both still laughing as they tugged on their hats, made sure the blackout was secure, donned their coats and let themselves out of the back door. They didn't need to switch on the small torches that they carried everywhere at night, for the sky was bright as great beams from the searchlights on the Common flicked back and forth, criss-crossing each other in the attempt to catch an enemy plane in their glare.

'Activity must be hotting up,' Amy yelled because the noise from the ack-ack guns were deafening.

'Yeah, we'd better run,' Patsy yelled back, as pieces of flak came raining down to hit the road with a clatter.

In Clapham Manor Street, before parting, they gave each other an affectionate hug. 'We'd better get down the shelter,' said Amy. 'God bless you, love.'

'You too, Amy,' Patsy answered. 'See you tomorrow.'

'Please God,' they both muttered, as they went their separate ways.

The whole family was there for Sunday dinner: Patsy, Eddie, Alex, David, Ellen, Emma, Ollie and Florrie. Kitty from upstairs had also been invited, and Vicky, as was normal these days. Patsy was warning everyone that there were plenty of vegetables but not much meat. 'You can fill up on afters, we've got three today.' Hardly had she got these words out of her mouth when young Vicky burst into tears.

'I was bombed out the other night,' she mumbled between her sobs.

Patsy got to her feet straight away, leaving Eddie, who was carving the meat off a rib of beef, to pass the plates down the table himself.

'Oh, love, don't cry,' Patsy urged, wrapping her arms around Vicky. 'You don't need to go to another hostel, you can come here.'

'Thank you, Patsy. I knew you'd say that.' She pulled a handkerchief from the sleeve of her cardigan and blew her nose into it, before she dropped her bombshell. 'I love you for saying that, but there ain't no need. I've joined up!'

Everyone started to talk at once.

'Gawd above, don't tell me they accepted you!'

Florrie cried, and when Vicky nodded she exclaimed, 'They'll be taking 'em straight from school next!'

'How? When you going?' the twins clamoured to know.

'Army or Navy?' asked Alex in his forthright manner.

'Had your medical, have you?' asked David.

Eddie took up one of the serving spoons that lay alongside each vegetable tureen and tapped the dish with it. The ringing sound caught everyone's attention and for a few seconds there was silence.

'Shall we eat this dinner that your mother and aunt have slaved all morning to cook, and hear all Vicky's news when we've finished? Not that we aren't interested, Vicky,' he hastened to add.

'Yes, that would be best, love,' Patsy said, quickly adding, 'There's no need to look so sad; it's always darkest before the dawn, and with tomorrow will come fresh hope and dreams.'

Alex glanced at his brother and stage-whispered, 'Aw, Gawd blimey, are we going to get treated to a dose of Mum's wisdom with our dinner today?'

Patsy couldn't looked vexed, not to save her life, and she laughed. Like most mothers, having her children gathered around her made Sunday the happiest day of the week.

Alex's statement brought a smile even to Vicky's

face. She loved this family, and felt privileged to be amongst them.

Seeing the moisture in Vicky's eyes, Patsy rushed in quickly with kind words to prevent the possibility of Ellen and Emma starting to weep in sympathy with her.

'Now don't start crying again, there's no need for that, it won't solve anything. Let's get this dinner on the plates before it goes stone cold.'

With the main course eaten there was a lot of laughter as Patsy set down a bread pudding in front of Florrie. 'Sorry, no custard today, not enough milk. Got a tin of evaporated milk though; you'll have to make do with that.'

'Sunday ain't Sunday without a jug of custard,' moaned Florrie.

'Luvverly,' said David.

'Special treat,' added Alex.

'Mum, they're taking the mickey,' said Emma.

'I know,' said their mother. 'I'll see they don't get a chance at me If-It pudding.'

'Oh, no,' sighed Ellen. 'We know what your Windmill pudding is, don't we, Emma? If it goes round, we all get some! But what in heavens name is If-It pudding?'

'*If you get a bit you're lucky!*' chanted Alex and David in unison.

'All right, all right, you pair of know-alls.' Patsy

grinned at them as she passed a pile of plates to Florrie and then got on with the job of serving the baked jam sponge.

Everyone tucked in until the pudding dishes were empty, and the boys had two helpings even if there wasn't any custard.

'I'll clear the table now, Mum,' offered Ellen.

'I'll put the kettle on,' volunteered Emma.

'I'll set the cups out, and get the milk in from the garden,' Vicky stated.

'Right, Vicky, now let's have all your news,' said Florrie ten minutes later, pouring tea into the last of the line of cups.

Vicky didn't look like someone who had recently been bombed out. Her light brown hair was squeaky clean, brushed until it shone. The freckles were standing out on her rosy cheeks though she wore no make-up, and her pale blue eyes were now dancing with merriment once again.

She must be coming up for twenty, Patsy thought to herself, making a mental note to find out the date of the girl's birthday.

'I went into town,' Vicky began. 'Browned-off, I was, what with one thing and another. Found myself in High Holborn, passed the Air Ministry Recruiting Office and there and then decided to join the WAAF.'

Patsy looked upset; it was such a sudden decision. Florrie shook her head in disbelief; girls didn't join

the Forces, not in her day they didn't – might have
become nurses, but the Armed Forces, never!

'Go on, Vicky,' Eddie quietly urged her. 'Tell us
what happened.'

'I had to fill in loads of forms, case history, the
officer said. Then they took me to another part of
the building where I was put through a complete
medical. Gave me two cups of tea and a Bath bun
while I waited, then told me I was accepted into
Radio Location. I've got a week before I have to
report for training.'

'Do you know where you're being sent to?' asked
Ollie kindly, breaking the stunned silence that had
settled over the kitchen.

'Yes. To a place called Bawdsey, near Skegness.
They said I'll get a travel warrant in a couple of days'
time.'

'Very quick,' Eddie said seriously. 'Must have
thought you were a good recruit. Congratulations,
Vicky.'

Alex and David teased her about joining the 'Bryl-
creem Boys', the twins kissed and hugged her, Kitty
said she hoped she'd be happy, Florrie said she must
be mad, Eddie and Ollie said how proud they were
of her and Patsy looked very sad.

'Where have you been staying these last few days?'
The thought of Vicky wandering the streets had just
come to Patsy, and it appalled her. 'Why didn't you

come straight to us? You know damn well we wouldn't have turned you away. You can regard this house as your home; I've told you that often enough, haven't I? Better let Eddie take you to get your things, wherever they are. You'll stay here till it's time to go into whatever it is you've joined, and I don't want to hear of you going anywhere else for your leave, when you get some. I'll write to the camp, that's what I'll do – tell them this address is your home and we're your next of kin.'

By the time Patsy stopped to draw breath, Eddie was staring at her as if she'd gone mad, Ollie was looking sceptical, Alex and David were taking the mickey, nodding their heads in mock agreement, the twins were cuddling up to Vicky and only Kitty and Florrie showed that they were totally on her side.

'Patsy, oh Patsy,' Vicky mumbled in a voice that was so funny it was hard to tell whether she was laughing or crying. 'I've been fine. The whole lot of us were taken to another Salvation Army hostel up at Blackfriars.'

'Aw, my Gawd!' cried Florrie, raising her eyes to the ceiling as if to beseech help from Heaven. 'Talk about out of the frying-pan into the fire! Bombed out at Vauxhall and what do they do? Take them poor little mites who ain't got no family of their own right up across the water into the thick of it. Silly bloody cows, the lot of 'em. Shouldn't be in charge of young children.'

Loud laughter erupted from everyone.

'Crikey, you're nuts, Aunt Flo,' declared Alex as he wiped the tears of laughter from his cheeks.

'What did you say?' Florrie turned on him in a flash.

'Nothing,' said Alex hastily. 'It's just that all the girls in the hostel with Vicky are about her age. They all go out to work.'

'Don't matter how old they are, they're still poor little mites with no family to look out for them, and something should be done about it. You should take heed of what Patsy's saying, Vicky, and come here for your leave. You don't mind that we regard you as one of our own, do you?'

'Oh, no, of course not,' protested Vicky, bursting into tears for real now as she went over to throw her arms around Florrie.

'And a happy time was had by all,' muttered Alex. Looking across at his mother, he gave her a saucy wink, then nodded his head towards the door as he said to David, 'Come on, kid, let's go and sell some flowers. Probably be a more 'appy bunch of folk up at the hospital than we've got here.'

'All right, clear off, the pair of you – and you, Alex, want to learn not to be so sarky,' Patsy told them as she handed a clean handkerchief to Vicky, but fondness was shining in her green eyes as she watched her two sons go.

'Shall I make us all another cup of tea?' asked Kitty as she piled the dirty cups on to a tray.

Ollie took one look at Eddie's face, got the message and said, 'How're the hens doing?'

'Come and see,' Eddie suggested with gratitude.

Outside in the garden, they both leant against the shed and packed their pipes with tobacco. Having cupped their hands around a match, they soon had the pipes well alight. With a sigh of contentment, Eddie turned to Ollie. 'No one will ever convince me that those women of ours don't enjoy a good cry.'

Ollie laughed. 'You're dead right. Shame though, isn't it, that young girls like our Vicky are getting dragged into this war?'

'Yeah,' agreed Eddie, wondering where it would all end and pleased that all the members of his family had shown Vicky so much affection.

Amy had done them proud. After all, as Ted had said, it wasn't often that they had a serving soldier to dinner – and a sergeant at that. She'd wangled some leg of beef and a piece of ox kidney from the butcher. 'Mind you,' she told Patsy, 'took a hell of a lot of cooking to get it tender, but I put two of those eggs you gave me in the pastry and it ain't half made a difference to the pie.'

Just the six of them were seated round the table: Amy, Ted, Patsy, Eddie, Mary and Stan Briggs. The clock in the hall chimed eight as Patsy helped Amy to clear away their soup plates and bring in the main course. 'There she goes,' said Ted as the now familiar wailing of the siren sounded through the thick black-out curtains.

It was a unanimous decision to stay where they were, eat their dinner and stop worrying. Thirty minutes later Stan Briggs got to his feet, raised his glass of beer and said, 'I propose a toast to our hosts and friends; the meal was wonderful and the company excellent. Thank you.'

Before sitting down he went to the chair where his coat was lying and came back across the room with a small parcel. 'My contribution to round off our dinner!'

Amy took off the brown paper, then a layer of greaseproof paper to find she was holding a piece of cheese that must, in her estimation, weigh more than three pounds. 'Canadian Cheddar!' said Stan, glancing round at everyone with a broad grin on his face.

Amy fetched a dish on which she first laid a paper d'oyley and then, almost reverently, placed the cheese in the centre. 'That must be about three month's ration for a family of six!' she exclaimed in delight.

Mary Briggs suddenly gave a tinkling laugh. 'I've got almost as much over at home,' she told them. They all, Amy and Patsy especially, looked at her in astonishment, for they were so used to handling small squares of cheese and even at the Canteen they didn't often get such a generous allowance.

'Go on, Stan, tell them the story,' Mary begged her husband.

'They'll never believe it,' he laughed.

'Try us,' said Ted, who by now was just as intrigued as the girls were.

'Well, it were like this, weeks ago now it was. German plane must have been scarpering for home, is what most of the boys reckon. Going across Beachy Head, which ain't far from where I'm stationed, it unloads a bomb which did a lot of damage to a merchant ship that was anchored there. Badly damaged, it was, but it managed to limp round to a place called Langney Point.'

Stan paused in the telling to accept a steaming cup of coffee from Amy. 'Sorry it's only bottled,' she murmured, not wishing to interrupt.

'The ship didn't sink,' Stan went on. 'Well not exactly, it beached. Come low tide you could wade out and walk round it, and believe me before it had hardly settled word had gone round and folk poured down on to the beach. Unbelievable it was. Like bees round a honey-pot! Whole cargo was washed out as her back broke and she split near in two. Dozens and dozens of these Canadian cheeses, well-preserved they were, layers and layers of waxed paper, and all in great ply-wood drums.'

Stan took a deep breath, laughed at the memory and drank some of his coffee before going on. 'The locals had a field day. Can't blame 'em, can you? Imagine if a cargo had been washed up on the banks of the Thames.'

'You don't mean to tell us that people actually made off with these cheeses?' Eddie asked, finding the whole story incredible. 'How much did they weigh, for God's sake?'

'Told you you wouldn't believe it but it's true, mate. About eighty pounds each drum weighed, and there they were, old and young alike, men and women and kids rolling these cheeses across the shingle.'

Eddie and Ted looked at each other in amazement. Amy and Patsy could picture the goings-on and were curling up with laughter.

'Weren't only cheese,' Stan took up the story again. 'Tinned fruit and tins of tomatoes were all over the beach; broken cases were lying out in the sea and single tins were being washed ashore.'

'How the hell did folk get the drums away, if they weighed so much?' Amy asked Stan, who had paused to light a cigarette.

'Wheelbarrows, carts, old prams and pushchairs – you never saw anything like it in your life. The family I got to know by having a drink in the local pub with the father, Alec Gibson, got one of these cheeses 'cos their ten-year-old boy Ronnie was down there, managed to roll a drum off the shingle on to the crumbles and hid it away beneath the bushes. I went with Alec late that night when it was dark, in his little old Austin Ruby. Took Ronnie with us; good kid, he remembered exactly where he hid it. We've been eating cheese ever since. Alec's wife Marjorie insisted I brought a lump home with me when she knew I was coming on leave. A nice family they are.'

'That can't be the end of the story,' Patsy cried. 'Tell us what happened to the rest of the stuff. Didn't the police get to hear about it?'

'They won't leave you in peace now,' Ted said sympathetically. 'Better put our coats on and disappear up the Bowery.'

'Oh no, you don't,' his wife Mary quickly interrupted. 'You're not going anywhere till you tell Amy and Patsy what happened then.'

Stan Briggs sighed, and grinned at Eddie and Ted. 'Won't take a minute, best to keep 'em quite! If you must know, girls, it weren't the police that were involved, it was Customs Officers. By daybreak next day they were swarming all over the place, and by midday the field opposite Pevensey Castle was a sight to make anyone laugh their socks off. Rows and rows of these drums of Canadian cheese were stacked high out there on the grass.'

'So were your friends the only ones to get away with it?' Ted asked doubtfully.

Stan threw back his head and roared with laughter, his thick-set shoulders heaved and it was his wife who intervened now.

'I thought that was the funniest part,' she told the girls. 'When Stan told me I couldn't stop laughing myself.'

Mary's face looked entirely different as she turned to gaze at her husband; there was a better colour to her cheeks and her eyes shone as they hadn't for months now. She's happy tonight, both Amy and Patsy were thinking, and what an awful war it was that took men from their wives and kids from their parents.

'Stan said, people got away with a load of stuff.' Mary took up the telling.

'If they had chicken-runs or allotments they dug up the earth and buried the cheeses in the ground. One man that Stan knew buried the one that he got in the old Pevensey churchyard.'

'Aw, my Gawd,' Amy's laughter was almost hysterical by now. 'Imagine getting the supper ready and having to creep out in the blackout to go to the Churchyard, dig up your cheese, cut a bit off, and then 'ave to bury it again, all by the light of a torch.'

'Trust you to think of something like that, you soppy cow,' Ted shouted at Amy, but the three women were falling about now and in the end Ted admitted the whole thing was comical. He produced a half-bottle of Johnnie Walker whisky from the sideboard, 'Might as well have a short here, they'll not have anything but beer up at the Bowery,' he said, handing round the glasses.

They drank to Victory, and to the homecoming of the Briggs's two little boys. After the telling of Stan's funny story, try as they might no one seemed to have the party spirit. 'Put your lipstick on, girls, we'll troop off up to the Bowery; never know, it might be lively up there tonight.'

Ten minutes later, with their hair brushed, their faces powdered and a dab of 'Evening In Paris' perfume behind their ears, the girls were ready. The short walk along Clapham Manor Street was depressing. Pitch dark, with the drone of the heavy aircraft almost above them, it was enough to frighten the daylights out of you, although they were supposed to be used to it by now. Walking three abreast, arms

linked, the three women flinched as the huge guns
on the Common opened up, so rapid was the firing,
the commotion was ear-splitting. Shivering, they
ran the last few yards to the pub and thankfully went
inside.

A blowsy type of woman with red hair and far too
much make-up was playing the piano, and customers
were standing round her singing loudly. The bar was
thick with cigarette smoke and the air smelt of stale
beer, but it didn't matter for the company was good.
Greetings were called to Amy and Patsy, and by the
time the men had been served with drinks for them
all, they had joined the throng. Arm-in-arm they too
sang lustily, 'We'll meet again, don't know where,
don't know when, but I know we'll meet again some
sunny day.'

Outside an air-raid was going on and the bloody-
awful war showed no signs of ending, but in here
everybody loved everybody else and if there was
going to be a bomb dropped tonight that had their
name on it, at least they'd go to meet their maker
happy.

'Same again, or would you girls like a port and
lemon?' Eddie called across to them.

'We'll have a port, please,' Patsy smiled with all the
love she felt for him evident in her eyes. Aren't I
lucky, she told herself. I haven't been left alone. For
the first time she was grateful that Eddie did have a

Chapter Seven

THE HOUSE FELT cold and damp when Patsy came in from doing a night-shift on one of the new mobile canteens they operated wherever and whenever they were needed. Wearily she took off her helmet and unbuttoned her coat; she was dead tired and filthy dirty. Christmas had come and gone again, and this war that folk had said would not last six months was still going on in 1941. There had been a lull in the air-raids until a fortnight ago, the middle of March, when the Luftwaffe had decided to resume its Blitz on London. The weather didn't help, winter seemed to be lasting for ever, and strong winds were making it bitterly cold. 'I'll get the fire going,' she said to herself, doing her best to keep her eyes open. 'Damn an' blast!' she muttered as she drew the shovel out from the scuttle almost empty. Eddie couldn't have been home all night or he would have filled it from the coal bunker and left the fire well banked up.

Longing to go to bed, she decided she must get things straight first. It wouldn't do for the twins to come home to a cold house. Her feet dragging, she took the scuttle and went out to fill it with coal.

Then an awful thought struck her: perhaps we haven't got any more coal, but surely we can't have burnt all our ration? She lifted the wooden flap and breathed a thankful sigh, for there was coal right to the brim of the bunker.

With a fire burning brightly and a mug of hot tea in her hand, Patsy was beginning to feel not only a lot better but decidedly drowsy. The opening of the back door made her start. 'Is that you, Eddie?' she called.

'No, it's me,' Alex's voice answered her.

'What are you doing home, this time in the morning?' asked his mother in a tired and subdued voice.

'Hmm, that's not a very warm welcome, Mother dear,' said Alex, 'especially seeing as you've got a lovely fire to sit in front of, thanks to me.'

'Sorry, my love,' Patsy murmured. 'It was a relief to find the coal bunker full. I'll get your father to bag some up and take it down to Aunt Florrie the minute he gets the time. She does feel the cold, you know.'

'No need,' Alex told her, showing a cheeky twist to his mouth. 'I dropped her off three hundredweight this morning before she was up.'

'How come you can make so free with the coal? It's right short at the moment – lucky to get our ration even, so George Fuller told me.'

Alex removed his trilby, which until now had

stayed tilted to the back of his head. Still only seventeen years old and looking so much older, this lively, perky son of hers was full of self-confidence. He has grown up far too quickly, Patsy told herself sadly.

'You haven't answered me,' she called after him as he went through to the scullery.

'Just getting myself a cuppa tea out of your pot,' he called back.

'Oh, sorry, son. I'll get you some breakfast in a minute, soon as I've drunk me tea.'

'No, you won't,' he told her quickly. 'You're to get yourself straight into bed, you're dead on your feet. Bad night, wasn't it?'

'Yeah, it was an' all. Where's David?'

'Left him in the café, he hadn't finished his breakfast.'

'Oh,' she sighed deeply. What was happening to her family? What kind of mother had she become when Kitty upstairs saw her girls off to school and her boys had to get their breakfast in a café, and God only knew where Eddie was and it was days since she'd been down to check on Florrie. That reminded her, she hadn't seen Ollie since last weekend, and she hadn't answered Vicky's last letter. Even three days and just one night on this war work was getting too much for her.

'What time did you go out?' she asked Alex, quite

aware that he still hadn't told her how he'd got them some coal.

'About four,' he said, putting down his mug and sitting down to pull off his shoes. 'Me and David gave a 'elping 'and to Len Simmonds, loading up his coal truck down the railway yard – works for the Royal Arsenal, he does.'

'So is that how you got our coal?'

'Kind of.'

'What d'you mean, kind of? Either you did or you didn't.'

'Leave it out, will you, Mum.' Now it was Alex who sounded too tired to argue. 'All we did after Len had got loaded up and gone on 'is round, was stay behind and sweep and clean the trucks. Naturally we bagged up the dust and small bits of coal that were left behind.'

'Yeah and I've got wings sprouting out of my back an' all,' Patsy told him, but nevertheless she was unable to suppress a smile. 'That'll be the day when you clean out coal trucks. You pinched a load, didn't you?'

'No I did not. I worked for it, so did David. You're one in a million, you are Mother,' he told her, still with a saucy grin yet letting her know full well that he loved her. 'I reckon they broke the mould the day you were born. If I'd sold the coal to you and Aunt Flo, you'd 'ave said it was profiteering. I got it for

you for nothing, so I must 'ave half-inched it. Can't
win, can I?'

'With you it's become a case of ask no questions,
hear no lies,' said Patsy.

'Listen, Mum,' said Alex, 'I don't hurt no one, you
know that, and what's more I never take nothing
without paying for it, in one way or another. Before
this war is over it'll be very much a case of the survival
of the fittest, and as long as I'm around I intend to
do me best to see that my family get at least a share
of what's going. All right?'

Patsy gave this eldest son of hers a reluctant look.
He was a good boy, and he was doing his best with
a life that had been forced on him. True he was
ducking and diving, but then hadn't this war already
produced a flourishing black market? For those who
could afford to pay through the nose there were no
shortages. She just wished that he hadn't become
quite so streetwise, not at his age when he should be
thinking of nice young girls.

'Come on, Mum. Get yourself upstairs and
between the sheets for a change,' said Alex, wishing
she wouldn't look at him with such evident anxiety
in her eyes. Then in a much lighter mood he added,
'Why the hell did God 'ave to give me such a high-
principled mother?'

'That'll be enough of your blasphemy, thank you
very much,' Patsy told him, yet he was aware of the

laughter behind the threat as she added, 'I can always box your ears, you know, and I will too if you go too far. You're not too big, my lad, and don't you forget it.'

'I won't,' he answered, pretending to cower away from her. 'All me mates know what a dragon you are, and that I'm terrified of you.'

'Cheeky sod,' she said, getting to her feet, but she offered no resistance as Alex gently placed an arm around her waist, put his lips to her cheek in a soft kiss and very quietly said, 'I'll come up with you, Mum, and tuck you in.'

'Oh, God give me strength,' she whispered, smiling, though tears were shining in her eyes. 'I'm sure at some time in your young life you must have kissed the Blarney stone!'

'Now who's being funny?' laughed Alex as they went up the stairs. He still had his arm around Patsy's waist.

Patsy couldn't believe it as she struggled to sit up and look at the clock. Four o'clock in the afternoon: she'd slept the whole day away! Her mouth felt awful and she scratched her head which was itching like mad. Her fingernails were now ingrained with red brick-dust. She shuddered as the memory of last night came back to her. Buildings had collapsed like packs of

cards and incendiary bombs had rained relentlessly
from the sky. No sooner had the Wardens turned
their stirrup pumps on to one than another fell only
yards away. Firemen had dragged their hoses across
piles of debris, pouring fountains of water at the
burning buildings. She had been on duty with
another of the volunteers, one of the stiff upper-class
brigade was how Patsy had viewed the woman up
until now – but not any more. She might speak posh,
but underneath she's as ordinary as the rest of us.
Scared to death last night, same as everyone else, but
she'd done her whack. Both she and Patsy had been
roped in. Everything else had been forgotten, except
fire-fighting. Those fires . . . she shuddered again. As
the driver of their mobile canteen drove them home
across London Bridge, it had seemed as if the whole
of London was ablaze.

In the bathroom Patsy put a match to the geyser
and the plug in the bath – a good old soak was what
she needed. Taking the stopper out of a glass bottle
which stood on the shelf above, she shook a handful
of coloured bath crystals into the steaming water.
Replacing the stopper, she ran her fingers along the
satin ribbon wound round the neck of the jar. This
had been her Christmas present from the twins. Emotion got the better of her now and she burst into
tears. A good cry probably did her the world of good;
half an hour later she was clean and refreshed.

Her long copper-coloured hair hung damp over her shoulders as she slipped into her cosy dressing-gown and put her feet into her slippers. Coming down the stairs she smelt something cooking and heard the voices of Emma and Ellen. They were good girls, both of them. They'd be getting the dinner ready. She hadn't yet reached the bottom step when the front door opened and all she could do as she stared at Eddie was sigh deeply. No words would help. Like herself and a good many more last night, he'd probably been to hell and back. He looked awful: his tin hat was askew, his face grey, his eyes red-rimmed and he was swaying with fatigue. After the initial shock, Patsy went quickly towards him and led him down the passage and into the warmth of the kitchen.

Around the supper table that evening the mood was sombre. 'Why were you so late coming off duty?' David asked his father, his voice sounding reproachful.

Eddie shook his head, making no reply.

They had hardly finished eating when the sirens sounded. No matter how often they went off, the wailing always struck terror into Patsy's heart. 'Get yourselves ready and go down to the shelter,' she quietly told the twins. 'Yeah, we must don our tuxedos and go and look after the rich ladies up in the West End,' said Alex, trying to calm his mother's fears by making a joke. Both he and David kissed her gently before picking up their gas-masks and leaving the room, calling to their sisters as they went, 'Keep your 'eads down, you two, see you in the morning.' David stopped, went back to the door of the kitchen and asked his mother, 'How about Kitty, shall I go up and bring her down now?'

Before Patsy could answer, Eddie called from the scullery, 'No, it's OK, son, I'm going up to her now. I'll see she's settled down all right.'

'Fair enough,' David called back. 'Night, see you both in the morning.'

'Do you think Alex and David are on fire-watch duty tonight?' Eddie asked Patsy as he finished draining his glass and placed it back down on the table.

Patsy nodded. She had her doubts, but she wasn't about to express them – not tonight. The twins were asleep, she and Eddie had had a couple of drinks and this was the first time they had been entirely on their own for ages.

'Let's leave the washing up till tomorrow,' she said with a glint in her eyes. 'We'll have an early night, shall we?'

Patsy needed him with a sudden desperation, needed to know that she was loved. She wanted to lie in his arms and shut out the whole world. Eddie got to his feet smiling and kissed the top of her head tenderly. Within seconds of climbing the stairs together they had put all thought of the war from their minds. Air-raids, rationing, everything was forgotten except the love that they had for each other.

Neither of them heard Ollie's slow footsteps when he came in . . .

A little after six o'clock next morning they came downstairs, renewed both in mind and body, braced to face another day, and were astonished to find Ollie sound asleep in the armchair, a cold cup of tea beside him on the edge of the fender. He too looked as if a jolly good bath would do him good. His bushy hair was thick with dust, the lines of his face and forehead ingrained, and he looked so old.

'Blasted air-raids,' muttered Patsy as she set about filling the kettle. It seemed as if not one of them had escaped the horrors of these latest attacks. Eddie switch on the wireless. 'Do you have to do that?' Patsy whispered, not wanting to wake Ollie yet. But there was also another reason: Patsy hated listening to the news, hearing about the ships that had been attacked, the convoys sunk, the young sailors lost. She tried to close her mind, bury her head in the sand, Eddie always said, but she couldn't help herself. The actuality was too terrible for her to imagine.

There was a peculiar feeling abroad as the weeks passed, as if folk were waiting for something unex-

pected to happen. What more was there, Patsy ruefully asked herself. The meat ration was reduced to
1/10d worth, clothes were now only available if you
had the necessary number of coupons. Even a pair of
lisle stockings needed two coupons, and silk stockings
had disappeared altogether. Fresh milk, bread and
potatoes were in short supply. But there was one bright
hope: Roosevelt, far away in the USA, decided to
send Lease-Lend to Britain, which meant that we now
had more dried eggs, dried milk and, among many
other very welcome items, Spam. Spam must be
America's answer to corned beef, Patsy decided as she
made spam fritters for the Wardens and ARP volunteers who were glad to be able to use the Canteen.

As the crocuses and snowdrops which had struggled
to survive the past bitterly cold weeks gave up the
ghost and were replaced by the sweet-smelling jon-
quils, daffodils and narcissi, the days of May became
warm, bursting with the feeling of a new spring.

She had not enjoyed an afternoon so much for
ages, Patsy decided, coming up from the bottom of
the garden. She scraped the worst of the mud from
the fork with the toe of her boot and propped it
against the wall, shaking the earth off her boots at
the back door and stripping off her gardening gloves
before going into the scullery. Eddie and Ollie were
standing with their backs to her listening to the news
coming from the wireless.

'The boys are on standby down at the Wardens' post and the girls are having their tea over at Amy's, so there's only us three for dinner,' she called out to them.

But neither of them was listening.

'Makes you feel sick, don't it?' said Ollie, unashamedly letting a tear run down his cheek.

'Whatever's the matter! What's happened now?' Patsy asked fretfully, dreading what their answer would be.

'The *Hood*'s been sunk,' Eddie told her in a voice that held nothing but sadness. There wasn't a person alive who didn't know someone – friend, relative or just an acquaintance – who had served on HMS *Hood*. The *Hood* was the pride of the British Navy.

Suddenly Eddie's mood changed to anger. 'Damn the dinner, let's go and have a drink!'

Half an hour later there was not a dry eye in the place as friends and neighbours gathered in their local, stunned by this awful news.

Three days later, at almost exactly the same time. Eddie and Patsy were alone in the kitchen when the droning voice coming from the loudspeaker announced that the Royal Navy had sunk the German battleship *Bismarck*. It was the *Bismarck* which had sunk the *Hood*.

'Yes!' shouted Eddie triumphantly, while Patsy thought she too should feel jubilant, but she didn't. She just wished that all the bombing and killing would stop and that someone would declare the war to be over.

An evening alone with Eddie was a real treat to Patsy. They hadn't spoken a word for the past twenty minutes: they didn't need to, each being utterly content with the other's company. She was thinking how much better his colour was since they'd had these few weeks of sunshine. Oh, but it was nice to have him all to herself for a change, she said to herself, pulling on the thick wool she was using to make a slip-mat.

Patsy's thoughts were interrupted by Eddie saying, 'Wonder how all your men are managing, without you to cook for them tonight.' He laughed playfully, thinking how dear she was to him. Coming up for thirty-seven now, she was still his lovely Patsy − a short arse, but slim with it and her hair was still gorgeous with those copper tints. She only had on an old cardigan over a cotton floral dress, but she still looked a million dollars as she sat on the floor, her fingers pushing the thick needle through the hessian, as contented as a tabby cat.

'I can always go and offer to give a hand, if you're

fed up with me,' she replied, pretending to be put out.

'Did they ever take on another paid worker after Vicky left?' Eddie asked in a more serious voice.

'No, but we're never that short of volunteers. Local women are good and most seem to fit in a few hours, lending a hand – those that are not on full-time war work that is. By the way that reminds me, we got a letter from Vicky yesterday.'

She laid her needle aside, untangled the thick wool from around her legs, knelt up and took down her handbag from the dresser. She had to rummage through the contents for a while before she came up with the letter.

'Here, you read it,' she said, handing him the envelope.

'I don't believe this address!' Eddie remarked, a half-smile forming as he read on.

'I know, I thought Vicky was having us on when I opened the letter. Arundel Castle! Wants some believing, doesn't it? WAAFs being billeted in Arundel Castle. Who lives there by rights?'

'Arundel, that's the home of the Duke and Duchess of Norfolk,' Eddie told her. 'Anyway, let's hope these digs turn out a darn sight better than where she's been up in Skegness.'

'Sure to be,' remarked Patsy. 'Can't be worse, that's for certain. According to Vicky's last letter if she didn't freeze to death it was a dead cert that she'd die from starvation. Turn the last page over, she's added a postscript.'

Eddie read aloud: ' "Huge great stone fireplace in the wing where six of us girls are sleeping, always a roaring fire going. BLISS!!! Seven days' leave coming up, will let you know when to expect me." ' He folded the letter and placed it back it its envelope. 'We must think of something nice to do while she's on leave. What d'you think about a party?'

'I'd love that,' said Patsy wistfully. 'Bet Vicky would too. D'you think we could manage it?'

'Don't see why not. Have to sort out the sleeping arrangements though. You can't leave Florrie out, and you won't get her going down the air-raid shelter.'

'Well, just so long as we celebrate in one way or another. Must let the girl know we love her, let her know this is her home.'

'Course we will. You make everyone that comes here feel welcome,' Eddie said happily, knocking his pipe out on the bars of the black-leaded grate.

'Listen!' he said grimly, two minutes later. 'Things are getting a bit rough out there again. Better put your rug-making away for tonight, we'll have a cup of something and then I'd better take a walk down to the post.'

'Yes, I'll put the kettle on,' Patsy agreed quietly. Damn the raids, she'd known it was too good to be true. A whole evening on her own with Eddie, followed by a whole night in their own bed together – it was a dream. A dream that kept hundreds of couples going, old and young alike. After the war! A phrase that rolled off the lips now. Oh, if only all the planning were to come true.

While Eddie drank his tea, Patsy filled his Thermos flask with boiling water into which she had crumbled two Oxo cubes. Eddie stretched his long legs and said, 'Ah, well, I'd better make a move now. Don't stay in the house on your own; get down into the shelter, Kitty won't be asleep yet.'

Patsy shuddered at the thought of another night spent deep down under the earth, but she gave no sign that she was frightened.

Eddie knew her too well. 'Promise me,' he insisted sternly.

'Yes, of course I will,' she answered. 'I'll take a drink down for Kitty and for the girls, just in case they wake up.'

Vicky was home, and just looking at her brought out all the maternal instinct in Patsy. She stood still, her arms stretched wide, as Vicky gave a cry of delight and ran to her. Patsy wrapped her in a great hug and Vicky threw her arms around Patsy's neck. They stood locked together for several minutes. 'It's wonderful to be home,' she said when Patsy released her, her eyes shining and her face wreathed in smiles. Even Eddie felt a lump in his throat as he gave her a kiss and told her. 'You're still as pretty as a picture.'

Neat as a button, was how Patsy would have put it. Slim and elegant, her uniform a perfect fit, neat bobbed hair peeped out from each side of her cap its shiny peak barely inches from her nose. 'Come on, get your things off,' Patsy insisted. 'Bet you're dying for a cup of tea.'

Vicky's cheeky grin came to the fore, lighting up her freckly face. Things hadn't changed around here. Patsy and Eddie would do everything they could to make this leave a happy one for her. How wonderful it was to have a home to come home to, to belong to someone, to have a family of your own.

'Will you all kindly stop talking and sit up at the table', said Patsy, ladling boiling-hot gravy into a jug from a saucepan, 'otherwise the dinner will be cold and then you'll all be moaning at me.'

'Poor Vicky,' Eddie sympathised. 'Let her eat her dinner, you can ask all your questions afterwards.'

No one heeded him, and Vicky only smiled.

'Why was it so bad in Skegness?' Ellen asked, 'Mum told us you were cold and hungry.'

'Your Mum's right' Vicky said, savouring her roast

beef before answering. 'Cold! I've never known any-thing like it. Six of us girls in a room at the top of a very old house. Air Force iron beds and blankets, no heating not even when it snowed. We all slept in jumpers, socks, gloves, anything we could lay our hands on. Our thick overcoats were never hung up, they were always on our beds.'

'Weren't the people who owned the house nice to you?' Emma queried.

'No, they weren't,' Vicky stated emphatically. 'The woman was a real tyrant, ruled the roost she did and no mistake. Every slice of bread that old cow begrudged us. Her husband was a weedy little man who wouldn't say boo to a goose, and her two daugh-ters – well, let's just say they'd never had a boyfriend in their lives and they were both turned thirty.'

Alex reached across the table and touched Vicky's hand. 'I'd 'ave set the cat amongst the pigeons in that house if I'd been up there.'

'You would an' all, you bugger,' said Vicky, feeling thoroughly at home in the midst of this loving family.

'Never mind all that now, tell us what it's like to be living among the aristocracy.' David had been list-ening but had concentrated on his dinner. Wasn't too often that they got roast beef these days. Maybe Mum had saved up their rations, or more than likely she'd used one of Alex's tricks and bartered something in return. Whatever, he had enjoyed every mouthful, even down to the last drop of gravy which he was now scraping up from his plate with a spoon.

'Heaven,' Vicky breathed the one word and all the family laughed. 'Which reminds me, Cook gave me some home-made jam, a box of dried fruit and a packet of tea to bring home to you. And I've got my special ration docket which you can change anywhere.'

'Tea! Oh, you're a godsend!' Patsy cried in delight.

'I don't think the staff at the Castle know the meaning of the word shortages,' Vicky said quite seriously. 'My lot were lucky, there weren't any quarters available for WAAFs, that's how we got billeted at the Castle. Separate wing, of course, and the beds are still Air Force issue, but the food is all cooked for us in the Castle kitchens by their own staff.' She gave Alex one of her cheeky grins. 'Make your mouth water if I told you our daily menu.'

'Well, they do say the Devil looks after 'is own,' he answered her in the same cheeky vein.

'You'll be rolling home, fat as a barrel, on your next leave,' David added to Alex's saucy remark.

'Well, there's no staff to wait on you lot here,' said Patsy getting to her feet and holding out her hand for their dirty plates. 'We've got apple pie for afters, thanks to your Gran; she got Blower to drop me off a nice few Bramleys when she knew you were coming home, Vicky.'

They'd finished eating their meal, but everyone remained seated around the table while Vicky told them story after story; her aptitude for mimicking others had them all roaring with laughter as she talked in an exaggerated imitation of her officers' voices.

'We do have one *lady* officer,' she said, hardly able to tell them because she too was laughing so much. 'Very well bred, don't you know. Bloody amusing actually! Bloody lovely morning. Bloody lovely meal. Top Bloody secret, our radar work is. We call her Lady Bloody Sarah.'

Eddie got to his feet and shook his head to clear it, still unable to stifle his amusement. 'I'm sorry, Vicky, I'm on duty tonight, I've got to get going.' Turning to Patsy, he gave her a hug. 'I'm only down at the post if you need me.' The twins were both still giggling as they kissed their father good-night and followed him up the passage to see him off.

After he'd gone, Alex said warmly, 'Vicky, would you like to come over to the Bowery with David and me? We could have a game of darts, if you like.'

'Would you mind?' Vicky asked Patsy.

'Not a bit, love. To tell you the truth, I'm dead whacked, so I'll take a book and get down the shelter with the girls.'

'Well, if you're sure . . .'

'Just so long as you remember you'll have me to answer to if you get up to any of your tricks,' Patsy stated, taking in both her boys with that stern look flashing from her green eyes.

'Oh, that's not fair,' said Alex, wrinkling up his nose at his mother.

'Course it's not,' muttered David. 'We wouldn't 'arm a 'air of Vicky's head, would we, brother? Furthermore, Mother dear, should the siren go we'll not bring her back here, we'll drag 'er by the hair into the nearest shelter!'

'Get yourselves off,' said Patsy, smiling in spite of herself. 'I've stood quite enough sauce from you two for one night.'

Vicky's leave passed all too quickly, but Patsy liked to think that they'd been a happy seven days. They'd given her a right good party in the back room of the Selkirk pub in Tooting, with practically all the Day family including Gran and Grandad Jack, Florrie, Ollie and all their neighbours from Strathmore Street, not to mention a lot of old coster mates from up at the Market, wishing Vicky well, drinking her health and heartily singing the old-time songs. It had brought back so many memories to Patsy that she had become very nostalgic, and for a few brief hours the war was forgotten. When Patsy had gazed across the bar and caught Eddie staring at her, each knew what the other was thinking. It was in this very bar that these same wonderful people had celebrated on the day when Patsy and Eddie became man and wife legally. Ollie had made it all possible, right down to the wedding breakfast which had been a complete surprise. All that and the party in the very same pub had been ten years ago. New Year's Eve 1931.

Now it was time to say goodbye to Vicky.

Walking back across the busy entrance hall of Victoria Station, Patsy heaved a great sigh. So many young men and women, wearing their different uniforms with pride, were setting off into the unknown. Should by rights be enjoying the best years of their lives, she told herself regretfully, not going off in various directions, to destinations that some of them had never previously heard of, in order to fight a war that was not of their making.

'Here, not much choice,' Patsy thrust a pile of magazines and a bar of chocolate (for which she had had to give up a whole month's sweet coupons) into Vicky's hands, forcing herself to sound much brighter than she felt. 'Make sure you write regularly,' she called as Vicky climbed the high step into the carriage.

Lowering the window, Vicky put out her head and shoulders and, smiling softly, she said, 'I will, Patsy. Thank you for everything, it's been a smashing leave.'

Patsy stood up on her toes, then reaching up her arms she cupped Vicky's face between both of her hands; having kissed her on both cheeks, she whispered, 'God bless you, love, take care, and come home again soon.'

The guard blew his whistle and waved his green flag, the engine hissed sending up a cloud of steam, and the wheels of the train began to turn.

Vicky remained leaning out of the carriage window, waving, while Patsy stood on the platform waving back until they could no longer see each other. Heaving another heavy sigh, Patsy turned to make for home.

Patsy looked at herself in the mirror and sighed. There was a Christmas lunch being given for the staff of the Telephone Exchange where Eddie worked, and she had been invited to go with him. A navy-blue suit and frilly white blouse, both some years old, were all that she had been able to produce by way of something smart for this unexpected event, and she felt rather faded. Still, she had put her hair up and was wearing tiny gold studs in her ears. This was supposed to be a time of peace and goodwill to all men, but still the war raged on. She wasn't in a very festive mood as she went downstairs, but her confidence was boosted by the admiration she saw on the twins' faces.

'Mummy, you look super,' said Ellen. 'Yes, really smart,' Emma added.

'Thank you my darlings,' Patsy smiled at them both, thinking as always that these two girls of hers were gentle and kind. They seemed to light up a room when they entered with their happy, glad-to-be-alive expressions, and the brightness of those green eyes which could dance with merriment at the drop of a hat. They spoke so nicely now, since they had been attending the private school run by Mr and Mrs Burgess. Miss Paula was an absolute saint, according to Ellen and Emma. They had just had their twelfth birthdays – no longer babies but quite the young ladies now when it suited them.

'Is this tie all right?' Eddie asked as he came into the kitchen.

'Looks fine to me,' answered Patsy, 'but ask your daughters; they're the fashion experts now.'

Oh, it was lovely to be going out to lunch with Eddie. He was still handsome to her, even if his hair was showing streaks of grey – more grey than brown, she decided on reflection, but it didn't matter. His huge dark brown eyes hadn't altered, they still had the power to mesmerise her whenever he looked at her in a certain way.

'Make sure you stay over at Auntie Amy's till we come for you,' Eddie said to the girls as he picked up his overcoat from the back of the chair and slipped it on.

'We shan't be late, we'll be home by tea-time,' Patsy assured them.

It was a lovely Christmassy lunch. They ate roast turkey with cranberry sauce, chestnut stuffing, roast potatoes and Brussels sprouts, with fruit salad and cream to follow, in a wood-panelled restaurant just off from Whitehall. Drinking their coffee and munching marzipan sweets, Patsy couldn't help wondering how such restaurants got their supplies.

'I suppose if you had the money you could eat in places like this every day,' she wondered aloud as she helped herself to another tasty sweet. 'Rationing need never bother you then.'

Eddie laughed. 'Trust you to think of something like that. It's more than likely that regulars have to give up their ration books.'

'I bet!' Patsy said with scorn. 'A case of who you know, not what you know, more likely.'

'Haven't you enjoyed your lunch?' Eddie asked.

'Yeah, course I have. Every mouthful. It made a lovely change.'

'Well, shut up, stop delving into things which don't concern you, or next time I'll take you to a pub for a beer and a sandwich.' He turned his gaze full on her and she could see a grin parting his lips. 'Finish your coffee, it's time I took you back to your humble surroundings, you obviously don't appreciate high living.'

'Cheeky sod,' she muttered. 'I was just wondering if you'd like to ask the manager if he could get us a turkey for Christmas – and while you're about it, perhaps he knows where we could get some decent presents for the kids.'

Eddie spluttered over his coffee and hastily put his cup back down on the table. 'I give up on you, Mrs Owen. You're daft, you know that, don't you. Can't take you anywhere.'

Still in this cheery mood they spent the afternoon walking along the Embankment. War or no war, there was plenty of traffic on the river. The cold weather didn't seem to matter as Patsy hugged Eddie's arm.

'Oh, Eddie, isn't it lovely to have time like this to ourselves?' she said.

Eddie bent his head. 'Yes, we should try to do this more often. Don't seem to have the time these days, do we?'

Patsy laughed. Nothing could take away the happiness this afternoon had given her.

'Well,' said Eddie as the daylight began to fade and the wind seemed to have become much colder, 'I think we'd better start making tracks for home.'

Patsy gladly agreed. She'd had a break from all the

wartime gloom, now she was ready to go home to her children, put her feet up in front of a roaring fire and best of all have a nice cup of tea.

The hush in the kitchen was frightening. One minute they'd all been talking at once, the boys taking the mickey as usual; Dad taking Mum out to lunch! The girls were interested in every morsel they'd had to eat. When the news came on, suddenly it seemed as if everyone had stopped breathing and you could have heard a pin drop. Japanese aircraft carriers, bombers and torpedo planes had attacked the American Pacific Fleet in Pearl Harbor, Hawaii.

Eddie rose from his armchair by the fire, went across the room and turned the sound of the wireless up higher. The voice of the announcer seemed to break for a second. 'This treacherous attack on US warships and fort installations took place while envoys from Japan were actually holding peace talks in Washington.'

It was hard to say whether Eddie was angry or sad. 'Bastards!' he said softly.

Now America was well and truly involved in this terrible war.

What a tragedy! This news certainly wouldn't help to make Christmas 1941 a very happy one.

Chapter Eight

PATSY AND THE twins had spent the afternoon with Florrie, and Patsy was worried about leaving her as she heard the sound of the siren starting to wail. They didn't get many daylight raids these days, and the few that did occur were more often than not short and sharp. Should they stay here in Tooting or make a dash for it and hope to God the trams were running? Florrie was sitting in her deep armchair, busily knitting school cardigans for the girls. In spite of arthritis in her fingers, she could still knit even intricate patterns. Her legs were bad and the pain she suffered in her knees made it difficult for her to get around. Patsy watched her carefully now; if she had *her* way, she'd take her home to live with them for good. But Florrie had other ideas. Independent to the last, Florrie would be. At sixty-four her hair was almost white, dragged back into an untidy bun from which strands continually escaped, but she was always jolly, ready for a laugh and a joke. The whole family adored her, though at times the boys teased her unmercifully, a treatment Eddie declared she enjoyed.

'Make a cup of tea before you go,' Florrie suggested. 'See then if it's going to be a bad raid or not.'

'I'll put the kettle on,' said Emma, making for the scullery.

Two minutes later she put her head back round the door and called. 'Auntie, the kettle's not out here.'

Patsy got to her feet and went to the fire range, but the big black kettle that usually stood on the hob wasn't there either.

'Where're your kettles then?' she asked, eyeing Florrie with a frown.

'The tin one out there got a hole in its bottom,' she said, not looking up from her knitting needles, 'an' I'm afraid I let me big one boil dry.'

'What, after all these years?' cried Patsy, picturing in her mind the black kettle she had known since she was a child.

'Afraid so,' Florrie said sadly. 'Nothing lasts for ever.'

'So, what 'ave you been using to boil water?'

'A saucepan, it's on the draining-board out there,' she called to Emma.

Oh my God! Patsy was appalled at the danger of Florrie pouring boiling water into the pot from an open saucepan. 'I'll come down again tomorrow and scout round the shops. Must be somewhere we can get hold of a kettle.'

'You'll be lucky,' Florrie said resignedly. 'Queenie's tried everywhere for me.'

January had been a horrible month, damp and cold with rain lashing down most days. Now on this first day of February, it was blowing a gale and cold enough to freeze the tip of your nose. Patsy pulled her coat tighter around her body, tugged her hat lower to protect her face a little and broke into a trot. As she reached the High Street a tram was waiting at the stop and she climbed aboard, thankful to be out of the wretched wind. She didn't relish the task of trying to buy a kettle for Florrie, but she had to try, she decided, handing her twopence fare to the conductress. Everything is getting so short, she moaned to herself. The meat ration had been altered. At least fourpence of the allowance had to be taken in corned-beef, eggs and fruit had practically disappeared, neighbours were always pestering her for any spare eggs from the chickens, and as for household goods – God help us. You needed a docket for every bloody thing you could think of. Ten yards of curtain material was all you were allowed to buy, providing you could find a shop that had some to sell – and even then only if you had a docket. Twenty square yards of linoleum – you needed a docket. To qualify for these dockets you either had to have been bombed out or to have just got married. Didn't the Government know that things wore out and had to be replaced at some time or another?

'I'll get off 'ere,' Patsy said to the conductress. 'Won't go on to the Broadway. I'll try the Co-op and see if I can get a kettle for me mum.'

The girl threw back her head and laughed, making her hair that was bunched up into a pretty snood bounce up and down. 'Rather you than me,' she said. 'I ain't heard of 'em having any.'

Patsy got off in the middle of the road and made her way on to the pavement, which brought her outside the Mayfair Cinema which was still advertising *Gone With The Wind*. Must get Eddie to bring me to see that, she promised herself. 'Good luck,' the cheery young girl called after her as the tram rattled off.

In the hardware department of Tooting Co-op, Patsy found an elderly, bald-headed, talkative gentleman. It took him a good five minutes to tell Patsy that the shortages of kettles and suchlike was due to the fact that these materials were needed to make munitions. 'Sorry I can't help you,' he finished.

'What's that?' Patsy asked, pointing to what seemed a nice piece of furniture and thinking it was probably a wireless set.

Very pleased at her interest, the gentleman opened the two small doors at the front of the cabinet. All

Patsy could see was what appeared to be a small bulging glass belly-shaped screen.

'This, my dear,' the salesman said with a flourish, 'is a television set.'

'And what the hell is that supposed to be – never heard of it.'

'Afraid you won't for a while. The war nipped the life of these sets in the bud, but just you wait, every house will boast one some day. We shan't need to go to the cinema, we'll be able to sit in the comfort of our own homes and watch a film.'

'Get on with you,' Patsy cried in disbelief, but because she was beginning to like the old gentleman she quickly added, 'I'll believe you, but there's thousands that wouldn't.'

She was about to walk away when she spied a stack of folding beds leaning against the wall at the back of the department. 'Are they for sale?' she asked, nodding her head in their direction.

She could hear the joy in his voice, 'Brand-new Z-beds. Folded away one can use the top as a table; set out, a comfortable bed with a reasonable mattress. Would you like me to show you one?'

Patsy couldn't help herself, she roared out laughing. It was infectious, and it was minutes before the pair of them stopped laughing, wiped the tears from their eyes and got down to business.

'Delivery only on Thursdays, will you be in?' he

asked as he wrote out the waybill. Placing the notes that Patsy had given him in the wooden cup, he screwed it into its socket, pulled the handle which sent the cup flying along the overhead wire to where the cashier sat high above the floor in her glass-fronted office.

'Isn't it funny,' he said to Patsy while they waited for her change to come back. 'We have to have a war before men like me can find a job. Would you believe that two years ago I walked holes in my shoes, tramping miles, and still couldn't find anyone willing to employ me. Decent wages to be had now and all. Anyway, my dear, you're pleased with your bed?'

Patsy told him that she was indeed, and was still laughing to herself as she left the store.

Walking down to the Broadway she passed Totterdown Street where a long queue of women were waiting in the hope of getting some offal, which was still not on the ration. Further along, a notice outside Blunt's the fishmongers said, 'Wet Fish at 12 o'clock'. She looked at her watch, it was ten minutes past ten. The queue was already very long.

The inside of the Market made her feel quite sad. More stalls were shuttered than were open for business. But her spirits rose and a smile came to her face as she heard Blower Day's voice boom out: 'Wotcher, me old cock sparrer, come an' give your old uncle a kiss.' The Day brothers' stall was nothing like it used to be. True they were displaying more than most, on the vegetable side at least.

'You've only just missed your two boys,' Blower told her as he spread a sheet of newspaper on top of a dirty box for her to sit down.

'What are they up to? Or shouldn't I ask?' she said, giving Blower a broad grin.

'Nah, they're all right, the pair of 'em. Get their selves out an' about a bit, they do. Still manage to run that truck – it's cos of the pig-swill that they get petrol. Brought me in half a ton of spuds, a few nets of sprouts and some 'eaven-sent leeks. Gold dust they are! Ain't seen an onion for weeks.'

Changing the subject, Patsy asked, 'You haven't any idea where I can get a kettle, have you, Blower?'

'Blimey, gal, I wish I 'ad. Queenie's been driving me mad about Flo not having one.'

'Oi, did you say you was wanting a kettle?' Ma Brown, from the home-made sweet stall, crossed the space that lay between them. ''Ow you doing, Patsy, gal? We ain't had the pleasure of seeing you round here lately,' she cried loudly, patting Patsy's shoulder with affection.

'I'm fine,' Patsy answered, leaning forward and kissing the old lady's cheek. 'Do you know a shop that might have a kettle?'

'Not for sure, but me grandaughter works at Ely's – you know, round at Wimbledon Broadway – and she told her mother they was getting a whole load of goods in today.'

'You're an angel,' Patsy said, kissing her again. Hugging Blower tightly, she said, 'Give Gran and Grandad a kiss for me. God bless,' and she was away running down between the stalls as Blower stood watching and thinking, 'That gal ain't changed a bit. Not from when she was a kid. Made of good stuff, our Patsy is.'

Ely's did have kettles and Patsy sent up a silent prayer of thanks as she joined the end of the queue. It took twenty-five minutes before her turn came. 'China cups or glasses?' the young lady in a brown overall asked and Patsy's heart sank. Oh, no!

'It was a kettle I was after,' she said in a timid voice, fearing that she would be told, 'You're too late.'

'Oh, hang on a minute,' and turning her head the assistant called across to where two older men were still unpacking wooden crates, scattering shavings all over the floor, 'Have you come across any more kettles?'

'Tin one, or a brown enamel with a black handle?'

Patsy breathed a deep sigh of relief. She didn't care if it was sky-blue-pink. The girl looked at her and raised her eyebrows.

'Sorry,' said Patsy quickly. 'I'll take the enamel one, please.'

As Patsy paid her three shillings, the woman behind her muttered, 'Daylight robbery! Bloody profiteering, that's all these shops are doing!' The shop assistant put the receipt inside the kettle and handed it to Patsy. She slunk away, ignoring the woman who was next in line. No chance of getting her precious kettle wrapped; bags and wrapping-paper had long since been dispensed with. Whether it was a fireside rug or a new coat, you carried your purchase home either under or over your arm.

Outside the wind was still blowing, and Patsy stayed in the shelter of Ely's doorway whilst she rummaged in her shoulder-bag for the brown paper carrier-bag that she had kept and used for so long that its handles were getting weak. Having got herself sorted out, she was about to brave the elements when she looked across the road to what she knew was a working men's café.

'I've earned a cup of tea,' she muttered, walking quickly across the pavement.

The café was very busy and Patsy couldn't see an empty seat. 'Here you are, love,' said the man behind the counter, wiping his hands down the front of his white apron.

'Thanks very much,' said Patsy as she paid him and accepted the plate which held a spam and tomato sandwich. She glanced at the marble-topped counter; both her hands were full, there was no way she could pick up her large mug of tea.

'There's a seat over there in the corner, beside me driver. I'll bring your tea over for you,' a Cockney voice from behind her told Patsy.

'Thanks,' she murmured gratefully, turning round.

She found herself face to face with a young woman wearing bus conductress's uniform, neat navy-blue trousers, white high-necked jumper and a double-breasted overcoat which was unbuttoned and hanging loose. They stared at each other, confusion showing on their faces.

Patsy took the empty seat, said hallo to the bus driver and was still feeling baffled by the time the girl came back with a tray bearing hot drinks for all of them.

Suddenly it came to her. 'Peggy Woolston!' she declared.

'Patsy Kent! We went to school together,' she told her driver.

'Patsy Owen for a long time now. How about you, Peggy?'

'Been married twice. On my own again now. I never would've recognised you. Can't believe me eyes. Patsy Kent! You were always so skinny, look at you now!'

'Well, you don't look so bad yerself. Working on the buses — d'you like the job?'

'Yeah, not 'alf,' said Peggy, giving her driver a nudge and a saucy wink.

'You two can't sit there nattering all day,' the bus driver said jovially. 'We only get fifteen minutes 'ere, so drink your tea and let's get going.'

'Come for a ride with us,' Peggy implored. 'We're on the 200s, only a short ride, through Raynes Park down to Coombe Hill. You can bring the sandwich with you.'

Patsy laughed. 'Why not?' she said as she gathered up her things and drained the last of her tea.

It was certainly a cheerful reunion. Good job it wasn't a busy route, though. They hadn't seen each other since those days in Strathmore Street when Patsy's mother had worked up at the Market and Peggy's mother had been the local money-lender. They certainly had a lot of scandal and news of old neighbours to catch up on, and Peggy still seemed to know everyone's business: 'Remember Elsie Shew? She married Jock from the fish shop. Her daughter got married last Saturday, wasn't 'alf a good do in the Mitre.'

'Her daughter married?' queried Patsy. 'How old is she, for heaven's sake?'

'Sixteen, but it don't matter these days – all the kids are doing it if they can find a serviceman who'll have 'em.'

'Whatever for? Seems daft to me, tying themselves up for life,' Patsy said.

'Cor, where the hell have you been? You ain't got

it, have you? It's for the marriage allowance, you silly cow, that's what they're after.'

Both Peggy and Patsy were sitting on the long seat just inside the single-decker bus. There were only half a dozen passengers on board and Peggy had collected their fares. Patsy fell about laughing, 'D'you mean to tell me that's what they get married for?'

'Course it is. That and the fact that if the bloke gets 'imself killed the girl is set up with a widow's pension.'

'Blimey! What a way to start out, eh?'

'Yeah, well, there it is! This bleeding war has made us all do a lot of funny things, ain't it?'

A moment later and Peggy was off again. 'You'll never guess who I saw in the Selkirk the other night: Audrey Watkins, Yeah, that's right – the one whose old man was always having it off with the barmaid from the Fountain! Well, she's certainly having 'er own back now. Done up to the nines she was, talk about mutton dressed as lamb; no, that ain't exactly fair, she didn't look too bad at all if it 'adn't been for the fact that her bloody jumper was about three sizes too small and she nearly poked me eye out with one of her tits. Still, the Air Raid Warden she was with seemed to like it. Couldn't wait to get her down 'is shelter!'

'Stop it, Peggy,' Patsy pleaded. 'I've laughed so much I've nearly wet myself.'

'Well, two more stops and we're there; you can 'ave a pee in the toilets and I'll show you some posh houses that'll make you want to spit. Remember our outside loos in Strathmore Street? An' what about the day we had a tram outing to 'Ampton court? We got lost in the maze, and your Gran came with us in a bath-chair.'

'Don't you ever run out of breath?' Patsy asked, wiping tears of laughter from her cheeks for the second time that day.

One thing was for sure, when she set out this morning to search for a kettle for Florrie, she'd never expected the day to turn out like this.

'They are fabulous!' exclaimed Patsy some minutes later as she stood beside Peggy staring at one detached house and a pair of semis. 'Show House', the estate agent's board declared. 'God, I'd love to see inside,' said Patsy, gawping at the looped lace curtains which hung at the bow-window.

'Why don't you, then? Stay here, go an' be nosy – go on, won't cost anything and we'll be back in an hour to pick you up.'

'Cor, what a good idea. Right, I will an' all – can't hurt me for looking, can they?'

Patsy stood on the grass verge of the tree-lined avenue and watched Peggy swing herself up on to the platform. The driver gave her a toot, Peggy waved from the back of the bus and suddenly Patsy was alone in what seemed to her to be an entirely different world. The silence for one thing – it was so quiet, even the wind only seemed to whisper as it moved the bare branches of the trees. The grass was so green, cleaner than the grass on Clapham Common. Don't be so daft, she chided herself, grass is grass, but she still thought it looked different.

It was a very apprehensive Patsy who walked in through the open front door of the detached house and across the entrance hall, the carpet of which she had never before seen the like, let alone walked on.

'May we help you, madam?' In a room to her right, a long-haired blonde young lady was seated in front of a typewriter which stood on a leather-topped desk. Behind her, his arm resting on the marble mantelshelf above a wide-open fireplace, stood the gentleman who had just spoken. A very elderly gentleman. The way he was dressed did nothing to put Patsy at her ease. Like a ruddy undertaker, she reflected. Dark grey pin-striped trousers, from which peeped pointed-toed black patent shoes, and a black cutaway coat worn with a white shirt with a winged collar. Suddenly he smiled in Patsy's direction and immediately she found herself liking him.

'I would like to view this house, please,' she said with a great deal more confidence than she was feeling.

'By all means, madam.' His tone was cheerful, even

kind, as he added, 'Would you like to wander round on your own? I will just finish dictating a letter to my secretary, then I'll join you.'

There was nothing he could have said that would have pleased her more. To be set free to wander around this beautiful house, all on her own! She liked it very much. The living-room and the kitchen, which was enormous, looked out over a garden that had at least three trees, besides flower-beds and lawns. The front room had French windows which opened out on to a paved area. Fancy sitting out there in a deck-chair on a lovely summer's day!

Upstairs was unbelievable. She kept going back into the bathroom, time and time again. Walls tiled from floor to ceiling, wash-hand basin, hot and cold water, and carpet all over the floor. Four bedrooms, all a good size, no box-room. An arch-shaped window on the landing looked out over a golf course of all things! Cold and blustery as the day was, it was a beautiful sight. Rolling greens that looked like velvet and a club house that was a mansion. Oh, she sighed, wouldn't it be lovely to live here? She could bring Florrie and look after her for a change; perhaps Ollie might like one next door? All together in these lovely surroundings. The twins would love it, it would be marvellous. Would it? a voice in her head challenged.

Florrie would be lost without her neighbours, chairs on doorsteps, chats with Gran, kids playing in

the street, drunks singing and barrow-boys shouting
their wares, not to mention the gossip. Take Florrie
away from all that and she'd die. And what about
herself? Be honest, the voice in her head insisted.
True! She'd miss Amy and Ted and the children, the
folk next door and up and down the street. And
the Canteen, especially having a laugh and a joke
with the men customers. What about a pub? 'Not
seen one of them round here,' she was saying beneath
her breath as she came back down the stairs.

'Would you like to have this copy of our brochure,
madam?' the gentleman with the wing collar asked
as he met her in the entrance hall.

'Yes, thank you,' Patsy said, holding out her hand.

'Our telephone number is in the top right-hand
corner. If we may be of further service to you, please
don't hesitate to give us a call. This is a price list,' he
added, holding out a sheet of typewritten paper
towards Patsy. 'This detached house is one thousand,
one hundred and fifteen pounds, freehold; semis start
at eight hundred.'

Patsy thanked him and turned to go.

He put a restraining hand on her arm. 'The pity
of it is this site was nearing completion when war
was declared. Prices have held well considering there
has been no house-building since 1940. Think of it
as an investment, madam. Come the end of the war
and the asking price for prestigious dwellings such as

these will soar sky-high.' He paused, shaking his head slowly before adding, 'People are afraid to take a chance, it being war-time. Sad so sad.'

Patsy felt uncomfortable, even a little sorry for the old man.

She thanked him again, shook the hand he held out, nodded towards the long-haired young lady and went out through the neat front garden, closing the gate quietly behind her.

She was very glad that she'd found the nerve to view that property – smashing to see how the other half lived – but, yes, she had to admit it, she'd be like a bloody fish out of water living out here. London was where she'd been born, and where she'd stay if only Hitler would stop trying to wipe London off the face of the earth.

On the journey back to Wimbledon, Patsy took a leaf out of Vicky's book and, mimicking a posh voice, she described the rooms in detail to Peggy.

'Gawd blimey, who the 'ell wants all those rooms? You'd be for everlasting on your knees cleaning the bloody place. Suppose you could always take in a few lodgers?'

The thought of labourers or suchlike coming home in their dirty overalls to a place like Coombe Hill, telling the neighbours they were lodging with Mrs Owen, made Patsy roar with laughter in which Peggy soon joined. They were still laughing as they parted, promising each other they'd not lose touch this time.

Patsy ran up the hill and climbed aboard the tram which would take her to Tooting Broadway. She was going to enjoy a cup of tea with Florrie! First she'd tell her about the Co-op and the new extra bed, then the effort of getting her a new kettle ... leaving Peggy Woolston until last. The Woolstons had never been Florrie's favourite people. Humming away to herself, Patsy knew she'd get a laugh out of Florrie; she could just hear her: 'Me live in a detached 'ouse on the edge of nowhere? Golf course! Coombe 'Ill! You've addled your brains.'

Sipping her tea later, her stockinged feet propped up on Florrie's brass fender, Patsy nearly choked with laughter. For that was almost word for word what Florrie was yelling at her now.

Still, as she said to Eddie later that night as she cuddled up to him, 'Florrie was pleased with her enamel kettle. You know, I wouldn't have been a bit surprised if she'd told me she'd rather have had the tin one.'

Chapter Nine

THE COMMON LOOKED better for last night's heavy rain. March had come in like a lamb and according to the saying would go out like a lion. Meanwhile daffodils were showing bright clusters of brilliant yellow as they nodded their heads beneath the trees. The great anti-aircraft guns, covered in their camouflage nets, and the huge silver barrage balloons that hovered above could still be described as sinister, but Londoners knew they were a necessary evil. Tired as she was, Patsy felt good as she swung her arms and took deep breaths of the fresh air. She had started her shift at the Canteen at six o'clock this morning, finishing at twelve noon, and was now on her way home.

The two corner shops in Clapham Manor Street, the dairy and the grocer's-cum-sweet shop, both had queues outside. Both pubs, the Bowery and the Manor Arms, were having a good clean-up; doors to the bars were propped wide open. Nearing the Bowery Patsy had to stop in her stride for a big woman in a tatty overall was shaking the doormat with great vigour, showering the pavement with dust.

What with the grime from that and the awful stale smell of beer and tobacco that was coming out from the public bar, she was thankful when at last she was able to pass. Nevertheless it was a beautiful morning, sharp and fresh, and Patsy was humming to herself as she fumbled in her bag for the key to the back door. Turning it in the lock she pushed, but the door stuck half-way. Reaching up she used her hands on the upper part and her bottom on the lower half; the door gave and she stumbled in, almost falling flat on her face. She chuckled as she straightened up and made to close the door, but the chuckle died in her throat and her hands flew up to cover her mouth. She desperately wanted to scream but she knew if she did it would be a long time before she stopped. Her head shook from side to side and she muttered, over and over again, 'Oh, my God! Oh, my God!'

Hanging on the inside of the back door was half a pig. She couldn't take her eyes off it. Through its hind leg was a metal S-shaped hook, and it was by this hook that it dangled upside-down. The whole animal must have been slit right down the middle. One back leg, half the trunk, one front leg with the trotter still attached, half the head, one glassy eye staring straight at her from beneath bristly eyelashes, one huge ear from which long white hairs were protruding, and half a snout swaying barely inches from the linoleum. As if that wasn't enough, her washing-up bowl was on the kitchen table, filled to the brim with pig's offal.

'Oh no, my lad, this is too much! You've gone too bloody far this time – you'll end up having us all carted off to prison.'

Clutching on to the edge of the table, she sank down on to the floor and clasped her hands around her knees. She couldn't look at the pig, it was giving her the creeps, but it was no good trying to dodge the issue: it was here, and something would have to be done about it. 'But what?' she yelled aloud. 'As if I haven't enough to worry about. Gawd knows what'll happen to this lot though.'

A terrific noise made by somebody thumping on her front door had Patsy jumping half out of her skin. This is it! she said, firmly believing the law had come to take her away. Her heart was hammering away nineteen to the dozen as she went up the passage. Cautiously she opened the front door. Her worst fears confirmed, all the colour drained from her face and the faces confronting her began to swim.

'Here steady on, Mrs Owen,' the local policeman said, putting out a hand to support her. 'It's not bad news. I'm sorry, love, if we startled you.'

Bert Higgins, Air-Raid Warden for the street, shook his head. 'Come to a sorry state of affairs, ain't it? When a copper's only got to show his face and folk fear the worst.'

'You all right now?' the bobby asked Patsy, 'or shall we take you back inside and get a drink of water?'

Jesus Christ! That was the last thing she wanted. 'I'm fine,' she said firmly.

'Well, if you're sure. It's just that the swimming-baths is expecting a lorry-load of sandbags and stirrup-pumps which probably won't get here till about eight, time they've unloaded an' all. We was wondering if the Canteen would be able to offer them a hot drink and maybe something to eat?'

'Only too pleased to,' Patsy assured him with the greatest sense of relief flooding through her veins. 'If the raids are not too bad, the manageress always sees that the Canteen is staffed until ten. Depends, though. There's always the mobile tea vans. Some might have to go up to the docks, but one of them will be around here somewhere.'

'Thanks, love, be seeing you.' Both men stopped at the corner, turned and gave her a cheery wave.

With the front door safely closed, Patsy leant against the back of it and let herself go limp. Whew! Her whole body felt as if it were soaked in sweat. Gradually her pounding heart began to slow down, her breath which had been coming in shallow, short pants steadied, and she was able to relax.

'I never want to have to go through anything like that again, not as long as I live,' she muttered as she went back down the passage.

'Well, I'll be buggered!' Her eyes nearly popped out of her head in amazement, for seated on each side of the kitchen table were her two sons. Bold as brass and twice as cheeky, they grinned at her. 'If I'd a poker in my hand at this minute,' she declared, 'I'd clobber the pair of you.' She couldn't believe it. 'There's me with the law on the doorstep and you two hid away in here while I cop all the flak.'

'Now, come on, Mum, it wasn't like that at all. We were listening, we saw Bert with the copper so we came in the back way. We'd have been out there like a shot if there'd been any trouble, you know damn well we would.' Yes, she knew well enough they'd never willingly do any harm to her, but she wasn't letting the pair of them off that lightly.

'Right, then, let's have the story, and while you're about it you can tell me exactly what you propose doing with that half a pig, *and* how you came by it.' Patsy's voice had risen to a scream and the anger was flashing in her green eyes.

'I'll put the kettle on and make us a cup of tea,' David said, giving Alex a sympathetic pat on the shoulder as he went by.

'Well?' his mother demanded, glaring at Alex.

'A present for you, Mum. I thought you might be pleased. Must make a change from bloody corned beef.'

He had taken the wind right out of her sails. What

did one do with a boy like that? How could she remain angry? He was such a nice easygoing young man, and at his age he really ought to be still studying at some college, not ducking and diving to make a living. A pity, it really was, this rotten war was ruining so many young lives. She gave in.

'You daft devil,' she said, whacking him on the back and planting a kiss on his cheek.

'You can be Lady Bountiful, doling out bits of pork to your friends,' he answered, concealing his embarrassment behind a joke.

'Is it safe to come in?' David called from the scullery.

'Just bring the tea and let's have less of your cheek,' Patsy called back, rising from the chair where she had been sitting close to the hearth.

'Christ, I'd forgotten that!' she cried as she had to lift the bowl of offal from the centre of the table to make room for David to set down the tray.

'Don't start again,' David was quick to defend Alex. 'You know, Mum, there's no rationing on offal, what's in that bowl is pig's liver and heart.' He poured the tea, and handing the cup to Patsy he asked, 'Well, have you made up your mind what you're going to do with all that pork?'

'Give most of it away, I expect,' laughed Patsy, adding more milk to her tea to cool it.

'Sod that for a lark!' Now it was Alex's turn to

raise his voice. 'Not after all the bother I had to come by it.'

'And just how *did* you come by it?' his mother asked evenly.

Alex didn't answer. He stirred his tea, made a grimace and added a spoonful of sugar.

'Presumably you got it from the pig-farmer you collect the swill for?' Patsy said trying to be discreet. 'Doesn't he mind, this pig-farmer, or is he running a racket that you've told us nothing about?'

'No, he don't mind, not if he don't see,' said Alex, grinning at her. "Sides, I take him stuff.'

'Gawd bless us,' Patsy sighed, not daring to ask what stuff.

'What about what Charlie said when he came off the blower this morning?' David suddenly said to Alex and they both burst out laughing.

'What's suddenly so funny, and who the hell is Charlie?' Patsy quickly wanted to know.

'You tell her, David, she's likely to box my ears for me if I do,' Alex pleaded with his brother.

'I will land you one, my old son, if one of you don't soon tell me what's been going on.'

'All right, I'll tell you,' said David, while Alex pretended to cower away from her but still showed a cheeky grin.

'Charlie is Charlie Bateman,' David began, now sure of Patsy's full attention. 'Yes, he's the bloke we get the swill for, his place is out Banstead way, through Kingston — got about a hundred pigs, all shapes all sizes. Supposed to inform the Ministry when he's about to have a kill-off and all they legally allow him to keep — do as he likes with — is the offal. Ministry takes the whole carcases.' David paused, drank from his cup and grinned across the table at Alex.

'Use your loaf, Mother. Even the blokes that come down to the farm wearing their bloody bowler hats can't be that green. They must *know*. Ain't a man alive that's going to breed all those pigs, let the Food Office march off with all that pork while the farmer and 'is family get a meat ration of one and tenpence a week, and a tannersworth of that has to be taken in corned beef. Give over, Mother; there might be a war on, but no one's that patriotic.'

Both boys laughed out loud. 'So. You still haven't answered my questions,' Patsy reminded them.

'Well, you must have guessed by now.' Alex took up the telling, 'When we're on our rounds we take orders for Charlie, only from blokes that he knows can keep their mouths shut.'

'Yeah, and we deliver an' all.' David spoke up.

'I suppose that hanging there was a bit of excess today, was it?' Patsy asked, nodding her head towards the back door.

'Something like that,' Alex grinned.

'You still haven't told me what suddenly set you both off laughing,' Patsy said, reaching for the teapot to give herself a refill.

'Well,' David was still grinning from ear to ear, 'early this morning we were out in the sheds helping Charlie to put up the orders. The phone rang three times in the space of about twenty minutes, and the third time when Charlie came back across the yard from the house he was effing an' blinding, wasn't he, Alex?' Alex nodded, chuckling away fit to bust.

' "Every bugger wants a leg of pork," Charlie was moaning away. "A nice bit of loin or a 'and and spring ain't good enough for the bleeders. How many bloody legs do they think an effing pig has got?" '

Even Patsy couldn't hold out any longer. Her face crumpled, her eyes filled with tears of laughter and she just threw back her head and roared. What on earth had she done to deserve two such sons! One thing she knew, she could swear and cuss at them till the cows came home – that was her right – but let anybody else call them names or try and do them down and Gawd help them! She was like a lioness with her cubs when it came to protecting her own – not that she was about to tell them that.

'Move yourselves, then,' she demanded. 'Get this table cleared. I'm off up the shop to see if Tilly Turner's got any packets of greaseproof paper stuffed away somewhere. Got to get something to wrap that

meat up in; perhaps if I give her the whisper that
there might be a couple of pork chops in it for her
and her old man, she might come up with some.'

The cutting-up of the pig was done in the midst
of much merriment. The hand and spring was ear-
marked for Patsy to take down to Gran in Tooting;
Pork chops for dinner tonight; and some chops and
pieces of the belly were wrapped and laid aside for
Amy and Mary Briggs. 'I shan't be a minute,' Patsy
called as she slipped three chops and a nice piece of
liver on to a dinner plate which she then covered
with one of her clean aprons. When Ada Nicholls
opened her front door in answer to Patsy's knock, a
smile came to her face as she saw Patsy standing there.
Since that Sunday morning when war had been
declared, Ada and Patsy had often stopped for a chat,
and also done each other favours by sharing anything
that they managed to get hold of that was in short
supply.

'Here you are, love, a little treat for you and Jim
to have for your dinners,' Patsy told her, drawing the
plate out from beneath the cloth.

Ada's eyes lit up. 'Cor! God bless you, Patsy, I was
at me wits end to know what to do for Jim's meal.
Needs something tasty when he gets home. You heard
he was working on the demolition, did you? Has to
get the unsafe buildings down — terrible what they
find in the debris an' all.'

Ada had lost a son when the *Hood* was sunk and since she received the dreaded telegram she had rarely smiled.

'You're more than welcome, you've done me many a good turn,' Patsy told her as she turned away. So sad, Patsy murmured beneath her breath as she went back across the road. A good many more families would mourn their dead before this lot was finished; it had been going on for two and a half years now, and showed no signs of slackening.

'Don't cut that leg in half,' Patsy said as she came back into the kitchen. 'We'll have it roasted on Sunday, with apple sauce, stuffing and all the trimmings. We'll make sure your Aunt Florrie and Grandad Ollie are here, have Kitty down, might even be able to persuade Gran and Grandad Day, even Queenie to come up and join us.'

Alex knew what his mother's next words were going to be, and he dreaded hearing her say them.

'Seeing as how it's your eighteenth birthday next Tuesday – it's the 2nd of April on Tuesday, I'm sure – we'll make Sunday the day of your party.'

He drew a deep breath, and said in a very quiet voice, 'Thanks, Mum. That'll be great. I report to the East Surrey Regiment Training Depot at Kingston next Wednesday. I've got my calling up papers; I'm going into the Army.'

The bottom dropped out of Patsy's world. She had

known in her heart that this would happen but hadn't let herself think about it. Not her Alex! Now, as she looked at his tall broad figure, and the young face so like his father's with those huge deep brown eyes, she knew she couldn't hold on to him. The Army was desperate for men and now he was eighteen the Army said he was a man. She would miss him. A feeling of nausea came over her as she tried not to visualise her Alex as a soldier.

Patsy had always believed in God, since she was a little girl and her mother had made sure that she went regularly to Sunday school. It was a happy, cheerful sort of belief, coupled with love and assurance. God was up there somewhere, ever-loving, ever-watchful, and his home above the sky was where all loved ones would meet eventually. If you didn't cling to that belief, then life had no meaning at all.

She prayed silently now, although she seldom asked God for anything, please, please take care of Alex, don't let any harm come to him. It didn't seem right for her to plead for the life of her son when there were so many other boys dying in this war, but she prayed just the same.

Chapter Ten

'Is that you, Patsy?' Eddie called, taking the grill-pan out from underneath the gas.

It was. 'Yes,' she answered, 'what are you doing up? It was turned three when you came home this morning.'

'Got fed up lying there. I'm just making myself a bit of toast, want some?'

'Might as well,' she said, gratefully taking the mug of tea he had poured out for her.

Patsy dumped her shopping-bag down in the corner of the kitchen. Coming home from a morning of endless queues, she was fed up to the teeth with all the shortages. Everything seemed to be getting on top of her at the moment; life was one long struggle.

'Take your elbows off the table,' Eddie said, putting a plate of hot toast down in front of her. 'Dripping or marmalade? Can't find any butter in the cupboard, so I suppose that means we've had all our ration.'

'Afraid so. I'll have dripping,' she said, getting up to fetch the pepper and salt from the larder.

'Are you feeling all right?' asked Eddie with concern.

All Patsy's misery came out in a shuddering sob and slowly and miserably she put out her hand to take his.

Eddie was really worried by now; he had never before seen her look so woebegone. He rose and came round to the side of the table where she was sitting and quickly hugged her. 'I'm being daft,' she muttered, her head pressed in tightly against his chest.

'No, of course you're not. You're just a bit off-colour, that's all. It's a wonder there's not more of us going round the bend when you come to think about it. What with the raids, rationing and the news, it's bound to get you down.' He stayed still, cradling her in his big, safe arms.

'I can't get Alex out of my mind,' she told him ruefully. 'We've not had a letter from him for nearly three weeks.'

'Well, you ought to know your own son by now, letter-writing was never his strong point. He'll turn up like a bad penny any day now, you'll see. What's David up to these days?' He wondered aloud, thinking to take her mind off Alex.

Patsy sighed. 'That's another thing that's worrying me to death. D'you realise that in another three months our David will be eighteen, and if things go on as they are he'll be the next one to join the Forces? Don't seem possible does it? Our Alex has been in the Army two years now.'

'Yes.' Now it was Eddie's turn to sigh. 'I'll say this for our David though – since Alex went, he knuckled down, took over from his brother, didn't he?'

At last a smile came to Patsy's lips as she thought about some of the recent capers her youngest son had got up to. 'Yes,' she admitted.

'Not actually a wide-boy, nor a barrow-boy, a bit of a mixture of the two!'

'That's better,' Eddie grinned with her. 'Come on and eat your toast. What say we pop over to the Bowery fer a lunch-time drink; make a change, wouldn't it?'

'You still on six to two today?' she asked, scraping the dripping to the side of the basin with her knife in order to get at the rich dark jelly that had settled to the bottom.

'Afraid so. I'll have to leave you about quarter-past two.'

'Flaming June,' Patsy muttered as she stood at the front door. The first few days of the month had been so welcome. Bright, sunny and oh so lovely and warm. Vastly different now. The sky had become almost as black as night and the rain was lashing down in torrents.

'Let's run for it,' Eddie called loudly.

Patsy held an old coat up over her head and shoulders, stooped low and ran. 'Whew!' she grumbled at the door to the saloon bar as she shook the rain from the coat. 'My feet and legs are sopping wet.'

'I'll get you a brandy,' Eddie offered. 'Warm you up and make you feel a whole lot better, a nice drop of brandy will,' he told her as she settled down on one of the velvet-padded bench seats, and he gave a tug to her long hair that was screwed back with an elastic band.

'Daft devil,' she grinned as he turned to go to the bar.

There's something different about this pub this morning! The thought suddenly struck Patsy and it must have come to Eddie at the same time for he stopped in his tracks and turned to look back at her.

The bar was so quiet. No music was playing, plenty of customers but no one was talking. Come to that, not a soul had called out a greeting to them when they'd come in, and that was unusual. Eddie raised his eyebrows in question and Bert Brown, who ran the shellfish stall outside the Bowery at week-ends, put down his pint and nodded towards the counter. The landlord had placed his wireless set on top of the counter and all the regulars were listening intently to the news.

'We will have our next bulletin at six o'clock,' the calm voice of the announcer stated, and everyone in the pub started to talk at once.

'What's happened? Tell us for Christ's sake,' Eddie demanded of the group of men who were gathered round the counter.

'Our troops have gone over,' a burly Council worker said. 'And about time too,' added his mate.

'Eddie,' Ted Andrews' voice cut above the din as he came across the bar. 'D-Day, eh!' Ted said solemnly, putting his glass of beer down on the top of the bar, 'What will you have?'

'No, I'll get them,' Eddie said, calling out loudly, 'Make that two pints, Gov, and better make the brandy a double.'

'Who the hell's drinking brandy at this time in the day?' asked Ted, giving Eddie a queer look. 'Not ill, are you?'

'No, it's Patsy. Feeling a bit down in the dumps, she is, and I've only got time for the one; don't sign on till six, but I'm down for shelter rota, three to half-past five. You just finished or just going?'

'Just walked in, about quarter of an hour 'fore you,' he said dusting down the jacket of his fireman's uniform with a hand that was far from clean. 'I'm off duty now for forty-eight hours, supposed to be anyway, though God knows what'll happen now with this latest news. Hope to Christ they give me time to have a bath if they're going to come and get me, I'm filthy.'

'I'll have to get going,' Eddie said to Patsy, gulping

down the last of his pint. 'Ted will see you back home all right. I'll try not to wake you when I come home in the morning.' Bending over her, he kissed her cheek. 'Cheer up, love, the girls will be home from school soon, have a game of cards or something with them.'

Patsy laughed. 'Go on, I'll be fine.'

She *was* fine, Patsy decided as she snuggled down in Eddie's big armchair, she wasn't going to do any work this afternoon, just be thoroughly lazy. The double brandy had been just the job. She felt warm and glowing, even a little light-headed as she pushed her head deep into a cushion, but she still wished there had been a letter on the mat from Alex when she came back from the Bowery.

Two years and two months since he'd been called up the minute he was eighteen. She couldn't understand it. I thought I'd got used to him being away, but this last fortnight I've not been able to get him out of my mind. He'd been lucky, had Alex; no doubt about that! But then when hadn't her Alex been able to manipulate any situation to his own advantage?

The first six weeks in the Army, according to Alex, had been spent foot-slogging, and then on to weapon training was how he'd described it on his first leave home. Then – and he'd told them he'd gone down on his hands and knees and given thanks to God – he'd been selected for the Royal Army Service Corps as a driver.

Both his father and his grandfather said his early years of mucking about with old vans and any motor he could lay his hands on had certainly paid off.

The brandy was still having an effect and soon Patsy had dropped off into a much-needed sleep. She was in such a happy, foggy state that the sound of someone banging on her front door didn't alarm her at all. Not minding in the least that her peaceful snooze had been disturbed she yawned, stretched and slowly made her way up the narrow passage.

A three-ton Army truck was parked in the kerb right outside her front gate, and on the doorstep stood Alex. He was in the uniform of a corporal, the double white stripes worn proudly on each arm. There he was, large as life, still with a saucy grin spreading across his face.

His arms came around her and she was lifted clean off her feet as this tall son of hers kissed her face over and over again. Then setting her back down he said, 'We've only got time for a quick cuppa, Mum.' Turning his head, he whistled towards the cab of the truck and another soldier with rosy cheeks and a mop of blond hair put his head out of the window. 'Come on in and meet my Mum,' Alex shouted.

Emotion had by now caught up with Patsy and as

she turned to go back inside the house she had to use the hem of her blouse to wipe away the tears. With hands that wouldn't stop trembling she filled the kettle and set out cups and saucers on a tray. Thank God Kitty made me this cake, though it hasn't got any fruit in it, she worried, as she cut it up into slices.

'This is me mate, Mum, Joe Davis,' said Alex as the young lad came into the kitchen. 'We've been together since day one, he's from Liverpool.'

'Pleased to meet you Mrs Owen,' he said politely, holding out his hand to her.

'Sit down, son, make yourself at home. Have you two had any dinner today yet?'

Alex roared out laughing and his mate grinned. 'What did I tell you?' Alex cried. 'Told you she'd think we were starving and want to start feeding us up. Sorry, Mum,' he said, turning to face her. 'We're fine. Honest. Probably better fed than you lot at home here are. A quick cuppa and we must be off. We're on our way back from Woolwich Ordnance Depot, been to collect stores, boots, capes and all that sort of gear.'

The words were barely out of his mouth when both doors to the kitchen were flung open. David came in through the back door and stood stock still, amazement and pleasure showing on his face. Faces flushed with excitement and panting from running,

Ellen and Emma came in through the other door and threw themselves at their eldest brother.

'We saw the lorry!' cried Ellen.

'Yes, and we ran like mad,' Emma added. 'How long are you home for? Will you give us a ride in your lorry? Oh look, Alex's been made a corporal.'

'Will the pair of you leave him alone. Come on, get down from his knee and go up and tell Kitty to come down and say hallo to Joe.'

Everyone laughed, Patsy was in such a fluster that she didn't know whether she was coming or going. She was so happy as she poured tea and handed round the plain cake. The house was alive again, with all her children together in the one room; oh, why couldn't Alex have arrived before his father went to work? What about the mother of the other lad? She was way up in Liverpool. God knows they've had their share of the raids up there, they wouldn't be able to pop in and see her. What a shame! But she was very lucky, wasn't she?

Soon everyone was crowding out into the street to see the lads off. Alex hung back, drawing his mother aside. 'Mum,' he said quietly, 'on our way up from Felixstowe this morning we had to make a delivery to a NAAFI depot, and somehow or other one of the boxes got left behind in the lorry. I've put it under the put-u-up in the front room.'

Any protest that Patsy was about to make was cut

off short by the fact that Alex bent his head and softly kissed her, then said, 'Mum, don't worry if you don't hear from me for a while. We're sure to be on stand-by now.' Outside on the doorstep he playfully punched his two sisters, gave Kitty a hug, shook hands with his brother and had a few quiet words before looking into his mother's face. 'Look after yourself, tell Dad I send me love,' he said briskly before striding down the path and climbing up into the cab of his Army lorry. Patsy never took her eyes off him as he let out the clutch and drove away.

Patsy laughed shakily. 'What am I supposed ter do with it all?' she asked David who was standing look-ing down at where she sat on the floor surrounded by the contents of the box that Alex had left behind. Eddie was still in bed and the twins had gone to school. Patsy had left the cardboard box where it was until the next morning before opening it up.

'Now don't give us that, Mum,' said David cheer-fully, 'And stop feeling guilty. You don't think the Army is going to starve just because our Alex pinched a few bits an' bobs from the Quartermaster's stores, do you?'

'You don't have to put it like that,' said Patsy angrily, giving him a look of disgust.

'How *would* you put it then, Mum?' asked David,

not in the least upset by her look. 'You're not going to suggest that our Alex bought and paid for that lot, are you?' He indicated with the toe of his shoe the four-pound tin of corned beef that stood upright on the carpet, bags of rice, sugar and tea resting up against it. There were also two pairs of thick Army socks to which a card had been pinned, which said, 'These are for my dad.'

'Course I'm not,' she retorted fiercely. 'I just don't want Alex getting in to trouble, that's all that's worrying me.'

'Well then, the best thing you can do is split those bags up, put the tea and stuff away in jars and tins, out of sight, and say nothing to nobody. And the quicker the better. Christ knows what you can do with the corned beef.'

Suspecting that he was taking the mickey, she glanced up at him and he gave her exactly the kind of cheeky grin that Alex would have done.

'Just don't serve it up to us seven days a week, will you?'

'If you don't get yourself out of here I'll end up throwing the tin at you,' Patsy said, regaining her sense of humour. 'Though on second thoughts, hang on a minute. Are you going down towards Tooting in the van this morning? If you are, you can give me a lift. I may as well take some of these goodies down to your Gran and Aunt Florrie right away, seeing as how I'm not on duty today.'

'What you mean, Mother dear, is will I run you down to Strathmore Street!'

'Well, yes,' mumbled Patsy, trying hard not to laugh.

'That's better, you're sounding livelier already, not so worried about receiving stolen goods,' he said, teasing her.

'There's not much to choose between you and your brother,' Patsy yelled at him, but all the same she was laughing. 'You're both a pair of cheeky bounders,' she said, determined to have the last word.

'Make us a cup of tea while I sort this lot out,' Patsy said to David as they carried the box of provisions through to the kitchen. Her worries had all gone and she was thinking of the pleasure that would come to Florrie's face when she set down a tin full of tea on her table.

The large cardboard box was repacked, tied with string and stood by the door ready to go.

'What the hell have you got in there?' asked David as he came in from the scullery.

'I've put in some eggs and a few nice vegetables from the garden,' said Patsy, accepting the cup of tea he was holding out to her.

'You know, Mum, you're a bit of a conniver

yourself when it comes to looking after all of us,' grinned David as he playfully patted her arm.

While Patsy drank her tea, David changed his clothes ready to take her to Tooting, but his mother was not too certain that she liked what she saw as he came back into the room.

I suppose you could say he was nattily dressed, she thought to herself, but it wouldn't have been what I would have chosen for him to buy. His grey trousers, pale blue shirt and navy-blue tie were fine. It was the jacket he was wearing that she objected to: 'Like a bookmaker's runner!' she muttered beneath her breath, staring at the loud check pattern of the cloth. His hat didn't help either. She didn't mind the dark felt trilby, it was the way he wore it, tilted to the back of his head.

'By the way, I've been meaning to ask you, have you got any clothing coupons to spare?'

David gave her an enquiring look. 'What d'you need them for?'

'Well,' she said, 'Florrie usually gives me all her clothing coupons to keep the twins well turned out, what with their school uniform and all. She's always said new clothes never bother her – got enough to see out her lifetime. But she needs shoes, and you know what a bugger she is with those. The last pair your father bought her, she cut the front leather almost away 'cause she said they hurt her bunion.'

'Why didn't you tell me before?' said David.

'Well, I've told you now. Have you got any to spare or not? It's not only her shoes, before long she's going to need a whole set of new underwear.'

David sighed. 'Course I've got some, but up until a few days ago I had a darn sight more. I got rid of them.'

'What do you mean, you got rid of them?' she cried. 'You didn't throw them away, did you?'

'Oh, Mum! There's times when you really do take the biscuit. Throw clothing coupons away!' He shook his head in disbelief, then opening his wallet he took out first one and then a second full page of coupons and laid them on the table. 'They were promised, but family comes first. I'll get you some more, but it'll take me maybe a couple of weeks.'

Patsy felt her face flush up. These weren't his own spare coupons; there was more there than any one person was allowed for six months. She was fighting down her guilt once again. These boys of her dabbled in everything. It really was a wonder that one or even both of them hadn't landed up inside Wandsworth Prison. War or no war, no one could get away with it for ever! She was eyeing the coupons with envy though. Besides Florrie, the twins could do with shoes; both Eddie and Ollie needed shirts; a new mac for Eddie was out of the question.

'You want to know where I got them from, don't

you?' David's question broke into her thoughts, but Patsy didn't answer. 'There's a woman who lives up Brixton Lane, got nine kids, no money but plenty of coupons. There's others like her. I know people who've got plenty of money but no coupons. Seems a fair swap to me.' David paused and the cheeky grin showed again.

'Is that a fact?' It was Patsy's turn to tease him.

'I've just told you, haven't I?'

'Yes, you have. Don't mean I have to believe you.'

'If you don't want them . . . David was leaning towards the table with arm outstretched.

His mother was quicker as she snatched them up. 'Oh, no you don't, my lad. It's needs must when the devil drives.'

David smiled. 'I'm sure God won't make you spend years and years in purgatory just because of a few clothing coupons.'

'And the rest,' Patsy muttered as she pulled on her hat and watched David pick up the heavy box.

Chapter Eleven

PATSY WAS SEETHING with rage as she and Mary
Briggs picked themselves up off the floor of the Canteen and dusted themselves down.

'As if the air-raids haven't been bad enough,' Patsy
groaned as she coughed twice to clear her throat,
'now Hitler has to start sending these bloody
doodlebugs.'

Mary was still fighting for breath, as she too
coughed and choked and finally spat into her
handkerchief. Suddenly they both sneezed loudly, and
despite the cloying dust they both laughed, which did
a lot to ease the tension.

These planes which were coming over without a
pilot and without any warning were, to most Londoners, worse than the bombers. No wailing siren
warned you to make for an air-raid shelter. There
was no steady boom-boom of anti-aircraft fire. Was
that something to be grateful for? Patsy wasn't sure.
Sometimes the guns on the Common sounded more
menacing than the bombs did. But the pilotless planes
were something else. Shooting across the sky, with
uncontrolled flames blasting out from the tail until

the engine cut out. Then came the silence. Everyone, young and old, prayed the same prayer, watching in horrified fascination as the plane glided on for a few moments before plunging to earth. 'Please God, don't let it fall down here.'

Just ten minutes earlier, Mary had come into the Canteen, looking bright-eyed and bushy-tailed, bubbling over with excitement because she had come home from a late shift last night and found not one, but two letters lying waiting for her on the mat. An air-mail from Stan in Italy, and one from her two boys in Wales.

'Give us a soapy cloth, Patsy, and I'll wipe these tables down while you see about that cup of tea we were going to have.'

'Right.' Patsy glanced quickly at Mary's face; it still had that yellowish touch, but it was ages since she had seen Mary looking so pleased and acting so cheerfully.

'Good job no one else was in here,' Mary remarked as she worked quickly to remove the loose grime from the table-tops.

'First lull I've had since I came on at eight o'clock this morning,' said Patsy. 'Had five firemen in for their breakfast; Ted was one of them, they all looked exhausted. Amy's off today, Ted said she wasn't going to do anything, just laze about. Why don't you pop in and see her on your way 'ome – she'll be just as pleased as me to hear all your news.'

'Yeah, all right, I will. There, all ship-shape once again, how about that tea?'

'Here, take these,' Patsy called, handing two large steaming mugs across the counter. 'I might as well make the most of this break and come and sit with you while we drink our tea, and you can tell me what's in your letters.'

'Wonder where that one fell?' said Mary as she set the mugs down. 'Must have been quite a few streets away 'cause we've got no damage, only dust – get used to that, don't you? I was scared enough of the raids, without these bleedin' things on top.'

Patsy grinned and Mary quickly went on, 'I know what you're thinking, I shouldn't be swearing, but it's enough to make a saint swear.

'We all do our share of it these days. Come on, tell me how the boys are getting on.'

Mary didn't need any coaxing to talk about her boys. 'Seven pages, five of them written by Sam but the other three young Joey had written himself. I'll tell you this much, Patsy, I was dead lucky the way it turned out – you know, having the boys evacuated. You hear so many horror stories, don't you – makes you wonder how people can be so unkind to kids, but they have been, that's for sure – look how many have come back to London. Fell on their feet, my two did. Even my Stan was amazed when he had his

embarkation leave and he took me down to Risca
for three days.'

Mary paused to sip at her tea and Patsy said, 'Risca?
I never knew that was where the boys are, only that
they had gone to South Wales. Is Risca a big town?'

Mary was a while answering Patsy's query. Her eyes
had a faraway look in them and Patsy didn't need to
be told that she was remembering that week-end –
so long ago, it seemed now – when Stan had come
home on leave looking so smart and proud in his
uniform, Mary had got permission to have a week
off from the factory and they had set off so happily
to see their kids.

'Course it's not a big town, it's a little village, nearly
all the men and even the young lads work down the
coal-mines.' Mary's voice continued, a little muffled
as she coped with the emotions the memory had
brought back. 'Honest Patsy, Mr and Mrs MacCarthy
couldn't look after our boys better if they were their
own flesh and blood. Got two boys of their own, but
they're both grown up and married. I told you, didn't
I? Besides the house they live in, they own a shop –
right next door on the corner it is. Sells everything,
even fish and veg. Guess what Joey wrote about most?
Uncle Mac – that's what they call Mr MacCarthy –
gave them both an orange. Cor, Patsy, what I
wouldn't have given to have been able to see my two
lads sucking away at their oranges!' Mary raised her

mug to her lips again and Patsy was thrilled to see her so elated.

'Didn't tell you about the working men's club in Risca, did I?'

'Don't think you did, Mary; we don't often get a chance to have a good old chin-wag like this, do we?'

'Well, love, that club was marvellous. Course we had a bed and breakfast, just down the road from the MacCarthys, but they took us to this club on the Saturday evening. I should think the whole of the village, kids an' all, was crammed into the hall that night. Mac, as everyone calls Mister MacCarthy, is a big man, not as tall as my Stan, but big-shouldered and has a big belly.' Mary added, laughing to herself, 'Funny, really, his wife Polly is quite small, but both of them are real dark-haired and dark-skinned as if they had lived abroad for years and yet they were typical Welsh, lovely lilt to their voices – and Patsy, you should have heard Mac sing. Great deep voice which seemed to rise up from his very boots. In fact, all the men had beautiful voices. At eleven o'clock when the club closed every man in that hall joined in singing, "We'll keep a welcome in the hill-side, we'll keep a welcome in the dales, this land you knew will still be singing, when you come home again to Wales." I tell you, Patsy, there wasn't a dry eye in that crowd – lovely, it was.'

Silence hung between them after that until Patsy gently asked, 'And how was Stan?'

'All right as far as I could tell. Can't say much on those flimsy air-mails, can you? And then they censor a lot of it. Still, at least you know he's alive and kicking which is something, God bless him!'

'I suppose you'll spend the afternoon writing letters and I'd better get on and do some washing-up before our lady volunteers come on duty.'

'How did you guess?' Mary grinned. 'I'm going to tell the boys that as soon as their father gets another leave we'll both be down to see them.'

Patsy's heart sunk. Blimey, that was wishful thinking. Stan Briggs get leave, from Italy! But she wasn't about to puncture Mary's balloon that was flying so high today for a change. She thought for a second and then blurted out, 'No. You can do better than that. Tell them you'll be down in two or three weeks' time. I'll come with you. I'll get Eddie to find out about the trains and all the connections, and Ollie will take us to the station. It'll make a nice couple of days' break. Ask Mrs MacCarthy to book us a bed and breakfast.'

Mary gave a long, shivering sigh and glanced sadly at Patsy. 'If only we could . . . You don't mean it, do you?'

'Course I do. Wouldn't suggest it if I didn't. Tell you what, you come over in the morning; it's Eddie's first

Sunday off since God knows when. We'll 'ave a chat about it and he'll help us get things sorted, you'll see.'

'Thanks, Patsy.' Mary was beaming as she gathered up her things and made for the door. 'I'll see you in the morning then, about eleven?'

'Fine' Patsy agreed as they hugged each other.

We will go down to Wales, Patsy vowed to herself as she watched Mary walk some distance and then step off the pavement and skirt a pile of rubble where a wall had collapsed. Turning back to start her jobs, she gave a muffled curse. We all seem to lead such regimented lives these days, queue for every bite of food, turn sheets side to middle, make coats out of blankets because there's nothing new to buy and, if there is, chances are we never have enough coupons. A real good peaceful night's sleep seems to be a thing of the past. Well, I've 'ad enough. A few days' break from all this monotony won't lose us the war; I'll even ask Amy if she wants to come to Wales with Mary and me. A night out in that workmen's club that Mary just described could be just what the doctor ordered for all three of us.

It was a quarter to eleven on Sunday morning when Mary rapped her knuckles on the back door and came in, still with eyes that sparkled brighter than Patsy had seen them in weeks. They were still sitting nattering, elbows on the table, when Eddie came in from the garden. 'Hallo, love,' he greeted Mary, then he said to Patsy, 'Still plenty of cabbages, swedes and a few carrots in the ground, but not much else. I must have known Mary was coming over, I've brought half a bucket of potatoes up from the shed.'

'Oh, I haven't come over for dinner,' Mary protested quickly.

'And why not?' Eddie wanted to know, 'A bit of company will do both me and Patsy a bit of good. Course you'll stay.'

Mary turned her glance towards Patsy. She loved these two people who had been her friends from the day she and Stan had moved into Clapham Manor Street, but she wasn't one to impose – after all, the Owens had a lovely family and loads of friends without her foisting herself on them for Sunday dinner.

'Come on, stay, have your dinner with us. There'll only be me and Eddie.' Then Patsy grinned. 'Maybe you won't want to stay when I tell you what we've got for today – rissoles!'

'Well, what's wrong with rissoles?' Patsy's grinning was infectious and Mary started to giggle, and even Eddie gave a throaty chuckle.

'For one thing they're off the ration, so God knows what's in them. I asked the butcher to let me have half a dozen 'cos I thought Ollie was going to be here, but then he tells me last night that he's taking some big-wig down to Windsor. "Oh, having your tea with Her Majesty, are you?" I asked him.'

'Yeah,' Eddie interrupted Patsy's yarn and, turning to Mary, he said, 'And Ollie told her she should show a bit more respect for her elders.'

The rissoles weren't at all bad, the vegetables were fresh and plentiful and the company was good even if the laughter at times was tinged with sadness, as the three of them each mulled over the terrible things that were happening so frequently.

It was six o'clock before Patsy stood at the front gate with Mary. ''Bye, love, thanks for today. I don't know when I've enjoyed a Sunday more and I think it's ever so good of Eddie to say he'll see that you, me and Amy get down to Wales to see my boys. Ta-ta, love, see you soon.'

'Oh, I forgot,' Patsy said as she returned Mary's hug, 'You'll see me in the morning. I'm not on at the Canteen tomorrow, so Ollie suggested I come with him on the coach when he takes you workers and then he'll drop me off somewhere near Oxford Circus. I mean to have a wander around the shops up there for a change.'

'See you in the morning, then, hope we get a quiet night.'

'Amen to that,' said Patsy as she watched until Mary reached the corner of Navy Street and turned and waved.

★

Patsy was sitting in the corner on the back seat of the coach as she watched the workers alight and walk in through the factory gates. Mary and her workmate Elsie were the last two to get off, and Patsy twisted her body round and raised her hand as Mary hesitated and looked back.

'All right back there?' Ollie called as he let in the clutch and moved off. They had travelled four streets when a deafening explosion shook the buildings around them, causing the coach to rock and the front nearside window to shatter. A piece of debris flung up by the explosion landed on the roof of the coach with a loud bang. Ollie rammed his foot down hard on the brake pedal, almost standing the bus on end as he brought it to a standstill, throwing Patsy hard against the seat in front.

'Come on, Patsy, let's get out of here,' Ollie shouted as he got himself out of the driver's seat and waited in the gangway for Patsy to come forward.

'Oh hell!' Patsy yelled as she climbed down to the pavement, having caught her hand on the jagged glass in the framework of the door. Blood gushed out splashing on to the roadway; hastily Ollie pulled a handkerchief from his pocket and wrapped it tightly round the wound. The blast had forced front doors open, broken glass littered the pavement. A young boy clung shrieking to his mother.

Ollie's main concern was to get back to the factory.

'Would you rather wait here for me?' he gently offered Patsy.

'No, I'm coming with you,' she declared, reaching out and clutching his hand. The doodlebug had fallen three streets away. The men on fire-guard duty had their work cut out dealing with the results of a direct hit on a garage. The damage from the blast was horrendous – a gaping hole at the entry to the munitions factory was hampering the rescue work.

Patsy watched in despair when, half an hour later, Ollie came back to where she waited with several other women, all of them were shivering, feeling desolate and utterly useless. Ollie looked dead-beat; he was covered in dust and his voice shook as he told the group of women, 'Three dead in there so far, about twenty injured, ambulances are lined up round at the rear entrance. You all know that tall gangly lad, all freckles and red hair? He's had a lucky escape; part of the roof fell in on him, he's got a broken leg, arm as well I shouldn't be surprised. Ruddy blast does almost as much damage as a direct hit with these damn things.'

Patsy was trembling violently. Intuition told her that Ollie was speaking fast to cover up something. Mary! He hadn't mentioned Mary. Before she could bring herself to drag out the question, he took hold of her elbow and drew her aside. Sounding as if he were scared stiff, he managed to say, 'Mary has been hurt and she's on her way to the hospital; they took her in the first ambulance.'

Patsy's sentences were disjointed, short, sharp outbursts. 'Where? What hospital? How badly is she hurt? I must get there . . . straight away. Can you take me?'

Ollie wiped his hand across his eyes; at the moment he couldn't answer one of her questions, not truthfully anyway. 'You'll have to hang on a bit yet, Patsy, love, until they get things organised in there. As soon as we are able to get some real information, of course I shall take you straight to the hospital. Be a good girl and try and calm down.'

Easier said than done. All around them was the smell of smouldering rubber and the air was thick with dust, soot and smuts. Glancing up, Patsy saw a pale sun in a sky that was clear and blue. How could it be? Death and devastation had just rained down on London. People had been having conversations, saying good morning, getting ready for another day's work at the beginning of a new week. Some were now dead; others maimed, perhaps for life. Patsy wanted to run, hell for leather − anywhere, somewhere where the air was sweet and scented by nature, where there was peace and people smiled and lived quiet but happy lives, whole families together. Was there such a place left on this war-torn earth?

This was the nearest she had been to death. She and Ollie had been just minutes away.

'Come on. We'll find a hot drink somewhere.' Ollie's voice sounded completely drained as he took her hand in his and led her between the various service vehicles which were now on the scene.

Within the hour Patsy was at St Thomas's Hospital. Listening to the clamour outside in the corridor as more casualties arrived, while sitting watching Mary in total silence made her feel worse. The time stretched endlessly. Please open your eyes, Mary. Squeeze my fingers, nod your head, anything to let me know you're still with us, she pleaded silently. Then in her mind she prayed: God spare her. *Please.*

A touch on her shoulder made her jump and she looked up to see Ollie's great frame bending down on her. 'I'm going for a while, to see if there is anything I can do back there. I'll phone Eddie, if the phones are working. I'll try and get hold of Amy too. See you later,' he whispered, planting a soft kiss on her forehead.

Much later a nurse came into the ward and handed Patsy a cup of tea. 'There you are, love, drink it while it's hot,' she said, her sallow, hollow-cheeked face showing compassion.

Patsy roused herself, thanked the nurse and gratefully sipped the tea, her eyes now fixed on Mary's pale face. Oh, Mary! Was it only yesterday we had that quiet lovely day together? And Saturday morning – had a good old natter, didn't we? Don't see each other for days and then we have that nice week-end. You were bubbling over with joy 'cause you'd got two letters. Oh, please, love, wake up and give me a smile, just a little one – don't just lie there . . . like a corpse, she almost muttered, then she banished that thought immediately. Mary was not going to die, she wouldn't let her. She's got two boys to live for. Patsy had the urge to take Mary by the shoulders and give her a jolly good shake. I would, too, she vowed with the tears now stinging the back of her eyes, if I thought it would give her a new lease of life.

At half-past nine that evening, Patsy was sitting with her elbows on the edge of the bed, her face cupped in her hands. Eddie sat despondently opposite her. Ollie had been back twice, the second time in his overalls to tell them he would be at the main Air-Raid Wardens Post.

About ten o'clock Amy staggered in and as Eddie stood up and offered her his chair, she thankfully plonked herself down. 'God, what a mess!' she whispered. 'How is she?' nodding her head towards Mary. How ill she looked; her eyes were closed, her face deathly pale.

'No change from the minute I got here; she hasn't moved, not even when the doctor or the nurses see to her.'

'Let's pray she's holding her own, eh?' Receiving no answer, Amy pressed on. 'Phew!' she groaned, looking up at solid, reliable Eddie. 'At least it's peaceful in here. I've been over to your house; Kitty and Ada Nicholls have taken Emma and Ellen to the shelter. There's no raid on at the moment, in fact it's so quiet it's bloody eerie, but there were several of them doodlebugs this morning. Nothing's back to normal yet, I had to walk 'ere. But I had to come.'

'Course you did,' Patsy agreed, heaving a great sigh. 'Who'd have believed it, eh? She was so happy yesterday, and on Saturday. On top of the world she was, full of life. Now look at her.'

A nurse came to the bedside and adjusted the drip tube that led into Mary's arm, then before leaving she indicated with a nod of her head that she wanted Eddie to follow her.

The young doctor was kind and sympathetic. 'Has she no relatives?' he asked. 'They should be here when she . . . His voice wavered and he couldn't continue. He was going through this dozens of times every week now, yet somehow he still wasn't hardened to it.

'Her husband is in the Army, his regiment is in Italy; her two young sons are evacuated to South Wales — have been there since the beginning of the war. Neither my wife nor I have ever heard Mrs Briggs speak of any other family.'

The doctor nodded his understanding. 'No one you think we should get in touch with locally?'

'None that I can think of. What about her husband?'

'The police will deal with that, get in touch with the War Office. His company commander will break the news of his wife's death to him.' There, he had got the words out and Eddie hadn't the heart to query that statement.

'It was the doctor that wanted to see you, wasn't it?' Patsy shot the question at Eddie before he had scarcely set foot back in the ward.

'It's the crack on the back of her head that's worrying the doctors,' Eddie told Patsy quietly, and as she lowered her head into her hands he looked across at Amy and silently shook his head.

'She'll be all right, won't she, Eddie? She will pull through?' Patsy's voice was no more than a whisper and it was more than Eddie could do to answer that question.

'They've told me, all we can do is wait and see. We must go home now, Ellen and Emma will be frightened if we stay much longer,' he chided her softly. 'There is nothing any of us can do, the medical staff are really wonderful, you know that, and I promise we'll come back really early in the morning.'

★

It was barely six o'clock next morning when they left Clapham, taking the same route as the previous day. Patsy shuddered and buried her head in Eddie's shoulder as Ollie drove on past the burnt-out garage.

There had been a nurse in the side ward with Mary when they walked in. 'I'm so sorry,' she murmured, and they all knew that Mary was dead. But she looked very peaceful lying there; her eyes were closed, her hair was still dusty and tangled, but an attempt had been made to brush it back from her forehead. Her arms lay at her sides on top of the bed covers. Patsy reached out and took hold of one hand; she stood there stroking her fingers until she could no longer hold back her tears and had to turn away and leave the room.

Ollie followed her. 'Don't, Patsy, love. Don't cry.' His arms drew her to him. She was shaking from head to foot and her crying got worse, beyond her control as her choking sobs turned to hiccups.

Ollie couldn't bear to see such misery. Mary's sudden death had come as a mighty shock. How could he, or anyone else for that matter, cushion her against the way she was feeling?

'She was so happy . . . we were going down to see her boys . . . she didn't believe me when I said I'd go with her, but I meant it. I did, Ollie.' Patsy's eyes pleaded with him to believe her. 'Oh, poor Stan!

Who will tell him? He's not likely to get leave, is he? Not from Italy.'

Tears were rolling unchecked down her cheeks when suddenly her mouth opened wide and she let out a wail, a moaning wail like the sound that might come from a hurt puppy. 'Ollie . . . oh, Ollie. Mary's boys!' Her hands were now clasped over her mouth and through clenched fingers she croaked, 'Who the hell is going to tell them?'

In the tiny ward the nurse had moved to pull the sheet up to cover Mary's face, but Eddie's outstretched arm halted her. 'Give me just a minute, would you, please nurse?' Sympathetically she nodded and left the room.

Hurting inside, Eddie stood looking at Mary, not knowing quite how to say goodbye. Such a nice woman. Honest and kind and good. Such a good mother, such a wonderful wife to Stan. Why Mary? It didn't make any sense. His eyes were full. He couldn't find his handkerchief and the tears trickled down his cheeks while he wished that everything could have been so different – that he could turn the clock back, that Mary hadn't gone to work yesterday and would have lived to see this damn war come to an end, and Stan get demobbed and Sam and Joey come back to live in London.

Eddie didn't think of himself as being romantic, but he had to do this for Stan. He took hold of

Mary's hand, held it between both of his for a lingering moment, raised it to his lips and gently kissed her wrist. He laid her hand down, brushed her cheek with his fingers and looked at her for the last time. It was several minutes before he felt able to join Patsy and Ollie. He was blinded by tears.

All the arrangements were made by Ollie and the funeral was to be the following Monday.

'You sure she ain't got no family?' Kitty, being the practical one, asked.

'Never heard her speak of any, and the police said they haven't been able to trace any relatives, only Stan and the boys,' Patsy answered.

'She did once tell us her mother and father died within weeks of each other – said it was the year her first baby was born. Remember?' Amy asked, jogging Patsy's memory.

'Only vaguely. I'll be glad when it's over now.'

'So will we all, love,' Florrie stated as she waddled in from the scullery bearing the inevitable pot of tea. ''Tisn't fair on them boys. Why the good Lord saw fit to take their mother away from them beats the life out of me. Ours is not to reason why, so they say, and I suppose He had His reasons but it don't make no sense – not to the likes of me it don't.'

There were many more women sitting in the pews

at the church than Patsy had imagined there would be. It was a service full of emotion. It could so easily have been any one of them . . . but it wasn't. It was Mary in the coffin that was slowly being lowered into the ground.

It was a fortnight before they all got their breath back and Amy and Patsy set off on their journey to South Wales. The MacCarthys had been marvellous, sincere and kind, saying there was no need for the two of them to make such a long journey. But they felt differently. They were going to keep their promise to Mary and hopefully they were going to keep her flat; even if the windows got blown out, they'd see to it that they were boarded up. There had to be a place waiting there for Stan to come back to, a home where he could raise his two sons.

Cold it was in Risca, even though it was supposed to be summer now. 'Nice and bright and dry, though,' Polly told them as she gave them rugs to carry over their arms and a basket packed with food.

'Now don't you be staying down by that river for too long. See you're back by four. It gets windy down by the water.'

'Make up your mind, woman,' Mac said sternly, though there was a twinkle in his eye. 'The amount of food you've packed, we could be forgiven for thinking you'd not be wanting us back till tomorrow.'

The boys burst out laughing. 'Get away with you

all!' Polly shooed them up the narrow passage. 'I'll have the table all laid and the hot-pot simmering in the oven, so mind what I've said – no staying down there too long.'

Patsy and Amy struggled to lift their feet as they crossed the damp field. Mac had already spread the blankets a few yards back from the river. Sam and Joey, both filled out and grown so much taller than either Amy or Patsy remembered, were already taking their shoes and socks off.

'It's too cold for them to be in that water,' Amy exclaimed.

'Leave them be, they'll be all right, they're obviously used to it. Look at them splashing,' Patsy said, never for a moment taking her eyes off the two boys.

'Yes,' Amy sighed. 'Look happy enough, don't they? Can't tell what they're thinking though, can we?'

'Let's just be grateful that they've got each other and that there are such people as Mac and Polly in this world.'

Back on the river-bank Mac was throwing a ball to the boys. Fast. Each in turn had to catch it and throw it back. Suddenly they heard Mac's deep throaty voice ring out. 'Butter-fingers!' and then they heard the boys laugh loudly.

Amy and Patsy looked long and hard at each other, and although there were tears in their eyes a great feeling of relief flooded through them. One more happy day was spent shopping, with the girls assuring Sam and Joey that all the gifts came from Eddie and Ollie and that the very special one was from their father.

Time to say goodbye. A last cuddle. The babble of talk and laughter died and the boys' faces dropped. 'They're just tired,' Polly assured the others.

Their shoes made an awfully loud noise as they walked across the pavement to the waiting taxi; they were going home on the train, back to their own families – it didn't seem fair that all this should have happened.

Mac hugged them both in turn, Polly kissed them and whispered, 'Sam and Joey will be fine, I promise. Me an' Mac, we'll see to them.'

Amy and Patsy sniffed back their tears. They were both touched and very grateful.

Patsy awoke slowly in a quite unaccustomed mood of optimism as she remembered it was Saturday. There had been enough gloom and doom and long faces in the house over the past weeks; she was going to make a determined effort to brighten things up, it wasn't fair on the twins to be so mournful all the time. It was half-past seven as she got up and pulled back the curtains, delighted that the sun was shining, the birds were singing and all in all it promised to be a lovely day. Having washed and dressed, she went downstairs, drank two cups of scalding, strong tea and ate just one biscuit. Then she laid the table with places for three, placing a long tin loaf on the bread-board in the centre and the butter-dish beside it. There wasn't any jam or marmalade, they'd had all their ration for that month. There weren't any baked beans either, which she knew both Ellen and Emma adored but which she herself couldn't stand. But there were eggs, thanks to the chickens in the garden, and still a few rashers of bacon.

The bacon was cooked, drained and put on to plates which were now keeping warm in the oven at the side of the range. Patsy pushed two slices of bread to one side of the pan and cracked an egg into the tilted other side just as the door opened and Emma came into the room still rubbing sleep from her eyes.

'Morning, darling,' she greeted her daughter. 'I thought we might go down and see Auntie Florrie and Gran today, seeing as everyone else is working.

'All right by me,' said Emma.

'And me,' piped up Ellen, who had just entered the kitchen.

'Shall we buy cut flowers or a plant?' Patsy asked the twins later as they stood outside the tube station at Clapham Common.

The girls considered the flower-stall carefully. 'Whichever,' sensible Ellen said quietly. 'We'd better get the same for Gran – don't want to ruffle their feathers, do we?' She smiled softly at her mother. They settled on some carnations because of their gorgeous smell and Patsy asked Minnie, the flower-seller whom she'd known for years, to put two penny-worth of gypsophila in each bunch.

'Lucky to have any gyp, me darling,' Minnie said, smiling broadly at the pretty sight the twins made in their floral short-sleeved dresses, their copper-coloured hair looking sleek and glossy with yellow ribbons holding it back from their faces.

'Sorry, ain't got no paper,' she said sadly to Patsy as she handed a bunch to each of the girls. 'By God, I miss your Alex,' Minnie murmured. 'There wasn't much that boy couldn't get 'old of. I just hope the good Lord sees fit to bring him back safe and sound.'

So do I, Patsy was saying to herself as they gingerly stepped on to the escalator.

Tooting Broadway was packed. Uniforms of all shapes, sizes and colours were to be seen amongst the crowd, and the loud drawl of the American soldiers could be clearly heard. The sun was high in the sky, the clouds only very few and they drifted lazily along looking for all the world as if they were made of cotton-wool. Women wore thin summer dresses and the children were free from their winter woollies. It was the end of June and the beginning of what promised to be a nice summer.

If only this wretched war would end, Patsy was thinking as they stood on the kerb waiting to cross the road. In Selkirk Road a thought came to her. 'I'll pop into the oil shop, see if Mr Anderson has any matches,' she said to her daughters.

'Can we go on?' Emma pleaded.

'Course you can. One of you go over to Gran with her flowers, I won't be long.' But she was talking to their backs for they were off and running, turning the corner out of sight.

The old oil shop had held a fascination for Patsy for as long as she could remember. She drew in a deep breath as she stepped into its dim interior and sniffed at the familiar smells — smells left over from her childhood. Paraffin! Many a time she had brought the can to be filled for her mother when coal had been too costly and they'd used a paraffin stove instead. Moth-balls, camphor, oily liquid Creosote which the Day brothers had used to weatherproof their barrows. Clothes-props, clothes-lines, wire netting for the chicken-runs — the shop hadn't changed at all and neither had the proprietor.

'Patsy!' Mr Anderson emerged from the darkest regions, as the door-bell jangled. He stood still, his arms stretched wide and Patsy went into them gladly. She laughed as he patted her back, over and over again, just as Ollie had done when she was a child. To come into this shop was always like coming home. Mr Anderson peered at her over the top of his steel-framed glasses. 'So how have you been?' he asked, pushing his thin white hair off his forehead. 'And that good husband of yours? He don't come to see me no more.'

'Don't be cross with Eddie, please,' she said softly, still holding on to his hand. 'He doesn't get much time to himself these days.'

'I know, I know,' he answered sadly. 'This war has spoilt so many things! Our way of life is so different, it has to be.'

'Crikey, look at that!' The nervous shout came from a boy who was about ten years old. Standing in the doorway of the shop, he pointed upwards. 'I ain't never seen one as close as that before.'

Stumbling with panic, Patsy was across the shop floor first. The chug-chug of the doodlebug's engine made her go cold with fear. It was directly above, with raging flames shooting out from its tail. She elbowed the lad backwards into the shop and slammed the door. 'Down, get down on the floor.' Too late – the noise from the sky had stopped. Now there was a deathly silence.

The twins! Patsy was praying like mad for what seemed an endless time. Inside her head she was screaming, then came the thunderous crash and she was thrown to the floor.

'Cor, that's close.' The boy was on his hands and knees crawling to where Mr Anderson lay against a pile of sacks, coughing his heart up as the choking dust filled the shop.

The door had been blown open and a mass of rubble blocked the doorway, but this didn't stop Patsy as she scrambled and clawed her way over. Keeping to the centre of the road she ran like the wind. It took her only moments to reach Strathmore Street.

'Better not go down there,' an ARP worker warned her. 'It landed in the next street but we've got a lot of the blast damage.'

'My kids are here,' Patsy insisted, brushing him aside and rushing forward.

Gran and Emma were on the doorstep, standing in the midst of fallen bricks and mortar. Emma screamed and ran wildly towards her mother. 'Ellen and Auntie are in that lot,' she cried in a voice from which all the breath seemed to have been sucked, as she pointed to the pile of rubble opposite.

'Stay with your Gran,' Patsy ordered as she ran across the road, pausing only to lift aside a twisted front door that lay in her path.

'It's not safe to get too close,' an ambulance worker told her. 'A lot more of that house looks like it's ready to go.'

Patsy caught his arm. 'My little girl and my mother are in there.'

'They're all right,' he said, heaving a thankful sigh. 'At least, they will be when the ARP men can get at them.'

'Mummy, Mummy!'

'Ellen!'

Ignoring the warnings, Patsy was climbing over the teetering plaster and window-frames and within seconds was peering down the opening the men had already cleared. Ellen's dirty tear-stained face looked up at her.

'Thank you, God. Thank you, thank you,' cried Patsy. 'Are you all right? Are your legs trapped? What about Auntie Florrie?'

'Don't panic, love,' a man wearing a tin helmet said coolly. 'The old lady's all right. We'll have them out of there in no time. I don't think either of them is really injured – they were lucky, only caught the tail end of the blast.'

Lucky! God above! Patsy knelt down and put her face right into the opening. 'I'm here, darling,' she said.

'When are they going to get us out of here, Mummy?' Ellen sounded so pathetic.

Patsy had to swallow twice before she could bring herself to answer. 'Soon, luvvie. Soon, I promise.'

Reluctantly she went back across the road and

waited. Emma held on tightly to her with a palm that felt smooth and soft, while Patsy's other hand was held by Gran's leathery, liver-spotted one. Each was trying to draw comfort and give reassurance at the same time.

'I can reach her now,' Patsy heard a rescue worker call, and if it hadn't been for Gran putting her fat, safe arms tightly round Patsy she would have sunk to the floor, so great was the feeling of relief that flooded through her body.

Ellen's head and shoulders came out, her face scratched and bleeding, her pretty dress torn to shreds. The ambulance man carried her to safety, gently lowering her into Patsy's outstretched arms as the street began to fill with people. 'You'd do better to go indoors and make yourselves a strong cup of something,' he said kindly, steering Patsy by the elbow towards Gran's front door. 'We'll let you know the minute we have your Mum free.'

Their feet made a crunching sound as they walked down the passage which was littered with broken glass. 'My God,' Patsy mumbled fearfully as she took stock of the mess the kitchen was in.

Lowering Ellen into Grandad's big armchair, she turned to Emma. 'Stay with her, I'll get you both a cup of tea as soon as I can.'

Now was not the time to panic either. Gran looked ghastly – should she run to the Selkirk? What the old lady needed was a good stiff brandy. Should she sweep the broken glass off the table? Should she wipe the chairs down? They were covered in thick dust. The broken window-frame was still hanging dangerously by its sash cords; she ought to cut it down and knock out the jagged shards of glass that were sticking out from the sides of the frame. Better if she filled the kettle and put it on to boil first. Oh dear God, help me, please!

As if in answer to her silent prayer the kitchen door opened and Ollie's massive frame stood there. The relief was so great that she burst into tears. Ellen and Emma were crying, so was Gran, as Ollie comforted each in turn.

'Leave everything,' he ordered. 'My place has only lost the front bay-window. Fall in!' he said, doing his best to make a joke of it all, as he swept Ellen up into his burly arms and led the way out of the mess. A strange procession they made as they walked the few yards to Ollie's house.

'Nice car!' A Warden nodded his head towards the huge black shiny car that stood at the kerbside as he held open the front gate for Ollie to pass through.

Patsy couldn't believe her eyes. It *was* a posh car, but before she had time to question what it was doing here the noise came again. Another V-bomb, a plane on fire shrieking through the sky. Ollie, Gran and the girls were all inside the house by now but Patsy stood, rooted to the spot, every limb trembling while she watched in terror as it rumbled above Tooting, shaking the old houses with its vibration. She waited in breathless silence as it continued on course and guiltily said a prayer of thanks that the engine of this one hadn't cut out in this area.

'Grandad's going to take us home in that Army staff car,' Emma told her mother as soon as she set foot inside the kitchen. Oh, bless you, Ollie, Patsy silently mouthed. Trust him to set the fear of the past hour at rest.

'Cor, aren't we lucky?' she said, reaching across the table and taking hold of their hands. 'Your Grandad always did have friends in high places. And now I'll make us all a nice cup of tea.'

'About time too,' said Gran, coming in with a warm wet flannel and gently wiping away the grime from Ellen's cheeks.

'Drop of brandy in it, Gran?' Ollie asked.

'I should think we've all earned it,' she answered enthusiastically. 'But make sure you keep a drop for poor old Flo. She's going to need it.'

A great cheer went up as willing hands reached to lift Florrie out into the daylight and on to the waiting stretcher. It had taken nearly three hours to free her. Barely had the rescue workers lifted the stretcher above the ground than the rubble began to slip, tumbling quickly, sending up clouds of brick-dust. A tin-hatted fireman cursed loudly as he tried to stop himself from toppling sideways while the bricks and stonework from the old house collapsed. He landed with a jarring thump.

'You all right, Bert?' one of the other firemen called. There was no answer.

Patsy was only feet away from where the fireman was lying on his back staring up at the sky, an odd dazed expression on his face. When he still hadn't moved a minute later two ARP men went to kneel beside him. Tentatively they touched his face. 'Let's get him to the ambulance,' one man muttered, taking hold of his shoulders while his mate took his feet, and as they lifted him the fireman's head moved slowly round until it was at an impossible angle to his neck.

Patsy, filled with sudden horror, stared in disbelief.

'Gawd almighty, he's dead,' one man shouted, and an ambulanceman rushed forward to feel his pulse.

'Oh, my God!' the woman standing next to Patsy whispered.

No one needed telling. Everyone knew. The fireman was dead.

A dreadful fear welled up inside Patsy, for Florrie wasn't making a sound as the rescue men did their best to be gentle with her. There was none of her usual repartee, no complaints, no swearing or cursing of the Germans. What if this had been more than Florrie could take?

Ollie saw the muscles of Patsy's face begin to twitch. 'Do you think she'll make it? She's not going to die, is she? Please, Ollie, tell me she won't die.' Patsy by now was hysterical.

No. This cruel war was getting more than anyone could stand. Was Florrie going to die? No! By God, No! Defiance was expressed in Ollie's face as he turned to confront her, saying quietly, 'You mustn't start thinking the worst, Patsy, you know as well as I do that our Florrie is made of sterner stuff than that. Come on now, let's go and tell Gran and the girls that Florrie is safely on her way to hospital. And I'll tell you another thing,' he said as they stood side by side and watched the ambulance drive away. 'Give her a couple of days and she'll have the whole ward in an uproar!'

Ollie was right. After having slept away two days Florrie was almost back on form. The doctors said she had been lucky. 'Thank God,' Patsy had breathed. Despite having a broken leg, a good many bruises and a deep cut above her left eye which had required eight stitches, she wasn't quiet any more.

It was almost six o'clock in the evening as Patsy and Eddie walked the length of the open-sided verandah at St James's Hospital. 'Oh No!' Patsy looked up at Eddie with fear showing in her eyes as the wail of the siren split through the air.

'It won't be much,' Eddie assured her. 'It never is when they come over this early.'

The black-out boards were in position at the windows, and patients who were able to walk were being escorted into the corridors when Patsy and Eddie reached the ward. They looked at each other and then at the three nurses who were straightening up, having wrapped blankets round the knees of their patients. None of them could help themselves; they all roared with laughter. From the ward, echoing right down the corridor, came the sound of Florrie's voice. Raised to full pitch, she was singing, 'Wish me luck as you wave me goodbye; Cheerio, here I go, on my way,' giving a very good impression of Gracie Fields.

'What are we going to do with her?' Patsy asked the young Sister in the neat navy-blue uniform and flowing white cap, who had come out of her office.

'Thank the Lord above, I should think,' she answered Patsy with a broad grin. 'Would that there were more like her. Your mother has stamina and a great sense of humour, and she is also a very brave lady.'

'Yes.' It was Eddie who agreed. 'She's one hell of a lady!'

Patsy looked up at him, he nodded, held out his hand to her and together they walked between the beds to visit Florrie of whom they were both so proud.

'Don't come 'ere weeping,' Florrie said to Patsy as she bent over to kiss her with eyes brimming with tears. 'And before you ask, I'm fine. It'll take more than a German doodlebug to finish *me* off.'

Patsy laughed and sighed at the same time. This was more like it, the Florrie that she knew and loved. A quiet Florrie with nothing to say for herself had had Patsy very worried.

After just two weeks Florrie was home, well and truly installed in Navy Street. Eddie had said that she would probably be happier if they turned the front room into a bed-sitting-room for her. After all, they only used the front room on high days and holidays. The room did look nice. The dark wood of the corner cabinets had been given an extra polish, all the Dresden ornaments had been carefully washed, and a double bed with brass head-rail had been placed against the wall facing the window so that Florrie could see the folk who went past. Not that Florrie lay in her bed all day – quite the reverse. With her leg still in plaster she got around fine with the aid of her crutches. She also used these crutches to emphasise a point if she didn't think enough attention was being given to her, much to the amusement of the whole household.

Patsy didn't have to wait for the month of August to arrive, for her worst fears became reality in July. One month before he was eighteen, and David was wearing a uniform! The Army still desperately needed men and no officer quibbled over four weeks in the birth date of a volunteer. 'How could you be so daft?' she wanted to ask him, but didn't dare.

Eddie wouldn't discuss it. It weighed on him heavily that his two sons were now fighting for their country, while he was no good to any branch of His Majesty's Forces. He shrugged and turned away whenever Patsy tried to bring up the subject.

After David had gone, and Patsy was seeing the girls off to school one morning, it struck her that both Ellen and Emma looked right down in the mouth. Until now she'd assumed that the pair of them were happy and proud for their brothers to have joined up. Now she realised that they were sad and that Ellen hadn't really got over being buried under all that rubble. Wish I knew what to do to cheer them up, she thought, but at least I have Florrie to talk it over with now.

Florrie was up and dressed, sitting in an armchair by the window, watching a Persian cat select a place on the garden wall that caught the warm rays of the sun before he stretched himself out full-length.

'Take 'em up the West End,' was her advice when she had heard Patsy's tale of woe. 'I know you won't be able to buy things, not unless you've still got some coupons – don't suppose there'll be much in the shops anyway – but you can take the girls somewhere nice for tea. It's not always what you have to eat that matters, you know, surroundings make a hell of a difference. Gawd knows those two kids ain't had much of a change lately, and besides it'll do you good as well. Tell you what, have tea in Park Lane! Yeah, that's it, The Dorchester, why don't you?'

Florrie went off into peals of laughter as she thought about her own suggestion. 'Tell you what,' she said again, wiping her eyes with the back of her hand. 'Go up to Oxford Circus on the 88 bus, then get yourself a taxi. Climb in as if you used taxis every day of yer life. "The Dorchester, please," is all you have to say. See the doorman come forward and open the cab door for you – the twins will be tickled pink. It'll be a lovely feeling, I can tell you that!'

'Florrie!' Patsy stopped laughing and stared at her in surprise. 'You've done this yourself – haven't you?'

Florrie's cheeks flushed up but she still laughed like a cat that had got at the cream. 'I ain't always been a fat old woman, you know. I was a young, slim girl myself once, though it takes a bloody good memory to know that. Can't complain, though. I did have me moments. Good job I did – Jack was killed on the Docks before we'd been married two years.'

Patsy's mouth opened wide. How sad; she'd never known this before.

'Now don't go all soppy on me,' Florrie said very abruptly. 'I've had a good life, at least he never lived to see me go to seed!' Again Florrie laughed but Patsy had the feeling that this time her heart wasn't in it.

Florrie's advice worked like a miracle. The Dorchester was so grand! No shortage of staff in splendid uniforms, even if they did all look about ninety years old, hovering to attend them.

They sat at a circular table, with a snowy-white damask cloth on which the loveliest of china was laid out.

'Don't seem like they know that there's a war on,' Emma said in a voice that was much too loud, as she stared at the plush furniture and the gigantic chandeliers. But before Patsy could reprimand her a young lady sitting at the next table with a naval officer leaned across, smiled gleefully at Emma and said, 'I agree, but isn't it all lovely!'

'Shall I call you a taxi, madam?' the doorman asked respectfully as Patsy and her daughters came down the hotel steps into the brilliant sunshine.

'No thank you,' she replied giving the elderly gentleman one of her sweetest smiles. 'We're going to take a walk in Hyde Park.'

'Very wise, on this lovely afternoon,' he said to Ellen and Emma, whose faces were still flushed with excitement.

'This is Rotten Row, used by the nobility for riding their horses,' Patsy told the girls, which set them giggling. 'Rotten Row,' they said in unison. 'Some way over there is the famous Serpentine, but I don't think we'd be allowed near it today. Probably surrounded by troops and anti-aircraft guns.' Patsy's voice sounded suddenly sad.

'Then we won't go,' declared Ellen. 'The war has been halted for us, just for today.'

Would that it was so, Patsy sighed to herself, then smiled quickly; nothing should be allowed to spoil this wonderful outing.

'If we turn here and go through those huge gates we'll be at Marble Arch,' she told them. 'And we can walk down Oxford Street, see Selfridges if you like.'

'Yes, please,' they chorused.

Neither of them was prepared for the mass of

people who were in Oxford Street nor yet for the number of foreign uniforms being worn by both men and women.

Patsy was walking between her two girls when suddenly she tugged at their arms, that were looped through her own. Her head nodded towards Lyons Corner House and she smiled a smile that was so different it set the twins wondering.

'Your father brought me to tea in there once,' she told them, still with a dreamy look in her eyes.

'When was that?' Emma demanded.

'A very long time ago,' Patsy murmured, more to herself. 'I wore a wool hat and scarf that your Aunt Queenie gave me for my birthday. Your father said I looked like a pixie.'

Wartime or not, Selfridges looked to Ellen and Emma like Aladdin's cave. Soft lights and sweet smells in the perfumery department had the girls drooling. A white-haired assistant, taken by the freshness of the pretty twin girls and their obvious excitement at being in the West End, generously sprayed them with a light flowery scent from a sample bottle.

'How much is this, please?' asked Ellen having held a whispered conversation with her sister. 'And do we need any coupons to buy it?'

The lady assistant took the box from Ellen: it held three tablets of Yardley's Old English Lavender Soap, each tablet individually wrapped in purple paper.

'Never mind about the coupons,' she whispered, smiling with them as a conspirator. 'It's three shillings and sixpence – have you enough money?'

'Oh, yes,' Ellen whispered quietly. 'And thank you very much.'

Not to be left out, Emma piped up, 'It's for our Auntie. Her house was hit by a doodlebug and she was hurt badly, but she's much better now and lives all the time with us. Her leg is still in plaster 'cause she broke it.'

The woman's eyes met Patsy's and they smiled knowingly at each other. What it was to be so young!

It was five o'clock when they joined the queue for the bus in a street at the back of Oxford Circus. It seemed suddenly different here, away from the big stores, and people looked weary. Jackets and raincoats were shabby, to say the least. How long, Patsy wondered before we'll all be able to have a new thick winter coat? Most in the queue were workers, on their way home. They had probably set out early this morning, and what were they going home to? Not a good roast dinner, that was for sure. This was wartime London as it really was – shabby and tired, but not beaten.

The bus came and they climbed the stairs, the twins flying along the gangway to reach the very front seat above the driver. It was funny the way things had turned out. Patsy felt so pleased that she'd had that talk with Florrie, and carried out her advice to the letter. The twins were different girls! Just listen to them! Seated behind them, she wondered if they were ever going to stop talking. This treat in the West End had done wonders for them.

'Auntie, look what we bought for you!' they were yelling before they'd hardly set foot inside the house.

'For me?' exclaimed Florrie in sheer delight, taking hold of the box with the picture on the lid of an old-fashioned lady holding a bunch of lavender. With one of her big arms around each of the girls, she looked over their heads and caught Patsy's eye. 'Worth it, was it?' she mouthed silently.

Patsy nodded, smiled and let her left eyelid drop in a cheeky wink. 'Clever old thing, aren't you?' she muttered to Florrie as she went past her to go and put the kettle on.

Chapter Twelve

IT WAS NOVEMBER before David had finished his training at Aldershot, and was granted just three days' leave. Winter was almost upon them, with the nights drawing in and the foggy, rotten air making it hard to breathe. Patsy was still doing her stints at the Canteen, but things were difficult. She often felt embarrassed at the poor quality food they now had to offer, and such little choice – especially when the men came in tensed up and dropping on their feet, having been on duty practically all night. She and the other women didn't ask questions any more, and the Wardens never volunteered information. She always made sure that she brewed them a good strong pot of tea the minute they walked in – it was the least she could do.

David's first night home was one of the happiest evenings she'd spent for a long, long time. The only person missing was Alex, and he was somewhere in France. Thank God they did get regular short notes from him and he always impressed on them how fit and well he was – but then, that was Alex. Ready to make the best of any situation. Never a moaner.

David had been drafted to the Royal Corps of Signals and now, with his training finished, he was being posted to Winchester. Somehow he seemed taller than ever and even more handsome, but I suppose every mother must think the same thing, she told herself. How much longer can this war go on? She climbed the stairs feeling utterly weary. She could still hear the voices of David, his father and grandad; it seemed only fair to leave them to talk men's talk, even though David was off again in the morning. His three days had flown by.

Patsy climbed into bed and pulled the clothes over her head. She wished she could drop off to sleep straight away, but she knew she wouldn't be able to. In the stuffy darkness of her bedroom she thought about 1939. What a wonderful summer it had been weather-wise. She remembered how she and Eddie had taken the kiddies on the Common for picnics and even down to the coast with Ted and Amy and their brood of children. Yes, children. That's what they'd all been when this awful war had started, and everyone had gone around saying it would all be over in six months. A bloody long six months!

Look at the kids now: Alex in France, God alone knows where David will end up, and young Vicky – look at her. On radar sites! Nobody had heard of radar before this lot . . . at least I hadn't, she muttered as she punched her pillow straight for the umpteenth time.

Amy wasn't feeling too bright these days, and who could blame her? Her eldest one, Laura, had joined the WAAFs the same as Vicky, and on her last leave had brought a Yank home with her. 'What if she marries him and goes off to live in America?' Amy had cried over it for days; didn't even listen when everyone told her it might never happen. George Andrews had finished up going in the Merchant Navy, one of the most dangerous jobs imaginable in wartime.

Thomas, born almost at the same time as Alex, but so different – what with his fair hair that automatically fell into a glorious mass of curls and waves when he was a youngster – had always been such a quiet boy. Not street-wise like her own two. Ted Andrews had told Eddie only last week that both he and Amy had dreaded the day Tom got his call-up papers. Can't believe it, can you? she asked herself time and time again. David had been just thirteen years old when all this started. Tomorrow morning she would have to put on a brave face, kiss her son goodbye and send him off to be what he was now trained to be: a soldier. It's not fair, she cried in anger, knowing there was nothing she and all the other mothers could do about it.

*

The pilotless planes, long known to all Londoners as doodlebugs, were still coming over practically all the time. These flying-bombs were so fast that anti-aircraft guns could seldom hit them, and their warheads were so powerful that any RAF planes attempting to shoot them down ran the risk of being blown up with them.

With Christmas approaching, the news did begin to improve. Since June when Allied troops had landed in Normandy and beach-heads had been established, there had been a build-up of troops, tanks and artillery accelerated. Daily now the papers reported that the German coastal defences had been breached and our troops were well into the Normandy countryside.

Of all the places to be, when the best news they'd had for ages came through they were in the Manor Arms pub. It was a Friday night, and reluctantly Patsy had agreed to come to a darts match with Eddie. The bar was packed as the clock on the wall showed it was almost nine o'clock and, as had become the habit, everything stopped for the BBC News. The wireless set which stood on the end of the counter in the saloon bar was switched on and everyone stopped talking. Disbelief was the first reaction. Then joy, laughter and a good many tears. Our troops had located and overrun the launching sites of the V1 flying-bombs. God was on our side after all!

★

'Why is it that there always seems to be a tragedy around Christmas time?' Florrie's reading glasses were perched lopsidedly on her nose as she peered over the top of the newspaper and spoke to Patsy.

The twins were off to their last day at school before the Christmas holidays, and Eddie had not yet come home from his night-shift. Patsy and Florrie had finished eating their breakfast but were lingering over a second cup of tea.

'What are you on about?' Patsy asked, only giving Florrie half her attention, for she was thinking of all the jobs she wanted to do that day and wondering where to start.

'That American dance bandleader, the one you and Eddie are always on about – the girls bought you one of his records for your birthday last year – well, he's missing presumed dead.'

'D'you mean Glenn Miller?' Patsy asked, surprise and shock both apparent in her voice.

'Course I do. I just told you, Glenn Miller.'

Patsy didn't argue but got up from her seat and went round to where Florrie was sitting. Leaning over her shoulder and reading from the paragraph that Florrie pointed to, Patsy learned that the band-leader had been on a flight to France when the plane he was travelling in just disappeared.

'How awful!' she exclaimed. 'That must be terrible

for his family, not knowing what really happened to him.'

'Might find out later,' Florrie said optimistically, 'Bodies have a way of turning up.'

'Don't be so morbid,' said Patsy, giving her a playful push. 'And for Christ's sake put that paper down and let's do some work, otherwise the day will be gone and we'll have got nothing done.'

There were pictures in the papers of girlfriends of German soldiers being chased through the village streets of France, barefooted and with their heads shaven. Surely that must mean that the Germans were no longer in control, Patsy thought as she studied the pictures of these women. The news from the Far East started to be much more favourable, and as 1945 dawned folk really did once again begin to hope that the end to this gruesome war was in sight.

May always was a lovely month. Now it was fantastic!

Germany surrenders unconditionally!

The whole country went mad with joy! Blackouts were ripped down and lights were switched on everywhere. There wasn't a street that didn't have a bonfire, people yelled, danced and sang. Cars and buses hooted their horns.

No more shift-work for Eddie. Alex and David

would be coming home, swaggering, cock-a-hoop – Patsy didn't give a damn, she'd hug them tightly and tell them how much she loved them.

Late that evening, the street was still packed with people who couldn't bring themselves to go to bed. Tilly Turner was still playing all the old songs on her upright piano that had been pushed out of her house on to the pavement, when Patsy crept away.

The door to Ada Nicholls' house was wide open and Patsy walked straight in and peered round the door to the front room. There was no light on, but the flare from the bonfire and the lamp-post outside enabled her to see that Ada sat in the bay with the window thrown up as far as it would go, and Jim, her husband, sat opposite her.

Ada rose to her feet immediately. 'Have a drink with us, Patsy,' she said, handing Patsy half a glass of light ale.

'We'll drink to peace, shall we?' Jim Nicholls said as he too stood up and clinked glasses with Patsy.

'Thanks for coming,' Ada whispered as she walked to the front door with Patsy. In silence the two of them put their arms round each other and held each other close for a while.

Back outside her own house where a row of chairs had been set in a line, Patsy sat down next to Eddie and reached for his hand. 'Just look at that lot,' he laughed. American soldiers had joined the throng and were leading a line of girls down the middle of the road, all doing the Conga. Ellen and Emma were in the middle of it all. Ollie poured another Guinness into Florrie's empty glass and told Patsy he'd got a bottle of champagne hidden away, and now was the best time for him to get it and open it up. Patsy was already half drunk, as much with relief and excitement as with alcohol, but she still had sufficient of her wits about her to be able to count her blessings: she still had all of her family.

Ada Nicholls' boy wouldn't be coming home. Neither would a good many other young men. And Stan Briggs would have to bring up his young sons without their mother.

In the Sunday afternoon quietness Patsy heard her front door open and close, then the voice of Amy calling, 'Where are you?'

'Out here in the garden,' called Patsy, and Amy came to sit in a deck-chair beside her. Patsy thought that Amy looked as if she hadn't slept a wink last night, and in all probability she was right.

'Your garden's looking great,' said Amy. 'Tom don't get much time to do ours, though he does try. We've had a fair amount of vegetables, thanks to him.'

'How is he?' Patsy asked sympathetically.

'Afraid to show his face, I think. Bloody fool! What

did he have to go and spoil our Laura's going-away party like that for?'

'Concern, I should think and Eddie agrees with me. After all, Amy, Laura is his only daughter and if we but knew the truth, he must be worried out of his mind with her going to live in America and all.'

'Hundreds of girls have married American soldiers,' said Amy, now on the defensive.

'Yes, of course they have,' Patsy agreed kindly, 'but Laura's going to have her baby soon and I expect Ted feels he's not only losing his daughter but his grand-child as well.'

'It's just as bad for me,' said Amy, brushing away tears from her eyes.

'I know, I know,' Patsy told her, leaning over and taking hold of Amy's hand.

'Was everyone disgusted with Ted's outburst?'

'No, they weren't,' Patsy told her firmly. 'Joe asked for it, spouting off in that loud way of his about how much better off your Laura was going to be living in Mount Tremper. Nobody had ever heard of the place, and Joe would insist that it was within easy reach of New York City. It was the way that he kept saying it: NEW YORK CITY!'

Amy smiled for the first time. 'Ted asked him if it was bloody Hollywood, didn't he?'

'Yes, he did.' Patsy smiled back at her friend, think-ing to herself that unfortunately some of these new

American wives would find out too late that their new homes were not in the least like the Hollywood-style houses they had been led to believe they would be.

'There's talk of cheap fares being sorted out so that parents can go over to America and visit their daughters,' Patsy said, doing her best to comfort Amy.

'Won't be much good me and Ted applying to go. We couldn't even ask directions as to where Joe lives – neither of us can pronounce his bloody surname.'

'Oh, blimey, if that don't beat all!' said Patsy. 'Can't go to America 'cause you can't pronounce your daughter's married name!' When they'd both had a good laugh, Patsy added. 'Well, Laura will just have to come home every so often, won't she?'

'Christ, I hope so,' said Amy.

Let that be the truth, Patsy silently prayed, thanking her lucky stars that it wasn't one of her daughters who was going off to live in America.

The ending of the conflict hadn't solved all the problems; in fact, some families now faced a whole lot more. This war had robbed youngsters of the best years of their lives, and now most of them were rebellious; they had a lot of living to do and were hell-bent on wasting no more time. Ellen and Emma were no exception! Suddenly they were staying out late and not giving straight answers to enquiries as to where they had been.

Eddie had said the girls should be working and Patsy had thought about that. In a way he was right, their minds had to be occupied, yet in another way it would be hard for her to see them go out into the big world. She couldn't bear to think of them travelling up to the City every day, especially in the rush hour. They had both done very well in their commercial courses – shorthand, typing and bookkeeping. Maybe they would settle down if they get jobs in an insurance office or even a bank, meet some nice well-educated young men, mix with a different crowd. Certainly she wanted to put a stop to them seeing those two brothers whose father had a dress shop in Clapham High Street. 'Flashy gits!' is what Florrie called them.

Eddie had made a few cautious attempts to warn the twins about the bad reputation these boys had gained for themselves. 'Hardly out of short trousers, they seem to think they're God's greatest gift to young women.' He had spoken quietly, taking care not to lose his temper.

'Dad, how did you get to know about the tales going around about the Woodley brothers?' Emma was quick to ask. 'Not that there's any truth in them,' she added just as quickly.

'Well, just you be warned. You're only a couple of kids still,' Patsy had said, pouring oil on troubled waters before they became too stormy.

'Anyway, we weren't seriously interested, were we, Emma?' Ellen looked to her sister for her agreement.

'Course we weren't. Mean to play the field now all these young men are getting demobbed,' Emma was grinning. 'So don't you go losing any sleep over us, will you, Mum?'

All that was easy to say, but what mother wouldn't worry over two seventeen-year-old girls as beautiful as her two?

For the past six years they had been prevented from leading a normal life because of the blackout and the air-raids. There were still shortages, and rationing would probably continue for a very long time, but London was free and the bright lights beckoned. Yet Patsy couldn't help wondering if either Ellen or Emma realised just how attractive they really were. Get themselves set up with the wrong man and their whole life would end up in a mess!

Patsy turned her attention back to Amy, who had fallen asleep.

Do her the world of good. Patsy's heart ached for her – to have to stand at Southampton and watch your only daughter go aboard a liner that would take her to America, to become part of someone else's family. Knowing it would be a long time before you'd get to see her . . . and what about when the baby was born?

What then? It didn't bear thinking about.

Chapter Thirteen

EDDIE OWEN FELT that he was one of the lucky ones. With the ending of the war Ollie had wasted no time in getting The Ace Trading Company up and running again. Thanks to Ollie's generosity both he and Patsy were directors, and the future looked all set to be worthwhile. Things had moved swiftly over the past four years for all members of his family. Whether all the decisions that had been made would prove to be the right ones, only time would tell.

Then again, it was the same the world over. India had gained independence and had been paying the price ever since. The Muslims had refused to join with the Hindus, demanding their own state of Pakistan. The newspapers were full of reports of riots in Calcutta. In February 1947 Lord Louis Mountbatten had been appointed the last Viceroy of India, but although the Mountbattens had excellent relations with the leaders of both parties and Lord Louis made earnest pleas for differences to be settled peacefully, horror stories were still being reported.

Neither was post-war Britain exactly what the men of the Forces had hoped it would be on their return

home from the fighting. There was still a great deal
of unemployment.

Ollie had wanted to bring both Alex and David
into the company, but neither of them had been
enthusiastic. However, their grandad had insisted on
giving each of them enough capital to set them up
in business. Wholesale fruit and vegetable importers,
they called themselves. Eddie smiled at the thought.
Patsy and he were in agreement that their boys hadn't
changed. Ducking and diving, thriving on deals – this
is what they did best, and God above knew there
were enough quick profit transactions flying about
since the war ended. Not least of which was Govern-
ment-surplus merchandise. A lot of money was being
made through stock such as this, and who could
blame the boys if they were going after a share?

Ellen and Emma had sprung a surprise on everyone
– they had both gone into nursing. When they were
accepted at Hammersmith Hospital, one of London's
great teaching hospitals, neither Patsy nor Eddie had
been sure that the twins would stick at the arduous
three-year training course. They had, both had passed
their exams and were now State Registered Nurses
still hoping to get further qualifications in specialised
subjects.

Many of the problems the company had to face
after the war were much the same as those they'd
experienced in 1937. Business didn't just come to

them for the asking. Coaches were the main problem; there were no new ones to be had. Leyland had promised that as soon as their production lines were rolling Ollie would be regarded as a valued customer. Meanwhile, he had purchased three single-decker buses and two coaches which he'd had renovated up to standard.

The yard at Vauxhall was back to being busy again, with two of the original men and two new employees. Garratt Lane premises had been another story, though. Anti-aircraft guns had been sited on Garratt Green and the Ace premises had been used to house troops. It was more than two years before Ollie was able to reclaim the property for his own business purposes. Now, Garratt Lane once more had a coaching station that was the pride of all who were associated with the Ace Trading Company.

When finally in the September of 1945, after two atomic bombs had been dropped on Japan, the Allied Forces had accepted the surrender of the Japanese and the war really was over, Eddie had felt that Patsy should take life more easily. But Patsy had thought otherwise. All the children were grown up and she had no intention of sitting at home twiddling her thumbs.

As time passed, Eddie knew she had made the right decision. With the war damage put right and the whole of the offices at Stockwell newly decorated and furnished, Patsy was in her element. She thrived on business problems, in Ollie's opinion. Another factor which served to brighten her days was that Vicky was back working with them.

Vicky had not been demobbed from the WAAF until 1947. She had eagerly agreed not only to have her job back but to take on the tenancy of the flat above the main office. This had been Florrie's idea, for at twenty-eight years of age Vicky was no longer a child. 'Give her a bit of freedom, for Christ's sake,' Florrie had yelled in answer to Patsy's suggestion that Vicky be invited to make her home with them.

All the family had tried to pressurise Vicky into finding a nice young man and getting herself married. Patsy had confided to Eddie that in her opinion Vicky was in love with Alex.

'Your intuition is right nine times out of ten,' he had told her. 'But this time you're way out. Vicky's five years older than our Alex!'

'Maybe she is,' Patsy said with a knowing smile, 'but what you've got to remember is that Alex was old when he was born. At fourteen, did Alex have a paper-round? Yes, he did. For how long? Not long. He got himself a pitch and then another and another, and before you knew it he had leased them all out. Grown men were working for our Alex – and happy to be doing so.'

Eddie admitted to himself that what Patsy said was

true. And come to think of it, Alex could do a lot worse. Vicky still sparkled, was a good-looking, attractive young lady with a sound head on her shoulders. But Alex didn't seem to be the slightest bit serious about her, though he did take her to the theatre now and again and Vicky was at their house almost every week-end. Perhaps Patsy is right, he thought. Time would tell.

Coming into the room, Patsy broke into Eddie's wandering thoughts. 'You're a bit late getting ready,' she said without much sense of disapproval.

'I know. I had my bath and I've just been sitting here dreaming. I'm going up now to get dressed.'

'Well, don't take too long, the taxi will be here in about forty minutes.'

Patsy looked at herself in the mirror to make sure she had not put on too much eye-shadow, and that her upswept hair-style really did look all right. Her long black velvet skirt felt great, and the white blouse with the silver sequin motif had been a good choice. Silver high-heeled sandals on her feet finished off the outfit well.

'You'll do!' Florrie had come into the kitchen and was inspecting her. 'What about me?' she asked, turning round slowly so that Patsy could get a good look at her.

'Fishing for compliments, are we?'

Florrie laughed. 'Well, it ain't often I get dressed

up these days. Come to that, it ain't every day my two great-nieces have a birthday and get themselves engaged. We having any entertainment after the meal?'

'You're an entertainment in yourself, Florrie.'

Florrie patted Patsy's shoulder and laughed again. 'You never know, I might hit it off with one of them nice doctors that'll probably be there.'

Looking at Florrie, Patsy wondered how she did it. She looked marvellous; her hair, though white and thinning now, had been washed and set into deep waves. She was wearing a navy-blue two-piece silk suit – the skirt of which almost reached her ankles, covering up her swollen legs – and for once she had a decent pair of soft leather shoes on her feet. I wouldn't put it past her to take them off half-way through dinner, Patsy said to herself. Florrie was incredible. She had only recently come out of hospital, having suffered an attack of bronchial pneumonia which at her age, seventy-one, was no joke. After two weeks of enforced rest in St James's she had had the whole place doing her bidding. Ollie and Eddie had gone together to speak with the doctor, offering to pay for any specialist who might have been able to help Florrie. 'Her will to live is what will pull her through,' he had told them, smiling broadly at the same time.

'Stop fussing,' Florrie cried now as Patsy tried to wrap a scarf around her neck.

'Wow! Two beauties for me to escort,' Eddie declared as he stood in the doorway giving them both a look of sheer admiration.

'You don't look so bad yourself,' Patsy said almost shyly. Eddie in his evening suit was something to behold.

'No, you'll do.' Florrie muttered. 'Probably be the biggest penguin there.'

'I've a good mind to make you walk for that remark,' Eddie chided her. 'I'll have you know these black suits and white stiff-fronted shirts are very expensive.'

'Yeah, well, let's hope you weren't robbed. And while we're on about walking – just remember, the pair of you, I'm quite recovered and I don't want you hovering around me all night. Enjoy yourselves, 'cos that's what I intend to do.'

'You'll be fine, Florrie,' Eddie told her, cheekily adding, 'Only the good die young.'

He was saved from a box round the ears by the sound of the taxi tooting its horn outside the house. Kitty was half-way down the stairs and Eddie and Patsy both stared at her in admiration.

'Another glamorous lady,' said Eddie, offering one arm to Florrie and the other to Kitty.

Patsy walked behind them proudly as they went out to the taxi.

The 'do' for the twins was to celebrate their twentieth birthdays, and also the fact that they were both using the occasion to announce their engagements. The catering facilities at Wandsworth Town Hall had been recommended to Eddie and he wasn't disappointed. The meal had been excellent.

The ballroom was nicely set out. Small tables around the wall all had a small floral arrangement and there were plenty of comfortable chairs for the older folk. The band on stage was grouped around an enormous set of drums. In front of the band a young blonde in a silver lamé dress was crooning a love song with her eyes closed and her hands clasped tightly together.

'Everything all right?' Eddie asked as he came up to where Patsy and Amy were sitting and handed them both a gin and orange. 'We can always scoot off early, once the speeches and announcements have been made, if you get fed up.'

'No, I'm finding it fascinating.' She pointed over to a group of young men and women standing with Ellen and Emma in the centre. Her eyes shone with pride; her girls looked marvellous.

'Have you seen the boys, and have you taken Florrie and Kitty a drink?'

'Ollie is seeing to both Florrie and Kitty, David is in the bar with Ted — but no, I haven't seen Alex, not since we left the dining-room.'

'I saw him going out on to the terrace with Vicky,' offered Amy. 'Did you want him?'

'No, I just wondered,' said Patsy, unable to conceal her delight.

The dance-floor soon became crowded and Patsy squinted, trying to pick out Ellen and Emma in the sea of made-up faces, freshly-set hair and glamorous dresses. Most of the young people here were friends who worked with the twins at Hammersmith Hospital; they seemed a very nice, well-spoken and well-mannered bunch.

Through a gap in the moving couples, Patsy saw Ellen and Emma gliding by, each held close in the arms of the young man they had declared they meant to marry. She swallowed hard. The girls had brought their young men home on several occasions, and they were as different as chalk from cheese.

Donald Langford, Emma's intended, was a nice, ordinary man: quite tall, with light brown hair and a complexion that showed he mainly worked out in the open air. He had been working on the hospital's rebuilding programme as a bricklayer when Emma had first met him. Invited to Sunday tea, everyone had scrutinised him and declared him to be 'a good bloke'. His folk were very friendly; Patsy had sat beside Mrs Langford during dinner and they had got on well. Mr Langford's health was not too good, he had a heart problem and so they had left once the meal was over, but not before they had kissed Emma and Patsy and said how nice it was that they were getting a daughter. Donald was their only child.

Patsy was at a loss to describe exactly how she felt about Robert Dellor. 'Suave' was a word that came to mind. About six years older then Ellen he was a junior doctor, well-educated, about five foot ten, slim, with dark sleeked-back hair and a pencil-thin moustache on his upper lip. Ellen seemed to be head over heels in love with him, but in a childish and obvious way. She was the one who worried Patsy the most. Kind and gentle herself, she saw no wrong in anyone.

'Oh, Patsy, he's so nice, he's a charming young man,' Kitty had said.

'You just fell for his flattery.' Florrie had made the accusation loud and clear. 'He fancies his luck a bit too much for my liking. He'd suit Emma more than Ellen – she'd see through him in no time. Our Ellen's too trusting for a cocky bloke like Robert Dellor.'

'And what do you really think of him?' Patsy had asked Eddie. 'Do you like him?'

'I don't know. Honestly and truthfully, I don't know. I certainly didn't take to him straight off, the way I did with Donald.' That had been Eddie's cagey way of dodging a direct answer.

Alex said it was none of his business, the girls were old enough to make up their own minds, and that his mother should stop acting as if she were a broody old hen afraid of losing her chicks.

David had declared that Donald was all right. Robert Dellor! Well, there was something about him, wasn't there? But he wouldn't be drawn further than that.

Eddie now came back and sat down next to Patsy, and Amy went off to find Ted.

'Do you really believe Robert's parents live in Geneva?' she asked, voicing her fears aloud. 'They could have sent a telegram, or written a letter to Ellen.'

'You're not still worrying yourself sick over Robert and Ellen, are you?' Eddie stared at her with a grin that spread from ear to ear. 'The twins have promised they'll not think about getting married until they're twenty-one, and that's a year away. A lot can happen in a year. Engagements have been broken before now, you know.'

Patsy raised a bleak face. 'Well, they're still so young.'

'Rubbish!' he said, pulling her to her feet. 'Come and dance with me, or are we too old?'

They were both laughing as they took to the floor and began to move to the rhythm of a slow fox-trot.

Chapter Fourteen

PATSY THOUGHT HOW right Eddie had been when he said that a lot could happen in a year. They weren't half-way into this new year of 1950, and life was hectic at times. Business was booming; with the coming of the fifties the holiday trade had taken off and Ollie now had eight coaches in operation – four of them brand new. This coming week-end was the Whitsun Bank Holiday and their order book was full. Not only did the Ace Trading Company do day trips to the coast and places of interest around the country, they were now committed to the holiday trade. It had been Eddie's suggestion that they should set up this package deal, and his proposal had been met with much enthusiasm – no sooner the thought than the deed. Ollie had gone to Ramsgate, having already dispatched Eddie and Patsy to Margate. The idea had been to find one or two hotels which would be interested in catering for parties of forty people for a week at a time. Hotels had to be able to offer full board and approximately 24–30 bedrooms. Ace would do the bookings in London and provide transport to the hotel, returning to pick up the party the following week-end for the return journey. Local coach firms would be only too glad to lay on outings to popular places of interest if folk felt they would like extra days out.

By the end of February two deals had been negotiated. The owners of the Esplanade Hotel at Cliftonville and the Gloucester Hotel at Ramsgate had become willing participants in the scheme. Advertisements in the local paper had been all that were needed and bookings flooded in. The fact that the holidays were to favourite seaside places and that the travelling would be almost door-to-door made the idea very popular with old and young alike. Starting this coming Saturday, they had two such holidays booked for every consecutive week until 3rd September.

On Whit Saturday afternoon, Patsy breathed a sigh of relief as she filled the kettle and put it on the gas to boil. Vicky had successfully seen off the six coaches that were going on day trips, while she and Eddie had taken on the task of seeing that their first venture into the weekly holiday trade got off to a good start. Patsy had stayed on the coach that was bound for Cliftonville until every pick-up-point had been covered and all the passengers were safely aboard. Eddie had done the same with the coach bound for Ramsgate.

Sundays were always precious days and tomorrow was going to be marvellous. Everyone would be home, the house would come alive, the boys would probably be boisterous but their laughter would be good to hear. With Monday being a Bank Holiday, they'd got an extra day.

Patsy looked out down the garden where Eddie was digging up vegetables for tomorrow's dinner. He'd only got home late last night, having been down to check last-minute details at both hotels. She was so glad he was back; he'd only been away three days, but she missed him terribly. There was too much room in their double bed without Eddie to cuddle up to.

'Potatoes, carrots, leeks and spring greens,' Eddie told her as he came into the kitchen and sat down at the table.

'That'll be fine. Amy got me two cauliflowers up at the market this morning. Want a cup of tea?' she asked.

'Yes, please,' he said, and she poured him one from the teapot on the table. 'All the kids coming home tomorrow?' he idly asked.

Patsy grinned. 'Not exactly kids any more, are they? Yes, they'll all be here. Ellen and Emma are staying till Tuesday – make a change for them to get away from the hospital and nurses' quarters. Alex and Vicky will be here by lunch-time and David, Valerie and young Timmy will arrive early in the morning.'

'Get the girls married at the end of the year and

we'll be a proper old Darby and Joan, won't we?'
Patsy didn't answer and Eddie didn't press her.

Ellen and Emma, she rolled their names around in
her mind lovingly. She was lucky to have been blessed
with two such daughters; they were beautiful, warm
and loving. Never a day's worry had they caused her.
Oh, there'd been the usual high spirits when they
were in their teens, but she was very proud of them
both now. She didn't really want them married and
off her hands, not if she was truthful, but she supposed every mother in the world must feel the same
when the last of her children leaves the nest.

The boys were both settled. No fuss, no arguments.
Just a clear-cut statement from Alex last Easter: we're
getting married, Wandsworth Register Office at
twelve noon. Hope you'll come, don't want no fuss.
Alex had married Vicky just as Patsy had predicted
he would. They lived in the flat above the offices at
Stockwell and were as happy as a pair of larks.

Both Eddie and Patsy had been a little apprehensive
over David's choice, but only in the beginning. Now
they thanked God that he too was happy and settled
with a really nice girl, and had a six-year-old son
named Timmy who called Patsy and Eddie Grandma
and Grandad and whom they both adored. Valerie
Simmons was a war widow with a four-year-old little
boy when David first brought her home to Sunday

tea, and Patsy had been doubtful as to whether her son's choice was a wise one. She had no doubts now.

Patsy wondered if there were many families who had managed to come through the war as lucky as she and her brood. Apart from Florrie and Ellen having been almost buried alive when the blast from a doodlebug had struck Strathmore Street, it was Alex who had fared the worse. The silence between herself and Eddie as they drank their tea was companionable and totally unstrained, yet she shuddered as her mind went back to the day when she had picked up that dreaded postcard from the front-door mat. All it said was that Alex had been wounded and was in an RAMC Field Hospital.

Desperate for news, she knew she had been hell to live with until the letter had arrived from Alex himself. He was alive! Alone in her bedroom she had sunk to her knees and not only thanked the Lord but praised his Holy Name. Things had been moving swiftly in Normandy at the time and being with the Royal Army Service Corps much of Alex's duties consisted of ferrying truck-loads of supplies to the forward units. On one such assignment his lorry had struck a mine. Joe Davis, the young lad from Liverpool whom Alex had brought home on a brief visit, had been killed instantly. Was it a guardian angel that protected Alex or did he just have the luck of the Devil?

Alex hadn't told them the details until after he was demobbed; only then had he admitted that he had been thrown clear but that he had screamed his head off when a swordlike piece of shrapnel had smashed into his right thigh. He had done his best to staunch the blood from this ghastly wound in his leg, then he had fainted. He was found by a medical orderly crawling around looking for the wounded amongst the dead and within a month he had rejoined his unit.

David had had one of the most dangerous jobs. Thankfully Patsy had never been made aware of the fact that his platoon of the Royal Corps of Signals was responsible for laying communication lines from Battalion Headquarters to companies up in the front-line areas. Once their boys were both home and safe Eddie had disclosed to her that he had spent more sleepless nights worrying over David than he would have admitted at the time.

Oh yes! She had many blessings to count and to be thankful for.

Stan Briggs had been left with two young sons to bring up without their mother, and a damn fine job he was doing. Many a mother had lost an only son like Ada Nicholls, but there had been divine intervention there, for he had left behind him a son yet to be born and a young mother who had become a real part of the Nicholls family. Sometimes Patsy felt her heart ached when she thought about Joe Davis's mother in Liverpool. Was Joe her only son? She had never met Mrs Davis but she had written to her, though the words had been hard to form. Joe's death could so easily have been that of her own son.

'Penny for them,' Eddie smiled at her. 'You were miles away, weren't you?'

'Yes, I suppose I was,' Patsy agreed immediately. 'But I'd better shake myself, hadn't I? There's plenty to be done before they all descend on us tomorrow.'

'Get away with you,' he said, sensing her secret excitement. 'There'd be hell to pay if you thought even one of them was going to desert you.'

Sunday was a lovely spring day, with blue skies and warm sunshine. The garden was alive with activity and sounds of laughter were coming from everywhere. The men were wearing sports jackets and flannels while the girls had put on pretty, light-coloured dresses. A ball was being kicked from one end of the grass to the other while Timmy did his best to halt its progress as they played piggy-in-the-middle. 'Men!' Patsy called out. 'You're a bigger load of kids than the boy is. I've brought you a brown ale each, and there's a ginger-beer for Timmy.'

Ollie and Eddie broke away and came towards her.

'Getting too old for these larks,' laughed Ollie as he took the tray from Patsy.

'Great to have them all here,' Eddie said, nodding his head in the direction of the game still being played with high shrieks of merriment coming from young Timmy.

Patsy leaned against the shed and watched her two sons and the two young men who were to become her sons-in-law before the year was out. Robert Dellor felt Patsy's eyes on him and looked across to where she stood. He flashed her a smile of such charm that she felt a stab of annoyance. Why did she always get this feeling that Robert was not all that he would have them believe he was? And another thing, why did she feel that she had to tread so carefully when he was around? Ask him questions, especially about his family, and all you got was excuses, no explanations. This irritated Patsy. But like it or not, this rather dazzling young man was Ellen's choice. Eddie was right, she would have to learn to live with that fact, or there was a danger that she might end up losing her daughter. That was something she couldn't bear even to think about, so she'd learn to keep her mouth shut, put a smile on her face and give a damn good impression that she approved of Robert Dellor as a husband for Ellen.

Laughing aloud at her resolution, she turned and

went down the garden, opened the kitchen door and almost knocked Florrie flying.

'For Christ's sake, Patsy, you're talking to yourself and you almost scalded the pair of us,' said Florrie, setting down the heavy saucepan on the wooden draining-board.

'Sorry, my love,' Patsy told her, turning the handle of the saucepan of boiling potatoes inwards so that it wouldn't get knocked. 'I was only laughing at myself about something I'd decided I must do in the future.'

'Never mind about the bloody future, this dinner is all ready to dish up. The girls have laid the tables in the front room. Who's going to carve the meat?'

In the weeks that followed there wasn't time for any of them to think about wedding plans. Not everything ran smoothly. The summer had turned out to be a very hot one, and there were days when tempers flared and no one seemed satisfied. This Saturday morning was proving to be a stinker.

Alan Thompson, one of their new drivers, had turned up twenty-five minutes late at Vauxhall. 'That's all right, we'll make up time when I get out on the road,' he had said, jeering at Patsy when she complained that folk waiting at pick-up-points would not be too pleased.

'Why does everything go wrong on a Saturday?'

Patsy murmured half to herself as she gratefully sipped her coffee. Vicky sat on the opposite side of the desk, the windows to the office were open wide but there was scarcely any breeze.

'Probably 'cause no one really wants to work; they'd all like to have the week-ends off,' Vicky said, breaking a shortbread biscuit in two and dunking one half into her cup of coffee. 'Must say, though, I agree with Ollie that when it comes to reliability we can't beat our old drivers.'

Patsy was stopped from making her own comment by the ringing of the phone. She listened quietly for several moments before she said, 'Tell me exactly where you are.' She made notes on to the pad which lay in front of her. 'Now, Bert, give me the telephone number of the call-box you're in, can you see it?' While she waited Patsy raised her eyebrows at Vicky and scowled. 'All right, Bert, we'll sort something out and one of us will phone you as soon as we can to let you know what's happening. Do your best to keep the passengers happy.'

'Coach broken down?' Vicky asked.

'Yes,' Patsy sighed. 'The other side of Canterbury.'

'Well, at least they got clear of London. Here's good luck to us,' Vicky said, draining her cup. 'I'll use the phone in the back office and we'll see who can get hold of Ollie first.'

That put an end to any plans that they had made

for themselves for this week-end. All their own coaches were out on the road and hiring one proved an impossibility. 'As you said, Vicky, no firm's got coaches standing idle in this weather,' said Patsy as she replaced the phone after making her sixth call. There was no hanging about once Ollie was made aware of the situation, though. Eddie's own car was in for a service and it fell to Alex to help them. He knew the route well, and the miles disappeared under the wheels of his van as he drove his father to Canterbury. The police had already called out a mechanic from a nearby garage; the trouble was the fuel line which had sprung a leak, and while it was not a major job to replace it the garage didn't have one to fit in stock.

'Will be Monday now before we'll be able to locate one,' the mechanic said ruefully.

The owner of the garage appeared on the scene and Eddie thanked his lucky stars as he heard this helpful man say he'd got hold of a local coach that was willing to take the passengers on to Ramsgate. Within half an hour everyone had been transferred, and a great cheer rent the air as the new driver let out the clutch and the coach moved off. Bert went with them, he would stay at the hotel until Monday when hopefully he would be able to pick up his coach again.

Eddie was shaking hands with Tony Parsons, the garage owner. 'I can't thank you enough,' he said.

'It never rains but what it pours, it happens to the best of us.'

'Yes, well, we'd have been well and truly up the creek if it hadn't been for you.'

In the middle of all this Eddie heard Alex say, 'I'll have a word with my father – my stomach thinks my throat's been cut.' He turned to his father. 'Dad, Fred here says he knows a great pub where we can get a decent meal and I said we'd all go. Least we can do is treat these blokes, ain't it?'

It certainly was a decent dinner that The Rose and Crown served up for the four of them. At closing time they shook hands and wished each other all the best, and Alex was laughing like a schoolboy as he climbed into his van.

'What's tickled you?' his father asked.

'Just thinking, it's an ill wind that blows nobody any good. I've just set up a great deal with that Fred. If I pull this one off, David and me will be set up for weeks to come.'

Eddie leaned back in the passenger seat, tilted his trilby to shade his eyes and decided it would be best if he didn't ask any more questions.

'Now don't start making out you're not interested,' said Alex. 'It's a damned good deal. I've told you time and time again, it's bartering that counts when you're ducking and diving for a living.'

'All right, don't show off,' his father said, then waited for Alex to tell him the details.

'That Fred's brother is a fruit farmer, I've just set up a deal with Fred for all the White Hearts that'll soon be ready for picking. Got in there just right — beat the big boys from the canning factories for once.'

'White Hearts?' queried Eddie.

'Naps . . . cherries, and the same will stand for the Bramleys come September; catch 'em before the hop-pickers wreck the orchards.'

'And what have you promised him? The Crown Jewels from the Tower?'

'Not quite,' Alex said, changing gears and slowing down to let a tractor turn into a farm gate. 'There's a bloke up at Vauxhall, foreman at one of the tyre depots, been a valuable contact to me for a long time and helped Ollie out more than once in the past. I happen to know that his firm are overstocked at the moment with Goodyear heavy-duty tyres. Just right for lorries and suchlike. Fred brought up the subject of tyres, mentioned the fact that they sometimes had difficulty in locating them, I had a word with Tony Parsons and we shook hands on it. Be a good profit all round on it, Dad. Well, a fair one,' he added cautiously.

'All above board, will it be?' asked Eddie.

'Seriously, yes,' Alex answered, keeping a straight face for once. 'You ought to know by now, Dad, I've

got more sense than to get myself involved in anything illegal. A middle-man's cut, a favour for a
favour, that'll do me – no messing, honest.'

'I'm glad to hear it, son,' said Eddie. 'Your mother
worries herself sick about what you and David get
up to – you know that, don't you?'

'Well, you know Mum, Dad, better than any of
us. Likes to make out she's a holy terror, but if she
didn't have us to worry about she'd be bound to find
something else.'

They were leaving the countryside behind, meeting
a lot more traffic. Eddie decided to let the matter
rest, and once again he settled himself back in the
passenger seat and closed his eyes.

A broad grin came to Alex's face as he glanced at
his father. Good job he wasn't always around when
he and David set up a deal!

The summer months sped by and the coming event
of the double wedding was now uppermost in the
mind of every member of the family. The only topic
of conversation seemed to be what was everyone
going to wear? With the twins' wedding day only six
weeks away Patsy was beginning to wish it was all
over. Eddie was nervous and even Ollie, who was
giving Emma away, seemed uneasy; it was to be a big
day for him too.

'Are you happy about all of this?' Patsy had asked one evening when she and Eddie were alone.

Eddie smiled. 'I keep telling you, the girls have got good heads on their shoulders and they haven't rushed into this. I think the pair of them will be all right. Couple of good blokes – they'll be able to look after our girls.'

The question of the brides' dresses had been settled months ago, when night after night had been spent looking at pattern books and samples of materials. In the end Ellen and Emma had chosen different styles to be made up in the same white silk with heavy lace trimmings.

Florrie had been a problem. 'You're not dressing me up like some floosie,' she had insisted. In the end she'd settled for a cream-coloured two-piece with a pale blue hat and gloves. But shoes for her! They still had to be bought.

'She'll probably come to the church wearing slippers, if we don't watch her,' Patsy had said irritably to the girls, having spent a whole afternoon going in and out of every shoe shop in Clapham.

Patsy was pleased with the outfit that Amy had helped her to choose for herself. Together they had gone to Oxford Street on the bus and spent the whole day trying on dozens of dresses and suits. Amy had bought a navy-blue suit and a very expensive silk blouse. Patsy had told her that she looked very attractive, but she must make sure that she bought shoes and a handbag that went with it. Her own choice had been a silver-grey coat and dress that matched and were edged with a trimming of dusty-pink embroidery. They'd laughed themselves silly as they tried on hats. The young lady assistant had entered into the spirit of things and had produced from a room at the back of the shop a saucy little number, all feathers and veil, which was the exact shade of pink to match Patsy's ensemble.

'You don't think it looks cheap and flashy?' Patsy whispered to Amy, as she held a hand-mirror to her face so that she could see the back view in the large wall mirror.

'Cheap!' Amy hissed. Then in a conspiratorial whisper she said, 'look at the price tag!'

The actual day had arrived. Patsy slid into the front-row pew on the right hand side of the church, pulled the hassock into position and sank gratefully down on to her knees with her hands over her face. 'Please God take care of them both,' she prayed. 'May they both have long and happy lives with the young men they've chosen to be their husbands. Help those lads to care as much for Ellen and Emma as Eddie has for me.'

The soft notes of the organ changed, bursting into the Wedding March, there was a lot of rustling as everyone stood up.

Patsy thought her heart would burst with pride and she was unable to hold back the tears which filled her eyes.

Eddie was staring straight ahead with a smile on his lips that said it all. Ellen, his eldest daughter by only a few minutes, had her hand tucked into the crook of his elbow. A few paces behind them came Ollie, proud as punch and beaming as he led Emma down the aisle. All eyes were on the twins. Had there ever been two lovelier brides? The full skirts of their dresses seemed to billow out as if they were crinolines. Ellen's dress relied on the lace to form an exquisite panel down the front and this pattern was repeated down the centre of the long sleeves. Emma's billowing skirt and the neckline of her dress were encrusted with tiny pearls. Their hair glowed; the whiteness of the chiffon veils served only to make the glints stand out all the more – a shimmer of rich chestnut in the middle of all that white.

The walk up the church was taking ages, Patsy thought, and then they were at the altar. Eddie handed Ellen to Robert, so handsome in his dark suit and white shirt and with the carnation in his buttonhole. He was looking down at Ellen and smiling with pride, but Patsy couldn't help herself; she still felt a tightness in her chest when she looked at him. Ollie had left Emma beside Donald and they all moved a little way up the pew to make room for him and Eddie when the time came for them to sit down.

Donald had reached for Emma's hand and his eyes danced with joy. They were so funny, these two. Donald had such an easygoing, nice temperament, asking nothing more of life than that which came easily.

Patsy looked across the aisle and smiled as she saw Lucy and Fred Langford. They looked eager and intense, all their concentration on their only son and Emma who was about to become his wife. They were nice people. Plenty of friends of Robert were attending the wedding, but no mention of any near relatives had been made.

Eddie took his seat next to Patsy and held her hand between both of his. They eyes met, they smiled at each other and settled down to concentrate on the ceremony.

'How many more?' Patsy sighed as she smiled yet again and shook hands with young folk whom she'd never set eyes on before today.

'It's all going very well, Mum,' Emma said. 'Aren't you pleased with it all?'

'I just wish we could sit down and get on with the meal, my feet are killing me.'

Now there were some of their older neighbours waiting to shake hands.

'Hallo, Ada, how nice you look!' Ada Nicholls was a different woman these days. Soon after the war had come to an end Barbara Wilson had turned up on the doorstep of the Nicholls house. She had with her a little boy, Clifford, who'd been born on 24th November 1941, six months to the day after HMS *Hood* was sunk. 'Your son was his father, we were going to be married on Tom's next leave.' The young, fair-haired girl with piercing blue eyes had said quietly to Ada. Ada hadn't needed to read the letters that Barbara had cherished for so long, one look at five-year-old Clifford and she had burst into tears. Now a great friendship existed, and Ada's grandson, all of nine years old, was a regular visitor in Navy Street.

Where everyone was going to sit had given Patsy nightmares. She had checked and double-checked that Gran and Grandad Day were seated at the top table, as was Florrie. They were all the family she had ever known, and with Ollie they were all the family that she had never needed.

'God knows who's running the stalls in Tooting Market this Saturday,' Patsy whispered to Eddie over the buzz of conversation as folk filed into the dining-room.

'Lovely to see so many old friends, isn't it? Bit different from when we got married, eh?'

'A lot of the same old faces, though. Good friends, the lot of them.'

'Come on, Mum, we've shepherded most of the crowd towards the eats.' Alex and David stood before her, both looking so well turned-out in their new suits, their faces shining and eager, and Patsy smiled happily at each of them. If only her girls' marriages could be as good as those of her two boys she'd have no complaints. Both Vicky and Valerie were like daughters to her. After all the worry and uncertainties as to how Alex and David were going to turn out she had been well rewarded.

Soup first, then a fish course and now the main dish was being served. The thought of how much all of this must have cost made Patsy's stomach turn over.

'You're not to give it another thought,' Ollie had declared when menus and prices were being discussed. 'The reception will be down to me, that's my privilege, besides which,' he had added thoughtfully, 'you seem to forget, Patsy, that you are not in the least hard up. As a director of our firm you can vote yourself any amount of money you need.'

All that was well enough on paper. Patsy tried not to look at balance sheets and suchlike, she was well aware that Ollie was rich, and he saw to it that both she and Eddie drew generous amounts for their wages, but beyond that she didn't delve.

The meal was over and the waiters were pouring champagne for the toast. The best man for each groom did a good job: telegrams were read out and both young men made a witty speech. Now it was the turn of the bridegrooms. Donald got to his feet first. He thanked his own parents for the happy life that they had given him, for their presence here today, and he promised them both that neither he nor Emma would be strangers and that they must feel that they could call on them in their new home at any time without waiting to be asked. 'The same goes for my new in-laws, who have so generously let me steal their daughter and for Ollie who gave her to me at the altar. I promise I will do my best to make her happy. Thank you.' He sat down and the applause went on for a long time.

'Ladies and gentlemen.' Robert Dellor was in his element. He said he now had a lifetime of penal servitude but that it would be a privilege and an honour with the lovely Ellen by his side. He thanked his friends and colleagues for changing their shifts and coming here today and for all their wonderful wedding presents. He had to consult his written notes before he was reminded to thank Ellen's parents. No mention was made of the girls' Grandad, although Eddie had made him aware of the fact that it was

Ollie who was settling the bill for not only the reception but for most of the drinks as well. He sat down looking well-satisfied with himself, but there was a moment of uneasy silence before folk began to clap. It seemed no time at all before the crowd was shouting for the twins to throw their bouquets. Two cars stood ready and waiting at the foot of the hotel steps. Stop hanging about and get going, was what Patsy felt she would scream any moment now. She couldn't bear this final moment of parting.

'Goodbye my darlings . . . take care,' whispered Patsy, blinking away her tears.

The moment had come. Eddie had an arm round each of his daughters, but he was too choked up to speak. Then the twins came over to where Florrie and Gran sat side by side. They each bent down and placed a cheek against an old and wrinkled face. 'Goodbye Auntie, Goodbye Gran,' they said in turn. 'Thank you . . . thank you, we'll see you soon.'

The old dears for once, were totally at a loss as to what to say. They had to swallow hard and only then did they manage to push Ellen and Emma gently away with the words that the girls had known all their lives: 'Gawd bless ya.'

Everyone cheered as the two cars moved off – everyone that is, except Patsy and Eddie. With his arm around her shoulders they watched until the girls were out of sight.

Chapter Fifteen

PATSY WAS DUMBSTRUCK! When Mr Topple had telephoned asking her to come and see him in his office he had aroused her curiosity, but at most she had thought it was a small matter that he wanted her to deal with in regards to the business.

Mr Topple sat behind his desk, Patsy sat facing him with her hands clenched tight on her knees. Disbelief was written all over her face. She still hadn't taken it in.

After forty-seven years her mother's sister wanted to contact her! She hadn't even been aware that her mother had *had* a sister.

'How the hell did she come to get in touch with you?' Patsy asked, trying to be sensible.

The solicitor swallowed deeply before answering. 'It is highly probable that your mother's family may have known of your mother's whereabouts from the beginning, or perhaps now her sister might have gone to an agency or suchlike.'

'I can't believe that her parents would have known where she was all those years, I just can't. Neither of them ever made contact with her while she was alive, and God above knows there were times when she could have done with a helping hand. True, I was only a kid, but even I knew that my mother was never cut out to be working like she did.' Patsy was rocking in the chair now, her temper getting the better of her, and her voice rose as she asked, 'And where were they when my mother was so ill?'

Mr Topple sat back in his chair, compassion flooding through him as he watched this woman whom he had known for a good many years now. She was torturing herself with memories of her childhood and the questions she was asking were not really directed at him. She was talking aloud, expecting no answer, flaying herself mercilessly.

He rose from his seat, crossed the room and went out of his office closing the door quietly behind him.

Patsy hardly noticed he had gone. Thoughts and recollections were racing around inside her head. Why now? How dare this unknown woman suddenly appear and think that she could intrude on her life? Well, she wasn't having it! They had never given a damn about her until now. If matters had been left to them when her mother had died, she herself would have ended up in the workhouse. Thirteen years old she had been, and it was then that they should have come forward, not now. No. She shook her head, furious with herself for getting so upset. Now it's too bloody late. I don't need them and I don't want them.

When Mr Topple made his re-entry, followed by his secretary carrying a tray set out with cups, saucers, coffee pot and a jug of hot milk, Patsy was sitting still, her face covered by her hands, and she was crying quietly.

'Take your time Patsy.' Her old friend and solicitor spoke kindly as they both sat sipping their coffee. 'All this has been a shock to you, coming after all this time, hasn't it?' he asked sympathetically.

She raised her tear-stained face and gave him such a sad look that it tugged at his heart-strings. He had seen her and that great tall husband of hers through a great deal of trouble one way and another, but they had come through smiling. Mr Alexander Berry, father to Patsy in every sense of the word, was now a very rich man, and Eddie Owen and Patsy were legally man and wife, with a lovely family to round things off. Now this . . .

'Think your decision through carefully, Patsy,' he said after some minutes had passed. 'No one is going to force you to meet your Aunt, but it might give you the opportunity to find the answers to some questions you must have wondered about over the years.'

Patsy sighed heavily. 'Life isn't fair is it?' and he answered her truthfully, 'No, Patsy, it isn't fair.'

As she stood and made ready to leave, Mr Topple handed her an envelope. 'Inside is a typed list of details. Your mother's maiden name was Vaughan, and the lady in question who has expressed a wish to meet you is Rosemary Rothstein, Rothstein being her married name.'

'Thank you,' Patsy whispered, taking the envelope and placing it in her bag. As they stood in the doorway of the building, Mr Topple put his arms around her and gave her a reassuring hug.

Rightly or wrongly, she had made her decision.

The Strand Palace Hotel was an impressive but comfortable building, a place where a good many people were having tea on this fine dry afternoon.

'Table for one?' a young man dressed in a maroon jacket edged with black trimmings queried as Patsy hesitated in the entrance of the vast lounge.

'No, I am meeting Mrs Rothstein, so a table for two, please.'

'Oh,' his manner which had been pleasant enough now changed to being almost deferential. 'Mrs Rothstein has already arrived. If you would follow me, please?'

He led her to a round table tucked away in an almost private corner, with a deep comfortable armchair placed on either side. A grey-haired, blue-eyed, well-dressed woman was seated in one of them and she rose to her feet as they approached.

Hesitant but smiling, she said, 'It is Patsy, isn't it?'

Oh God, Patsy thought, I wish I hadn't come. Then she said to herself, stop getting so worked up, you soppy thing, she can't eat you and you don't even have to stay and listen to her if you don't want to.

'Yes,' Patsy said, the colour rising in her cheeks and her heart beating nineteen to the dozen. There was a moment's awkwardness as they stared at each other, then the stranger took charge. 'Do sit down,' she said. 'Shall I order tea?'

Rosemary — Patsy couldn't bring herself to think of her as Aunt — had soft hair that had been set by experts, and a remarkably young face which was heavily made up. Patsy knew from the details she had been given that she was seventy-two years old, about three years older than her mother would have been had she lived. Money could even keep old age at bay, Patsy thought spitefully to herself.

Oh God, this is my mother's sister! Patsy turned her full attention to the woman, watching her closely as she held out her hand in greeting. Patsy took off her coat and slipped it over the back of her chair, then aunt and niece took stock of one another.

Conversation was going to be hard; Patsy's feelings were hostile. Rosemary Rothstein looked very well off. Her jewellery alone must have cost a fortune.

'You look very much like your mother,' said Rosemary, giving Patsy a hesitant smile.

'I'm surprised you even remember what my mother looked like,' Patsy answered vindictively, thinking, it's no good, I'm not going to like her. There is no earthly reason why I should.

A waitress appeared with a loaded tray, setting out two cups and saucers and placing a two-tiered silver cake-stand in the centre of the round table. The sandwiches were dainty, the cakes small and fancy. They drank their tea in silence, cautiously watching each other as they nibbled at the food.

'Forty-seven years!' said Patsy suddenly.

'I beg your pardon,' Rosemary sounded nervous.

'Forty-seven years,' Patsy repeated, 'since my mother was cast off, rejected and forgotten. So why now?'

'Your mother was never forgotten.'

'No! Well, she wasn't remembered very well either, was she?'

Rosemary winced, her expression now melancholy. 'Listen to me,' she pleaded. 'You would have to have known my father to understand why he acted as he did. He and our mother were always so proper, so God-fearing and we children were brought up that way. Father would hardly allow us to breathe without his permission, and our mother was thought of as saintly.'

'Hmm,' Patsy sniffed. 'Saints don't disown their

children when they are in trouble, nor turf them out to fend for themselves.'

'It wasn't like that,' Rosemary protested weakly. 'None of us, not even my mother, dared go against my father – he made all the decisions. Ellen was not turfed out, she could have stayed with us if she had agreed to have you adopted.'

Patsy was lost for words for the moment, so appalled was she by what this woman was saying.

'Your mother chose you. She must have loved your father dearly to give up all the advantages she had been brought up with.'

'What a horrible man your father must have been – my poor mother! What a choice to have been given.'

By now Rosemary was perturbed and she raised her cup and drained it in one gulp, hoping to calm herself. Patsy kept her eyes on her thinking, by heck you've really set the cat amongst the pigeons now – that is what Florrie would say if she were here. Just look at the woman, you've really made her hackles rise. And a good job too, she answered her own thoughts.

'That's how things were at that time.' Rosemary was still doing her best to be agreeable. 'Father did what he thought was right. He had to hide Ellen away at the top of the house because of the shame, and it would have got to the stage where her bulge couldn't be hidden any longer. None of us would have been able to hold our heads up again. Don't you see, dear, Ellen's behaviour could have ruined our father?'

Patsy was sick to the teeth already with this pompous woman. 'I ask you again, if what my mother did was so shameful, why after all this time did you feel the need to contact me?'

Rosemary took a laced-edged handkerchief from her handbag and wiped her nose. 'It must be difficult for you,' she said, 'meeting me like this after all these years but it is painful for me too.'

'Feeling guilty are you?' Patsy asked showing no respect for the woman who was by rights her aunt. She was beginning to get an unpleasant impression of this mysterious family of her mother's.

'I was very young and it was horrid. Ellen going off like that. It upset me a lot at the time.'

'Horrid?' Patsy practically screamed the word. 'And I suppose you imagined that everything in the garden was lovely for my mother. No one to turn to. A baby due within days and you've got the bloody cheek to sit there and tell me that her leaving home was horrid for you.' Now she had done it. Swearing in a posh hotel in London. If she didn't hold that temper of hers in check, the staff would be asking her to leave in a minute.

'Perhaps I shouldn't have used the word horrid but there was a lot of gossip you know. The servants spread the word that Ellen had gone and they knew the reason why. Some people were very unkind.' She finished the sentence on a sob and looked as if she was about to cry.

Patsy stared at this woman who was her mother's sister and felt nothing for her. She was an impossible old lady whose guilt had caught up with her. Or was there more to it than that?

'Both your grandparents are dead,' her aunt said apologetically. 'I'm sorry you never met them. One of my brothers, your uncle, was killed during the war, the other one lives in Scotland and I rarely see him or his family. My husband died young, soon after we were married, but I do have a son, Richard, he also is married, though his wife and I don't exactly see eye to eye.'

Good God! The penny dropped. Aunt Rosemary was a lonely, lost soul. There was no love in her life while love was the most important thing to Patsy. She couldn't imagine life without the love of her family. Well, as you sow so shall you reap, was her quick thought.

Rosemary became bolder and reaching across the table she took hold of Patsy's hand, 'I had hoped . . . what I mean to say is . . . I thought we might become friends, get to know each other. Maybe you would like to visit me now and again, to stay, have a holiday if you'd like to. Maybe I could meet your family?'

No chance, was what Patsy wanted to scream at her as she practically snatched her hand back. The silence between them became long and heavy. Each meditating on what the other had said. Patsy's mind was concentrating on the difference between the way her mother had been treated by the people of Tooting and those of her own family. The comparison was unbelievable. Oh, Mum! Poor Mum, she was whimpering the words silently. Frustration surged through her body. You stood by and watched my mother abandoned, never lifted so much as a finger to help her, and now you want to be friends with me? I'll see you in hell first! Patsy only just stopped herself from yelling the words at her.

Then she had to gulp because of the lump in her throat, telling herself that she mustn't get upset, for if she got upset it would be a victory for this aunt who would more than likely think she was crying for the good life she imagined Patsy had been deprived of.

Quite the reverse, was the truth. It was Rosemary who had been deprived. Deprived of the most important thing in life where Patsy was concerned: *Love.*

Ellen, her kind, gentle, loving mother, so different from this vinegary warped woman who sat opposite her now. I was a bastard, not wanted by my mother's kith or kin. Well, if they did but know it they must have done me the biggest favour possible. And that's the truth. Patsy jerked her chin up and held her head high. On the death of her mother the authorities were insisting that she was a waif, and as such had to be found a place in an institution, but they hadn't reckoned on Florrie. Florrie, her second mother in every sense of the word, had fought for her as a tiger would for its cub.

Then there was Ollie! She pursed her lips as she turned to this aunt who had turned up out of the blue and broke the silence that had settled between them.

'You think that I never had a father, don't you? Well, I suppose you are right in a sense, for my mother never denied that I was illegitimate, but to tell you the truth you couldn't be more wrong.'

'Oh . . . oh, I don't understand.' Rosemary was flustered and she put out her hand towards Patsy again, saying, 'But if you'd like to tell me . . .' her voice trailed off, then she said, 'Things are not going the way I had hoped they would.'

No I wouldn't like to tell you and I'm not going to neither, Patsy defiantly resolved. Ollie was her father, from the day she had been born. And it was by choice, determined by love. Always there to put his arms around her and hold her head against his broad chest; to listen to her troubles, to wipe away her tears, to laugh and play with her. Ever ready with a kiss and a cuddle, grandfather to her children, children who adored him and loved him. See, love was everywhere in her family. Without Eddie's love she wouldn't want to live. Love between Eddie and herself was total. This relation of hers could never begin to understand that.

What about the Day family? Patsy felt the laughter roar up inside her as she imagined Rosemary visiting Strathmore Street in Tooting and having tea with members of the Day family. Yet for all their coarseness and loud mouths they had hearts as big as footballs. They had befriended her mother from the start – helped to bring Patsy herself into this world, had Gran. Given Ellen a job when no one else would, seen to it that she and her mother never went hungry – and most of all the whole family had *loved* both her and her mum. See, there it was again, *love*! Try explaining that to Rosemary. The silence now uneasy, Rosemary looked uncomfortable and Patsy was dangerously tense.

'Shall we meet again, give you time to get used to the fact that I am your aunt?' Rosemary asked, leaning across the table towards Patsy. 'I've been thinking all this while that I've missed such a lot by not keeping in touch with Ellen.'

'No, I don't think so,' Patsy said as kindly as she was able.

'Are you sure? Won't you think it over? Perhaps

even write to me.' Patsy just couldn't bring herself to form an answer and didn't even look back as they made to go their separate ways.

Florrie was the only person Patsy told about this meeting and after having been unusually quiet for some time, Florrie began to laugh – a great belly guffaw that shook her whole body. It took some time for this spasm to settle down until, still grinning broadly, she made an effort to speak.

'I've been called a few things in my time, Patsy, but an hypocrite ain't one of them. Gawd above, what I wouldn't have given to have been a fly on the wall when you two met! I said it often enough when Ellen, God rest her soul, was alive. Yes I did, I told her over an' over again she'd live to see her day with that toffee-nosed family of hers. Well, sadly she didn't, more's the pity, but if she's been looking down on you all this time – and you can bet your bottom dollar she 'as. I know damn well she's laughing her socks off right this minute.'

Florrie's chuckling started all over again but this time she held her arms wide and Patsy went into them. The pair of them stood there, rocking back and forth, tears of laughter streaming down their faces.

★

For three nights now Patsy had lain awake, wondering if after all this time it had really happened. This aunt turning up, it was all like a dream. Not quite a nightmare but not a nice dream either. To make matters worse she was feeling guilty. Unbearably guilty. She and Eddie had never kept secrets from each other. She had to tell him.

That evening, like most week-day evenings, Eddie sat in his high-backed armchair on one side of the fireplace and Patsy sat facing him, carefully sewing up the hem of a skirt that was too long for her.

'Last Wednesday I had tea in the Strand Palace Hotel, met a lady who was sister to my mother,' she said as an opening to the story.

Eddie listened in silence as Patsy used jerky sentences to outline what had taken place. Even when she had finished speaking and was making a pretence of being occupied with her needlework, some time passed before he spoke.

'You went to a West End hotel, to meet a relation of your mother and . . .' he didn't know how to go on, he shook his head. 'On your own?'

'Yes, I did,' she said modestly.

'Why didn't you tell me?' Eddie seemed almost cross.

'I didn't know whether to or not. I didn't know how it would turn out.' She looked apologetically at him, feeling embarrassed.

'Well, I'm glad you've told me now.' He said quietly as he folded his newspaper and set it aside to give her his full attention.

Patsy shot him a grateful look, and whispered, 'Thanks, Eddie.' At least now they could talk about it, as they had with every problem that had cropped up since the day they met.

'I can't put it into words, Eddie, but she meant nothing to me. I wanted to hate her for what she and her whole family did to my mother, but somehow I couldn't. She was pathetic; she was dressed up to the nines, you could have scraped the make-up off her face with a knife, and the jewellery – it was a wonder she could use her hands her fingers had so many rings on them. Maybe I even felt a little sorry for her, but not much. Not enough to let her suddenly intrude into my life, share my family.

Eddie had never loved Patsy more than he did at this moment when she was so fiercely protective of her brood.

'She wanted to come and meet my family! Can you believe that? They're our kids, their name is Owen, or it was till the girls got themselves married.' Now she was able to look across at Eddie and give him a broad smile. Well, it irked her that this unexpected relation had made such an issue of it all, going on about them becoming friends, stressing how it had become so important to her to have contact with her sister's

child. Why couldn't the old biddy have come straight
to the truth? She had no one to share her life with,
no affection, let alone love, and she had sought her
out with the sole idea of having a living relative who
might at least provide her with some company from
time to time.

As the seconds went by and Eddie made no further
comment, Patsy regretted her outburst. Was Eddie
reproaching her?

'Eddie, do you think I was cruel? I suppose, thinking back I could have given her a bit more of a
chance. There could have been so much we might
have talked about, so much I could have learnt, if I'd
been willing to listen to her explanations.'

Eddie was proud of the way she had handled this.
He was always proud of her, her values were right,
their family came first. Yet something bothered him
and he couldn't fathom what it was. This stranger
popping up as she had was connected with Patsy's life
before he had ever met her. The hardships she and
her mother had suffered were caused because Ellen's
family had cast her off. Ashamed of her. So why now
did an unknown sister want to make contact? His
heart ached for her as he said, 'Patsy, stop being so
hard on yourself.' And then, as an afterthought, 'You
should talk about this to Ollie – you know that don't
you? I think you have done exactly what I would
have done in your place. This woman has no right

whatsoever to approach you after all these years and the decision as to whether or not you wanted to have an association with her was entirely up to you.'

She looked happily up at him, feeling the guilt of rejecting her aunt slip slowly from her shoulders. He had reassured her. Dispelled all her doubts. 'I love you very much, Eddie Owen' she whispered.

'I love you too, Patsy,' he said standing up and drawing her into his arms.

It was Saturday evening. Eddie had gone with Stan Briggs to the Bowery for a pint and a game of darts. Ollie and Patsy were seated at the kitchen table playing crib. Patsy played the five of clubs and Ollie matched it with the five of diamonds, giving him two points for a pair which was all he needed to win the game. 'Beat you again,' he laughed, taking the pegs out of the holes on the cribbage board ready for the next game.

'I'm sure you must cheat.' Patsy teased him. Then becoming serious, she asked, 'Ollie, d'you mind if we don't play for a bit? I want to talk to you.'

'Of course not.' He smiled, gathering the cards into a pack and giving them an expert shuffle.

'Ollie,' Patsy began in a voice that held a slight tremor. 'What would you say if I told you that a member of my mother's family had been trying to get in touch with me?'

'Bloody hell! Have they?' His tone was suspicious.

'More than that, I had tea with my mother's sister.'

Disbelief spread over his face and Patsy's conscience troubled her as she watched. It wasn't fair to spring it on him like this. She should have told both him and Eddie what was happening before she had gone to the Strand Palace Hotel. It was too late to worry about that now.

'I'm so sorry, Ollie. I shouldn't have sprung it on you like this. Will you listen if I try and explain how it all came about?'

Their eyes met but there was no smile on either of their faces as he gently nodded his head. Solemnly she told him every detail of that encounter. Frustration, hurt and anger all combined in Ollie as his fist came crashing down on the table-top, sending the pack of cards scattering to the floor. 'I'd have told her to go to the devil! After what that family put Ellen though!' Then the tone of his voice softened. 'If only I had asked Ellen to marry me when we first met. All those years, I always meant to, but your mother was out of my class.'

They were both silent . . . Remembering.

'You're too nice for your own good.' Patsy looked up at him with a warm smile.

'That's as maybe.' This big man who to Patsy never seemed to age had tears in his eyes as he softly spoke now. 'I can't help thinking how incredible it is the things that happen in people's lives. The pain, the suffering, the tragedies even miracles sometimes – things that change a person's whole life.' He paused and sighed, then his eyes brightened as he said, 'I might never have had you in my life. Out of bad does come good. If your mother hadn't become pregnant or your father hadn't died she and I would never have met. My life would never have been so richly blessed. It's odd to think Ellen lived in Tooting, worked on market stalls and took care of you for nearly fourteen years without asking help from anyone.' It was as if he was talking to himself and Patsy kept quiet, not daring to interrupt. 'Ellen,' he said her name with reverence. 'She was so gentle and yet so strong, and too young to die. I wanted her, and you – for us to be a family. It is more than thirty years since she died and I have lived with my regrets all that time. Yes, I loved your mother dearly and I always will. I've never wanted any other woman for my wife and I am truly grateful that I have you, Eddie and the children to call my family.'

For a long moment, Ollie closed his eyes and Patsy saw a tear squeeze out between the lashes and roll down his face, then he leaned forward and touched her cheek. 'Let me tell you something, my darling Patsy, your mother never regretted leaving her family and holding on to you. That's the truth, I swear it is. The thirteen years she had you were happy years. Hard, yes, but happy. She loved you so much.' Tears were now running unashamedly down his cheeks.

To think of Ellen was still sad, and kind of beautiful at the same time. 'No other woman was or could be like your mother was,' he whispered. Patsy was crying too now, as she clung to Ollie's hand: the look of love and gentleness he gave her said it all.

After a while they both wiped their eyes and Ollie smiled. 'Weren't you tempted, just a little, to have well-to-do relations?' he teased.

Patsy playfully swiped him on the shoulder. 'I'm too old to want to know my mother's background or to need a new family.' She looked at him sadly, but there was a twinkle of mischief in those green eyes. 'I'll be forty-seven come Christmas.'

He threw back his head and laughed loudly. To him she still looked about twenty-five.

'You did well, Patsy,' he firmly told her.

'Thank you, Sir.' She gave him a brief bow and they both laughed.

'You know you're a lot like your mother was. Strong and kind and very stubborn, but she could play cards a whole sight better than you can. Shall we have another game?'

As Ollie bent to retrieve the playing cards from the floor, Patsy, not for the first time, was fully aware that she could count herself amongst the lucky ones.

Chapter Sixteen

'I'VE BEEN WONDERING what to get the children for Christmas,' said Florrie coming in from her scullery and plonking herself down in the armchair that was nearest to the fire.

'Toys and sweets,' Patsy suggested.

'Oh, very funny, but not very helpful.'

'Sorry,' Patsy said immediately. It wasn't fair to tease Florrie but it did seem a bit daft to refer to Ellen, Emma, David and Alex as if they were still about six years old.

'Will you take me shopping some time this week, or will you get things for me and I'll give you the money?'

'Me buying for you is not the same. You come round the shops, see all there is to see, get a bit of the Christmas feeling. I'll take you Thursday, we'll have a bit of lunch out. I can't today, I've got to go in a minute.'

'Well, I wouldn't want to be any bother to you. Where you off to now?' Patsy laughed, 'come on now Florrie don't play the martyr, making out you're so ill-done-by.'

'Cheeky bitch,' Florrie said trying hard not to laugh herself.

'If you must know I'm off to Vauxhall. Ollie's laying on drinks and eats for the men: you can come if you want to, it'll be all very informal.'

'If you had really wanted me to go with you, you would have said so before now, not just asked me out of the blue like that when I ain't even dressed properly.'

Patsy laughed again, and this time she got up from her chair and put her arm around Florrie's shoulders. 'Got out of bed the wrong side, did we?'

'Sarky this morning, are we?' Florrie quickly retorted, grinning broadly.

'I could stop and help you wash and dress yourself if you'd really like to come and have a drink with the men.'

'No, love, you get yerself off. I'll be ready about ten on Thursday.'

Patsy went up the passage and came back with her hat and coat on. 'Right, I'll be here on the stroke of ten Thursday, my love, and I hope to God you'll be in a better mood.'

'You're getting to be downright disrespectful,' Florrie called after her, and then for good measure she added indignantly, 'And the day ain't come yet when I need help to wash and dress meself.'

'Bye,' Patsy called back, still laughing as she closed the front door.

It was very informal. Vicky was seeing that the men's glasses were kept filled while Patsy made sure that they had plenty to eat. From time to time Patsy saw Eddie and Ollie with their heads close together and glancing at her proudly. The men seemed happy and relaxed.

Ollie called for silence and said, 'I'm not going to make a speech.'

Eddie cheered, then so did everyone else.

Ollie told them the business had done well during the year and that there would be a bonus for each of them. 'We've plenty of theatre work for the winter, pantomimes and shows through all of January, so there'll be no question of laying off drivers.' More cheers.

'One point I would like you all to think about. The Esplanade Hotel at Cliftonville is being put on the market for sale. Any new owner may not want to accept our weekly package deal and this would cut our business considerably.' The men shuffled their feet and there were a few nervous groans.

'Mr Owen and myself have discussed the possibility of the company owning the Hotel. Maybe even leaving our coach and the driver at the resort for the seven-day tour — on the spot, so to speak, to do our own daily trips. It would mean most of you taking it in turn to be away for a week at a time.'

'Can I be the first volunteer?' quipped Bert Franklin.

'Fair do's, I reckon, get away from the Missus once in a while,' said Cecil Woodman.

'All right,' said Ollie, laughing with them. 'I reckon we'll have some definite news for you early in the new year. It only remains for me to wish all of you a very merry Christmas.'

Patsy took stock of Ollie as he stood shaking hands with each of his employees. He's a good man, she muttered beneath her breath. He was wearing a formal, dark grey suit, a really nice tie, and he still had a good head of hair even though most of it was grey by now. Oh God, I know this much, I'm damned lucky to have had him for a father.

All the hard part had been done yesterday on Christmas Eve. Eddie had drawn the sinews from the legs of the turkey, Patsy had simmered the giblets, made the stuffing and the gravy. She had also washed and chopped all the vegetables. Florrie was bringing the Christmas pudding, one of three she had made months ago, boiling them in her copper for six hours. Kitty had made the mince-pies. Two tables pushed together and covered by a white sheet took up most of the floor space in the front room. Patsy was just putting the finishing touches to the dinner-table, which was set for sixteen, when Eddie put his head round the door.

'That looks really Christmassy,' he said, nodding towards the table.

'Glad you like it,' she smiled.

Patsy had arranged crossed red and green crackers at each place. The centrepiece was white Christmas roses, holly and silver fern. Tall red candles at each end of the table stood in silver candlesticks that had once belonged to Eddie's mother.

'I came to see if you'd like a drink,' Eddie said.

'I'm coming now – are there any more presents to go round the tree?'

'Of course there are. Young Tim is out at the car now with David, bringing in a whole pile. That boy is going to burst if someone doesn't allow him to open at least one of his presents.'

Together they went down to the kitchen which by now was a noisy, happy scene of females clattering dishes and stirring saucepans, while gorgeous smells were coming from the oven.

Patsy gazed around the table and counted her blessings. Her two sons were both big and strong, she couldn't have had better. But her mouth twitched as she thought of some of the capers the pair of them used to get up to. Still did, if the truth were known. She loved both her daughters-in-law and there weren't many mothers-in-law who could truthfully say that. As for young Tim he was a lovely little boy.

Ellen, well, she still worried about her. She would give a lot to be able to say that her fears regarding Robert Dellor had been groundless, but she couldn't even now admit that. Robert had bought a detached house out at Tolworth and on the couple of occasions when she and Eddie had visited everything seemed fine. Ellen wanted for nothing, or so it looked on the surface; the house just hadn't felt like a home, was the only way she could put it. Eddie said she was being daft and she prayed that he was right.

Emma was Emma, she never changed. She'd whispered that she was pregnant and Patsy had wanted to scream from the roof-tops that she was going to be a grandma. Donald had bought a semi-detached house on the Kingston bypass, a house where she felt entirely at home. Donald was a hard worker, a good husband and a good son; he wouldn't have agreed to spend Christmas here with the family if his parents had not been included in the invitation.

Both she and Eddie got on well with Lucy and Fred Langford, while Florrie sang the praises of them both which said a lot.

When everyone declared they couldn't eat another morsel. Lucy and Kitty said they would do the washing-up.

'Oh no, you won't,' said Patsy, 'we women are going to relax and enjoy a nice cup of tea. My sons and sons-in-law can do it.'

'Trust you, Mum, to spoil our Christmas,' said Alex as he got to his feet. 'I thought Christmas was meant to be a time of enjoyment, but there's a fat chance when we've got a slave-driver for a mother.'

'We'll have none of that,' she told Alex, pretending to be cross but slyly winking at young Timmy.

'Favouritism, that's what it is,' said David, throwing a cushion at Valerie's head.

They sat round the fire opening their presents and soon the carpet was covered with torn wrapping-paper and ribbons which had been used to make fancy bows. The men drank brandy while the women had their tea and ate the Christmas boxes of chocolates, nuts and dates. The four young men were engrossed in helping Tim to make working objects from the Meccano sets he had been given for his Christmas presents.

What with the big dinner and the heat of the room, Eddie and Ollie were both feeling sleepy, but it was Fred Langford who dropped off first. His brandy glass clenched firmly in his hand and his mouth slightly open, he suddenly gave a loud snore and Tim roared with laughter.

'Oh, sorry,' muttered Fred.

'Don't be daft,' Patsy said quickly. 'Shows you feel at home if you're able to drop off and have a bit of a sleep.'

'It's been a really happy Christmas,' Patsy said to Eddie as they stood on the doorstep waving goodbye to everyone.

'It certainly has,' he agreed.

The front room felt empty and cold when they went back indoors. 'Shall I light a fire?' Patsy asked.

'What for?' he said, grining at her. 'We've got our bedroom back to ourselves now, haven't we?' For the past three nights it had been a case of all women in some rooms and all men in the others.

'Oh, you Eddie Owen, you've got a one-track mind. You didn't mind them all staying here, did you? It was a lovely holiday, wasn't it?'

'Yes Patsy, very lovely. The best I've ever known.'

Chapter Seventeen

WITH CHRISTMAS OVER and January just beginning, the weather was absolutely foul. 'I'd much rather it was freezing cold, even snow,' Patsy said to Vicky.

'Yes, I've just about had enough of this damn rain, it hasn't let up for two days now – can't be much more left up there.'

Patsy was having her usual morning coffee with Vicky. 'Is anything settled yet?' Vicky asked.

'No, and if it isn't soon we're going to be right up the shoot. How can we even think about accepting bookings when we've no idea what hotels we'll be able to use?'

'I heard Eddie saying something about Ollie putting in bids for both the Esplanade and the Gloucester.'

Patsy knew there would be no problem in finding the cash. The inheritance which Ollie had received on his brother Jack's death had seen to that.

'I know. He told me that was his intention and asked me to dig up all the details, but he's not discussed it since. I've got all the facts and figures and I think we should collar both Eddie and Ollie today and pin them down to a decision, otherwise we won't know whether we're coming or going. What do you think?'

'Too true.' Vicky spoke quickly. 'We don't want to be turning business away – you know, day trips and such like – and then find that the coaches aren't going to be away seven days at a time. Either we are still doing weekly holidays or we're not – about time we were told where we stand.'

Leaning forward Patsy looked at Vicky; she was a good ally, who had learned the business well. She also managed to keep Alex on the straight and narrow – well, as much as anyone ever could. Alex was still very much his own man. Still lived in the flat over these offices, through Patsy had an idea that Vicky would have preferred a house, more so since David and Valerie had bought one very near to where Emma and Donald lived. Alex had no intention of tying up capital in property at the moment. He had his fingers in so many pies – barrow-boys, stallholders, even a warehouse she had been told. Both he and David checked every load that came in or went out, and at the end of the week they both collected their dues from the men who worked for them.

'When you've finished your coffee, you get on that phone and you tell those two men of ours that we want a meeting, here in this office this afternoon. And don't take no for an answer!'

Much to Patsy's surprise, Vicky burst out laughing. She couldn't help it, the thought of her mother-in-law, no more than five foot three, delivering an ultimatum to Eddie and Ollie, both well over six foot, well!

'Oh, blimey, Patsy!' she cried. 'You should see your face.'

Suddenly Patsy saw the funny side of the situation and she laughed, then having hesitated for a moment she tossed her head defiantly. 'I'm going to get a straight answer one way or another today,' she said, more to herself than to Vicky.

Normally, Patsy had a light lunch in her office or, on occasions, she and Vicky went to a nearby restaurant. Today she wasn't going to bother with anything. Eddie and Ollie had promised to be at the office by two o'clock and she intended to have all the relevant papers laid out.

The four of them were seated around the table which stood in the alcove by the window of the large office. Patsy glanced over at Vicky sitting opposite her, her pad in her hand, pencil poised.

'Here you are,' Patsy said, opening one of the folders which lay on the table in front of her. 'All the figures and information you asked me to get on the Esplanade at Cliftonville.'

Ollie took the folder, paused and looked at Patsy. 'I suppose you agree that we're doing the right thing – buying hotels.'

Lifting her head, Patsy looked at Eddie and at a nod from him she leant forward and smiled at Ollie. 'Yes, I do,' she said, 'I don't think we have any choice, not if we want to continue with our package holidays. But you said hotels; I thought it was only the Esplanade that was on the market.'

'It was, but a little whisper I heard told me that the Gloucester at Ramsgate had learned that we'd started negotiations for the Esplanade and they wanted to get in on the act. Eddie and I decided, in for a penny in for a pound.'

'Did you now?' Patsy exclaimed, allowing surprise to come out in her voice. She could handle these meetings and any situation that arose much more easily now. Although she hadn't wanted to be made a company director and been afraid she wouldn't be able to cope, now she thoroughly enjoyed her job and had learned her lessons well.

'It pays to keep one ear to the ground,' Eddie said, smiling at her.

'Besides, we're in a much stronger position if we own the hotels we're using, rather than relying on owners to tell us which weeks we can have. Might even be able to drum up some winter trade: if we put managers in and have to keep the places heated from October to spring, it make sense to offer reduced rates to semi-permanent residents. What d'you think?'

'Nice of you to ask me,' said Patsy a little sarcastically.

Ollie burst out laughing. 'Now you've ruffled her feathers,' he said to Eddie.

'Well, you do seem to have it all cut and dried,' she complained.

'No, we haven't,' Ollie told her, still with laughter in his voice, but with all the affection he felt for her apparent in his bright eyes. 'We have settled on the Esplanade, completion date is three weeks today and before you bite my head off we only knew ourselves this morning. That's where we were, at the solicitors.'

'I wasn't going to bite your head off,' Patsy said meekly. 'At least now we know where we stand on Cliftonville.'

'I thought we'd leave the decision of Ramsgate to you and Vicky,' Ollie said to them both. 'Send you off for the weekend – look the place over on the spot, not from a distance.'

'You'd be wasting your time and money,' Vicky interrupted bluntly. 'What do we know about hotels and buildings?'

'Now don't be so hasty,' Patsy laughed. 'It isn't often we get told we can have a week-end at the seaside, all expenses down to the firm; of course we'll go.'

'Good, at least that's settled. You can take yourselves off this Friday.'

As he stood up, Ollie said, 'Now, if there's nothing else you girls want us for, we've a hell of a lot of work waiting for us up at Vauxhall.'

'Hang on a minute,' Eddie said good-naturedly. 'How come the pair of you get a week-end away? You'll have to pay attention to a lot of details – you know that, don't you?'

Vicky looked across at Patsy and they both grinned.

'We'll certainly do that,' was Patsy's parting remark.

Having caught an early train, it was only a few minutes after twelve on this bitter cold January morning when Patsy paid off the taxi-cab driver outside the Gloucester Hotel. She and Vicky stood for a moment looking up at the building. The structure was very old, yet the architecture was beautiful and the masonry a work of art. The wintry sun disappeared behind a cloud, and Patsy thought sadly that the old brickwork had a dejected air.

The hotel was not open for business but they were obviously expected. A tall, thin young man wearing a heavy polo-necked jersey came down the front steps, picked up their suitcases and with half a smile said, 'Morning, ladies. Let's get you inside out of this biting wind.'

Inside the entrance hall they were greeted cordially by a couple in their late fifties. 'Bill and Mary Yates,' the man said, holding out his hand, 'and that's our son Peter,' he nodded towards the younger man.

'Feel free to wander wherever you like and we'll do our best to answer any questions,' Mary Yates told them as she handed them a key. 'We've made up two single beds in one room, and put an electric fire in there for you.'

While waiting for the lift, both Patsy and Vicky glanced around. Already, they could see small but noticeable signs of neglect. The room allocated to them was in the front of the hotel, spacious and high-ceilinged: the bathroom that led off was very tiny. The furniture was old but good. Wardrobe and dressing-table were mahogany, so too was the bed-head, the bed-side tables were oak. Each of the double wall-lights held only one bulb that worked.

'Might have run a duster round,' Vicky said, rubbing her hand along the bed rail and disturbing the dust.

'At least the bed-linen is clean,' Patsy told her as she straightened the bedspread back over the sheets, blankets and pillows. 'But it's like a bloody ice-well in here – for Christ's sake plug that fire in, if you can find a socket that works.'

Vicky crossed the room and found a socket set into the wainscoting. Having plugged the fire into it, she straightened up and gave a cry of pleasure. 'Come and look at this view – and it's starting to snow.'

The view was marvellous. 'The position of this place must be its best asset,' Patsy murmured half to herself.

Right opposite the hotel was a long, wide stretch of lawns and beyond was the sea. Great waves, topped by foaming white horses, were rolling in to crash on the beach, sending showers of spray high into the air.

'Isn't it wonderful?' cried Vicky.

'It certainly is,' Patsy agreed as they stood there fascinated by a scene that was totally unfamiliar to both of them.

Next morning there were more loud cries of pleasure from Vicky.

'You'll catch your death of cold standing there in your bare feet and nothing on but that flimsy night-dress,' Patsy yelled at her. Then she too let out a cry as she went towards the window. 'Good God!'

It was as if someone had laid down white blankets over everything during the night. Every sound was muffled, the tide was out and the snow lay thick on the lawns and the beach. To their right stood a long low building, maybe a shelter of some kind that old folk rested in during the summer. The snow was piled high around it and was inches deep on the roof.

'Must have been snowing all night.' Vicky shivered and Patsy pushed her towards the bathroom. 'At least there's plenty of hot water,' Vicky called.

Patsy was fishing about in her suitcase. 'I brought two jumpers with me, I think I'll put them both on,' she called back.

By the end of that Saturday, they would both have loved to have gone home. They had seen all that they wanted to, and they were finding it almost impossible to keep warm.

'You go home in the morning,' Patsy said to Vicky as they sat in the deserted lounge drinking their after-dinner coffee. 'We'll phone Alex to meet you. I bet he'll be over the moon, he's sure to have been lost without you.'

'Why can't you come as well – don't see the point of you hanging around any longer. The Yates are not exactly friendly, and we've seen all we need to see, surely?'

'I want to check out a few things at the Council offices. Land registry, make sure the property is free-hold – and I can't do that till Monday morning. Make no mistake, though, I'll be on the first train as soon as I've got all the answers that Ollie will need.'

'Well, if you're sure.' Vicky was unable to conceal her delight and Patsy laughed at her.

'Miss Alex, do you?'

'Not half. Especially in bed, there's no one to cuddle up to.'

By eleven o'clock on Sunday morning Vicky was on the train bound for London and Patsy was seated in a corner of the café which was at the entrance to the municipal park.

'You the lady from the coach company? Come to look over the Gloucester, have you?'

Patsy had been lost in thought and the voice and the hand tugging at her arm startled her for a moment. Seated at the next table were three frail old ladies and one elderly gentleman.

'Yes . . . I suppose I am,' Patsy stammered. 'How did you know?'

'We all used to live in the Gloucester,' the gentleman answered. 'The staff at our place told us someone from Ace Coaches was coming to view the place and we saw you arrive.'

Patsy turned her gaze on to the lady who had spoken first. 'Is there something that I can do for you?'

The lady flushed slightly and looked away, avoiding Patsy's eyes.

'Perhaps I'd better introduce everybody,' the gentleman said quietly. 'I'm Mr Stapleton, this lady who spoke to you is Mrs Wright, and her two companions are Mrs Webster and Mrs Brookes. Mrs Wright lived at the Gloucester for eleven years.'

Leaning across, Patsy took hold of the offered hands and said, 'How d'you do,' to each of them in turn.

After the introductions were over, there was a prolonged silence and Patsy wondered why Mrs Wright had spoken to her. She shifted in her seat and leaned forward urgently. 'Look, Mrs Wright, is there something I can do for you?' Her voice was calm but strong, and it seemed to give the old lady a degree of confidence.

'Are you going . . .' Still she hesitated and Patsy smiled encouragingly. 'Are you going to buy the Gloucester?'

Patsy couldn't think how to answer. What difference could it possibly make one way or the other to this group of elderly folk?

'Why are you so interested?' she asked.

Mrs Wright hung her head and the motion held such dejection that Patsy felt tears sting at the back of her eyes and was tempted to stand up and put her arms around her. The old lady's lips trembled; she was near to tears as she fumbled in her bag for her handkerchief.

Just then a jolly-looking woman in a flowered overall plonked a tray down on the table and, with a happy smile, asked the old people, 'Finished?' Then without waiting for a reply she gathered up the four cups and saucers and stacked them on the tray.

'I've finished with mine, thank you,' Patsy said, holding out the empty cup. 'Do I have to go to the counter for more coffee?'

'No, that's all right, my love, I'll bring you one in half a jiffy.'

Patsy gave the assistant one of her sweetest smiles, opened her purse, took out a ten-shilling note and holding it out, she said, 'Would you mind making that five coffees, please?'

'My pleasure,' said the woman as if she truly meant it, marching away with her tray of dirty cups and humming 'Onward, Christian Soldiers' to herself as she went.

Patsy got to her feet and lifted her chair. Guessing her intention, Mr Stapleton moved nearer to Mrs Brookes, making a space for Patsy to set down her chair and join them at one table.

While they were waiting for their fresh coffee Patsy looked hard at these three small, grey-haired ladies. Their clothes were good, but decidedly dated; the hands of each were heavily veined and spotted by dark brown liver spots. Mr Stapleton was a large man with a ruddy complexion and thin white hair that barely covered his bald head; his general manner and his clothes suggested that in his early days he had been a man of means.

They all said 'Thank you' as the overalled woman placed a steaming cup of coffee in front of each of them.

'Shall I try to answer your question? But before I do, would you like to introduce yourself to us?' Mr Stapleton ventured.

Patsy felt her cheeks flame up. 'Oh, I'm so sorry. My name is Mrs Owen and yes I have come from the Ace Trading Company which is owned by my family.' Again there was a long pause as the sugar-bowl was passed around the table and everyone stirred their coffee.

'You've been sending weekly visitors to the Gloucester for some time now and that was why Mr Yates gave us all notice to leave.'

Patsy stared in amazement at Mrs Webster, perhaps the most frail of the three ladies, for it was she who had made this statement.

'Because you could pay more money per week for summer visitors than he was getting from us,' said Mrs Brookes, who had decided to be brave and add her comments to the conversation.

Without giving Patsy time to reply, Mr Stapleton took up the story. 'What they are telling you is the truth. We, and twenty others besides, were residents in the Gloucester before Mr Yates purchased the premises. Mrs Wright and two other ladies were living there for most of the war years. That was when

Dorothy Jameston, a nursing sister, owned it; she allowed the place to be used for wounded servicemen, and after the war, she ran it as a rest home. Then Dorothy died, the Yates bought it but didn't make enough as a rest home. Can't blame him for having turned to the holiday trade, just a bit hard on those who had come to look on the place as their home.' He sighed heavily as he finished speaking.

By now Patsy was utterly bewildered; it was a ludicrous situation she had got herself into and she couldn't think straight. She felt so sorry for these dear sweet people, but what did they want her to do about their situation? 'Where do you all live now?' she asked, almost dreading to hear the answer.

'In the Maplehurst Rest Home,' said Mrs Wright.

Patsy looked at her wrinkled face which was gentle and kind, but decided that there was uncertainty in her eyes. 'Aren't you happy there?' Patsy asked with a sudden burst of courage.

'Yes we are,' four voices said in unison.

'That's the trouble.' Mr Stapleton spoke again. 'As things turned out, it was a move for the better. Of course we all miss living on the sea-front — Maplehurst is three streets back — but the owners, two sisters, have been goodness themselves.' Suddenly he was overcome with emotion and it was Mrs Wright who explained.

'Anita Gould, the elder of the two, is very ill. She

hasn't too long to live, so her sister Harriet has decided she must sell the rest home and devote herself to caring for Anita.' Mrs Wright's voice dropped to a mere whisper and mournfully she said, 'I thought I would end my days in the Gloucester, we got turned out from there and now it's happening all over again.'

'You see where it leaves us, don't you, Mrs Owen?' said Mrs Brookes, and when Patsy made no reply she said, 'Well?'

'Well what?' prompted Patsy.

'Your company wouldn't consider buying Maplehurst, would they?' Mrs Brookes blurted out in a moment of bravado.

Patsy looked around at all of them in utter disbelief. Buy a rest home? Full of elderly folk? Commit themselves to being in charge of them if not responsible for them? She could just see Florrie's face if she were to go home and relate this conversation to her. 'You've gone bloody daft, girl,' is what Florrie would say, 'Not safe to be let out on your own.'

Patsy spent the whole of Monday rushing around from one office to another. She visited borough clerks, surveyors, and a branch of the bank of which the Ace Trading Company was an important client. She even had a talk with two of the town's main tradesmen. The ideas forming in the back of her mind were exciting.

By the time she reached Ramsgate railway station and found herself a corner seat in one of the carriages of the London-bound train, she had decided that the Gloucester had character. At one time it had probably been a first-class hotel. It certainly needed a lot of changes, but modernisation and renovation weren't the only things that Patsy had in her mind as she opened her case and began to read through the notes that she had made.

Patsy stopped talking, heaved a great sight of relief and leaned back in her chair. She had been telling Ollie everything that had happened while she had been in Ramsgate. Not once had he interrupted her.

Ollie studied her thoughtfully for a moment, feeling great admiration as well as a deep love for her. Since he had set up this business Patsy had proved she had a quick mind and a great determination to learn. He had never for a moment thought that she might flounder, though Patsy herself had feared this. If when she was a child circumstances had been different, if she had been given the benefit of a good education, there was no telling what she might have achieved. As it was she had certainly showed that she wanted to learn anything and everything about the trade that he had chosen. Eddie had laughed when Vicky arrived back home on her own. As they'd talked about Patsy, he had remarked on her lively sense of humour.

'She'll delve into the council archives, drive them all mad if she doesn't get the answers she's after,' Eddie had said. He hadn't known then what she was going to propose when she did get back.

'If you don't want to get involved, if you don't think it would be a good thing for the company, or even if you think I've gone a bit doolally, please, Ollie, just say so. I'm not going to try twisting your arm. Just forget this conversation. Only there is one thing – you don't have to tell Eddie, nor Florrie, that I came up with some mad idea about you buying a rest home, do you?'

There was a pathetic edge to her voice, but Ollie could read Patsy like a book. Had been able to do so from the day she said her first words and fluttered her big green eyes at him.

'What are you grinning at?' she cried.

Ollie's hearty laugh rang out as he got up from his seat and came round the desk to where Patsy sat. He pulled her to her feet and picked her up in his arms, just as he used to do when she was a child.

Patsy giggled. 'Put me down, Ollie, I've got a load of work I ought to get started on.'

'You don't have to put on that broken-hearted act

for me,' said Ollie in his forthright way. 'There aren't many things I could bring myself to refuse you. And you know it,' he added, with great delight.

Patsy's face lit up in a bright smile as Ollie set her down on her feet. 'Then you will think about buying Maplehurst Rest Home?'

'I'll do more than think about it, I'll get Eddie to come down to Ramsgate with me as soon as possible. Can't let all that digging you did go to waste, can we?'

'You're not having me on, are you?' demanded Patsy suddenly.

'Course I'm not, I promise. Might be a very good investment now I come to think about it. Who knows, you might be very glad to have a place down at Ramsgate where you can shove me and Florrie out of sight when we become too much for you to handle!'

'That'll be the day, when I can't sort the pair of you out. Neither of you will ever go in a home while I'm alive, and you'd better bloody well believe it.'

'Oh, I do,' Ollie said, doing his best to keep a straight face.

'That's all right then,' she said.

They both began to laugh loudly and Vicky, coming into the office at that moment, was struck not for the first time by the strong bond of affection there was between them.

Over the next few weeks, Patsy learned that money talks all languages. Having set all the facts before Ollie and used her powers of persuasion on Eddie to get him to agree that making an offer for the Maplehurst Rest Home would be no bad idea, she had spent a couple of sleepless nights worrying whether she had done the right thing.

The purchase of the Esplanade went through without a hitch, and with what Ollie described as a very capable husband and wife installed as manager and manageress, they were all set for a grand opening in time for Easter. The acquisition of the Gloucester had not been quite so straightforward; it would be Whitsun before they could send their first coach-load of visitors to Ramsgate. Patsy felt that the delay would be well worthwhile. Carpenters, decorators and plumbers had been working in the hotel non-stop since the day the contracts were signed.

Alex and David had played their part. 'Good as gold, they've both been,' said Eddie to Patsy one evening when they were discussing a wholesale purchase of dining-room and lounge furniture that their two sons had acquired on very reasonable terms. Patsy looked worried and Eddie's smile became a frown. 'You always think the worst of Alex, don't you?'

'No, I don't.' Her eyes flashed and she banged the fresh pot of tea that she had just made down on the table. 'It's just that whenever we need something, Alex always knows somebody who has exactly what we want at way below the normal price, and if that fact alone doesn't make you suspicious then it damn well ought to.'

'Now you're just being silly,' said Eddie, reaching for the milk jug and then pouring out his own tea.

Patsy gave him a mutinous look. 'Most of the deals the pair of them do must cost a tidy bit of money. Where do they get it from? That's what I'd like to know.'

Eddie felt his temper rising. 'What you're insinuating is uncalled-for. Both Alex and David have always managed to stand on their own two feet. Haven't ever asked us for much. They could have been lay-abouts, even got a cushy job with Ollie. You should think about it. They haven't got a bad reputation; if they say they'll handle something, you can guarantee they'll keep their word.'

Patsy sat up straight and asked, 'Are you telling me all they do is above-board, all the time?'

'Well, I suppose I must admit they're not exactly a pair of angels,' said Eddie. 'But I still don't think they overstep the mark. Not much anyway, not these last weeks.'

Patsy's annoyance struggled with her sense of humour and lost. She giggled. 'Fine father you are, you encourage them.'

'Oh, blimey, don't tell me you're going to start on me now.'

Patsy was still trying not to laugh outright. 'Well, I just like to know what's going on in my own family, I don't fancy having to visit my boys in Wandsworth Prison.'

'I give you my word that the boys don't get up to anything that is really illegal,' Eddie said quite truthfully. 'They're just always in the right spot at the right moment to do a bit of price-cutting, and they've got some very useful friends.'

This time Patsy had to laugh out loud. 'What you mean, Eddie Owen, though you won't admit it for all the tea in China, is that our boys are in with a load of conniving buggers.'

Within a month of Ace Trading Company becoming the new owners of Maplehurst Rest Home, the whole operation was a runaway success. Everyone connected with the running of the place was delighted. Eddie and Patsy had to do a lot of organising to get a free Sunday, and they were really pleased to see Mrs Wright and her friends waiting at the door when they arrived at the home at midday on Whit Sunday. Ollie and Florrie were with them.

In the entrance hall there were cuddles and pecks on the cheeks from the old ladies. When they were all seated in the lounge it was Mrs Brookes who first elected to tell them how happy and grateful they all were.

'Two more of our old friends are moving in once the bank holiday is over,' she said, which brought happy exclamations from Patsy, Eddie and Ollie.

Mrs Wright put out her hand and gently touched Florrie's arm. 'We're having a late lunch, we waited for you to arrive. I feel I know you as Mr Berry has spoken of you.'

Florrie smiled, but was strangely quiet for her.

'Florrie,' said Patsy fondly, 'Why don't you let Mrs Wright show you her room?'

'I think you'll like it,' Mrs Wright was saying as she and Florrie slowly crossed the lounge.

By the time the gong sounded for lunch Ollie and Eddie had become firm favourites with the old folk, and as Florrie came and took the chair next to Mrs Wright she was beaming as if she had been treated as a celebrity. On the journey home Patsy sat in the back of the car with Florrie and was subjected to an inquisition.

'Now,' Florrie began, 'tell me exactly how you

came to meet that dear old soul.' Patsy faced up light-heartedly to all of Florrie's questions.

'Gawd 'elp me,' muttered Florrie as her eyes became heavy and her lids began to drop. 'That old people should have to come to that. Turfed out of the only home she'd known for eleven years. The good Lord sent you down to Ramsgate, Patsy – you know that, don't you? Thank God he did an' all. They'll be all right now though, the lot of them – lovely place, is Maplehurst.'

'Heaven be praised,' said Eddie irreverently, as Florrie's head dropped forward and she gave a contented snore. 'I thought she might want to roast us alive. Think we were giving her a preview before we suggested she went there to live?'

'She knows better than that,' Patsy told him firmly, 'but I am glad she and Mrs Wright hit it off. See, you never can tell. As different as chalk and cheese, yet they swore they would keep in touch with one another.'

Chapter Eighteen

WITH THE COMING of September there was sad news from Buckingham Palace. Surgeons had operated to remove one of the King's lungs. He was, said the bulletin posted outside the Palace, 'as satisfactory as could be expected'. These bland words were meant to reassure the people and they succeeded.

The long, dry, hot summer was almost over, the leaves of the trees on the Common were changing colour and soon the nights would begin to draw in.

Child bearing had brought few problems for Emma. Strong and healthy, she had sailed through her first pregnancy with no fuss or bother and in the first week in September gave birth to a fine baby boy. Born with dark hair and enormous brown eyes, he was a miniature of his grandfather.

'We have to name him Edward,' Emma had declared as she lay propped up on a pile of pillows.

'You'll get no arguments from me so long as you give him Frederick for his second name. Please my Dad, that will,' said Donald, acting the proud father.

About the same time Vicky got her way and she and Alex moved out of the flat above the offices in

Stockwell. They chose a detached house at Shannon Corner – the same area where David and Valerie and Emma and Donald had set up home. The houses were relatively new, with fair-sized rooms and a garden back and front. The 152 bus ran all the way down the bypass to Hampton Court, and if Patsy didn't feel like driving herself she could pick up the 152 bus at the Cricketers in Mitcham which would drop her off very near to all three of them. It was Ellen that she was still concerned about.

'She really does worry me, our Ellen,' Patsy confided to Amy one Saturday morning as they did their week-end shopping together. 'Not many Sundays when the other three don't turn up for their dinner or their tea, but weeks can go by and we don't get to see anything of Ellen and Robert.'

'Perhaps they're both working; she phones, doesn't she? You'd have heard if there was anything wrong.'

'Well, let's hope so,' replied Patsy. 'It's not as if I can just drop in on her like I can with the others. Robert told me outright that he'd rather we let them know when we'd like to visit.'

'Bloody cheek!' exclaimed Amy. 'You never told me that before.'

'Yes, well. Eddie said some of it's my own fault. I can't help it, I just don't feel right in his company. I miss Ellen, though.'

'I know what you mean,' sighed Amy. 'I sometimes think I'll never get to see our Laura again.'

'Oh, sorry love, I'm a selfish cow, going on about not seeing much of Ellen – and there's you with your girl off in America.'

Saturday was always the noisiest and busiest day of the week but today the market was unusually crowded. 'What's up?' asked Amy, turning her head to glare at a lad who had just bashed into her.

'Don't know,' said Patsy, 'but there seem to be a hell of a lot of police about.'

Suddenly they were swept along with the crowd. Despite their struggles they were pushed and pulled past the vegetable and fruit stalls, the wide-boys selling carpets, doormats and china, and the open-fronted fishmonger's and butcher's shops.

'Thank God for that,' said Patsy as they came out on to the wide pavement of the High Street and saw policemen forming a line on the kerb.

'What the hell is happening here this morning?' Amy asked in some confusion while rubbing her sore shin-bone.

'Don't you read your papers, darling?' a stocky bald-headed man asked. 'Churchill's coming!'

He didn't need to explain any further, because a big black open-top car had appeared and a great cheer went up from the crowd. Churchill was a sight to behold as he campaigned for the Conservative Party in the election that was to be held in October. Larger than life, he stood up as the car moved slowly through Clapham High Street. In black overcoat and top-hat, with white silk scarf, his chubby face wreathed in smiles and an enormous cigar clenched between his teeth, he didn't for a moment forget his famous wartime 'V' sign for which he had become renowned.

The Conservatives subsequently won the election by a narrow margin and Winston Churchill was once again the British Prime Minister.

As the year moved towards its end, the latest acquisition to the family was the apple of Patsy's eye and the star in Eddie's sky. Edward Frederick Langford was, as Florrie put it, 'A bloody lovely baby'.

At times Patsy felt guilty about her feelings for young Edward. Perhaps she poured out her love on him because he was their first grandchild – not that she would ever voice that thought aloud. Valerie was a marvellous daughter-in-law and young Timmy was loved by every member of the family. Or perhaps it was because the new baby had inherited all his features from Eddie. Whatever it was, she loved that tiny mite and seeing Emma just nursing him brought tears to her eyes. If only Ellen could be as happy . . . but Patsy knew she was not.

When Ellen did visit now, Robert hardly ever came

with her, and if Patsy attempted to ask questions of Ellen she would close up like an oyster. Patsy wished there was someone she could talk to about her daughter. She still couldn't determine in her own mind the extent and nature of her suspicions. How could a man act like Robert Dellor did? He was odd, queer, tight as a drum when it came to his family background. It wasn't natural, was it? The only person who would argue the pros and cons of the matter was Florrie, but she was the last one Patsy could go to, seeing as how she had hated Robert's guts from the moment she'd set eyes on him. The fact that Emma said when she saw Ellen she rarely spoke of Robert did nothing to quash Patsy's suspicions.

'And what have you got to go on?' Alex asked, when Patsy had broached the subject to her two boys.

'He's different to us, Mum, a doctor, very refined.' That had been David's summing-up.

'Yeah, thinks we're as ignorant as pigs,' was Alex's final word.

So there she had left it. It wasn't that Alex and David didn't love Ellen, there was deep affection between all four of her children, thank God; it was just that she had nothing explicit to confront Robert with. At least she had no worries about the marriages of her two boys; she couldn't have chosen better if she'd hand-picked their wives. All she would like from Vicky and Valerie were more grandchildren.

She'd been about to go into the scullery this morning when the door had been pushed open again and Alex had thrust his head through and said, 'You want to know something? It could just be that you're an interfering old mother-in-law.'

'Aw, Alex!' She burst out laughing. 'Go on. Get going.' Quickly she had picked up a tea-towel from the dresser and thrown it at him.

'On the other hand, you're a marvellous, kind and caring mother,' he'd said, laughing as he closed the door.

The business was doing so well it almost frightened Patsy. Did they all deserve to be so prosperous? Of course, full credit had to go to Ollie. If it hadn't been for him she wondered what sort of job Eddie would have ended up with after the war. Then again, without the money from his brother Jack, none of it would have been possible. From an outsider's viewpoint, everything had seemingly come to the Owens, through Alexander Berry. Not only did he have the two coach stations but he had extended the Vauxhall yard by acquiring two business premises to the right of it and a shop to the left. The business premises had served to enlarge the coach station, and the shop had been converted into offices downstairs and a flat above for one of the mechanics. Two more staff had been taken on to man that office. Both were men, which made for a great deal of friendly rivalry between them and Vicky and Patsy.

You didn't need brains to read the balance sheets for the Esplanade and the Gloucester at the end of the first summer season. Both had shown a profit. Patsy especially was more than pleased with the way things were progressing at Maplehurst too. Even Alex grudgingly agreed that it had been a wise move to buy the rest home. They had also been extremely lucky with the staff they had found; Mrs Wright and her cronies would soon have let them know had they not been entirely satisfactory. They assured her that the staff, from the Matron to the room orderlies, were kind and considerate. Nothing was too much trouble and the food provided was always delicious.

How was it, Patsy asked herself over and over again, that such a strong friendship had been struck between Florrie and the genteel Mrs Wright? Crikey, with the difference between them it was amazing.

Oh, that Florrie of ours. Was there ever another like her? Yet for all her bossy and cantankerous ways, she was a marvellous person, with a heart of gold and a reputation for never refusing to help anyone in need. On the other hand, Patsy was only too aware that Florrie couldn't express herself without swearing. It didn't bother Patsy; she had grown up with it and knew Florrie only had to get excited and her language became colourful. Rub her up the wrong way and Gawd 'elp you! Patsy laughed to herself as her mind went back years to the day when the Relieving Officer had come to Strathmore Street and suggested to Florrie and Gran that she, only thirteen years old, had neither kith nor kin, and he'd see to it that a place was found for her in an institution. A workhouse! Florrie's language that day had turned the air blue. None the worse for all that, Florrie was a good-tempered old softie – well, most of the time anyway!

With the coming of the new year, sadness struck the nation, and Patsy, in a very personal way.

On 6th February, a brief bulletin on the railings of Buckingham Palace announced that King George VI had died peacefully in his sleep.

Britain now had a new Queen. Princess Elizabeth was Queen Elizabeth. What would it be like having a Queen on the throne after all these years? The country was flourishing, bad memories of the war were receding, clothes were no longer rationed and the 'New Look' was ready to make its mark. Longer skirts and dresses, hats with veils, and new fashionable colours of yellow and green were what the young Queen had to look forward to, once she put the grief of losing her father behind her. May she reign as long as Queen Victoria did, was the general feeling of her people.

On the day when the funeral procession of King George VI was on its way to Windsor, Gran Day died peacefully in the front room of her house in Strathmore Street.

When Eddie came home and told Patsy she didn't say a word, but ran into the kitchen and, laying her head on her arms on the table, she burst into tears. She felt such a sense of loneliness. Try as she might, at this moment she couldn't imagine life without Grandma Day. To Patsy's way of thinking she had been the head of a large family, loving, kind and generous but never slow to speak her mind. She counted herself very lucky to have been part of that family. She rubbed her wet face along her crossed arms and Eddie heard her whimper like a child, 'I wish Gran hadn't had to die.'

Eddie put his hand on her shoulder and murmured softly, 'Oh, Patsy, Patsy, I'm so sorry.' His arms went round her and her sobbing grew louder. 'There, there, it's all right. It's all right,' he whispered softly, patting her back just as Gran, Ollie and Florrie had done when she'd been a child.

When she had cried it out and her sobs were quieter she raised her head and looked at him. Then she felt his fingers brush her damp hair away from her forehead and she shivered.

'Feel better now?' he asked.

She brushed the back of her hand across her eyes before saying, 'I'm sorry.'

'Oh, Patsy, don't be so bloody daft, what have you got to be sorry for? Don't you think I feel like bawling my eyes out?'

'Yes, I suppose so,' she sniffed.

'We won't be the only pair that's having a good cry this day. Grown men as well as women and kids are going to feel a great gap in their lives with Gran gone. She might have ruled the roost with a rod of iron, but even a blind man could have told how much she was loved – yes, and respected in more ways than one.'

'Oh, Eddie, thanks.'

'What the hell for?'

'For saying just the right thing at the right time. I feel all kind of empty like, but sort of more peaceful. She was a wonderful person wasn't she?'

'Never be another like her,' he said aloud but to himself he thought, only Florrie! Right well-matched pair, had Gran and Florrie been. Christ, Flo will be cut up. The worst thought that struck him now was what the hell would happen when they lost Florrie. He wouldn't relish the task of breaking *that* news to Patsy. By all accounts it was Gran and Florrie who had been there when Patsy was born. As it turned out, apart from Ellen – her mother – they and Ollie were the only family Patsy had ever known. It was understandable her being so upset; the three of them had fought tooth and nail for her when she was a kid.

They stood staring at each other and Eddie's voice was grim now as he said, 'I think we'll go and spend the evening with Florrie, she'll probably be glad of our company.'

'I bet Ollie will be there already,' said Patsy, reading Eddie's thoughts as she went off to wash her face and get ready to go to Tooting.

Chapter Nineteen

'THIRTY-THREE IS still a bit old. Course I'm happy about it, but I still say our Vicky will have to take care. Carry on like you've all been doing this summer, and I'm telling you, my girl, she'll never carry to nine months. Anyone would think we were all starving, hadn't a penny to our names, the way you lot dash about from one job to another, seven days a week. I ask you! Just look at you, forty-eight you are and the way you're carrying on you won't live another ten years. Oh, our Ollie, he needs his bloody head seen to. The bugger is sixty-nine, he started all this company lark but hasn't got the sense to slow down and leave most of the work to others.'

Patsy sighed; if she didn't stop her, Florrie would rant on for the next hour. 'Oh, for Christ's sake, Florrie. I come dashing down here to tell you that Vicky's pregnant and all you can do is lead off the deep end at me. Stop getting yourself up the wall; sit down, I'll put the kettle on and make us a cup of tea.'

'You'll do nothing of the sort. I ain't paralysed yet. Get out of me way.' She playfully pushed Patsy towards an armchair, then lifting the kettle from the hob she went towards the scullery, saying, 'I'll put it on the gas, it'll be quicker.' She pulled a face at Patsy as she went by and Patsy had to laugh.

Settling herself back against the soft cushions, Patsy closed her eyes for a moment. She did feel dog-tired; it was nice to have Florrie bossing her about for a change.

After a moment Florrie called out, 'Apart from Vicky's news, how's things?'

'Fine. Like you say, though, we've got more work than we can cope with.'

'Yeah. I heard 'em talking up the market about the day trips. Do well from the Leather Bottle, don't you?'

'Yes. You should be there one night when the coach draws in. Free-for-all it is. What with the kids waiting to greet their parents and old Harry Quinton putting on a band to encourage them all to stay and have even more booze, it's a wonder some of them ever make it home.'

Florrie's head came round the door and her voice rose still louder. 'Don't tell me you have to be there of a night-time to check the coaches home?'

'Course I don't. Once now and again Eddie and I have been down there for a drink.'

At this statement from Patsy, Florrie let out a roar of laughter, crossed the room and pushed Patsy's shoulder. 'Who are you trying to kid? Go down for a drink! What with Ollie and Eddie, between them they've got you on a bit of string. Like I said, you tell 'em you're going to ease up and, while you're about it, tell 'em I said it's about time they gave themselves a break an' all.'

Now it was Patsy's turn to put her head back and laugh. 'I'll tell them all right. By the way, kettle's boiling, scullery's full of steam.'

Florrie's body wobbled as she turned round quickly, crying as she did so, 'Go on, laugh, take the mickey, but don't come crying to me when you drop down dead.'

God! the things Florrie came out with, she really was a tonic! I'd have a job to come crying if I'd dropped down dead. Florrie had a store of sayings like that which never failed to make Patsy smile.

When Florrie brought the tray of tea into the kitchen Patsy said, 'How d'you feel about a holiday?'

'Not given it any thought. What've you got in your mind now, gal?'

'I thought if we went down and stayed at the Gloucester for a week, we might kill two birds with one stone. See for ourselves what the food and room service is like at the Gloucester, and do a bit of spying on the Maplehurst at the same time.'

Florrie came towards Patsy now, and bending over her, wagged a finger in her face as she said slowly,

'You ain't going to upset the apple-cart there, are you? Promise me there'll be no talk of closing the place if it's not showing a profit. Jesus only knows those poor old dears have been through enough, pushed from pillar to post, without you going down there to start meddling. I hear from Mrs Wright every other week, and she tells me they've never been so well treated.'

'Oh, you, Florrie!' Patsy pulled herself up straight in the chair. 'What d'you have to go and say a thing like that for?'

'Well, all I've been hearing for years now is how much profit this one makes and how much another one makes, but there's a darn sight more to life than making money. It isn't places that matter either, you know that, Patsy, it's people.'

'Florrie, trust me. Aren't you forgetting that it was me who found Mrs Wright and her friends – or rather, they who found me? Didn't I come home and nag away at Ollie and Eddie till they went down to Ramsgate to see for themselves? Though to be truthful about it, they didn't need much nagging.'

'Aw, I'm sorry, Patsy, love. I didn't mean to have another go at you. I know you've done real good for those folk; I wasn't knocking you. What can I say, it's just that . . .'

'Stop saying anything and pour out the tea.'

'Now look,' said Florrie as she handed over a cup

of tea. 'Did you mean it? That you'd take me down to Ramsgate for a week?'

'Well, not till I can find the time,' said Patsy, teasing her rotten.

'I knew it! Work bloody mad! A holiday, she says, but not till she can find the time. This year, next year, some time, never. What d'you want to ask me for in the first place?'

'Well now, Mrs Holmes, if you'll just shut your trap for a minute, I was about to say that we'd go not this coming Monday but the one after. Give you time to write to your friends and tell them we're coming, and that we'll have a right old rave-up with them while we're there.'

'Go on with you!' Florrie gave her a wide grin and said, 'D'you mean it, really?'

'Course I do. And I tell you what – we'll take them out and about every day, and I'll even buy them an ice-cream cornet.'

'I'll get me case out from under the bed then. Gawd, I'd better do some washing and ironing before I think about packing.'

Again they were laughing, only Florrie's laughter was still mixed with distrust; then suddenly she stood up and, throwing her arms about Patsy, whispered, 'Christ, I shouldn't have doubted you for a moment. You're good and kind, you are, Patsy. You've grown

so much like your dead mother, Gawd rest her soul
– more so every day.'

'Well, praise from the highest,' Patsy said, doing
her best to be flippant but not succeeding. Then in
a voice that was very soft, she went on, 'That's one
of the nicest things you've ever said to me.'

'It's true. Time and again, Gran and I used to say to
each other, you grow more like Ellen as time passes.'

The very mention of Gran and the conversation
came to a dead stop. Grandma Day! She had left such
a void in their lives.

'Come on, Florrie, I miss her too, but she wouldn't
have wanted us to be so upset. Life has to go on;
think about all the good times we had with her –
please, Florrie, please.'

The last words were a plea and they brought Florrie's eyes up to meet Patsy's. There was a pause then
before Florrie cleared her throat and in a gruff voice
said, 'Yeah, lass, I know what you mean.' Moments
later she banged her cup back down on its saucer.
'Bloody tea's stone cold,' she cried. 'Go on with you,'
she nodded her head towards the scullery. 'Move yerself and make a fresh pot for Christ's sake; you don't
expect me to drink that muck, do you?'

Suddenly it was the promised Monday morning, and
Eddie was saying goodbye to Florrie as he helped her

into Patsy's car. Feeling wistful because she was leaving him on his own for a week, Patsy hugged him warmly.

'It's only for seven days,' she told him.

Eddie said nothing, but continued to hold her close to him, pressing her head to his chest and stroking her shiny hair. Eventually he released her and stood back. He took his pipe from one pocket and his tobacco tin from the other, all the while watching her as she put her hand luggage on the back seat.

Patsy knew exactly what he was thinking. 'Why don't you come with us?' she said cheerily. 'Do you good to have a break – Christ knows you need one!'

Eddie's face changed ever so slightly. 'You know I can't, Patsy. Ollie's got that Peter Crawford coming over from Australia again, we've a hell of a lot of business to sort out with him.'

'Yes, I know. Sorry. It was just an idea,' she murmured softly.

His huge brown eyes stared down at her. 'I'll miss you, you know.'

Patsy had to laugh at his hangdog expression, which had brought that endearing little-boy-lost look to his still handsome face. 'Get on with you, you'll be out every night with Alex, having the time of your life.'

'Some hopes! Alex is a reformed character since

Vicky became pregnant. You let me know the minute you get there, and I want to talk to you every night. All you have to do is pick up a 'phone and call me. I'll be in. Promise me you'll do that.'

'Anyone would think we were going half-way round the world to hear you going on.'

'Promise?'

'I promise, Eddie,' she said, suddenly very serious.

'Drive carefully.' He bent low and kissed her tenderly.

Long after the car was out of sight he stood gazing into space. Even after all these years he hated Patsy to be away from him, and all he knew at this moment was that it was going to be a very long week.

With the coming of October Ramsgate wouldn't be so crowded, Patsy thought as she drove through the countryside. The autumn foliage of the hedges and trees was glorious — russet, red and gold mingled in the bright sunshine of an Indian summer. It was early afternoon when they reached the town and as Patsy drove along the cliff road she and Florrie were having the same thoughts. The bay looked magnificent, with the lovely view out to sea and the long line of cliffs glowing white and green in the autumn sunshine.

Florrie wound her window down. 'Cor, smell that

sea,' she said, taking a deep breath of the clean, fresh air. 'And listen to the seagulls.'

Patsy laughed at Florrie's excitement, as she too watched the gulls glide gracefully in, circling the shore, their cries echoing over the land.

'It's all a bit different from London, ain't it?' Florrie asked, then without waiting for a reply added, 'Everything looks so clean and bright.'

Yes, thought Patsy to herself, but put you down here to live and you'd soon be pining for the dirt and grime of dear old London. Like a fish out of water you'd be!

It did not take long for them to settle in. Patsy was really pleased with everything she saw, and although she was shrewd enough not to question the staff outright, over the next few days she did keep her eyes and ears open. Florrie would have been content to spend every minute of every day at Maplehurst. 'They've done wonders here,' she informed Patsy when she came to pick her up one lunch-time.

The elderly residents of the rest home fascinated Florrie, and in her chatty, friendly way she got to know them all and soon had them eating out of her hand.

Mrs Wright almost wept as once again she thanked Patsy for having been instrumental in securing them all such a lovely safe place to live. 'We've never been so happy, not for years,' she told Patsy as she sat with her friends in the lounge grouped round a log fire.

'D'you see what they're doing?' Florrie asked in a loud voice, a smile a yard wide on her face.

'Well, some of these ladies are knitting and others are crocheting,' Patsy observed.

'Yes, but can't you see, gal, they're all making baby clothes for Vicky; look at this beautiful dainty shawl.'

'How? They can't do that,' Patsy protested, but got no further.

'Who says we can't?' Mrs Wright challenged her and everyone in the circle smiled. 'I share Florrie's letters with all my friends,' Mrs Wright explained with a smile. 'There isn't much that we here at Maplehurst don't know about you and your lovely family, Mrs Owen. We are all hoping that Alex's wife has a baby daughter, seeing as how you already have two grandsons.'

Patsy was at a loss for words. She decided that the whole lot of them were a kindly, gentle bunch of saints. Then came their invitation, and although Patsy gazed at Florrie and protested, it was to no avail. They were giving a special dinner in Patsy's honour on Friday evening.

Mrs Wright reached over and rested her hand lovingly on Patsy's arm. 'You will come, won't you?' she implored. 'Please, everyone – including the men – has been planning this evening ever since Florrie wrote and said you were coming to Ramsgate for the week.'

Patsy shifted nervously in the chair and crossed her legs. She didn't need all their thanks, had done nothing to deserve it, and she felt extremely uncomfortable at the thought of all the effort they must have put into preparing for this invitation. Desperately wanting to let them know how much she appreciated their kindness, she smiled. 'Thank you,' she said, looking round at the whole group. 'I shall be very happy to come.'

Patsy didn't know whether to burst out laughing or to sit back and cry. It was just as if she had stepped back in time, for everybody present was attired in formal dress. The ladies had an appearance of faded elegance and each wore a sprinkling of jewellery, whether fake or not Patsy couldn't tell. Not all the men were in evening suits – some had dark trousers and a dinner jacket, others a dark blazer – but each wore a white shirt and a black bow tie.

Mrs Wright walked the length of the room with Patsy and made the introductions. Then, holding out a gallery-edged silver tray on which stood a solitary glass, she said, 'Will you take a glass of sherry with us, Mrs Owen?'

The motion was made with such dignity that Patsy

was tempted to put her arms around her, and felt near to tears as she accepted the sherry. As Mrs Wright moved away Patsy stared after her – such a small lady, her clothes were good but decidedly dated. Having joined Florrie, Patsy watched as they raised their glasses to each other, and for the umpteenth time asked herself what these two totally different women had found in common. She couldn't stop herself from smiling with amusement at the very thought of the genteel Mrs Wright and her beloved Florrie hitting it off so well.

When everyone had a glass of sherry Mrs Wright rose and said, 'Mrs Owen, we have elected Mrs Bradford to tell you of our reasons for asking you to join us for dinner this evening. So, without more ado, Mrs Bradford, you have the floor.'

A tall, elegant lady now stood in the centre of the room. The very simplicity of her black dress told Patsy that originally it must have been very expensive.

'Mrs Owen, we are all of us old but none of us are senile. We were lost but now, thanks to you, your husband and Mr Alexander Berry, we are safe in a very warm and comfortable haven.' She paused and looked around at her companions, her wrinkled face gentle and kind. 'We would like to show our appreciation in the only way we know.'

Every one of the residents got to their feet, then

Mrs Bradford raised her glass high. 'To Mrs Owen, our benefactor and our friend.'

Suddenly everyone was talking to her at once, but Patsy couldn't have answered to save her life. Her eyes were stinging, there was a lump in her throat big enough to choke her and all she wanted to do was get out of this room. She felt alarmed – was she now responsible for each and every one of these old men and women? No, I'm not, she told herself angrily, but she knew this was not true.

'Well?' Florrie was standing in front of her and her face was wreathed in smiles.

'Well what?' Patsy prompted.

'Don't you feel bloody good?'

'Should I?' Patsy hedged.

'Course you should. God works in mysterious ways his wonders to perform, and this time he used you to set this place up and to see to it that these old darlings had somewhere to 'ang their 'ats for the rest of their lives.'

In the face of such logic, Patsy asked herself, what could she do? She feasted her eyes on Florrie, still fat and blowsy, still loud-mouthed when it came to airing her views, but a mine of information and with a heart as big as a balloon. Nudging Florrie hard, she told her, 'I cottoned on to you a long time ago – you know that, don't you? You manipulate people into doing what you want them to, and you always seem to get your own way.'

'Not always, I don't,' Florrie argued with a glint of amusement in her eyes.

Patsy looked at her carefully, smiling a knowing smile, and said nothing. There was a tightness in her throat again as she wondered whatever she would do when she lost Florrie, because there would never be another like her.

Back at the Gloucester, Patsy decided she ought to ring Eddie before going up to bed.

'What's wrong?' she queried as soon as she heard his exhausted voice.

'Peter Crawford never arrived. There was a car accident on the way to the airport.'

'What? Where? An accident?'

'Yes, yes,' Eddie repeated. 'In Australia.'

'Oh. I'm so sorry.' Patsy straightened up, pulling her thoughts together. 'Was it bad?'

'Very bad, from what Ollie has been able to find out. Peter is seriously injured and Ollie is making arrangements to fly to Sydney.'

'Ollie is!' Patsy exclaimed, 'On his own?'

That was when Eddie dropped his bombshell. Patsy's hand holding the telephone receiver shook uncontrollably, and her heart began thumping against her ribs. In an unsteady voice she said, 'Did I hear you right?'

'Patsy, darling, what else can I do?' There was no mistaking his extreme agitation. 'I can't let Ollie go all that way on his own.'

'When? When will you be going?'

'Nothing's settled yet. Mr Topple is in touch with the offices in Melbourne. Depends when the travel agency can get us on a flight.'

By making a great effort, Patsy was in control again, aware that she had to cope with this tragic emergency just as much as Eddie did. 'Shall I come home tonight?' she asked, wishing she were back there right now.

'No, Patsy, there's no need for that. I don't want you setting out at this time of night. See to it that you and Florrie get yourselves a good night's sleep, then you can leave after breakfast in the morning.'

'All right, love, we'll be home by lunch-time.' She heard Eddie sigh and clamped her mouth shut, afraid to say any more.

'Good-night, my darling. See you tomorrow. I do love you.'

Patsy dropped her voice and whispered, 'I love you, Eddie. Good-night. God bless you.'

The idea of Eddie going to Australia and leaving her in London on her own horrified her – and Ollie would be going as well. I don't know how I'll ever be able to manage, she said to herself, yet she knew that not only would she have to but that she could and would, much though she would dislike it.

Chapter Twenty

PATSY RESTED HER arms on the dressing-table and stared into the mirror. She looked a mess: her face was drawn and her hair needed washing. For Christ's sake pull yourself together, she sternly told herself as she went downstairs to the kitchen and put the kettle on to boil. She made a pot of tea, drank one cup and stood staring down the garden, reflecting on the fact that they were now into November and it was almost a month since Eddie and Ollie had gone to Australia.

The days were bad enough, even though she had plenty to keep her occupied at the office. It was the nights that were so lonely. She couldn't get used to sleeping on her own, and no matter what anyone said she missed Eddie like hell. Her glance went towards the letter-rack, and she leaned across and took down the last letter she had received. Looking at the Melbourne postmark and the colourful stamps, she held it against her cheek for a moment, feeling the rush of tears to her eyes.

Eddie's news had covered five pages and Ollie had added two of his own. Gran had been fond of saying that when you have the sweets of life you have to put up with the sours. So she shouldn't moan really. All her family had benefited from the death of Jack Berry in one way or another. What a man Jack must have been! He had certainly had the courage of his own convictions when it came to business, and his interests had spread far and wide between New Zealand and Australia. Even all these years later things were still not completely sorted out.

Peter Crawford hadn't died, but with the terrible injuries he had suffered in the crash it might have been more merciful if he had. Patsy cast her mind back to when he had come to England soon after Ollie had heard of his brother's death. About the same age as herself, a stocky well-built man, tanned and good-looking, with bright blue eyes that always seemed to be laughing – that was how she remembered him.

Over the years, with Ollie having constant dealings with Australia, she and Eddie had learnt a lot about Peter Crawford. Apparently there was nothing that Peter didn't know about J. & B. Enterprises. At the time of Jack Berry's death Peter had been working for him for twenty-five years, and Jack had trusted him implicitly. Peter had been the young, go-ahead type for whom there was always room at the top. Now he had been struck down and very likely his business career was at an end. Patsy raised her eyes heavenward and prayed. Poor, poor Peter, help him, she pleaded.

Her thoughts were quickly scattered as she heard Kitty's voice calling out from the top of the stairs: 'Yoo-hoo, Patsy, love.'

Turning quickly, she rubbed at her eyes, went out into the passage and looked up into Kitty's face.

'I've got a nice bit of oven-buster, thought I'd do it with a batter pudding, just the way you like it. Seeing as how it's Sunday, we may as well have our bit of dinner together before all your tribe arrive for their tea. Come up about one o'clock, will you?'

'That sounds good. You've been busy this morning, haven't you, love? I'll be up before one, I'll pop along to the off-licence and get us a couple of bottles of stout. See you later,' she called over her shoulder.

With a flash of her usual smile Patsy thought about Kitty, who had taken on a new lease of life just lately. The doctor had suggested sun-ray treatment for her legs and hip joints. Now an ambulance picked her up regularly twice a week and took her to a clinic in Earlsfield. Whether it was all in Kitty's mind, or the heat treatment really was working, Patsy couldn't decide. Whichever, it had certainly made a vast difference to Kitty, if only that it gave her regular outings. These days Patsy was often glad of Kitty's company and felt a lot happier knowing there was someone else living in this big house besides herself. As she rinsed her cup and saucer under the running tap, the thought struck her that if treatment was available for an old woman such as Kitty, maybe her prayers might be answered and something could be done for Peter Crawford. If that happened, if Peter did start to improve, then perhaps Eddie and Ollie would be able to come home that much sooner. You're a selfish bitch, she chided herself as she fished her purse out of the dresser drawer and made for the back door to go and buy their stout. Life isn't like that; you can't make bargains with God. Please let Peter get better so that my Eddie can come home? Not very nice thoughts, especially it being Sunday and all.

With the two pint bottles of milk stout standing on the kitchen table and the clock on the mantelshelf showing it was still only a quarter to eleven, Patsy decided to wash her hair. She had let herself go to pot these past few weeks, and with the whole family coming for tea it wouldn't do for her hair to be so drab-looking. But with her head bent low over the scullery sink and her fingers deep in the froth of shampoo, Patsy suddenly began to sob. Eddie usually poured jug after jug of warm water over her head whenever she washed her hair, and she was thinking how she would sit on the floor between his knees while he dried it for her. When the long, thick hair was dry and sweet-smelling, Eddie would run his hands through it, letting it cascade over his fingers, and more often than not this would become a tender prelude to their love-making. Oh God, she missed him!

It was just three o'clock when Patsy opened the front door to Vicky and Alex, the first to arrive.

'You look pretty today,' Patsy murmured to Vicky as she bent down to push the door-stop in place, making sure the door would remain wide open.

It was true. Pregnancy obviously suited Vicky; in a loose floral dress, with her short hair brushed till it gleamed, she looked really bonny, and the fact that she adored Alex was there in her eyes for all to see.

'There's nothing to do,' Patsy told them as she ushered them into the front room, where the big old mahogany table was laid for tea. 'So sit yourselves down and you, Alex, can tell me what you've been up to that's kept you so busy you haven't found time to pop in and see me this week.'

'There you are,' Alex cried as he turned to Vicky, 'Would you Adam and Eve it?'

'What the hell's the matter with you?' his mother asked.

'Mother,' Alex began slowly, 'I told you last Sunday that I would be away all the week, down at Clifton-ville. Remember? Dad asked me to keep an eye on the way the extension to the Esplanade was shaping up.'

Patsy's cheeks flushed. Alex regarded her with a saucy grin and a mischievous twinkle in his eye and quietly said, 'Missing Dad, are you, Mum?'

She was saved from having to answer by the arrival of Emma and Donald. 'Grandma,' – chubby little hands reached out and Patsy went down on her knees so that Edward's arms could go around her neck. Next through the door came Tim, quite the young man with his fair hair sleeked back and wearing his Sunday suit with long trousers. As he placed a pot of deep pink cyclamen in her arms and held up his face to be kissed, Patsy hugged him tight.

Then Valerie, David and Florrie were next to come through the open door. Florrie went straight over to Vicky and dropped a daintily wrapped parcel into her lap. 'Baby clothes from Mrs Wright and her friends,' she said.

Vicky's eyes were swimming with pleasure as she got to her feet and placed a kiss on Flo's weather-beaten cheek. 'I'll open it after we've had tea,' she said in her quick, impulsive way.

Patsy was tactfully pretending to be looking up the stairs, waiting for Kitty to come down and join them, but in reality she was looking up the street, hoping against hope that for once Ellen and Robert might come for their tea. With a twinge that was almost a pain, she turned and went down the passage to make two large pots of tea. Why was it that one member of her lovely family always had to be missing?

Oh, Ellen . . . Only once had Ellen started to open up her heart. Patsy recalled how her face had lit up when she held Edward after he'd been born. Your turn soon, she'd told her, and Ellen's face had turned bright red. 'Robert doesn't want any children,' she had simply said.

So filled with pent-up emotion was Patsy that she almost scalded herself when she lifted the big black kettle from the gas stove and took it to where the teapots stood on the draining-board.

'I'll do that, Mum.' Alex reached across and carefully took the kettle from her shaking hands. She hadn't heard him come into the kitchen. 'All the tea this family gets through,' he said. 'Still, I suppose it's better than booze.'

Having filled both pots and placed the lids on them, Alex looked directly at his mother whose big green eyes were swimming with tears. 'Come on, Mum,' he said. 'It's not as if Dad was gone for good: he'll be home for Christmas, you'll see.'

Alex was drawing his own conclusions as Patsy made no answer. He wasn't that daft – sure, Mum missed Dad, but he'd bet a pound to a penny that it was Ellen she was worrying herself sick over. He didn't want to interfere, felt that he had no right, and what made it worse was that he had heartily disliked Robert Dellor from the moment he'd set eyes on him. Wasn't the kind of man that you could have a straight up-and-down argument with. He'd twist your words, you'd never get to the truth with that slimy bastard!

Before joining the family in the front room, he promised himself that he'd see how David felt about this matter and then the pair of them would make it their business to go and see their sister. If she was all right and wanted to be left alone, so be it, but if there was anything wrong with their Ellen, then Gawd help that husband of hers, for the least he could do was to let their mother know.

Patsy felt much better as she poured the tea and Emma handed the cups around. She loved this happy atmosphere; Sunday wouldn't be the same without her lot coming to tea. Everyone stayed with her until nine o'clock, and when all the goodbyes had been said she stoked up the fire and sat down to write her weekly letter to Eddie and Ollie.

Tuesday morning came and Patsy was seated behind her desk by nine o'clock. Today, however, her mind was not on business matters. For the third time that morning she reached into her handbag and took out the letter she had read twice already since the postman had delivered it to the house at half-past seven that morning.

'Dear Mum,' it started. 'Every time I see you I mean to talk to you about Ellen. I'm so worried about her and yet I can't put into words exactly what I feel is wrong.' She knew the contents almost by heart now. The last few lines had seared themselves into her brain: 'Mum, I tried to tell you on Sunday, when I last saw Ellen she looked so ill.'

Patsy sighed heavily. The times when she had wished that Emma had a telephone! Ollie and her father had both offered to pay to have it installed, but Donald had refused. She admired him, really; not a one to get himself into debt. His job on the buildings relied very much on the weather – couldn't lay bricks if it was frosty – and that meant he saved when he was earning it and didn't squander money unnecessarily. Still, she'd give a lot right now to be able to pick up the phone and have a good old heart-to-heart talk with Emma. The letter had only brought her own fears out into the open, and she knew something would have to be done. As soon as she had sorted out the pile of papers that lay in front of her she made up her mind that she would take the day off, go over to see Emma and then, whether or not Robert Dellor liked it, she would go on to Tolworth to see for herself just what was going on between him and her gentle Ellen.

Moments later the door to her office opened and Vicky entered carrying a tea-tray. 'Morning, Vicky, bit early with a cuppa, aren't you?' Patsy said mechanically, not really looking at Vicky, her mind still on the letter she'd had from Emma.

'Morning, Patsy, thought you could probably use a cup of tea.'

Patsy looked up quickly – this didn't sound a bit like Vicky. 'Is something wrong, Vicky?' Clearly the question was absurd, the very look on Vicky's face told Patsy that something was *very* wrong.

'Emma's been on the phone. She tried the house first, but she must have just missed you.'

Patsy had to beat down her panic. 'What did she say? It's Ellen, isn't it? I knew things weren't right, oh, why for Christ's sake didn't I do something about it before now?'

Vicky poured tea for both of them, her heart aching for her mother-in-law. Emma hadn't said much, but she had got the gist and she hoped against hope that things were not as bad as they sounded.

'Are you going to tell me what Emma said?' Patsy asked, her voice fraught with anxiety.

Hedging for time, Vicky crossed the room and held out a steaming cup of tea. 'Emma's going to phone back.' The shrill ring made Vicky jump but she breathed a sigh of relief. Thank God, now Emma could be the one to tell her mother what had happened to Ellen.

Patsy flung her arm across the desk and grabbed the receiver from its stand. 'Emma? How are you, love? Is little Edward all right? What are you phoning this time in the morning for? You're not ill, are you?' She knew she was being ridiculous, but she didn't care.

'Mum, Mum, will you calm down and listen to me?' Emma's voice was strangely quiet as she pleaded with her mother, and it brought Patsy back to some degree of normality. 'It's Ellen, Mum. She's in hospital.'

'How bad is she? What happened? Which hospital has she been taken to?'

'Mum! There's no way to dress it up. Ellen has tried to commit suicide.'

Patsy's heart stopped thumping against her ribs, the colour drained from her face and she had to open her mouth wide and gulp in a great breath of air. Dear God, don't let her die. Please.

The sound of Emma crying came clearly down the line, and Patsy fought hard to control herself. 'I'm coming,' she said firmly. 'I'll be there as soon as I possibly can.'

'I'm coming with your mother,' Vicky shouted into the mouthpiece, before taking the receiver from Patsy and replacing it.

Patsy almost ran down the stairs and Vicky had a job to keep up with her. By the time they reached the garage where she kept the car, Patsy was calling herself all the silly fools under the sun. Her decision had been to go straight to the hospital; now, regretfully, she admitted she had no idea which hospital Ellen had been taken to. The weather had turned colder and a stinging, icy wind tore at Vicky's hair, whipped her face and made her eyes water as she waited while Patsy fumbled to get the car unlocked.

'We'll have to go to Emma's first,' Patsy muttered as she let out the clutch and moved off. Trying to stifle a sigh, Vicky sat back, pushed her hands in the pockets of her coat and prayed hard that Ellen was not as bad as Emma had told her.

Neither of them spoke much on the journey and as they turned off the Kingston bypass Donald Langford appeared on the pavement before the wheels of the car had stopped. Patsy was relieved that he was at home and that he welcomed both her and Vicky with his usual warmth and friendliness. She was suddenly glad, after all, that they had come to Emma's first. Maybe Donald could tell her exactly what had happened to drive Ellen into doing such a terrible thing.

Emma was waiting in the narrow hall, fresh bronze chrysanthemums were arranged in a copper pot on a wall shelf, and suddenly Patsy's face was wreathed in smiles. This was a happy home, she told herself as her grandson toddled, arms outstretched, towards her. Dark-haired, with those enormous brown eyes, he certainly was a miniature of his Grandfather.

Patsy swept him up into her arms, cuddling him tightly. Emma held the door to the living-room open wide and, still carrying Edward, Patsy moved in from the hall.

'Oh, how lovely,' she said to Emma.

A blazing coal-fire was burning in the open grate. Patsy put the baby down and looked around, feeling as she always did when she came here: at ease. The furniture was nice, though not expensive, the curtains and carpet toning in well. Everything was spotlessly clean, but homely. Toys were scattered on the floor.

'Is Ellen going to be all right? Shouldn't we be setting off for the hospital?' Patsy began to bombard Donald with questions.

He put a restraining hand on her arm. 'Mum, slow down, take it steady. Ellen is going to be fine. Our next-door neighbour is going to look after Edward. Emma will make us all some coffee, we'll have a long talk and then after that we'll go and see Ellen.'

'I don't want any coffee,' Patsy said stubbornly.

'Okay, Mum,' Emma smiled thinly as she butted in. 'Just give me a few minutes to take Edward next door.'

Patsy waited as patiently as she could, wondering how much Donald was going to divulge about Ellen's married life. Undoubtedly he and Emma knew more than they had ever let on, and probably that was what they wanted to discuss with her now.

As if he had read her mind, Donald now cleared his throat and blurted out, 'Things haven't been right between Ellen and Robert for a long time. Emma's been out of her mind with worry. Honest to God, it got to such a pitch we didn't know what to do. The truth is that Robert's been on a path of self-destruction and he's managed to drag Ellen down with him.'

Patsy jumped to her feet. 'What d'you mean, self-destruction?'

'The way he's been carrying on, the situations he gets himself into and the diabolical stunts he pulls to get himself out of these scrapes. It's gambling mostly that's his main trouble.'

Donald saw the fear in her big green eyes, the pain washing across her face, and wished with all his heart that his father-in-law were here now instead of being half-way across the other side of the world.

As Emma came back into the room, Patsy flung one word at her. 'Well?' Emma exchanged a long, worried look with her husband, but made no reply.

'Tell me,' Patsy demanded. 'Is Ellen in Kingston Hospital?'

'She was.' Emma's voice was no more than a whisper.

'What d'you mean, she was?' Patsy screamed. 'For Gawd's sake, one of you tell me where she is.'

Donald fidgeted uncomfortably. He could see that he was going to be the one who would have to tell her. 'In a special hospital, out at Belmont,' he said as calmly as he could.

'Never!' Patsy yelled. 'That's not true.'

Both Vicky and Emma tried to put their arms around her but Patsy would have none of it. She bent double and put her head into her hands. Agonized sounds, like those of a wounded animal, came from between her fingers. Belmont! They weren't hospitals out there, they were madhouses. Her lovely gentle Ellen, the quietest and most timid of all her children, locked away in a madhouse. No, No, No, Dear God, don't let it be true!

It was some time before Patsy could raise her head and bring herself to ask, 'Is she a voluntary patient?'

'I'm not sure, Mum,' Emma answered, biting her bottom lip to stop it trembling.

Donald was watching Patsy closely. 'Oh, Jesus,' he muttered.

Emma gave him a quick frightened look.

'This beating about the bush has got to stop. For Christ's sake, let's tell your mum the truth.'

'You tell her,' Emma moaned.

'One of you'd better tell me,' cried Patsy.

Heaving a heavy sigh, Donald said, 'All right,

Mum. You'll have to know some time. If I begin at the beginning, will you hear me out?'

Patsy nodded her head while her thoughts ran riot.

With a nod to Vicky, Emma said, 'Come and help me make that coffee.'

Left alone with Patsy, Donald swallowed hard, brushed his hair back from his forehead and made a nervous gesture with his hands.

'Get on with it,' Patsy said impatiently, rubbing hard at her eyes with a handkerchief.

'Bob wasn't a bad bloke, not in the beginning he wasn't.' Donald's voice got lower as he continued, 'As I said, gambling was at the root of all his troubles. Each time he lost, he risked more money, hoping to recoup his losses. But of course, he never did. The bookies never lose, do they?'

Patsy flared up then. 'What has all this got to do with Ellen being out at Belmont, for Christ's sake?'

'Wait, Mum, please. You said you'd hear me out.'

'Sorry,' she murmured, clutching her hands so tightly that the knuckles showed white.

'Bob got himself into such a state, money wise. That led to him drinking, and things went from bad to worse. He . . . he started knocking Ellen about.'

Patsy couldn't remain silent. 'What! And none of you thought fit to tell me or Eddie about it?' Her poor Ellen, she must have been going through hell! Oh, Ellen, love, why did you have to pick someone like Robert to get married to? She couldn't bear the thought of Ellen suffering on her own, with no one to smooth the hurt away. Alex and David will kill the sod!

Suddenly she was crying without any restraint, a lot of the tears due to sheer temper by now. She turned her eyes to Donald's face and felt pity for him; it wasn't his fault. 'Please, go on.'

'Right, I'll do my best to cut it short.' His forehead was covered with cold sweat as he continued. 'With the bookies threatening God knows what, Bob took out a second mortgage on their house. He couldn't keep up with the repayments and after several warnings the Building Society gave notice that they were about to foreclose. Ellen was in the house alone when the letter arrived, and she opened it. It must have been the last straw. She hadn't even known about the second mortgage, and later when she taxed Bob with the letter he ran true to form – went out on a pub crawl, came staggering back in the early hours of the morning and laid into Ellen.'

Donald got up from his chair and Patsy felt the touch of his hand on her hair. For a moment she stayed quite still, then she raised a tear-washed face. 'Why, oh why didn't I know about all this before now?'

Donald took a great gasp of air. She thinks that's the end of the story. Bugger me, I wish to Christ we'd had the sense to get hold of Alex instead of letting her come here on her own. He gave a twisted smile. Too late. He couldn't stop now, or else he'd never be able to tell her the rest. Suddenly he raised his voice, startling Patsy. 'Mum, there's a bit more.'

All the colour had drained from Patsy's face and Donald thought she was going to pass out. 'Are you all right?' he asked, as he knelt beside her chair and took both of her hands between his own. All she could do was nod her head. Well, there was no way he could dress up the facts. So here goes, he said to himself, and his words began to tumble out in a rush.

'When Bob started punching Ellen, she had to do something to ward off the blows and she grabbed the nearest thing to hand, which happened to be a knife. Luckily or not, I don't know, she only managed to slash his arm. Really badly, though. The sight of the blood, or maybe the pain, whatever, he went mad. He kicked Ellen half to death.'

The silence was deafening: only the sound of Patsy crying and the crackling of the fire. Emma and Vicky hesitated in the kitchen doorway. 'Coffee's made,' Vicky mouthed to Donald, but he waved her to wait a while yet. Still not a word from his mother-in-law. He would have given a great deal not to have to say any more, but knew he had to. So, very quietly, Donald told her the worst part.

'Robert phoned the police and told them his wife

had gone berserk and tried to kill him. Ellen crawled to the bathroom, locked herself in and cut the veins in both of her wrists.'

Emma flew across the floor, put her arms around her mother's shoulders and clung to her. Trying hard to control her own sobs, she began to whisper, 'Ellen will be all right, Mum. You'll see.' Then, talking more to herself, she added, 'If the neighbours hadn't broken the bathroom door down, Ellen would have died.'

Patsy held tight to Emma's hand, but she couldn't control her own limbs. One foot was beating rapidly against the leg of her chair and she was unable to stop the tremor. It was a while before she could bring herself to speak, but finally she asked, 'Have either of you been allowed to see Ellen?'

'Yes, Mum, we both have,' Donald assured her. 'The police came and told us what had happened and then they took us both, in the police car, to Kingston Hospital.'

'She didn't know we were there,' Emma whispered.

'That was only because she was under sedation,' Donald was quick to tell Patsy.

'And since?' Patsy asked firmly.

Donald shook his head and Emma cried as if her heart was breaking.

'How did you learn that Ellen had been transferred to Belmont?'

'The police came here again early this morning.

That's when Emma went up the road and telephoned you.'

It took a great deal of will-power for Patsy to pull herself together. Eventually she stood up and smiled weakly at Vicky, who was still hovering in the kitchen doorway. 'Shall we have that coffee now, then you and I will go and find a phone box. Any idea where Alex will be today?'

'Yes. Funny thing is, Alex wrote down most of his movements for this week. I think he worries about me and the baby, though I keep telling him there's weeks and weeks to go yet.'

Donald Langford felt great admiration for his mother-in-law as he watched her take charge and pour out the coffee. He also felt a great sense of relief that the whole matter of poor Ellen and Robert Dellor was now out in the open. One thing though, he didn't give much for Robert's chances when the Owen brothers heard the full story. Bashing their sister was bad enough, but calling the police and suggesting that Ellen had tried to murder him! He might wish she had by the time Alex and David were through with him. He shook his head as he thought about this Cockney family he had married into. The whole bunch of them could be wonderful friends, but he'd bet his last penny that they could also be deadly enemies.

Chapter Twenty-one

SHORTLY AFTER THREE o'clock, David turned into the gravel driveway and brought his car to a halt. Patsy looked ahead at the hospital building for a moment before she stepped out. The grounds were well kept and even on this grey November afternoon the various evergreens and shrubs were a bright spot of colour.

The place seemed strangely quiet. She had expected noise, hustle and bustle, but nothing stirred and no people were about.

'Try not to upset yerself, Mum,' David said, then quietly added, 'You know, Mum, these places must do a lot of good. They're not half as bad as people tend to paint them.'

Patsy looked at her youngest son sharply. 'And you'd know, would you?'

David smiled grimly to himself. No, he didn't know. In fact he was wishing that he was anywhere other than in the grounds of this loony-bin. Why the hell did Alex have to be tied up this afternoon? Not that it would have been any easier for Alex to have to drive his mother out here to visit Ellen – that's if the doctors let her see her. David's head moved up and down a few times, jerkily, as though he was trying to wipe out the things he had been told. He had been horrified at some of the capers his brother-in-law had pulled, but to harm Ellen and drive her to the brink so much so that she had tried to kill herself – bloody hell, the bugger wasn't going to get away with that, not by a long chalk he wasn't.

Again Patsy glanced up at David's face and for the first time she realised just how upset he was. He was such a kindly young man himself.

'You go in with Mum,' David said, turning to look at his sister. 'Donald and I will wait here in the car.'

'Is that all right with you, Mum?' asked Emma.

'Of course,' her mother assured her, fully understanding both David's and Donald's reluctance to enter such a place.

Emma's conscience was troubling her as she walked beside her mother. She felt so guilty. Could she have done more? Could she perhaps have prevented what had happened to Ellen? She and Donald had known for a long time about Robert Dellor. She squeezed her mother's arm and smiled gently at her. Though relieved she was here, Emma wished with all her heart that her father was not so far away, nor her grandfather. God knows they'd soon take charge, and Robert Dellor would rue the day he'd hurt her twin sister.

Patsy didn't smile back. Her green eyes looked unhappy, distant. Only grim determination showed on her face.

Up the steep flight of wide stone steps, Emma rang the bell set in the wall beside the huge double oak doors. They had to wait a few minutes before the door was unlocked by a nurse.

Patsy's fears increased and she could hardly get the words out. 'I telephoned earlier. I'm Mrs Owen.'

Nodding her head slightly, the nurse smiled. 'Yes, of course. Doctor Leigh is expecting you. This way please, Mrs Owen.'

The cold chill to the inside of the hospital was different from the bitter cold outside. It was a chill that ate into one's very bones. The entrance hall was large and pleasant, the floor of polished wooden blocks. There were long, comfortable-looking sofas set against the walls and groups of armchairs set around small, circular tables. Patsy hadn't expected anything like this. It seemed more like an hotel than a hospital, but the sign at the gate had stated exactly what this place was and she was under no illusion.

'You can go right in, Mrs Owen,' the nurse told her as she opened a door on their right. Emma clutched at her mother's sleeve. 'I'll wait out here,' she whispered.

It was a good twenty minutes before her mother came out again and as Emma watched her shake hands with the doctor she could see Patsy had been crying.

Patsy took a handkerchief from her coat pocket, blew her nose hard and managed to smile weakly at Emma. 'Come on, love,' she said, taking hold of her arm. 'Doctor Leigh said we may see Ellen, just for a few minutes.' They walked behind the nurse, neither of them able to control the shudder that went through their bodies when they continually had to stand and wait while the nurse used a key to open heavy doors. Waiting again on the other side, the sound of these doors being relocked behind them seemed sinister. Finally, after a long walk down endless corridors, two doors were slid open to reveal a long ward containing many beds. There were no patients in the beds, all were neatly made up and crease-free. A group of women were seated around a central table, huddled together, staring listlessly into space.

A young girl came limping towards them, only to be waved away by the nurse. An older nurse stood by the window, and with her sat a sweet-faced young woman probably no more than twenty years old. Blonde hair and lovely blue eyes, she was humming quietly to herself, all the time gently swinging a rag doll by its leg.

Patsy's heart was aching. Her lovely Ellen, with her sunny, outgoing disposition, the exact replica of Emma, without the tomboy mannerisms yet with the same green mischievous eyes and the shiny dark brown hair that held chestnut glints. To think that she should be incarcerated in such a place as this!

At the far end of the ward, the nurse stopped at a glass-fronted side room. The heavy curtains at the window were tightly drawn and for an instant the nurse hesitated. With her hand still on the door handle she looked back over her shoulder and very quietly said, 'Mrs Dellor won't know you're here.' Then, still hesitating, she gave them a sorrowful smile and added, 'She's not a pretty sight!'

Patsy had thought about this on the journey. Kicked half to death, Donald had said. Now, from having listened to Doctor Leigh, she knew the explicit details of Ellen's injuries. Taking a very deep breath, she gritted her teeth and followed the nurse and Emma into the side ward. She heard a switch flick and a single centre light came on. Even so, it was moments before their eyes became accustomed to the dimness.

The room had no furniture other than one armchair discreetly placed in the farthest corner. The bed was central, but even that could scarcely be termed a bed; it was just a thick mattress raised only inches from the floor. The walls of the room had been padded and covered with a soft, pale blue fabric.

Patsy couldn't move. The nurse's hand on her arm broke through the shock and forced her forward. 'Sit down, sit down,' the nurse urged, pressing Patsy into the only chair. For several minutes Patsy hung her head between her knees, fighting the nausea rising from her stomach and the fear gripping her heart. Eventually, she dragged herself to her feet and stumbled towards the bed. Dropping down on to her knees, she stared at the face of her daughter.

It was true . . . God help her, it was true. Nothing had prepared her for this.

'Ellen!' The word came out as a sob. Tears gathered in Patsy's eyes and rolled down her face, into Ellen's hair that was all matted with blood, and on to the pillow as she faced the truth: Ellen was at death's door.

Emma stood trembling at the foot of the mattress on which her twin sister lay, and felt the blood drain from her face. The very sight of Ellen was dreadful, terrible, no one deserved to suffer such a beating as she had had to endure. She wrapped her arms around herself and shivered as the minutes ticked by.

Patsy had to press her fingers over her mouth to stop herself from screaming. 'Ellen.' Once more she whispered her daughter's name.

Ellen lay like a dead thing. Her forehead was bandaged, her face the colour of alabaster. Her lips were cut and swollen and her cheeks severely bruised. Her closed eyelids were ringed around with black and blue discoloration, all the more stark because of the strange whiteness of her skin. Both wrists were wrapped in bandages.

Leaning across Ellen's still body, Patsy lifted the hand that was lying limply on the sheet and held it to her own cheek. She waited for some indication of movement, for Ellen to speak or even just to sigh, to show some sign of recognition. Nothing.

'Please,' Patsy pleaded aloud, 'Ellen, love, open your eyes.'

Still nothing. She laid Ellen's arm gently back down on the bed as, unrestrained now, her tears fell on to Ellen's hand.

With two fingers Patsy lifted the edge of the sheet which was all that covered Ellen. Her body was naked, not even a nightdress.

Staring long and hard at the bruised body of her daughter, she almost choked and then squeezed her eyes up tightly, recoiling from the horror of it.

Patsy moved, shook herself, made a supreme effort to quell the queasiness that was rising in her throat, and with great deliberation laid the sheet back over Ellen. She no longer wanted to cry.

Anger, blind rage, hate for Robert Dellor, these were the emotions that were now tearing away at her inside. She remained there, on her knees, her head lowered between her hands as she prayed. Prayed like she had never done before in the whole of her life. *Please God, don't take Ellen. Please don't let her die.*

Prayers said, she made a vow: Robert Dellor was going to pay for this, by Christ he was! When Ellen had first met Robert she had been so young, bubbling with irrepressible laughter and filled with optimism about their future life together. Although she had never taken to Robert herself, Patsy had watched Ellen follow him around like a devoted puppy-dog, her eyes gazing at him full of adoration. She must have been seeing him through rose-coloured spectacles. Oh God, how could he have beaten and kicked her like that?

Patsy remained kneeling there, her head lowered between her hands.

The touch on her shoulder was gentle, but it still made her wince. 'You'll have to leave now, Mrs Owen,' the nurse said, her eyes full of compassion.

'What are we going to do, Mum?' Emma pleaded as they walked back to the main entrance through the long corridors.

For a fraction of a second Patsy wanted to scream out, 'Kill Robert Dellor, for a start.' Instead she said, 'All we can do is pray.'

Bad news travels fast. It was seven o'clock, the front room of Patsy's house held all her family, and several of her friends and neighbours had already called in to express their sorrow for Ellen and their loathing for her husband.

Stan Briggs and Ted Andrews had been all for going to Tolworth there and then. 'No bastard's going to beat Ellen senseless and get away with it,' Ted had declared.

Patsy had grimaced. For the moment she was doing her best to force her mind to work on practicalities, though to be honest all she wanted to do was confront Robert and tear him limb from bloody limb.

Alex was being unusually quiet. He was standing with his back to the bay-window, jangling his money in his trouser-pocket and seemingly staring at nothing. His eyes were red-rimmed, but they were dry, and on the surface he appeared to be calmer than David and very much in control.

'No visitors to Ellen for two weeks. Is that what the doctor himself told you, Mum?' Alex's question broke the silence that had settled over the room.

'Yes,' Patsy said bitterly. 'She'll be under deep sedation for at least fourteen days – that's what he gave as the reason.'

Alex nodded, understanding. 'Perhaps it's for the best, Mum,' he said. He went over to the cabinet, poured whisky into three glasses and carried them to the coffee table. 'Help yourself,' he nodded to David and Donald as he picked up one glass and drank most of the whisky in one gulp.

'Stop crying,' he ordered Florrie, his voice very abrupt. 'Crying is not going to help Ellen one little bit. We've got to make up our minds what's best to do, and do it quickly.'

'That's the problem,' cried Patsy. 'What the bloody hell *can* we do? Do I let your father and grandfather know?'

'Better not,' David interrupted. 'They'll go beserk. Besides, they're bound to feel right useless stuck thousands of miles away. No, we'll handle things somehow, and let's hope to Christ that Dad soon writes or phones to say that they're coming home.'

'Yes, I agree,' Alex said. 'Wouldn't be very fair. What could we tell them? And more to the point, what could they do about it? If they were to get reservations on a plane it would be days before they arrived. I promise you, Mum, we'll get it sorted.'

Patsy noticed that Alex's voice was very low and his hands were clenched into fists. Her eyes moved to David – he had gone crazy when Emma had quietly told him how Ellen was. Not a day would go by now when her boys wouldn't be seeking revenge for what had been done to their sister. Their grief at the moment was raw and if Ellen were to die! That was a possibility Patsy couldn't bring herself to face.

★

'Don't suppose any of you have had anything to eat today?' Valerie's tone was brisk as she held open the door with her bottom and Emma moved to take the tray of sandwiches from her.

Patsy made a face. 'It's good of you, love, to go to so much trouble, but I don't think I could get anything to stay down.'

'Nonsense!' Florrie struggled to her feet, glad to have something to do. 'You must try. You should put something inside you.'

'All right.' Patsy couldn't be bothered to argue, and she was very pleased as Vicky followed on bringing cups and saucers.

'Kettle's just coming up to boil, I'll make two pots, shall I?' Vicky asked.

Alex held the bottle of brandy over the rims of the cups, adding a generous nip to the hot tea. 'Here, drink this, Mum. It'll help you to sleep,' he said in the softest of voices, handing her the cup and saucer. 'Would you like me and Val to stay the night with you?'

'No, honestly, Alex. Thanks anyway,' she said, smiling up at his serious face. 'I'll be fine, really I will.'

Her hand trembled as she raised the cup to her lips. She blinked back the sudden rush of tears and wished that she could blot out the picture of Ellen lying almost on the floor, battered and bruised as if she'd been savaged by a wild dog.

Nobody had much more to say for the next half

hour as they drank their tea and ate their sandwiches. A deadly calm seemed to have settled over Alex, and David was exercising an iron control: even Donald was finding it hard to disguise how upset he was. Even so Patsy was well aware that all three were preparing in their minds exactly what plan they intended to put into operation.

As far as Alex was concerned his mother was right. Nothing he could do tonight, just see that Florrie stayed and that both she and his mother got a rest even if they couldn't sleep. Come the morning, that would be a different thing entirely. He made himself a solemn promise: there would be no idle threats. Posh Doctor Robert Dellor. Too high and mighty to come to tea with the family in Clapham on a Sunday. Well, that had never bothered him. The farther Robert kept his distance the better he'd liked it.

Now Alex thought about all the hours his mother had spent worrying over Ellen. How he'd never taken any notice when she'd tried to tell him how vulnerable and fragile she was. In spite of himself he shivered as he went over in his mind the details Donald had related to him of Ellen's injuries. You've gone too far this time, you bugger, Alex said to himself, far too far. Ellen had slashed his arm, had she? Well, that was a minor scratch compared with what he was going to do to bloody Doctor Dellor!

Sons were sons and they could make all the plans

they liked, and Patsy promised herself that this was one time when she wasn't going to interfere. One thing she was adamant about though: she was going to be at Tolworth tomorrow morning to confront Robert in person.

'Excuse me,' Patsy said as everyone was preparing to leave. 'No one's bothered to ask so I'm telling you, I'll be at Ellen's house in the morning.'

'Oh no, you don't want to put yourself through that,' exclaimed Alex. Patsy gave him such a look that he sighed. There would be no point in trying to argue with his mother.

'I'll take Florrie to Emma's; she won't mind staying with Edward, and then Emma and I will meet you at Tolworth. Just say what time.' Patsy firmly stated her intentions.

Inwardly Alex sighed again. The last thing he wanted was women around when he caught up with Robert, especially his mother! He looked at his brother who nodded slightly and resigned himself to the fact that his mother would brook no argument. In the end he said grudgingly, 'I'll meet you at the roundabout at twelve o'clock.'

'Mum, why must you always have your own way?' David whispered as he gently kissed her good-night.

★

Florrie was in her element as she lifted young Edward up to sit on the draining-board and let him dangle his chubby little hands in the soap-suds. Patsy left them to it and went back into the living-room. It was barely ten o'clock yet, and it wouldn't take them more than twenty minutes to get to Tolworth. Now she stood watching her daughter. Emma was seated on the edge of an armchair, her elbows on her knees, her face buried in her hands. Patsy realised that Emma had had a rotten night and probably not slept a wink – and no wonder, having seen the awful state her twin sister was in, knowing that she'd more than likely be locked away in that terrible place for a very long time.

'Come on now, love. You mustn't go on blaming yourself.'

Even as Patsy spoke the words, she was taking most of the blame on herself. The signs had been there and she had chosen to ignore them. Didn't want to be classed as an interfering mother-in-law, so she had done nothing. Ellen was and always had been such a gentle person. Although she and Emma were identical twins, there was a vast difference in personalities and of the two, Ellen had always been the more sensitive.

Like Emma, Patsy had found sleep impossible, had tossed and turned all night long. The shock of seeing Ellen as she was was indescribable. She felt utterly weary . . . so inadequate. She so badly wanted to do something, she must do something, but what?

'Oh, Mum.' Emma raised her head, tears welling from her eyes and trickling slowly down her cheeks.

'You look as sad as I feel, darling,' said Patsy, putting her hand out and touching Emma's wet cheek. She lowered herself down to sit on the floor at Emma's feet. They took hold of each other's hands and stared at each other until Patsy said, 'Life is full of regrets, my love. We can all be wise after the event, and with hindsight, recrimination always comes, but you mustn't be so hard on yerself.'

As Emma let go of one of her hands and brushed hastily at her eyes, Patsy took the opportunity to ask, 'How long has it been going on?'

Emma shook her head. 'I don't know, Mum. I've never been sure. More than likely for some time. I wish I'd plucked up the courage to talk to you before, then perhaps you and Dad could have put a stop to it and Ellen wouldn't be in this bloody mess. But to be honest, I did try tackling Ellen and she said I should stay out of it.'

Patsy nodded. 'I should have done more, I've had my suspicions long enough.'

Emma shifted in her chair and leaned forward slightly. 'Now I've made you feel guilty, Mum, but it wasn't your fault. I've only ever had little things to go on. Ellen never complained, and whenever me and Donald broached the subject she would never give us direct answers. She always gave what at the time seemed plausible explanations for her bruises. As for coming to see you and Dad, the times I've pleaded with her to come for tea on Sundays! "Robert doesn't like family get-togethers," was all she'd say.'

Patsy was by now wrapped up in misery and she fought it off by getting angry. 'What the hell was wrong with her? Why the bloody hell did she put up with the sod?'

'Honestly, Mum, I think Ellen worships the ground that Robert walks on. She must do! She's overlooked so many things, things that anybody else in their right mind would have walked out on him for years ago.' Seeing disbelief in her mother's eyes, she raised her voice and said with great firmness, 'I'm not exaggerating, honest I'm not, Mum.'

'Has he always had this habit of hitting her?' Patsy asked bleakly.

'I don't think so; he's too crafty for that. Though, looking back, Ellen often had nasty bruises. Another reason why I think she has covered up for him so often is because she didn't want to cause trouble between Robert and Donald. They've never been bosom pals, but Robert never seemed to object to her coming here to see me and he would always collect her in his car. Always came in and had a chat with Donald. Don't suppose Ellen wanted to change all that.'

'Alex is parking his car round the back,' Florrie said, her voice tinged with relief, knowing that Patsy was in no fit state to be driving on to Tolworth – and Gawd knows what she'll be like when she's had a set-to with that sodding husband of Ellen's, she thought.

Alex came straight through the back way into the living room, and threw himself down in an armchair. 'I was early, thought I'd pick you up from here – don't need to take two cars!' He nodded his head at Florrie but before he could say, 'how about a cuppa?' Florrie beat him to it.

'I'll put the kettle on and you can all get yourselves ready while I make a pot of tea.'

'Put a bit of make-up on your face,' Florrie called up the stairs to Emma. 'And do your hair nicely – don't want that sod to think you've been awake all night because of 'im.'

Patsy was putting her hat on, checking in the hall mirror whether it was straight, when she heard a key being turned in the front door and Donald came in. He saw the quick look of apprehension that flashed between Florrie and Patsy. 'It's all right,' he quickly reassured them, 'David couldn't get here and I'm only coming to make the numbers up.'

'Thanks, Donald,' she said gratefully, aware that he would do his best to see that Alex didn't overstep the mark.

*

Patsy sighed heavily as she got out of the car and looked at the house. It was a detached home in one of the best parts of Surrey. All this going for them, and still the marriage hadn't worked.

When Robert Dellor first opened the door to them, Patsy almost felt sorry for him. His arm was bandaged high to the armpit and held up by a sling. Shock registered on his face and he fidgeted nervously with the lock of the door.

Without saying a word, Alex pushed him aside and once inside the hallway he motioned with his head for all of them to come into the house. Then he led the way, past a hall table with an arrangement of pot-plants, into a room at the front of the house – a huge room with a wide bow-window which had leaded lights set into it.

The state of the room shocked them all. The mess was awful. Every chair and most of the floor was littered with cast-off clothing and old newspapers. The grate held nothing but the dead and grey ashes of a burnt-out fire.

Robert stood in the doorway, stammering and stuttering about what he was going to do. When Patsy crossed the room and stood face to face with him, she could hardly believe what she saw. It was some time since she had set eyes on him and the change was awful. His face was bloated and he had put on so much weight.

'I'll ring the police if you don't all leave my house at once,' he managed to say at last.

Patsy, Emma, Alex and Donald all stared at him in disbelief, and he had the grace to let his shoulders slump and his head drop.

Pushing his mother aside, Alex had to force himself to speak rationally. Robert's threat had sent a feeling of shock surging through him which could so easily erupt into blind anger. 'Fond of the police, aren't you? I hear you're bringing serious charges against my sister.'

'You're dead right I am,' he answered with a sudden dash of boldness. 'Ellen tried to kill me.'

'Pity she didn't succeed!' Emma spat the words at him.

Robert turned angrily to where Emma stood and as she watched him coming towards her every muscle in her body stiffened.

Alex's arm shot out but Donald's move was faster, putting himself in front of Robert with his back to his wife. 'I wouldn't if I were you, Bob,' he said, his voice deceptively quiet. Quickly but very firmly he placed one hand under Robert's armpit and tightened the other on Robert's wrist, wrenching the hand backwards until the fingers were almost touching his shoulder-blade. Holding the grip, Donald pushed Robert back until he was forced to sit down in an armchair.

Robert did his best to struggle, even taking his bandaged arm out of the sling, but gave up and swore. Donald bent low until his face was almost touching Robert's. No one else in the room heard the words that he spoke, he uttered them in such a low voice.

Slowly, very slowly, Donald loosened his grip and straightened up. Contemptible! That was the only word that came into Patsy's mind as she watched the cowardly bugger cringe back into the cushions of the chair. Suddenly he put out a hand to grab at Patsy's arm. He was blubbering now. 'It's not been all my fault. I . . . I . . . I had a run of bad luck.'

Oh, Patsy groaned to herself as she listened to him whine. How can anyone cope with a man as twisted as he is? She knocked his hand from the sleeve of her coat.

Alex and Donald had retreated to the far wall where leaning back, hands in pockets, they both kept silent.

Robert was mumbling away to himself. 'Nobody knows the amount of debts we've got. We're going to lose this house. I don't know what we'll do. A lot of it's been Ellen's fault.'

'*Shut up, you lying bugger!*' The words spurted from Emma's lips. All her bottled-up feelings had now come to a head and there was no stopping her. 'This sanctimonious act you're putting on for my mother won't wash. *Tell my mother – go on – tell her.*' Emma's voice was high-pitched now as she screamed at him, but no one made any attempt to stop her.

'Tell my brother too, while you're about it. Tell him how Ellen's gone back to nursing: twelve-hour night shifts she's been doing, seven days on the trot. *And for what*? To pay off your damned bookmaker's debts!'

Patsy heard herself gasp, but she was more concerned about Alex's reaction. He was staring at the carpet; she couldn't see his face but his clenched fists were beating against the sides of his legs.

Hatred was blatant in Robert's eyes as he gaped at Emma, but one glance at Donald and he made no further move towards her.

Emma hadn't finished, and the accusations came pouring out. 'Don't forget to tell my family all about your drunken bouts. The excuses Ellen's had to make to the hospital time and time again, because the only way you could have got there would have been if you'd have crawled on your hands and knees. Tell them what happened to the silver photo frames our dad bought each of us when we were twenty-one. Like a lot more of my sister's personal belongings, you bloody well sold them!'

The pins had fallen from Emma's hair, her face was bright red and her breathing sounded laboured as she flung her final words at him. 'Seeing as how my father's not here – and you should bloody well count your lucky stars that he's not – why don't you finish the story and tell my family about your other women?'

While Emma stood gasping for breath, with her chest heaving, Patsy, Alex and Donald watched Robert's face flush a deep red and then slowly turn a pasty grey. They saw his hand come up, clawing at the air, and for a moment they all thought he was having a stroke. Then he seemed to recover slightly. Keeping a tight rein on her feelings, Patsy went out of the room to the kitchen to fetch him a drink of water.

Her worst fears had been confirmed. Why, oh why, had Ellen put up with it for so long?

The draining-board was littered with dirty crocks. Patsy turned on the tap and rinsed a cup beneath the running water. She wondered if there was any ice in the fridge.

'Smoke salmon and caviar!' she muttered, as she saw what lay on the shelf. 'I've a bleeding good mind to sling it all down the toilet. All I hope is that if it doesn't choke him, at least he'll get sodding food poisoning.'

Back in the sitting-room Patsy had a strong urge to throw the water over Robert's head. Instead she handed him the cup and he had the grace to say, 'Thank you.'

All Patsy felt was loathing. She was so angry, she wanted to hurt this fat bastard – hurt him as he'd hurt Ellen. Given a weapon, she could so easily kill him!

'I think we'd better get going.' Alex's voice, hard as steel, broke the silence. 'A word of warning, Robert,' he said, standing his ground directly in front of the other man. 'Now is not the time nor place, but you'll get your deserts. From the law? Well, grievous bodily harm will do for starters. From me and my family? We'll take care of you, that's a promise.'

Again Robert Dellor looked as if he were about to have a heart attack. No one took any notice as they left the room and went out of the front door. Patsy and Emma thankfully took a deep breath of cold air. They both felt drained, and they stood still on the gravel driveway to recover.

'Clear off!'

Robert's voice calling from the still open doorway made Patsy start, it sounded very menacing as he persisted. 'Clear off, go on, get off my property and don't any of you ever dare to come back. You're scum! The whole lot of you.'

Alex swivelled on the ball of his foot, his elbow came up high and his clenched fist was drawn back over his shoulder. He covered the distance to the front door in two long strides; his arm swooped through the air and the 'Whack' as his fist made contact with Robert's face had Patsy recoiling in horror. She watched as Robert staggered backwards until his legs met the staircase and he crumpled to the floor. His head lolled to one side and the lower half of his face was a bloody mess.

Alex took a clean handkerchief out of his pocket, folded it lengthways and wrapped it round the knuckles of his right hand. Donald looked at him, they both grinned, then Donald took a firm hold on the handle of the letter-box, gave it a sharp tug and slammed the front door shut.

Chapter Twenty-two

'ALEX BRINGING YOU here was in answer to a prayer, Florrie. I didn't realise just how lonely I was,' Patsy said as she pushed her empty plate to one side and leaned back in her chair.

Even the living-room looked different now that she wasn't spending hour after hour on her own. Instead of eating off her lap, Florrie had insisted that she lay the table, placing a clean starched white cloth over the dark green chenille cover on the scrubbed table top. The fire was well banked up, the big black kettle singing away on the hob, plants in pots on the edge of the dresser and fresh flowers in a jug on the window-sill. Everything looked so right . . . but the truth was that everything was so wrong.

Florrie had been up at Clapham for two days and had every intention of staying put until Eddie came home. Left to her own devices, it would have been Patsy who'd be the next one to end up in hospital; cups of tea and slices of toast was all that she'd been living on. I'd take a bet a decent meal hadn't passed her lips for days till I set foot in this kitchen and got the oven going, she mused as she set an apple pie down on the table.

Florrie's heart ached for Patsy. God knows what she'll do if Ellen dies. Come to that, what if Ellen has suffered brain damage? Ends up being nothing more than a vegetable? It didn't bear bloody thinking about. She knew Patsy would rather die than voice that fear aloud, but she was well aware how Patsy was spending her nights. Walking about her bedroom, coming downstairs in the early hours of the morning so that I wouldn't hear her crying, but of course I hear her sobbing her heart out. I'm not deaf, not yet I'm not.

The anger was rising in Florrie as she watched Patsy now. Worn out with worry, not allowed to see Ellen for fourteen days and still eight days to go. Alex and David popped in and out every day; the first words they said were, 'Have you phoned the hospital, Mum?'

Course she'd phoned the bloody hospital, if you could call it that. Dress it up how you like, it's still a bleeding loony-bin that sod has put our Ellen into.

'Holding her own,' was what the nurse on the other end of the phone said every damn time. What was that supposed to mean, for Christ's sake?

If Florrie had spoken aloud what she was thinking about Robert Dellor, the very air in the kitchen would have turned blue. The man was a bully and a coward 'n' all. Kicking Ellen! Indignation flared across Florrie's face. She grabbed the pie slice in her work-roughened hands and began to jab away at the pie.

'Steady on, Florrie, you're spoiling all the pie-crust,' Patsy said, knowing exactly what was going through Florrie's mind.

'Yes, I know. I was thinking about what Robert Dellor had done to our Ellen. Treated her like a doormat, and she put up with it for so long. I know I shouldn't be talking about him, you've enough on your mind without me putting me two pennyworth in, but I can't 'elp it. I wish to God I could get my 'ands on him. By Christ, I'd have a go!' A great sob burst from Florrie's throat. 'We just got to keep on hoping and praying that Ellen will come through all of this.'

It was no use, Patsy broke down. The tears held tight inside her until now, suddenly overflowed.

Florrie held out her fat arms and drew Patsy against her large bosom. 'There, there, love, let it all out.'

And out it did come, pouring out. 'I knew Ellen wasn't happy. The few times I did get to see her, there was always such a terrible hurt expression in her eyes. I knew I wasn't imagining it, yet I did nothing about it. Now look what's happened. Robert's half killed her, she's gone for him with a knife and now my poor Ellen is locked away in a mental home. I have to live with all of that now. I'll never get the picture out of my mind. I can see her, Florrie, I can, lying there on that floor and him kicking her, having already used her face as a punch-ball. That wasn't bad enough, was it? He kept on at her so much that she dragged herself off to the bathroom and slashed her wrists. Then lying there, waiting to die. She didn't deserve it, did she, Florrie? Ellen never did an unkind thing to anyone in her life.'

Florrie looked long and hard at Patsy as she drew away and went out to the scullery to wash her face. By God, she was glad she was there. Who else could Patsy talk to? Who was there to listen? She cringed at the thought of how Patsy was torturing herself. Why wasn't Eddie here? There'd never be a time when he was needed more – and him half-way across the other side of the world and Ollie with him. Christ Almighty! Neither of them knows! Leaning forward, she poked the fire so fiercely that a piece of coal dislodged itself and fell through the bars of the grate on to the hearth, sending up a shower of sparks.

One thing was for sure – there would be a great many more sparks flying when Eddie and Ollie did set foot back in this country.

Patsy had forgotten what a miserable month November could be. It was very much winter now, with damp short days and always the threat of the old fog rolling in off the Thames. The last fourteen days were the worst that she had ever had to live through. Thank God they were over and she was on her way to Belmont now to see Ellen. She was so looking forward to seeing her, to being able to tell her how much her sister and brothers loved her, that they would be coming to see her as soon as she was allowed more visitors. Hoping against hope that Ellen would be awake, no, more than that, Ellen must be able to talk to her, to smile up at her with those eyes no longer showing fear or pain. What would she find when she arrived? God, she was dreading going into that awful place!

She drove slowly through the big iron gates, parking her car on the gravel path with its front wheels touching the damp grass. Inside her there was a burning anger, an emotion very different from the despair she had been feeling when she left home. The police had called very early that morning and after going round and round the subject had finally got to the point, which boiled down meant that the charge of attempted murder against Ellen was being dropped. Thanks very much, she had managed to mutter, albeit very sarcastically. What about the injuries her daughter had sustained? They would be dealing with that matter at a later date, when they had the Doctor's full report. Well, she might have to be satisfied with that for the time being, but nothing – and I mean nothing – or no one is ever going to hurt Ellen ever again, she vowed, not while I'm alive.

She hadn't left much room between her own car and the one next to her, so she had to go round in front of the bonnet and slither down the grass bank. Oh, hell! Her high heel had caught in the mud and she'd splashed her stockings as she wrenched it free. 'Sod it!' she swore out loud. She hoped it wasn't an omen that nothing was going to go right today. Angrily she took out her handkerchief, spat on it and rubbed the back of her leg.

A little way up the drive Patsy fell into step with a small red-faced woman in a coat that looked as if it had been made during the war from an army blanket. Her hat didn't look much better either.

'Haven't seen you here visiting before,' the woman said in a kindly, polite voice.

'It's my first time,' Patsy told her, giving the woman an uneasy smile.

'Oh well, you'll get used to it. Two and a half years I've been coming here. Don't know why I bother sometimes. There's times when my daughter don't know the time of day, never mind whether I've been to see her, but when it's your own flesh an' blood, what can you do?'

The forlorn look in this mother's eyes frightened Patsy. 'You mustn't give up hoping,' she said, trying to step round her.

God above! Two and a half years!

She was going to stay angry. Angry at Robert Dellor, angry at Eddie and Ollie for not being there when she needed them both so badly, angry at the police for not locking Robert up and throwing away the key. She wasn't going to try, as Florrie kept telling her, to look on the bright side, because there wasn't any bright side as far as she could bloody well see. Anyway, being angry – she decided as she climbed the stone steps and entered the main hall that smelt strongly of wax polish and disinfectant – was a thousand times better than the numbing misery she'd been wallowing in for the last two weeks.

'Mrs Owen, would you like a cup of tea before we set off for the ward?' Patsy wasn't given a chance to reply as gentle hands pushed her to an armchair and the same nurse was saying. 'Here's your tea. Drink it while it's hot.'

Patsy's hand trembled so much that the nurse took the cup away from her and the Sister in the flowing cap who had steered her to the chair spoke for the first time. 'I think it will be best if I take you to see Ellen and we'll talk later.'

You haven't let me see my daughter for fourteen days, and now I am here you think I want to sit and talk! Patsy risked a quick glance up at the stern face of the Sister who was obviously in charge, and thought it was a good job that she hadn't voiced the words aloud. In a place like this it would probably be better if she did her best to keep on the right side of the people who were taking care of Ellen. At least for now, she muttered to herself.

Ellen was in the end bed on the right-hand side of the long ward. As Patsy walked by she saw that at least a dozen beds were occupied today. Visitors sat at the bedsides clasping the hands of the patient between their own. Any conversation was being carried out in whispers. She couldn't help wondering how long it was, if ever, since any laughter had echoed through these long wards.

Ellen lay, as if asleep, propped up high on a mound of pillows. Quickly Patsy put down her bag which held all the fruit, presents and letters from the family, friends and neighbours. Very gently she leaned across the bed and put her lips to Ellen's forehead. She might have been kissing a wax model, there was no reaction from Ellen at all. Patsy felt as if her heart was breaking as she drew back and stared at Ellen's face. She certainly looked a damn sight better than she had two weeks ago, but the bruises on her face were now a sickly yellow, giving her a jaundiced look, and her mouth was still swollen and bit lopsided where Robert's fist had cut her lips.

Patsy drew a chair to the side of the bed and sat down. She undid the buttons of her navy-blue jacket and smoothed down the front of her white silk blouse, then she took hold of Ellen's hand that lay lifelessly on top of the sheet. Quietly she began to talk to her daughter.

'You're looking so much better, my darling, we'll soon be able to take you home and when you're really feeling fit your dad and I will take you on a long holiday. Where would you like to go? Grandad will be in to see you as soon as he gets home. You love your grandad, don't you? He adores you, even though you and Emma twist him round your little fingers. Your brothers were going to come today, but as it's the first time the doctor said only one visitor. It'll be different next week, you'll be up and about. I'll bring you some nice new clothes. Alex said he thinks you're skiving – fancied a rest, a few days in bed. I boxed his ears for you.' She broke off, she had to. The lump in her throat was choking her and despite all her good resolutions not to cry her eyes were brimming over. Bending down she reached into her bag, but it was some time before she could go on.

'Look,' she laid a book near to Ellen's hands. 'Timmy sent you *Wind In The Willows*, he's doing it at school; he says his Auntie Ellen will love it.' Lifting up a small posy of yellow freesia, Patsy held them near to Ellen's face. 'Smell them, Ellen. Aren't they beautiful? Emma said to tell you they're from young Edward, as he misses you so much.'

It was no good. She wasn't getting through and

fear swamped Patsy as she contemplated the fact that perhaps Ellen might never be normal again. She spread her arms out, laid her head down and just let the tears flow. When the bell rang, telling visitors to leave, Patsy wasn't sorry.

'I'll walk with you to the entrance,' the stern-faced Sister told Patsy as she firmly grasped her arm. 'The doctors are sure that there'll be no lasting scars to Ellen's face.' She spoke kindly, but her next words confirmed all Patsy's fears. 'It will be the mental scars that will take time to heal.'

Driving home, Patsy cursed Robert Dellor and again, for the umpteenth time, she wished that Ellen had never met him.

Chapter Twenty-three

THREE WEEKS HAD drifted by and Ellen was no longer heavily sedated. Still in the long-bedded ward, but up and walking about during day-time and still only allowed visitors once a week, on Sunday afternoons.

Each week, Patsy longed to put her arms around her and hold her close but she had to curb this longing. Fear was a terrible thing and Ellen was still filled with it. There were times when it seemed as if she was still thrashing about in torment – in darkness so deep that even her own mother was not able to penetrate it.

Tragedy had struck at Patsy many times in her life, but nothing had caused her so much heartache as the waiting and watching for some sign that Ellen was on the mend.

'She needs something to jolt her out of this apathy, give her the will to live again,' the doctor had kindly explained to Patsy.

'A miracle wouldn't come amiss,' had been the only answer that Patsy could come up with.

Two more days and we'll be into December, was

Patsy's savage thought as she heaved herself out of bed that morning and gave up all thoughts of trying to sleep. Downstairs she filled the kettle and stood watching the birds in the garden while she waited for it to boil. There was a robin amongst the sparrows and his bright red breast made her think of Christmas cards. Strange she hadn't given a single thought to what they would be doing for Christmas.

'What the hell?'

With Ellen as she was and Eddie and Ollie still in Australia, she'd no heart for making preparations to celebrate.

Most women would be busy making puddings and mince-pies, touring the shops day in day out seeking presents for their children and grandchildren, getting in a store of logs, cleaning the house till it shone, hanging paper chains and tinsel in the front room and, most important of all, the tree. Everyone had a Christmas tree: set in the bay-window, covered with glass baubles and fairy lights, for all the neighbours to see and admire.

She made a pot of tea, came to the conclusion that it was too early to take a cup up to Florrie, drank two cups herself and decided to go for a walk. It had started to rain, but then it seemed to rain every day lately and each day was grey and bitterly cold. She tucked her chin down into the collar of her coat and pushed her hands deep into her pockets.

A bus came along and she got on it. 'We're only going as far as the Embankment,' the conductor informed her.

'That'll do me fine,' she answered, holding out the change for her fare. As she walked alongside the river, her thoughts were all mixed up. Happy memories, some even amusing, sad ones. She sat down on a wooden bench beneath a great oak tree.

Try as she might, Patsy still felt so disheartened. Ellen wasn't going to get well: she was only a fragment of her former self and achingly thin. Her lovely hair didn't shine any more or hang loose over her shoulders. It was always scraped back and tied with a piece of tape. She hardly ever spoke, but it was the way she looked at you with those huge green eyes, not a fearless gaze, certainly not that, more a wary look. There was no doubt about it, to Ellen the future seemed dark and menacing. She was afraid of life now, afraid to trust anyone, even those who loved her.

What Patsy longed for at this moment was for Eddie to come home. Ollie too. Between them they'd think of something, they always had. Just look at how Ollie had sorted out the authorities when she'd been a lass. How Eddie had stuck to her through thick and thin for years, even though she hadn't been legally married to him.

Another thing, Ollie had become rich only because

of his brother's death, but how well he'd used his inheritance. He'd had houses built at Mitcham, let them to the Jacksons and deliberately allowed them to avoid paying the rent. At that thought Patsy found herself laughing. Artful bugger! What a thing to do! Ollie had put all those properties in her name and she had practically blackmailed Johnny Jackson into giving her a divorce by threatening to evict the whole bloody lot of them!

Ollie had also started the coach business, which had done so well that all members of the family now benefited from it one way or another. There wasn't a kinder man on this earth. He hadn't quibbled for a moment when she'd asked him to think about buying Maplehurst Rest Home at Ramsgate so that Mrs Wright and her companions could feel safe and happy for what remained of their lives.

My God! Why didn't I think of it before? Patsy raised her eyes to the clouded sky and thanked God. She had the solution crystal-clear in her mind. Ellen needed a purpose in life, a reason to make a new beginning. She had to feel that she was loved and, more important still, that she was needed. Well, Patsy had the answer now.

She had to wait a long time until a bus came that would take her home, and she had hardly given a thought to just how wet she was. As she came up the garden path, Florrie opened the door.

'Look at you,' she cried. 'You're soaked to the skin. Come on, get by the fire. Take those wet things off. Were you trying to catch your bloody death? Stay there while I find you some dry clothes.'

Water was trickling down in little channels from both sides of Patsy's sodden coat, making puddles on the hearth-rug, but she didn't mind one bit. She smiled to herself. Florrie was in her glory, mothering her, and she was going to do the same for Ellen. Her plan had to work. She'd *make* it work.

Sunday had come around again at last. Thank goodness it was a nice dry day. Today Patsy didn't walk the corridors with dragging steps and fear in her heart, she almost ran.

Today she wasn't going to sit in the visitors' canteen where people were coming and going all the time and the noisy chatter often seemed deafening. Today she was going to have Ellen all to herself.

It took a great deal of persuasion to get Ellen to put on an outdoor coat and to allow Patsy to tie a scarf over her head, and quite some time to convince her that it was safe to go out into the grounds, but somehow Patsy managed it.

For the first few minutes they walked in silence. Ellen keeping her head down, her eyes seeing only the pathway. Patsy took her hand and drew her towards a bench seat. She resisted strongly, but Patsy was determined and after a short struggle they were seated side by side.

'Ellen,' Patsy began cautiously. 'If you could have one wish, what would you wish for?'

Ellen sat perfectly still, studying the ground at her feet. She looked so miserable that Patsy could scarcely bear to look at her.

'All right, Ellen,' Patsy said after a moment. 'You needn't talk if you don't want to, but I want you to listen to me.'

Still Ellen didn't move. She still sat staring at nothing.

Patsy tried to speak calmly. She reminded Ellen of how she and Vicky had gone down to the Gloucester for a holiday, how she had come to meet Mrs Wright and her friends. 'You remember, love, how excited we all were when your grandad told us that everything was settled, he had signed the contracts to purchase Maplehurst? It was a kind thing to do, wasn't it?' She paused, hoping for a reply but getting nothing. She was struck again by the pitiable way Ellen slouched. She had always had such an air of quiet dignity, a joy of living even when her life had been anything but. Patsy felt a choking sensation as she compared Ellen now with what she had been before she was married.

She had got to make Ellen see that there could be happiness for her in the future.

'I made a whole lot of promises to those old folk and you could help me to keep those promises. With your nursing experience you'd be such a great help down there. We'd all be happy to know that we had someone on hand that we could rely on if any of the residents were taken ill. Of course you could have your own flat, your own bit of privacy. We'd be down to see you often – doesn't take long to get to Ramsgate, you'd probably get browned off with the sight of us all. David and Valerie would bring Tim, and, yes, what about Vicky and Alex? They'll have their new baby early in June. Did I tell you that all the ladies at Maplehurst were making baby clothes for Vicky?

'Emma thinks it's terribly funny the way your Auntie Florrie and Mrs Wright have become such great buddies. Mrs Wright is a bit frightfully-frightfully, but the pair of them get on like a house on fire. You'd have your Aunt Florrie on your doorstep more often than you'd want. Come to give you a bloody helping hand, is most likely what her excuse would be. Your dad and me and your grandad wouldn't want to be strangers, so perhaps you'd better take over the job of getting tea for everyone on a Sunday. Save me the job.'

After all that, there was still no reaction from Ellen.

Anger flared up again in Patsy, fierce anger. In that instant there was murder in her heart and God help Robert Dellor if she could have got hold of him at that moment.

'I mustn't fail,' she muttered to herself. 'I'll make you speak, Ellen, if it's the last thing I do. If I give up now, they might just as well throw away the key. You'll be spending the rest of your life in this God-damned awful place.'

Brave words, but it was no good. She couldn't go on, she couldn't think of anything else to say. Time hadn't counted. She had rambled on as if her life depended on it; well, Ellen's did, and a lot of good it had done. Nothing had changed. Ellen still hadn't moved a muscle or uttered one word. Patsy put her hands between her knees and hung her head as dry sobs racked her body. She couldn't do any more. She had reached the end of her tether . . .

Gentle fingers were plucking at her sleeve. She didn't believe it! It was all she could do to keep quiet as she raised her head and stared at her daughter. A gurgling sound was coming from Ellen's throat, her eyes were screwed up tightly, her hands were fluttering, beating the air with such urgency that Patsy was afraid. Should she go for help? She decided, No!

It seemed to take ages for this spasm to pass, a lifetime it appeared to Patsy as she forced herself to keep calm. Suddenly Ellen became still. Very, very gently Patsy drew her daughter into her arms and for the first time Ellen made no resistance.

It was as if all Ellen's grief and fear had come to a head at once and was bursting from her in tears. Patsy cradled her, smoothing her hair back from her damp forehead. Then when the tears changed to racking sobs, Patsy pillowed her head on her shoulder, all the time patting Ellen's back and rocking her as if she were a baby. Gradually she became quiet.

Patsy spoke softly. 'There, there, my darling, you're safe now.'

For a long time Ellen didn't speak or move, then Patsy felt her head jerk up and forwards. Her lips brushed lightly against her mother's cheek and her hands slid slowly around her arm and tugged her nearer.

Patsy wanted to clear her throat, but she was afraid to do even that. Instead she pressed her cheek against Ellen's hair. They both stayed still. Neither of them spoke. They held on to each other as if afraid one would collapse without the support of the other.

If anything, Patsy was more frightened than before. This was the answer to all of her prayers – more than she had hoped for at one time. Nothing must be said or done that would push Ellen back into that twilight world she had been living in.

At last they drew apart and sat up. Ellen's eyes were still shining with tears, but Patsy could see beyond, into their depths, and was instantly reassured. It was her turn to weep.

'It won't happen overnight, Mrs Owen,' Sister said, with a hint of a smile on her face for a change. 'But, yes, from here on in it can only be good news. I'm sure of that.'

'And I'll be able to take her home any day now?' Patsy argued.

'Whoa! Not so fast. We must see what the doctors have to say about that. You could ring up tomorrow and make an appointment to see them.'

I'll do better than that, Patsy vowed to herself. I'll be here before ten in the morning. I need to know how much longer they think Ellen will have to stay in this place.

Nevertheless, when Patsy arrived home and called out, 'Are you there, Florrie?' and both Florrie and Kitty appeared in the hallway they knew straight off that the news was good.

Patsy couldn't wait to take off her hat and coat before she told them all about it. 'Ellen's going to be all right. She's turned the corner, she spoke to me, she let me hug and kiss her. She even kissed me! Oh, Florrie, isn't it wonderful?'

Florrie beamed at her, nodding her head, quite unable to speak, and Kitty's face was flushed bright red with pleasure. Patsy smiled and squeezed Florrie's arm. 'I'll tell you all the details if you give me a chance to get my clothes off – and I wouldn't say no to a cuppa.'

For the next half-hour Florrie flung instructions at Patsy. 'Get an appointment with the top man. Don't waste time talking to the house doctors. Make sure you let them know our Ellen's got a good 'ome to come to. Tell them she'll be safe and well looked after by her family.'

'Yes, Florrie,' Patsy said emphatically. Then for some reason, she heard herself say. 'What if they won't let her come home?'

'Now don't start that! Everything will be all right – you told us that yourself as soon as you got in the front door.' Florrie took out a handkerchief, wiped her eyes and blew her nose.

'You've just got to have faith now,' Kitty told her as she too began to weep. 'After all, this is the best news we've had round here for many a long day.'

''Tis an' all,' Florrie agreed.

'Then why the hell are we all crying?' Patsy managed to say, knowing full well that these were vastly different from the tears that had been shed in this house over the past few weeks.

Chapter Twenty-four

PATSY WAS AWAY and gone to the airport before Florrie came down to the kitchen. Florrie was relieved. What with the letter arriving to say that Eddie and Ollie were coming home, and the doctors at the hospital saying that Ellen could come home in time for Christmas, even though she would still need treatment, Patsy had been like a flea on hot bricks this last four days. Not that you could blame her, poor little cow. She sniffed. Life had dished out some hard knocks for that young girl – woman now I suppose, but always my young Patsy to me. Gawd above, but she'd coped well these last few weeks. She closed her eyes briefly at the memory of those details Patsy had given her of Ellen's injuries, when it had been touch and go as to whether Ellen would live or die.

Now, please God, with Ollie back and Eddie home things around here might just get back to normal. There'll be all the family here for the holiday. She added three spoonfuls of sugar to her steaming cup of tea. I'll have a word with Emma, yes, and Valerie and Vicky. See that they keep an eye on Patsy, don't let her go overdoing it in the rush to get things cracking now. What does it matter if everyone ain't got no presents this year? Enough thanks should be offered up that one of us ain't missing. Oh, blimey! She moved her bulk away from the kitchen door to enable Alex and David to come in.

'What the hell are you two doing here this time in the morning? Up to no good, I'll be bound,' she declared, doing her best not to smile and show the pair of them how pleased she was to see them.

'Now as if we ever get up to mischief, Aunt! We're too old for such larks now.' David grinned at her, while Alex made straight for the dresser and reached down two big breakfast cups.

'There's not enough tea in the pot to fill them great things, you'll have to make a fresh brew,' Florrie complained, knowing full well that she'd be making the tea for them and cooking them a good breakfast more than likely.

'Is Mum upstairs getting ready?' Alex asked. 'It's about time she was leaving for the airport. Me an' David tossed for it and I won. I'm taking her in my car.'

'Well, you could have both saved your time and energy. Your mum's long gone. Thought she'd creep out of the house so damn quiet, but I heard her the minute she got up and I watched her from the window as she drove off. As excited as a kitten, she was.'

'Great, isn't it, Aunt Flo, Dad and Grandad coming home at last? Course Mum's pleased,' said David as he settled down in what was his father's armchair.

'Oh well, with Mum out of our way we might as well bring all those things in,' Alex said, giving David's feet a kick.

'What things?' Florrie wanted to know.

'A mixture of sorts – you don't object, do you?' The concern in Florrie's eyes made both the boys laugh.

'It's all right, you silly old thing. They never fell off the back of a lorry,' David assured her.

'No, the lorry drove straight into our yard,' said Alex, teasing her unmercifully.

It took them three trips up and down the passage before David said, 'That's the lot. If you promise to feed us, Aunt Florrie, we'll take all this lot up to your room and you can sort it out in your own good time.'

'Yeah, there's plenty of wrapping paper in the bottom of one of these boxes. You'll have a great time sorting out who's going to get what.'

There was no telling with these boys. Hearts of gold really, but try telling them that! Presents for everyone and more, she'd be bound. No time for Patsy to go rummaging round the shops, but thanks to these buggers there'd be a smile on everyone's face come Christmas morning. For two pins she'd kiss the pair of them. No, better not, she decided, instead I'll go to the trouble of giving them fried bread with their eggs and bacon; they'd like that.

The destination board showed that the plane from Sydney would be landing shortly. Now as Patsy waited she was nervous. What will Eddie have to say when I tell him about Ellen, and how will Ollie react when he hears that Robert laid into her? She fiddled with the buttons of her coat, her restlessness growing by the minute. Will they be angry because I never let them know? she asked herself, and immediately dismissed such a daft idea. Backwards and forwards she paced, moving her handbag from one hand to another, working herself up into quite a state. She went into the toilet, more for something to do than because she needed to spend a penny. Having washed her hands, she glanced in the mirror, saw that she had bitten off most of her lipstick; her fingers trembled so much that she didn't make a very good job of trying to replace it.

Another twenty minutes passed and at last the people were pouring through the barrier. She had no job spotting her husband and her father. One dark head and one bushy one that was almost pure white, they both towered well above the heads of other men. Momentarily she hesitated. How tanned they looked, and how attractive Eddie still was. As she pushed her way through the crowds, suddenly Eddie's eyes locked on to hers and the look that passed between them said it all.

Eddie stopped pushing the trolley that held their cases and stood still, holding out his arms to her.

Patsy ran the last few yards and the breath went from her body in a huge sigh as his arms came around her, gathering her to his chest. Not a word did either of them utter as they stood locked together in each other's arms.

'How about me? Don't I get a kiss? I've brought him home safe and sound, haven't I?' Ollie's voice was gentle as he watched them tear themselves apart.

'Hallo, Ollie. Welcome home! Cor, I've missed you!'

'I've missed you too, my love, but not half as much as this great lout has done. He's been like a dog that's lost his tail.'

Patsy broke away from Eddie's grasp and flung herself at Ollie, who hugged her tight. 'Don't go away again, either of you,' she pleaded, holding her face up to be kissed.

As they walked through the terminal building Patsy held on tight to Ollie's hand. Eddie was occupied with seeing to the luggage, but that didn't stop Patsy from frequently turning round and, with a beaming face, giving him that special look that said 'I love you.'

All her worries and anxiety had gone. She was safe, her men were home and they would take care of everything and everybody. She felt now that she could face the prospect of Christmas with a lot more pleasure, safe in the knowledge that all her family would be together.

COCKNEY WAIF

Elizabeth Waite

London, 1918. Patsy Kent is only thirteen years old when her dear mother dies and leaves her an orphan. But when the authorities try to take her away from Strathmore Street, and the warm happy-go-lucky Londoners who regard her as one of their own, they have a fight on their hands.

As she becomes a young woman, and starts work in the local market like her mother before her, Patsy discovers all too soon the pain of first love, when cruel Johnny Jackson plays with her emotions and then casts their marriage thoughtlessly aside. Only the support of the market traders and friends who have always stood by her can raise her characteristic cockney spirit, and fortune smiles on Patsy when a real, deep love grows between her and the shy, thoughtful Eddie Owen. But the pointed fingers of the gossips, and the shame of living in adultery may prove too high a price for Patsy to pay, and it seems her only hope for happiness is to leave London and the very community she has come to call her family.

SKINNY LIZZIE

Elizabeth Waite

South London, 1932. Times are hard for ten-year-old
Lizzie Collins and her family. With her father dead, it is
up to her mother, grandmother and aunt to scrimp and
save to rear Lizzie and her three siblings. But the whole
family is blessed with the indomitable Cockney spirit –
and in particular the physically frail but strong-willed and
intelligent Lizzie.

So it is only her strong instinct for survival that sees Lizzie
through the snobbish school to which she wins a
scholarship, through the life-threatening horrors of
consumption, and through the dark storm clouds of
impending war. After school and a stint as a butcher's
clerk, she goes to work as a bus-conductress and, through
hard work and an inheritance, manages to save enough to
invest in property. And then fortune smiles on her in the
game of love. Happily married after the war to Charlie
Wilson, she relishes the prospect of a now secure future
with her family. But Charlie has other ideas. Ideas that
will take Lizzie to a lonely life in Devon, to the challenges
of a new career, and away from her beloved London . . .

Other bestselling Warner titles available by mail:

☐	Skinny Lizzie	Elizabeth Waite	£5.99
☐	Cockney Waif	Elizabeth Waite	£5.99
☐	Second Chance	Elizabeth Waite	£5.99
☐	Third Time Lucky	Elizabeth Waite	£5.99
☐	An Apple From Eden	Emma Blair	£5.99
☐	Flower of Scotland	Emma Blair	£5.99

The prices shown above are correct at time of going to press. However, the publishers reserve the right to increase prices on covers from those previously advertised without prior notice.

WARNER BOOKS

WARNER BOOKS
Cash Sales Department, P.O. Box 11, Falmouth, Cornwall, TR10 9EN
Tel: +44 (0) 1326 569777, Fax: +44 (0) 1326 569555
Email: books@barni.avel.co.uk.

POST AND PACKING:
Payments can be made as follows: cheque, postal order (payable to Warner Books) or by credit cards. Do not send cash or currency.

All U.K. Orders	**FREE OF CHARGE**
E.E.C. & Overseas	25% of order value

Name (Block Letters) _____

Address_____

Post/zip code:_____

☐ Please keep me in touch with future Warner publications

☐ I enclose my remittance £_____

☐ I wish to pay by Visa/Access/Mastercard/Eurocard

Card Expiry Date

_____

Tower HILL

A chill breeze blew from east of the City, carrying on its breath the rancid taint of glue works and tanners' yards. It filled the sails of merchantmen and barges and shivered the surface of the Thames. It twisted the weather vanes on the turrets of the Tower of London and ruffled the black drapes on the scaffold on Tower Hill.

Grim-faced soldiers gripped their pikes and sword hilts while the crowd shifted their feet and blew on their hands to ward off the cold. There was a general muttering and grumbling about the wait, and the occasional chuckle and guffaw about the news that Lord Nithsdale had escaped from the Tower the day before dressed as a woman.

And in among the crowd was Tom Marlowe, fifteen years old – though he was soon to be sixteen – and the assistant of the man who stood at his side: the brilliant Dr Josiah Harker. Dr Harker had given no explanation why he wanted them to come to Tower Hill, but Tom had been through so much with the doctor in recent months that he would have followed him into a burning house without question.

A murmur ran through the onlookers as the Earl of Derwentwater finally mounted the scaffold. Tom wondered at how calm he looked, and his voice sounded clear when he turned to the crowd and spoke. After saying a few prayers, Derwentwater retracted his guilty plea and spoke warmly in praise of the exiled son of James II: James Francis Edward Stuart, the man he believed should rightfully be sitting on the throne now occupied by George I.

Tom listened as Derwentwater told the crowd that there would never be peace in the country until the Stuarts were restored to the throne, but few in England would have shared that view. They wanted no more papists on the throne.

The new King George may have been German, but he was a Protestant. Better a foreigner than a

Catholic. There would be no James III despite all the efforts of his supporters, the Jacobites.

'I die a Roman Catholic,' said Derwentwater. 'I am in perfect charity with all the world – I thank God for it – even with those of the present government, who are the most instrumental in my death.'

There were more murmurs, though Tom could not tell whether they were murmurs against Derwentwater or against the government.

'I freely forgive such ungenerously reported false things of me,' continued Derwentwater. 'And I hope to be forgiven the trespasses of my youth, by the Father of infinite mercy, into whose hands I commend my soul.'

He handed the paper on which his speech had been written to the sheriff and looked at the wooden block in front of him. Laughter rippled through the crowd as he asked the axeman to chip off a splinter of wood in case he hurt his neck. Then Derwentwater took off his coat and his waistcoat and kneeled down. A hush fell as he laid his head on the block.

'Lord Jesu receive my soul,' he prayed as the axe was raised. 'Lord Jesu receive my soul. Lord Jesu receive my soul—'

The axe fell and Tom shut his eyes and wished he could have shut his ears to the noise of the axe's striking. But when he opened his eyes there was even more horror and he turned away from the sight, but not before he had caught a glimpse of the axeman holding Derwentwater's head aloft for the crowd to see.

'Behold the head of a traitor!' he shouted. 'God save King George!'

The crowd erupted into cheering and booing, but again, Tom found it impossible to tell whether they were cheering Derwentwater or the king, or booing a traitor or the government that killed him.

The body was wrapped in black and taken away and then Lord Kenmure appeared. Tom thought how much harder it must be to come to the scaffold when it was already damp with blood. Kenmure had pleaded for mercy at his trial; but he stood bravely now, though he made no speech. He prayed, said a couple of words to the axeman and kneeled before the block.

This time Tom turned away and watched Dr Harker's face. He heard the axe come down once, then again. The doctor did not flinch either time, but looked straight ahead, even when the executioner once more said the words, 'Behold the head of a traitor,' and Tom knew what his friend must be seeing. Still he stared fixedly while the cheering and jeering broke out once more. His gaze did not waver, even when the crowd, encouraged by the soldiers, began to move away and disperse. Tom had to tug hard on the doctor's arm before his trance was broken, and when he turned to Tom he had tears in his eyes. He closed them and shook his head.

'I should not have brought you here, Tom,' he said. 'You should not have seen this. I am sorry, truly I am.'

'Why were you so determined that we came?' asked Tom.

'Well, Tom, I wanted—' began the doctor, but he was interrupted by a man standing behind him.

'Josiah Harker, as I live and breathe,' he said, clapping a hand on Dr Harker's shoulder.

'Who the devil . . .? I don't believe it! Daniel . . . Well, how are you, man?'

The two men embraced like long-lost brothers, slapping each other's shoulders and laughing like schoolboys. It seemed a long time before Dr Harker remembered that Tom was with him.

'Daniel, Daniel,' he said, slightly out of breath. 'You must meet my very able assistant and good friend Thomas Marlowe. Tom, this is a very old friend of mine, Daniel Thornley.'

'I am delighted to make your acquaintance, Tom,' said Thornley, shaking Tom by the hand.

'And I yours,' said Tom.

Thornley was tall, and though he was probably a similar age to Dr Harker, he was leaner and fitter. He had a huge bright smile, his cheeks pulling back in curved creases to accommodate it. He had a relaxed air about him that put Tom immediately at ease, but his clothes were cheap and ill fitting, at odds with his voice and his bearing.

'What brings you here, Josiah?' asked Thornley, nodding his head towards the scaffold that was already being stripped of its black drapes.

'I might ask the same thing,' said Dr Harker.

'I have a professional interest in these matters, as you know, Josiah.'

'Yes, of course.' Dr Harker's smile faded a little. 'I suppose I had hoped you might have changed trades.'

Thornley smiled and then narrowed his eyes as he seemed to catch sight of something over Tom's shoulder. Tom followed his gaze but saw nothing but the remnants of the dispersing crowd.

'Let us not rekindle this old debate, Josiah,' said Thornley. 'I must go now, in any case. Shall we meet again? Do you still frequent The Quill coffee house?'

'Yes, I do,' said Dr Harker. 'But how do you know—?'

'Splendid, splendid. Then I shall see you in there very soon, Josiah. Very nice to meet you, Tom.'

Thornley walked off into the crowd and, with what seemed to Tom an almost supernatural ease, disappeared into it.

2

Monsieur PETIT

A golden haze lay across London like a silk scarf, softening the shapes of buildings, muting the colours. It conjured up something beautiful and dreamlike out of the cold, damp morning. Even the usual forge-like clatter and clang of the city seemed to have stilled itself in sympathy with the scene.

Frost silvered the grass of St Bride's churchyard, twinkling as it began to melt, and made the shadows in the carvings on the gravestones shimmer blue. Cobwebs glistened, strung with pearl-like beads of

7

water. The wrought–iron gate creaked at Tom's touch.

He left the slippery flagstone path leading to the church, walked across the wet grass and stopped in front of a headstone. The stone looked fresh save for a light coating of London grime; a year had not much weathered it and the carving was still as sharp as the day it was chiselled. A blackbird landed on a nearby railing, its tail rising as it rocked first forwards then back. It opened its yellow beak and sang out loud and long, its throat quivering, its wings twitching. Then it flew off, chattering away into the distance. Silence returned.

HERE LIES THE BODY OF WILL PIGGOT. Tom still found it hard to read the words, and even in the reading of them he found it harder still to accept that his friend really did lie beneath his feet and that he would never again see his face or hear his voice. It was hard to bear and Tom closed his eyes and hung his head.

'Here I am, Will,' said Tom without looking up. 'Here to show I haven't forgotten you. Nor ever will.' He opened his eyes and looked at the headstone once more.

On these visits to Will's grave, Tom increasingly found himself talking to the slightly startled-looking cherub that was carved into the top of the headstone above a scroll with REST IN PEACE written across it. It made him smile. Will could not have been farther from a cherub in life, and yet . . . and yet, there was something of Will in that carved cherub: the crooked smile, the long jaw and the deer-like alertness that had served him so well. Until the day of his murder, that is.

Will's friendship and, more especially, his untimely death, had changed Tom Marlowe's life for ever. Though Tom would have given anything to have Will standing there with him again, the tragedy had set Tom on an adventure that had made his life a thousand times richer than before. It was something that made him feel more than a little guilty: that he should have gained in any way from poor Will's terrible death.

If Will had not been murdered he would probably still be apprenticed to his father at the Lamb and Lion printing house, and he would certainly never have met the amazing Ocean Carter. Will had been Ocean's friend too, and Ocean had joined forces with Tom and Dr Harker to track down his killer. He was like no one Tom had ever met before; a cat-like visitor from London's underworld, quick-witted and fearless.

And now Ocean worked for Tom's father in his place and Tom worked for Dr Harker, cataloguing the doctor's enormous collection of artefacts collected on his travels and adventures around the world, living in an attic room at the top of his house in Fleet Street.

'You used to love to hear about Dr Harker's travels, didn't you, Will?' said Tom. 'You'd have loved to see all the things we've been cataloguing. We used to talk about how we'd run away to sea one day, didn't we? We used to say we'd go to America and seek our fortunes. I wonder if we ever would have done?'

Tom sat down on the cold stone tomb nearby, looked at the cherub smiling back at him and closed his eyes against the tears.

'Morning, Tom,' said Ocean as Tom walked into the printing house. He wiped as much ink from his hand as he could and offered it to Tom, who shook it warmly, slapping him on the arm.

'How are you, Ocean?' Tom asked. 'Father still keeping you busy?'

'I should say so, Tom,' he replied. 'It's all right for you, sitting around all day looking at books and the like. Some of us have real work to do.'

'I've done my share of work in this place,' said Tom, patting one of the presses warmly. 'I miss it sometimes, though. Is he about? Dr Harker's fussing about his books.'

'He's in the shop, Tom,' said Ocean. 'He'll be glad to see you.'

Tom walked through the door and found Mr Marlowe sitting deep in concentration, surrounded by piles of prints.

'Tom!' Mr Marlowe looked up from a print he was

reading. 'Just reading this sermon about how we are all about to be consumed by hell fire. "The Day of Judgement is upon us . . . These are the Last Days." I can't think how many of these I've printed in my life; yet here we all are.' He chuckled to himself as he got up and clapped his huge hands on Tom's shoulders. 'It's good to see you, son.'

'And you, Father,' said Tom. 'Dr Harker wondered if his books were back from the binders yet.'

'Not yet, no. Tell him they'll be done by Friday.'

'I will, Father,' said Tom, dropping his voice to a conspiratorial whisper. 'How's Ocean getting on?'

'He's a godsend, to be honest, Tom,' said Mr Marlowe. 'You'd think he'd been in the business all his life. He's a deep one, though. A bit like you in that respect.'

Tom returned Mr Marlowe's smile. 'I do believe you're growing fond of Ocean, Father.'

'I am,' said Mr Marlowe, as if the thought had only that instant entered his head. 'I believe I am.' He blushed slightly at the realization that not so long ago he would never have countenanced even employing a man of Ocean's shady background. He had disapproved of Tom's friendship with Will Piggot, and taking Ocean on had been a kind of penance after Will's murder. But now he found that he simply liked having Ocean around, and it helped sweeten the loss of Tom to Dr Harker. 'And by the way,' he went on.

'What's this I hear about Dr Harker taking you to Tower Hill, Tom?'

'To the execution, yes,' said Tom. 'It was horrible, Father.'

'I can't say that I approve, Tom,' said Mr Marlowe. 'I don't have any great sympathy for those Jacobite traitors, but even so . . . It's a grim piece of entertainment for a lad of your age. Why did Harker feel the need to go?'

'I'm not altogether sure,' Tom replied. 'He said we would be witnessing history, but I'm not sure there wasn't more to it than that.'

'These Jacobite rascals are everywhere, Tom. Mr Finch was in yesterday – you know, the baker on Goat Lane whose brother is a turnkey in Newgate? He says that London is crawling with them. He says that people think they're all Scottish, but they have scores of sympathizers in England . . . and in this very city. Think of that, Tom: in this very city. He says you can't tell who they might be, neither. It might be someone you've known for years. They'll get more than they bargained for if they come here, I'll tell you that for nothing.' Mr Marlowe picked up a hammer and weighed it in his hand. 'You can't trust anyone, that's what Finch says. You can't trust anyone. That's what the world's come to, Tom. It's all good for business though, I have to say. The printing house has never been busier, with all the pamphlets and sermons being churned out.'

'You don't think that . . .' began Tom and then shook his head.

'What is it, Tom?'

'You don't think it possible that Dr Harker might be a Jacobite sympathizer, do you?'

'Dr Harker!' said Mr Marlowe with a laugh. 'Never!' But then he saw the serious look on Tom's face and furrowed his brow. 'Why would you think such a thing?'

'It's just that . . . it's just a feeling I have about the execution. There was something more to it than Dr Harker was saying.'

'Come on, Tom,' said Mr Marlowe. 'After all you've been through with Dr Harker, you can't believe he would lie to you? He doesn't seem the type for secrets. He probably just thought seeing an execution would be educational. You can't get everything out of books.'

When Tom turned the corner into the courtyard of Dr Harker's house, he took out his watch and remembered that the doctor had said that he had some business and would be out until ten o'clock. However, the maid, Sarah, would let him in and Tom was more than happy to while away the time in Dr Harker's study.

To his surprise, though, when Sarah opened the

door she said she was sure the doctor was in because she had heard him walking about as she cleaned. So Tom climbed the stairs to the study. Above him, he heard raised voices: one was Dr Harker's, but the other he did not recognize. He was about to lay his hand on the brass doorknob of the study, when he paused.

The door was very slightly ajar and Tom could just see Dr Harker. He was talking to another man who was seated with his back to Tom. As Tom peered into the room, the man handed something to the doctor. Tom could not see what it was, save that it glinted as it caught the light from the nearby window. Dr Harker studied it and then put it in his waistcoat pocket. Tom knocked at the door and walked in. The stranger jumped up and reached into his pocket. Dr Harker grabbed his arm.

'Tom!' said the doctor with a rather forced laugh. 'Come in, come in. I would like you to meet my friend, Monsieur . . . Petit.'

The two men exchanged a furtive glance and then the stranger smiled and held out a hand. '*Bonjour*, Tom,' he said, with a thick French accent. 'I am very pleased to meet you.'

The man was tall and broad shouldered. Although the clothes he wore were stylish – verging on the foppish even – and obviously expensive, his appearance was a little dishevelled. As he took Tom's hand Tom noticed that his lace cuff was frayed and grubby.

Monsieur PETIT

He seemed an unlikely friend for Dr Harker.

Monsieur Petit's broad and handsome face was unshaven, the bristles, like his eyebrows, fair, and though his smile was warm enough, his clear grey eyes studied Tom with a wolf-like intensity. Tom was forced to look away and turned to Dr Harker.

'Monsieur . . . Petit is in London for a few days on business,' said the doctor, once again exchanging a glance with his guest that Tom felt he was not supposed to see. 'He is in the silk trade, with family in Spitalfields.' Tom thought that a man in the silk trade ought to have cleaner cuffs. 'He was just leaving.'

The stranger bowed and shook Dr Harker's hand and they spoke earnestly to each other in French for a couple of minutes, Tom's frustration at not being able to understand them growing by the second.

'*Au revoir*,' said Monsieur Petit, turning to Tom. '*Au revoir*, Josiah.'

'I'll see you out,' said Dr Harker, and the two men left and descended the stairs.

Tom crept to the stairwell and peered down. At the bottom, instead of making for the front door, they turned towards the back of the house. Tom went to the window to see the stranger leaving by the back courtyard. As he lifted the latch of the door in the courtyard wall, the stranger turned and looked up. Tom leaped sideways out of view. Had he been seen?

15

He was not sure.

Tom could hear Dr Harker's footsteps as he began to climb the stairs and he retreated back into the study. When the doctor entered, Tom was doing a very good job of looking fascinated by a book of geometry.

'Sorry about that, Tom,' said Dr Harker, taking off his wig and scratching at his scalp. 'Ah – that's better. Haven't seen Petit there for years.'

'Really?' said Tom, trying to sound uninterested. 'Have you known him for long, then?'

'Oh yes. For many years.'

'How do you know him?' Tom asked.

'How?' said Dr Harker, looking a little flustered. 'I don't know, Tom. I . . . erm . . . You know how it is, Tom.'

Tom had no idea how it was, but said nothing.

'But enough of Monsieur Petit!' The doctor slapped his hand down on a pile of books. 'It is your birthday tomorrow, is it not? Your sixteenth birthday?'

'Well, yes it is, Dr Harker,' said Tom.

'Then we must mark it in some way, don't you think? Of course we must! What do you say, Tom? What shall we do?'

'Well, sir, I should love to go to the theatre. My father never wanted to go and—'

'Excellent!' said Dr Harker. 'The theatre it shall be! We'll have a marvellous time.'

'Thank you, Dr Harker,' said Tom. 'But what shall

we see?'

'Well, I really think that ought to be for you to decide. What will it be, Tom? Shakespeare? Johnson?'

'I rather thought that I might like to see . . .' began Tom.

'Yes?' said Dr Harker with a smile.

'Well, I rather thought I might like to see an opera, Dr Harker.'

The doctor's face fell. 'An opera, you say?'

'Yes,' said Tom. 'But if you would rather . . .'

'No, no,' said Dr Harker, regaining his good cheer. 'If you want to see an opera, then an opera you shall see.'

Tom grinned.

'Excellent,' the doctor added, a little hesitantly. 'Excellent . . .'

Tom and Dr Harker were soon hard at work on the doctor's collection. Shelf by shelf, drawer by drawer, item after item would be taken out and dusted down and given a label with its own number. Tom would ask Dr Harker what the item was called and would then make an entry in his best script in a huge leather-bound ledger on the doctor's desk.

Of course, this process was not a swift one, as every time Tom asked what an item was, it would trigger a lecture about its history and the people who made it and a lengthy reminiscence about the adventure connected with collecting it. Neither Tom nor the doctor in any way minded this, though; for Tom it was an education and for Dr Harker it was a chance to relive the excitement of his youth and give vent to his enthusiasm for his treasures.

Tom dreamed of travelling, and Dr Harker's tales of his own travels fed his dreams. Normally, Tom would listen intently to every word the doctor said, sailing away with him in his imagination, paddling canoes along twisting rivers, riding horses across wide open plains, but today he found himself letting the words drift away into the background while the voice of the stranger he had met earlier grew in volume.

For Monsieur Petit might have been speaking French when he left, but he was speaking English when Tom arrived at the study door, he was sure of that. And more – much more strange than that, he had been speaking with a very particular accent: a *Scottish* accent.

3

Temple BAR

Italian opera was all the rage and Tom was eager to see what all the fuss was about. Dr Harker, however, was not at all keen on this new craze. To him the London stage seemed full of pantomimes and harlequinades and a lot of trilling Italians singing utter nonsense, but he kept his views to himself for once, as he and Tom braved the evening crowds and headed west for the King's Theatre in Haymarket. Mr Marlowe hated all kinds of theatre and, as Tom had expected, had politely turned the offer down.

19

As they walked along the Strand, a newspaper seller sucked in a wheezy breath and yelled for all he was worth in a thin, rasping voice: 'The White Rider strikes again! Ghostly highwayman robs another coach!'

Dr Harker's interest was aroused immediately. He bought a paper and pointed to the story. 'Do you see this, Tom?' he said. 'I've been following this story for the last few weeks. Do you see? The White Rider is a highwayman ... but not just *any* highwayman. Witnesses say that he is a kind of spectre or phantom, with a skull for a face—'

'A skull?' asked Tom.

'Yes,' said Dr Harker with a smile. 'Imagine that! It's intriguing, is it not? And there is more. He is said to be able to kill simply by pointing at his victims. Now what do you make of that?'

'I ... I ... don't know,' said Tom. 'Maybe the witnesses are mistaken.'

'Maybe. But this is the sixth such incident, all in different locations with different witnesses. They all seem to have seen the same thing.'

'Maybe the newspapers have made the whole thing up,' Tom suggested. 'Father said they do that all the time.'

Dr Harker laughed. 'Mr Marlowe may well be right,' he said. 'He often is. This White Rider has been striking around London. Perhaps we shall find out for ourselves whether he is a phantom or not.'

Tom was not quite as keen on this idea as Dr Harker seemed to be. Besides, he had been trying to work up the courage and find the right time to ask Dr Harker a rather delicate question.

'Dr Harker,' he said, 'can I ask you something?'

'Of course, Tom. Anything, you know that.'

'Is Monsieur Petit a Jacobite?'

Tom had not known how Dr Harker would react, but he had certainly not expected him to grab him by the collar and nearly pull him off his feet.

The doctor bundled Tom into a nearby alleyway. He looked about him and his manner was so excited that Tom was actually frightened of him.

'Listen to me, Tom,' he whispered. 'There is deadly danger in that question. Deadly danger, Tom. Do you understand?'

'Yes,' said Tom, though he understood nothing save Dr Harker's utter seriousness.

The doctor edged him to the corner of the street and pointed back the way they had come, towards Temple Bar and Fleet Street. 'Do you see, Tom?' he asked. 'Up on Temple Bar?'

Tom followed Dr Harker's pointing finger. On metal spikes above the arch of Temple Bar, silhouetted against the evening sky, were the boiled and tarred heads of Derwentwater and Kenmure.

'Do you want my head up there, Tom?' said Dr Harker.

'No, sir,' said Tom. 'Of course I don't.'

'Then, understand that we must never speak of Monsieur Petit again.' The words sounded like a threat.

'I understand,' said Tom.

Dr Harker suddenly saw the fear in Tom's eyes and allowed his face to relax into a smile. 'If I keep things from you, it is to keep you safe, Tom.'

Tom nodded and Dr Harker brushed Tom's coat down, adjusted his lace cuffs and tapped his cane loudly on the pavement. 'Good,' he said, regaining his previous relaxed manner. 'Good. Then let us away to the theatre.'

Tom had been so frozen by Dr Harker's words and fierce attitude that everything else in the surrounding world seemed to freeze along with him. In the alley there had seemed to be no sound other than that of Dr Harker's intense whispering voice, but as they emerged again, the rich cacophony of London life rolled back in like a mighty wave and crashed over them.

Carriages rumbled over the cobbles, shoppers milled about, staring in windows and chattering. Tom recovered his good spirits as they walked past Charing Cross, and the deadly danger Dr Harker spoke of seemed already a world away as they turned into the Haymarket. Tom was determined to enjoy himself.

Dr Harker had the use of a box that was reserved

by a friend of his from the Royal Society, so they could avoid the scrum of people as they tried to find their seats. Once in their box overlooking the stage, they could look down on the rowdy benches below and the crowded galleries behind them.

An orchestra was playing but it could not be heard above the noise of young rakes yelling drunkenly at each other, friends hailing each other from yards away and a general thunderous rumble as the audience chattered and gossiped. A group of men in the gallery began singing – a bawdy song unconnected with the music the orchestra was doggedly playing.

A hat was taken from an old man's head and flung across the theatre, to loud cheering from the gallery. A half-eaten orange flew past and hit a young lady on the side of the face, prompting her beau to get to his feet with his hand on his sword hilt, but as he had no idea where the fruit had come from he was forced to sit down again, to loud, derisive laughter.

The opera was called *Harlequin in Love*, and Tom wondered how it was going to compete with the drama the audience had created before the performance, but he need not have worried. Though Dr Harker shook his head in dismay, Tom was spellbound, as the singers appeared in ever more elaborate costumes in front of extravagantly painted backdrops. Cymbals crashed, small explosions flashed and banged, and a flock of small birds were released and flew in panic around the theatre, settling on wigs and spattering hats with their droppings.

Tom had not the faintest idea what was going on, of course, as the words, even if he could have made them out, were sung in Italian, but the spectacle of it enthralled him. He was particularly taken with the actress dressed as a man who sang a particularly sad song towards the end of the opera.

'Did you enjoy that?' asked Dr Harker when they were outside afterwards.

'Yes,' said Tom. 'Immensely. Though I could see that you were not impressed.'

'No, no,' began the doctor with a sigh. 'Well . . . Actually, Tom, the truth is, I hated it.'

Tom laughed and Dr Harker joined him.

'I'm sorry, sir,' said Tom. 'I hope it was not too much of a trial for you.'

'I think I will recover soon enough,' said Dr Harker with a smile. 'But I must say I could do with some air. The night is still young, Tom. What say we take a stroll by the river?'

'I'd like that, sir,' said Tom, who was hoping he would be brave enough to broach the subject of the mysterious Monsieur Petit again.

'So what was it you most enjoyed?' asked Dr Harker as they walked besides the Thames.

'Oh, the actress who sang the song near the end.'

'The astonishingly plump one?' asked Dr Harker in a baffled voice.

'No, sir,' said Tom, surprised that there could be any confusion. 'Not her. The one who was dressed as a man.'

'The one who . . . was . . . dressed . . .' the doctor began. He stopped and looked at Tom with raised eyebrows. 'The one who was dressed as a man!' he repeated, and to Tom's surprise he collapsed into roaring laughter and had to support himself on his cane.

'Dr Harker?' said Tom, a little annoyed now. 'What is it that is so funny?'

The doctor pulled himself upright and, taking a silk handkerchief from his pocket, dabbed at the tears in his eyes. 'Oh dear, oh my word,' he said, taking deep breaths to control himself. 'That was no actress, young Marlowe. That was a castrato.'

Tom could see it was taking an effort of will for the doctor to stop himself laughing again. 'A cast— cast— A what, sir?' he said in exasperation.

'A castrato, Tom.'

'So she was a castrato? And what is that, if I may ask?'

'It's *he*,' said Dr Harker with a sigh and a grin. 'A castrato is . . . Well . . . a castrato is . . . How can I put this . . . ?'

Dr Harker's words petered out and he squinted

over Tom's shoulder into the distance. Tom turned and saw that there was a small commotion some way off ahead of them. A group of boatmen and passers-by were clustered around some steps leading down to the river and the ferry boats moored there. Dr Harker walked purposefully towards them and Tom followed.

As they got nearer they could hear that the voices of the boatmen, usually so raucous and curse-laden, were strangely hushed. Two of them held lanterns over their heads and the light from them swayed back and forth, making the shadows flex and stretch, as if the quay itself were afloat on a choppy sea. As Tom and Dr Harker reached the top of the slimy steps, they could see that one of the boatmen had a punting pole and was prodding about between the ferry boats with great concentration.

'He's gone under again . . . No, no, there he is . . . If I can just get the pole under him and . . .'

The water was as black as strong coffee. Suddenly something bobbed to the surface between the ferry hulls. Tom could not make out what it was at first. It was covered in lank brown hair. A dead dog perhaps? Another prod by the ferry men left no doubt, as the thing spun round in the water. It was a human head, and the rest of the body rose up to the surface with a sickening whoosh, its clothes billowing around in the inky waters.

4

T*he* SKEAN-DHU

Tom shuddered and let out an involuntary groan as the body bobbed up and down in the black water, its bloodless face as white as the lace at its throat.

An old man standing nearby turned and grinned gap-toothed from under his crumpled, broad-brimmed hat. 'Another what's had a bit too much of the Geneva,' he said and cackled. 'Eh? Eh? I said, another what's had too much of the gin.'

Tom did not answer and the old man cackled

again. The ferrymen heaved the body up onto the quayside and it slapped down wetly onto the stonework like a pile of newly washed clothes.

Just as they did so Under-marshal Hitchin appeared, silver baton in hand, with his motley guard of thugs and ruffians. Tom and Dr Harker had had previous dealings with the odious Hitchin, and he in turn remained deeply suspicious of them both. He smiled wolfishly at Tom as he passed by, and Tom moved a little closer to Dr Harker.

The under-marshal shoved the old man aside and made his way forward. 'Make way, make way,' he said. 'Let me through, let me through. What have we got then? Another drunk gone swimming?'

'That's what I said, ain't it?' said the old man, turning to Tom with a self-satisfied smirk. 'Too much of the gin!'

'Anyone gone through his pockets?' said Hitchin, ignoring him.

The ferrymen shook their heads despite the fact that Tom had seen two of them doing just that only seconds before Hitchin arrived.

'Anybody know him?' No one answered. 'Well, then,' said Hitchin, turning to one of his men and waving in the direction of the body. 'Fetch a cart. The surgeons can play with him. And make sure you get paid this time!'

'Wait,' said Dr Harker.

Hitchin looked up. 'I do not much like being interrupted in my business, Doctor,' he said coldly. 'What is it?'

'And I apologize, of course. But I do not think he drowned,' said Dr Harker. 'Or at any rate, he did not *just* drown. I believe he was a Jacobite and I believe he was murdered.'

Hitchin paused for a minute and then laughed loudly, joined a moment later by his men. 'That's very good, Doctor.' He had stopped laughing now and looked coldly once more at Dr Harker. 'Now where's that cart?'

'Look at his arm,' said Dr Harker. 'His right forearm.'

'What has any of this got to do with you, may I ask?' Hitchin took a step towards Dr Harker.

'I am a citizen of London,' said the doctor. 'And you are in its employ. I need no other qualification. Now I ask you again, will you look at his arm – or do I have to send for a Justice of the Peace?'

Hitchin squinted at him and then reluctantly dropped onto his haunches to inspect the arm, grabbing a ferryman's light. Tom could see clearly now what the doctor had already spotted. There was a word, or at least some letters, tattooed on the arm: JAFRED. But what did it mean? The puzzled look on Hitchin's face asked the same question.

'It is a composite word,' Dr Harker explained. 'I've

seen it before. It is made up of the first two letters of his leader's forenames: James Francis Edward. He is a follower of James Stuart, the Pretender; a Jacobite agent.'

A murmur went round the group of ferrymen.

'Even if this was true,' said Hitchin with a bored sigh, 'what makes you so sure he was murdered?'

'Turn him over,' said Dr Harker.

'Do it,' ordered Hitchin.

Two of them rolled the body onto its front with another sickly wet-fish slap. Sticking out of its back, next to the shoulder blade, was the hilt of a small dagger. It seemed to Tom that everyone present turned to look at Dr Harker in amazement.

'I happened to see it as the body rolled over in the water,' said Dr Harker.

Hitchin pulled the dagger out and inspected it. The lantern light flickered across the wet blade. 'You mean to tell me that this little darning needle killed him?'

'It's possible,' said Dr Harker. 'But I think the fatal blow was probably struck with something larger.'

Sure enough, one of Hitchin's men found a tear in the man's coat that was probably a sword cut.

'Then why the dagger?' Hitchin asked.

'It is a skean-dhu,' said Dr Harker. Hitchin squinted in bafflement. 'A Scottish dagger,' the doctor continued. 'Someone wanted it to be known that this was a Jacobite rebel. They wish his colleagues to know he has been killed.'

'You seem to know a great deal about these Jacobites, Dr Harker,' said Hitchin suspiciously.

'I know a great deal about a great many things. I make no apology for it.'

'But one might wonder where your true sympathies lie,' said Hitchin. 'These are troubled times, are they not? Knowing about Jacobites is one thing but—'

'I know a great deal about fish,' interrupted Dr Harker. 'Does that make me a trout?'

One of Hitchin's men laughed for a few noisy seconds until a glance from the under-marshal silenced him.

'Don't think to bandy words with—' he began, but he was interrupted by the noisy arrival of a carriage and a group of armed men on horseback. They dismounted and ran down towards the steps, their boots clattering across the pavement. Two of them grabbed the body; the rest pointed cocked pistols at Hitchin's men.

'What's the meaning of this?' shouted Hitchin. 'Do you know who I am?'

Another knot of black-clad men came forward, holding pistols up to their chests. Several others took up positions around the carriage, watching the nearby building, pistols cocked. One of the men approached Hitchin and, without even looking at him, held out a letter.

He snatched it, read it, squinted at the messenger and handed the letter back. 'What do I say if someone comes for the body?' he asked as the man walked away again.

'What body?' came the reply as four of the men carried the body to a waiting carriage and threw it in. With a couple of shouts from the driver and a clatter of hooves the carriage and horsemen were gone, leaving Tom, Dr Harker, Hitchin and the others standing rather foolishly around the puddle that was the only tangible sign that the body had ever been there.

'Who was that, Hitchin?' said Dr Harker.

'That's Under-marshal Hitchin to you!' snapped Hitchin. 'And don't nobody forget it!' Then quietly, almost to himself, he said, 'I don't know. Government men.'

'But what about the murdered man?'

'Who cares?' said Hitchin. 'He was a Jacobite, like you said. It's just one of the vermin we won't have to hang.'

He gathered his men together and they began to move off, shoving bystanders out of the way in a transparent effort to regain some credibility in the face of such a public humiliation. But just as he was leaving, one of the ferrymen pointed up at the sky to the north-west over Tyburn and Hampstead beyond and shouted, 'Look at that!'

'Lord save us!' said another.

Everyone, including Tom and Dr Harker, turned to follow the ferrymen's gaze, and there in the sky was a weird floating pale light with rainbow colours at its edge, flickering and drifting in and out of visibility.

'Extraordinary!' said Dr Harker. 'Look at this, Tom!'

'What is it, sir?' said Tom.

'I have no idea. Some freakish effect of nature. Some sort of optical marvel. Isn't it wonderful?'

'Come on,' said Hitchin to his men, sounding nervous and eager for this troubled night to end. 'Let's get out of here!'

'Extraordinary,' said Dr Harker, shaking his head and smiling up at the sky in wonderment. 'Quite extraordinary.'

$\mathcal{D}$eath ON A PALE HORSE

$\mathbf{A}$ few days later, Tom and Dr Harker were walking through Ludgate on their way to The Quill coffee house. Tom had been over and over in his mind the events of recent days. During his many sleepless nights, his mind raced with images of axes and daggers, severed heads and floating bodies. People were now calling the strange lights in the sky Tom had seen that night 'The Earl of Derwentwater Lights' after the executed Jacobite lord.

It seemed to Tom that the whole Jacobite business

was pressing in around him, and he had failed to come to any conclusion about Dr Harker's involvement. He did not want to believe that the doctor was mixed up in the Jacobite cause, but the more he thought about it, the more there seemed to be no other sensible explanation. Tom had resolved to watch and wait.

Dr Harker seemed to sense Tom's troubled mind and put a hand on his shoulder as they walked. 'This is a great country, Tom,' he said, 'but it is also full of terrible darkness. Remember always that I care a great deal for your safety and would not see you harmed for all the world.'

Tom smiled and nodded. Dr Harker opened the door to The Quill and waved Tom inside with a theatrical flourish. 'After you, sir,' he said with a bow of his head.

Tom smiled weakly and went in, spoiling the effect slightly by tripping on the step and almost falling into the coffee house. Dr Harker scowled, but not at Tom's clumsiness. Someone was sitting in the doctor's favourite seat, his face hidden behind the newspaper he was reading. They were just looking for other seats when the newspaper dropped and Tom recognized Dr Harker's friend Thornley from Tower Hill.

'Dr Harker,' said Tom. 'It's Mr Thornley.'

'Josiah,' said Thornley, getting to his feet.

'Daniel.' Dr Harker smiled and shook the hand

he was offered. 'You have met Tom Marlowe here.'

'Pleased to meet you again, Master Marlowe,' said Thornley, shaking Tom's hand in turn.

'And I you, sir,' Tom replied.

'Splendid, splendid,' said Thornley.

Tom noticed that Thornley was quite changed since he last saw him. He was clean-shaven now and wore expensive clothes. Even so, they were black and sober and in no way flamboyant. Tom gained the swift impression that Thornley seemed almost to dress for the occasion in order to seem as inconspicuous as possible. It was certainly impossible to tell what trade he was in, let alone why it was that Dr Harker had hoped he might have changed it.

'Come – let's all sit down,' said Thornley. 'I can see why you come here, Josiah. The coffee is excellent.'

Dr Harker and Tom sat down and Thornley ordered drinks for them all, again remarking on the pleasant surprise of seeing them again so soon.

'Why are you here, Daniel?' said Dr Harker with an expressionless face.

'Same old Josiah' – Thornley smiled – 'always to the point.'

'Why are you here?' repeated Dr Harker. 'What do you want? It is wonderful to see you, of course, and I hope we shall have a chance to talk about old times and dine together, but please – why have you come? It certainly is not to tell me that the coffee here is excellent. Though it is.'

The smile disappeared momentarily from Thornley's face. 'These are dangerous times, Josiah,' he said. 'I wonder if you realize how dangerous?'

'I was saying something similar to our young friend here, not ten minutes ago,' Dr Harker replied.

'And yet I hear you were openly speaking Scotch the other night. Do you think that wise?'

'I was not speaking "Scotch", as you put it, Daniel. I merely gave the correct name for the dagger the poor unfortunate man was stabbed with. Is that a crime now, in this great country of ours?'

'Yes!' snapped Thornley, thumping his hand down on the table. Customers nearby turned and frowned at them. There was a tense pause before Thornley calmed himself and dropped his voice once more. 'Listen to me, Josiah. You are a very clever man, but you need to show more common sense. Have you had any visitors?'

Tom looked at his friend and thought of the strange Monsieur Petit.

'No,' said Dr Harker. 'I have had no visitors.'

Thornley looked hard at him and then at Tom, but Tom said nothing. Just then a huge commotion erupted at a nearby table.

'It's a disgrace!'

'Hang the lot of them!'

'It's not safe to leave the city!'

'It's not safe *in* the city either!'

'If they spent as much time chasing highwaymen as they do chasing Jacobites the country might be a better place for honest folk. What say you, Dr Harker?' The speaker was a stout, red-faced man at the next table.

'If they spent a little more time mending the roads, life would certainly be better for honest backsides,' said Dr Harker, to some laughter. 'But I see you are not in a joking mood today. What has especially upset you?'

'My brother here has been the victim of highway robbery,' said his friend.

'Then he should be grateful,' said Thornley, settling back into his chair.

'Grateful? How so?'

'For escaping with his life,' replied Thornley with a broad smile that was not returned.

'You must forgive my friend,' said Dr Harker, giving Thornley a weary look. 'He means no harm. He enjoys playing the cynic. But there is something in what he says, after all. Whatever was stolen, at least your brother is safe and well. That at least is cause for some cheer.'

'Yes, Dr Harker,' said the brother, still looking suspiciously at Thornley. 'I am of course grateful that I was not harmed. But another fellow traveller was not so lucky.'

Dr Harker shook his head. 'What is this about your fellow passenger?'

'Murdered, he was,' said the man. 'Murdered in cold blood.' As he spoke, he suddenly looked a little self-conscious: the whole coffee house was now looking at him and hanging on his every word. Everyone, that is, Tom noticed, except Thornley, who had half closed his eyes as if the whole subject bored him.

'Go on, sir,' urged Dr Harker.

'Well,' said the man, 'I had some business to attend to in Oxford – I am a clockmaker by trade – and was returning to London by stagecoach. We had not travelled long before I fell into conversation with my fellow passengers: an innkeeper from Southwark, a haberdasher from Cheapside and a tobacco grower from the Americas. The innkeeper was an enthusiastic talker, entertaining us with a great many colourful stories. It seemed a long time before anyone else had a chance to speak.

'The fellow from the Americas, when he did speak, was equally entertaining. The Americas were far more dangerous than England for the traveller, with not only bandits to fear, but bloodthirsty savages to boot. He said he always carried a pistol just in case and was an excellent shot. I confess I found it a comfort to have him aboard, as I for one had no experience of bandits and had no wish to gain any.

'He had many fascinating tales of the Colonies and

made the journey fly by. His charm was only increased by the knowledge that he bravely carried some deformity in his right hand. Though he wore a glove to conceal it, it was evident the hand was ruined in some way. Yet here was a man who was brimming with confidence and self-reliance. He was an inspiration, sir . . . and yet we were to see him shot down like an animal.' The clockmaker looked down and wiped his brow, the tips of his fingers disappearing under his wig as he did so.

'A brandy for my friend here,' said Dr Harker.

'No,' said the clockmaker, raising his hand. 'Thank you, but no. I do not drink intoxicating spirits. I am well, thank you. But I am not used to such scenes. It has disturbed me a great deal.'

'It is perfectly natural,' said Dr Harker. 'I should not have pressed you to report the matter. Forgive me.'

'No, I will speak. If only to tell you of the extraordinary nature of our attacker.'

'Extraordinary? Extraordinary in what way?'

'Well' – the clockmaker took a breath and seemed to search for the words – 'the man – if man he was – had no face . . . or no face to speak of. Where a face should have been there was only the white bones of a skull. Even as I say the words I doubt the powers of my own senses, but I swear to you that I saw what I say I saw.'

'The White Rider!' exclaimed Dr Harker. 'I knew

it!' There was a murmur of recognition. The doctor was clearly not the only customer of The Quill to have been following the story.

'You know of this creature?'

'Only by reputation,' Dr Harker replied. 'Come, tell us everything, my friend. Omit nothing. You were talking to another passenger. Then what happened?'

'Well, sir, the first inkling we had that anything was amiss was when we heard a loud bang, which I now take to have been a pistol shot, and the coach skidded to a halt. Then a voice outside shouted for us to stay where we were if we wanted to live. I leaned out of the window, looked in the direction of the voice and that was when I saw—'

'You saw a highwayman,' suggested Dr Harker. 'The skull-faced highwayman? The White Rider?'

'Yes. He was sitting on a white horse, and a strange glow was emanating from the ground in front of him and from the smoke billowing about him, so that he looked more like a creature from hell than of this world. Then he rode towards us. It was a fearful sight.'

'Did this apparition speak?' asked Dr Harker.

'Yes, it did,' said the clockmaker. 'In a loud voice, he shouted, "Gentlemen! Do as I say and none will be harmed, but be sure that I will punish any misbehaviour most speedily. I only want your valuables, but I will take your life if needs be." Then suddenly the man from the Americas shouted, "This is outrageous! We will not give in to such knavery!" and made for the door. I struggled with him and pleaded with him to stop. I should have fought harder to restrain him.' The man looked down into his lap and shook his head.

'You must not blame yourself,' said his brother.

'Please,' said Dr Harker gently. 'What happened then?'

'Well,' said the clockmaker, looking up, 'my fellow passenger shouted at the fiend who had attacked us and stood his ground bravely, refusing to give up any of his valuables. He pulled the pistol from his coat pocket and fired it straight at the brigand. Straight at him . . .'

'Yes?' said Dr Harker.

'Well . . . I . . . the highwayman simply sat there unharmed.' A murmur rippled round the customers.

'The man missed?' said Dr Harker.

'Yes . . . No . . . I do not see how he could have missed so completely,' said the clockmaker. 'But in any case, as our fellow passenger stood there, with the smoke still rising from his pistol, the highwayman suddenly—' He broke off and stared ahead, trying to come to terms with the memory.

'What is it?' asked Dr Harker.

'He . . . he . . .' continued the clockmaker, as if in a trance. 'He suddenly pointed at our fellow – merely pointed, mark you – and the American emitted a strangled cry and a scream, and then to our amazement a glow began to emanate from his body and he dropped to the ground. Smoke seemed to be rising from his chest. His eyes were open and staring.' He looked around the coffee house at the faces of his listeners and said quietly, almost to himself. 'He . . . was . . . dead.'

Tom looked at Dr Harker for some comfort, but the doctor's face was as inscrutable as ever. Thornley's face too was mask-like. How could a man be killed in such a manner? Tom wondered. How could someone be killed merely by the pointing of a finger? There was no reason to doubt the man's story. There were other witnesses, after all.

'What happened then?' asked Dr Harker.

'Then?' said the clockmaker, surprised by the question and wondering how much more of a tale Dr Harker wanted.

'Did the highwayman speak again?'

'Yes,' he replied. 'The fiend shouted at us triumphantly that the same fate would befall anyone who did not obey him immediately. You may not be surprised to learn that we co-operated most readily after that. We are not brave men, sir. We are not fighting men.'

'There is no shame in being robbed,' said Dr Harker. 'Or in choosing to live.'

'The rider came closer and threw a sack into the

carriage for us to fill and we all did so with a fearful energy. He reached out for the sack and I handed it back to him. I saw eyes twinkle in what had seemed empty sockets as he took it from me. He then bellowed for us to move on. I looked at the lifeless form of my fellow on the ground, but to my shame we left him there. Forgive me, Lord.'

'Try not to judge yourself too harshly,' said Dr Harker. 'There is nothing you could have done. We should all have done the same in your place.' Gentlemen around the room nodded in agreement.

'Thank you, sir,' said the clockmaker, smiling weakly. 'And I must own that I am not a total wretch in this regard. I did seek out the sheriff when we reached Camden and rode with him and his men to the spot where the attack had taken place.'

'Good man,' said Dr Harker. 'And so you were able to take the body back. Were you able to discover who the poor man was?'

'But that's just it,' he answered. 'He wasn't there.'

'Wasn't there? Could you have been mistaken about the location?'

'No,' said the clockmaker. 'There was a milestone next to the carriage where the man fell. There can be no doubt that that was the place. But there was no sign of the body.'

'Perhaps some passer-by found it?' suggested Dr

Harker.

'Perhaps.' The clockmaker opened his mouth to continue, but a strange high-pitched whine suddenly screeched out and everyone winced and turned to look for its source.

Reverend Purney from Newgate prison was rubbing his bony finger round the rim of his brandy glass. ' "And I looked, and behold a pale horse," ' he quoted. ' "And his name that sat upon him was Death, and Hell followed with him. And power was given unto them over the fourth part of the earth, to kill with sword, and with hunger, and with death, and with the beasts of the earth." Revelations, chapter six, verse eight.'

'Do you honestly believe that the end of the world will be signalled by a highwayman?' said Dr Harker. 'Really, Purney. You seem to be positively eager for the Apocalypse.'

'These are strange times,' replied Purney. 'Did you not see the strange lights in the sky? Does the Lord not give us signs and wonders? Is the country not crawling with papists? Do you not wish to be prepared for the second coming? All your clever words will be of little consequence on the Day of Judgement, Doctor. "Blessed is he that watcheth, and keepeth his garments, lest he walk naked, and they see his shame." Revelations, chapter sixteen, verse fifteen. Perhaps you need to read your Bible a little more and your science books a little less.'

Dr Harker shook his head and turned back to the clockmaker, who was already getting up to leave. The doctor stood and shook his hand. 'It was good to meet you, sir,' he said. 'I hope these events do not trouble you long.'

'Thank you, sir,' he replied. 'You have been very kind.' He bowed and put on his hat. The clockmaker's brother got up too, shook his head and patted Dr Harker on the arm before making for the door.

Tom looked around the room and saw the customers turn back to their coffees and newspapers: all except for Purney, who continued to scowl at Dr Harker as if trying to bring the wrath of the Almighty down on him that instant.

'Quite a tale,' said Thornley, whose eyes were completely closed now.

'You do not believe him?' said Dr Harker.

'I neither believe nor disbelieve him. He does not concern me. Frankly, Josiah, I am a little surprised at the interest you take in these people.'

'I thought you took an interest in everything,' said Dr Harker. Thornley smiled. 'You never did say why you were here, Daniel.'

Thornley opened his eyes and leaned forward. 'I am here to help you, Josiah, if you'll let me. But first I need you to stop playing games with me.' He looked at Tom and then back to his friend. 'You said earlier that you had had no visitors but that is untrue.' Dr

Harker said nothing. 'You were visited by a mutual friend of ours. Please do not deny it, because I know it to be true.'

'Then why ask? It seems to me that it is you who are playing games. And I am not aware of needing your help.'

'That,' said Thornley, getting to his feet, 'is precisely why you do.' With that he tipped his hat to them both, smiled his wide bright smile and left.

Tom looked at Dr Harker, but the doctor seemed to be in a world of his own. Above the clatter and clink of the coffee house, Tom heard Purney mutter, as if to himself: '"And his name that sat upon him was Death."'

A VISITOR *from* AMERICA

It was a troubled Tom Marlowe who entered the churchyard of St Bride's on a cool March morning a week or so later. He was still plagued by seemingly unanswerable questions, and Dr Harker was being as inscrutable as ever.

'I wish I could talk to you, Will,' said Tom. 'Really talk to you. Dr Harker has said I mustn't say anything about the things I've seen, but I can't just pretend I never saw them. For a start, who is Monsieur Petit and why was he pretending to be French when I'm sure he was Scottish?' The cherub on Will's headstone looked back with its usual blank smile. 'And who is Daniel Thornley? How does Dr Harker know him? Something is going on, I'm sure of it . . . but what?'

Tom dropped onto his haunches so that he was level with the cherub and reached out his hand to rest on the cold stone above its carved curls.

'Oh, Will,' said Tom with a sigh. 'What shall I do? All this secrecy is choking me. Besides, suppose Dr Harker is in trouble and needs my help but won't ask?' This last thought seemed to stir him into action. 'I've got to talk to someone, Will, but who? Who can I trust?'

Tom stood up and snapped his fingers. 'Of course! Ocean! If there's any man in London I can trust, it's him. Ocean will know what to do! Thanks, Will.'

With that, Tom walked briskly towards the church-yard gate and headed off towards the Lamb and Lion printing house.

'Ocean,' said Tom. 'How are you?'

'Me?' said Ocean without looking up from the pamphlets he was sorting. 'I'm fine. How's everything going with Dr Harker? Is he teaching you everything he knows, then?'

'Actually, Ocean, it's about Dr Harker that I've come,' said Tom. 'You see—'

'Tom,' said Mr Marlowe, who had just appeared in

the doorway with another man, who was dressed in expensive clothes. 'I . . . I wasn't expecting you.'

'Tom!' said the other man.

'Excuse me,' said Tom. 'Do I know you?'

'Does he know me?' said the stranger, turning to Mr Marlowe, whose face bore a strange, heavy expression Tom had never seen before. 'Does he know me indeed?' The man turned back to Tom. 'It is to my shame that you do not know me, Tom. Had I been a better man, you should have known me well, but what's done is dead and I say best bury it and be done. I'm here now and that's the news, eh, lad? All the way from America.'

'I'm sorry—' began Tom, utterly perplexed.

'Sorry? You? Sorry? Why, there's no need for you to feel sorry. There's only one in this room that needs use of that word, eh, Marlowe, and that's the man you see before you now, but I say, what use is all the sorrys in purgatory if you don't make amends, eh, lad? I could stand in the pillory for days, Tom – weeks, even, but it wouldn't make things right, now would it?'

'Make what right?' Tom asked. 'Who are you, sir?'

The man stopped with his mouth wide open, looked first at Tom, then at Mr Marlowe, then back to Tom, before slapping his palm against his forehead. 'But of course. I was forgetting that Mr Marlowe here – fine upstanding man that he is—'

'Be careful, Greaves . . .' began Mr Marlowe ominously.

'Who is this man, Father?' said Tom, seeing the anxiety growing on Mr Marlowe's face.

'Ah, but isn't that just the nut of it, Tom? Haven't you just put your finger right there on it?' said the man with a grin. 'The man there,' he said, pointing to Mr Marlowe; 'that man there, he's not your father at all, lad.'

Tom looked at Mr Marlowe in disbelief, but Mr Marlowe said nothing to contradict it. He looked at Tom with tears filling his eyes but kept his peace.

'And you might ask how come I know these facts pertaining to your good self, Tom,' said the man. 'Well,' he went on, 'the short of it is that I know that he ain't your father because *I* am. I am your father, Tom, and right proud to be finally making your acquaintance.'

The man held out his hand for Tom to shake, but Tom looked at Ocean, who stood as if in a trance, and then at Mr Marlowe, who opened his mouth to speak – but whatever words he hoped would come failed to arrive and he closed his lips again and screwed his eyes shut. When he opened them again, Tom was gone.

Tom wandered out into the street and walked like a blind man, shoving his way through the crowd, oblivious to the complaints and curses. He didn't think about where he was going; he didn't think about much at all. His mind was numb, as if the blow of hearing that news had deadened it.

Suddenly, like a rush of wind, the sound of the world around him came flooding back in. Tom looked around like a sleepwalker, waking to find himself in Smithfield Market. Cattle were lowing, sheep bleating, pigs grunting and a cart full of chickens in wicker cages rumbled by spraying a shower of feathers in its wake.

Mr Marlowe had closed up the shop but Ocean let him in. Ocean patted him on the back but neither of them said a word, and Tom climbed the stairs to find Mr Marlowe seated at the old oak table; the table he had eaten at every day of his life until his move to Dr Harker's house.

'Tom!' said Mr Marlowe, rising a little unsteadily to his feet. 'I thought . . . I don't know what I thought, son.'

'Don't call me that!' snapped Tom.

'Tom! I've lied to you, I know, but I only ever did what I thought was best.'

'How could it be best for you to pretend you were my father? To tell me how you loved my mother? Who are you?'

'I'm your uncle, lad,' said Mr Marlowe. 'Your uncle. And I did love your mother. More than anything in the world. She was my sister. My dear sweet sister, and there's not a day goes by when I don't miss her. Not everything was a lie.'

'Not everything?' shouted Tom. 'I have called you Father for as long as I can remember and now I find you're my uncle, and you say not everything is a lie. Well, it feels like it to me!'

'I'm sorry, Tom,' said Mr Marlowe. 'You don't understand—'

'Then make me understand,' said Tom coldly. 'For I dearly wish to learn.'

Mr Marlowe motioned for him to sit and, after a moment's delay, Tom sat down and his uncle sat opposite him. Mr Marlowe drew the flats of both palms down his face, as if he were wiping away sweat. Tom had seen that gesture a thousand times before; seen those huge hands etched with ingrained ink that no amount of scrubbing would ever get out.

'Oh, Tom,' said Mr Marlowe with a sigh. 'I don't know where to begin.' He looked at Tom but Tom said nothing. 'I was six years older than your mother. Our parents died of smallpox when I was only ten, and Jane and me we were sent to the workhouse school. They were tough times, Tom, but me and your mother, we looked out for each other and we got through.

'Even in a place like that, there's sometimes kindness, and there was a lady that used to come and visit and her husband ran a printing house and one day she said would I like to come and be apprenticed there? Would I like to be apprenticed? Oh, Tom, it was like a dream come true. And Jane came too, of course, and the lady said she could be a maid.

'And that's what happened. That's what we did. I worked there as happy as anyone might, and a better master or mistress a body never could have found. Jane and me, so long without any happiness, were now as happy as sunshine.' Mr Marlowe looked at Tom's face and saw that the coldness of his expression had not melted even with the warmth of these memories. He realized he ought to speed his tale along.

'So, anyway, the years passed and I worked through my apprenticeship and Mr Godfrey asked me to stay and work on at his printing house, an offer I gladly accepted. And things might have continued that way, had your mother not met . . . not met your father.' Mr Marlowe gave Tom another glance, but Tom remained expressionless.

'All of a sudden, there he was – your father, Nathaniel Greaves. For the life of me, Tom, I can't recall where and how your mother ever met the man, for she was rarely out of my sight and I had got into the habit of looking out for her since the workhouse days. But meet him she did, curse it all. Meet him she did.' Mr Marlowe stopped and suddenly smiled at the thought that had just come to him. 'Of course, Tom, if she hadn't met him, you'd not be here, so there's good in everything.'

Tom stared on as if in a trance.

'Anyway, in no time at all Jane is saying he wants to marry her and that she loves him, and what could I do? He came round, all proper like, and spoke to me and my master and mistress and told us all how he was an engraver and how he had great prospects. He was a charmer all right. Thing is, Tom, he really *was* an engraver, and a fine one at that. If he had put the effort into that that he put into . . . into other matters . . . he would have been someone.

'Him and Jane got married and I was happy for her, though I was sad to see her go. I shook your father's hand and told him to take good care of her and he swore he would. Swore it on the Bible there in the church, curse him. Then you were born, Tom, and Jane was so happy. I never saw her so happy as when she held you. But Greaves – your father – he was already breaking his oath . . .' Mr Marlowe slammed his hand down on the table. 'No, Tom, it ain't right. It's not for me to tell you this. Greaves should tell you himself.' He got up and made for the door.

Tom didn't know what to do or where to go. Mr Marlowe stopped for a moment and turned back. 'Greaves said he would wait for you,' he said. 'He's staying at The Eagle.'

Nathaniel GREAVES

Tom walked into the brick-paved courtyard of The Eagle. It was deserted except for two mangy cats, who were squaring up to fight until Tom appeared and now ran off in opposite directions, shooting nervous glances over their shoulders as they went. Greaves called down from the gallery that ran all around the courtyard, supported by carved wooden posts.

'Up here, Tom,' he said. 'Glad you decided to come!'

Tom climbed the stairs and Greaves showed him to his room, where he saw a jug of beer and two pewter mugs on a side table.

'Sit yourself down, Tom,' Greaves said. 'I suppose Marlowe has been painting my portrait in all its boils and wrinkles?'

'Actually,' said Tom, 'he said that it was up to you to tell me what I needed to know.'

Greaves raised an eyebrow and then laughed a bitter laugh. He poured them both a beer. 'Did he now? Did he? So he told you nothing then?'

'Nothing,' replied Tom. 'Though he made it plain he did not like you.'

Greaves laughed again. 'Well, nothing's changed in that regard,' he said. 'But I suppose he's right, old Marlowe. I suppose you deserve some history. What is it that you'd like to know? Anything at all, lad. Ask me anything you like. We've got a lot of catching up to do, eh, lad?'

'Why did you go?' asked Tom coldly. 'If you are my father, why did you leave?'

'Cut straight to the bone, don't you, boy?' said Greaves with a smile.

'Why did you leave?' Tom repeated.

'Tom!' said Greaves, clenching his fist. 'Do you think I don't feel a devil's crop of shame for leaving you, boy? Do you think I don't wish I could change things? Do you think I wouldn't like to wipe those sins away?' He looked into Tom's eyes; Tom could not hold his gaze and looked away.

'I was a different man then, Tom. I was a hard man and a weak man. But things is different now. Life has shoved me in its furnace and beat me on its anvil and I'm a changed man. It near broke me, Tom, but I come out stronger for it. And I come to make amends.'

'How can you?' said Tom. 'I've been brought up with lies, and all because you left. And you still haven't told me why!'

'Ah, Tom,' said Greaves. 'You probably won't understand. Look at you. Fine upstanding lad like you. You don't need to have dreams.'

'Dreams?'

'Yeah, dreams. Old Marlowe could never under-stand why I wanted more than this.' Greaves waved his hand round at the whole London scene. 'Me, I used to look at them ships in the dock and wonder where they'd been and if I'd ever see anything but the inside of these city walls and the stinking Thames. You ever felt like that, Tom?'

'Yes,' said Tom, for he had felt like that very often. 'But I would never leave my wife and baby.'

Greaves smiled. 'Be careful what you say you'll never do, Tom. You might surprise yourself one day.'

'And is that what you did?' asked Tom. 'Surprise yourself?'

'Look, Tom. What do you want me to say? I was a wretch. Where a good man would have seen a beautiful wife and baby, I saw my coffin. I saw my life stretched out, nailed up, finished. I was a fool.'

'So it's my fault that you left?'

'No, Tom!' said Greaves. 'Now I didn't say that. It was me at fault. There was nothing but good in you and your mother.' He glanced away and sighed, and then looked back at Tom. 'I fell in with ill company. I took to drinking more than is wise and spending more money than I had. The business began to fail as I did less and less work. And the less I worked the more I drank and the more I spent. Well, anyway, the long and the short of it is that I went from bad to worse and became the kind of wretch a lad like you would cross the street to avoid.'

'And what about us?' said Tom. 'What happened to my mother and me?'

'It came so that I barely saw you, Tom. Even in the state I was in, I could not bear the shame. And not because your mother chided me, but because she never did. Through it all she only ever saw the good in me. Old Marlowe saw straight through me, curse him, but she would have none of it. She was all goodness, Tom, and if there was any good in me at all, she was the only one as could see it.'

'But you left her all the same. And me too.'

Greaves looked at Tom with tears in his eyes.

'You've a hard heart, Tom,' he said. 'But I dare say that's my doing too.'

'Why America?' Tom asked. 'Why go so far?'

Greaves sighed and took another drink. 'So Marlowe really did not tell you then?'

'He told me nothing,' said Tom. 'I wish someone would.'

'I was transported, Tom,' Greaves told him. 'I was a convicted felon, lucky not to hang, if the truth be known.'

'Convicted? Convicted of what?'

'Thievery,' replied Greaves. 'I was as poor a thief as I was a husband and father and got caught too easily. My only luck was in having my trial before a soft-hearted or soft-headed judge who saw fit to spare me the noose. In its stead he sent me to slave in the tobacco fields of the Americas. Your mother came to see me off on the quayside as we were taken aboard, with you in her arms. I thought I would die of shame as I shuffled along in those manacles and chains, Tom. I cursed myself for the weak man I was and for the trail of pain I left in my wake.

'And so I left London for the first time in my life and sailed across the sea to Annapolis in the place they call Maryland. Imagine it, Tom: me, who had never been further than the other side of the Thames.'

'But did you never try to keep in contact? We were your family, after all.'

'No,' replied Greaves. 'I felt it was better that I died out there and your mother might forget me and marry again and you might have a father to be proud of. Of course, your mother, bless her dear heart, she stayed faithful and true to me and only ever hoped that I might return. But at least I was not around to drag you down with me, Tom.'

'Are you trying to say I was better off for having you leave?' asked Tom.

'Yes,' said Greaves. 'I suppose I am. With me out of the way, Marlowe could step in and interfere as much as he'd always wanted to.'

'Without his "interference" we would have ended up in the poorhouse,' said Tom.

'True enough. But that's my point. Marlowe did a better job of bringing you up than I ever could, and that's just how it is. I was no good to you then, Tom.'

'And why should you be any good to me now?' said Tom.

'I'm your father, Tom,' said Greaves.

'You were my father then.'

Greaves looked down at the tabletop and when he looked back at Tom there were tears in his eyes. 'I worked hard in those tobacco fields, Tom. Harder than I needed to. And the owner, Mr Bellingham, noticed the effort I put in. He gave me responsibility over other slaves, even though he knew I was a thief myself. He trusted me – though he had every reason not to. It was a kindness I never would forget.' Greaves paused, clearly moved by the memory. 'Then one day a letter come from Marlowe telling me your mother had died. I felt I was damned, Tom. All that lay ahead was the gates of Hell and any torments I might face there would be well deserved.'

'But you didn't come back,' said Tom.

'I couldn't, Tom. If I had come back before my time, I'd have been hanged.'

'But your time came to an end and you still didn't come back.'

'True, Tom,' said Greaves. 'Don't imagine I didn't think about you, because I did. But Marlowe had told me he was looking after you. I knew you were all right. And when my time was up Bellingham asked me to stay and paid me wages. Things were better how they were.'

'For you,' said Tom.

'I can't change the past, Tom.' Greaves sighed. 'What's done is done. I can only do something about the here and now and the years to come. I'm a different man. I'm not the man who left you. Won't you give me a chance?'

'To do what?' asked Tom.

'To try and make amends,' said Greaves.

'How? Why have you even come back? What have you got to offer me after all these years?'

'A chance to get out of this heaving ant hill and

come with me to America. A chance to see something better than the other side of the street.'

Tom looked at him and Greaves grinned. 'America?' said Tom. 'But . . .'

'I'm a wealthy man, Tom,' said Greaves. 'I dreamed my dream. When Bellingham died he left me land and then . . . Well, it doesn't matter how; the long and the short of it is I've made my fortune and I want you to share it with me. What do you say?'

The TOMAHAWK

The afternoon sunshine filtered into the study, lighting up the floating specks of dust as Dr Harker lifted down boxes from cupboards and searched shelves for books. Tom opened up the ledger and turned to the page showing the last entry. He smoothed it down and picked up his pen.

'I saw Mr Marlowe yesterday, Tom,' said Dr Harker nonchalantly as he rummaged around in a large wooden chest.

'I'd rather not talk about it,' said Tom. 'If you don't

mind, sir.'

'No, Tom. Of course, of course. And how is everything going with Mr Greaves? It must have been—'

'With all respect, sir,' said Tom, a little more forcefully than he had intended. 'These things are private. We all have things that are private, don't we, sir?'

Dr Harker looked long and hard at Tom. He could hear the tone in his voice and the hurt there too, but he did not respond to it. He knew Tom's temper and was happy to drop the subject. 'As you like, Tom. Back to work then.'

The doctor picked up a large package wrapped in calico and tied with string. 'I think you will find this interesting. A friend of mine sent it to me from Maine.' He pulled the string and the calico fell away to reveal a small hatchet with a metal blade inscribed with geometric designs set into a wooden handle with black feathers tied to the shaft. He picked it up. 'It's an Indian tomahawk, Tom. Iroquois probably. It's rather wonderful, is it not?'

Tom agreed that it was rather wonderful, though he doubted it would be quite so appealing in the hands of its original owner.

'Could you run downstairs, Tom,' asked the doctor, 'and ask Mrs Tibbs for a cloth and maybe a little vinegar and we can see if we might clean this up a little?'

Tom was almost at the bottom of the stairs when

there was an odd sound at the front door: a strange scratching and tapping. He drew the bolt and opened the door and to his horror found himself inches away from a face that was horribly beaten and bruised, with dried blood across the forehead and fresh blood streaming from the nose and lip. One of the eyes was closed behind blue and swollen lids. It took Tom a few seconds before he realized it was Daniel Thornley.

The door had been the only thing holding Thornley up, and now he slumped across the threshold and fell to the floor. Sarah came out from dusting the dining room and screamed, running to the kitchen for Mrs Tibbs, the housekeeper, and bringing Dr Harker down from his study.

'Dr Harker!' shouted Tom. 'Come quickly!'

Sarah reappeared, clutching a handkerchief to her face.

'Close the door, Sarah,' said Dr Harker as he crossed the hall, but Sarah did not move. 'Come, girl,' he urged, kindly but firmly. 'Be brave, now.'

Sarah inched her way past the fallen Thornley and closed the door.

'Now, Tom; help me here. Let's get him to the kitchen.' As they lifted him up Dr Harker asked, 'Can you walk, Daniel?'

'I think so, yes,' said Thornley, before hissing in pain.

'Who did this?'

'Could I – Aaah! – Could I trouble you for a

brandy, Josiah?' asked Thornley as they eased him into a seat.

'Sarah, fetch a bottle of brandy, will you? Mrs Tibbs, could I trouble you for a bowl of hot water and some linen?'

'Yes, Dr Harker, sir,' said Sarah, now restored to her usual efficient self. She brushed into Thornley as she left the room and he yelled after her, cursing loudly.

'I apologize for my friend here, ladies,' said Dr Harker. 'He is in some pain.'

'Of course, sir,' said Mrs Tibbs, tutting to herself.

'Now.' Dr Harker held a candle up in front of Thornley's face and inspected his injuries. 'Off with your waistcoat and shirt, man, and let's see what's amiss.'

Sarah shrieked again when she came in and saw Thornley stripped to the waist. She put down the brandy and hurried out of the room, blushing. Thornley was covered in red marks.

'Will you stop that infernal shrieking, you silly girl!' he shouted.

'I'll thank you not to talk to Sarah like that, Daniel. You will be black and blue on the morrow, but there does not appear to be anything broken. You must stay here for the next few days. You are a lucky man.'

Thornley laughed a wry laugh and instantly regretted it as he clenched his teeth in pain. 'Much more of this good fortune and I'll be a dead man,' he said.

Sarah reappeared with the bowl of hot water and left as hurriedly as before.

'Pour us all a drink, would you, Tom?' asked Dr Harker. 'And Daniel here will tell us what happened this evening.'

Tom poured the drinks and Thornley settled back in the chair, wincing again.

'Who did this to you, Daniel?' the doctor asked again.

Picking up his glass, Thornley cast a quick glance at Tom. 'Can we talk in private? No offence, young man, but my life hangs in the balance here, as you can see. It has nothing to do with you, I promise you. I simply do not know you, and this is too serious to rest on politeness.'

Dr Harker looked at Tom and Tom could see what was coming. 'I am sorry, Tom,' said the doctor. 'I must ask you to leave. It is for your own good.'

'Is it?' said Tom sharply. 'Never mind. I'll go. If you don't trust me—'

'Tom!'

But Tom was already in the hall and reaching for the front door. He wrenched it open and looked out at the courtyard. The earlier sunshine had been replaced by thick grey clouds and torrential rain. It was then he realized he had forgotten his coat and would have the embarrassment of going back to fetch it.

He slammed the door and then tiptoed across the hall to collect his coat from the hook by the stairs, hoping that Dr Harker and Thornley would not hear him. He did not want to talk to either of them. He just wanted to get out of the house as quickly as possible. As he edged past the door to the kitchen, he heard Dr Harker's voice.

'Who did this?'

Tom held his breath to hear the answer.

'It is best we do not talk about it, Josiah,' said Thornley. 'You know my life. You know the dangers. The less you know of this specific incident the better.'

'But surely—' began Dr Harker.

'I must insist. Secrecy is everything in my trade. Perhaps it would be better if I left—'

'Be still, Daniel,' said Dr Harker calmly. 'You are going nowhere in that condition.'

'I will be fine, Josiah,' said Thornley. 'There is something far more pressing to attend to.'

'And what is that?'

'They have McGregor,' Thornley replied.

Tom craned nearer at the sound of the name McGregor. So it was true. Dr Harker was somehow mixed up with the Scots. But was this McGregor a Jacobite?

'Jamie?' said Dr Harker. 'When?'

'Yesterday. He was arrested and taken to Newgate.

He is in the Red Room awaiting his fate. He'll hang for sure unless we help him.'

Tom had to stop himself gasping when he heard this. So it was true. Dr Harker and Mr Thornley were trying to aid a Jacobite. Tom wondered if this Jamie McGregor was the Monsieur Petit he had met.

'But how can we help him now?' asked Dr Harker.

'I have arranged it so that when Jamie is taken out of the Red Room to be interrogated, he will break free from his guards and escape. I was able to persuade the turnkeys that he is a spy working for the British government, and with the encouragement of a little cash, they were happy to play along. Once out he will need money.'

'How much?'

'A lot,' said Thornley. 'He must get out of the country and join his fellow exiles on the Continent. He will be safe there. A hundred pounds should do the job.'

'I will get the money first thing tomorrow,' said Dr Harker.

'Splendid,' said Thornley.

'Do you think Jamie can get away safely?' asked Dr Harker.

'If any of them can, he can. But I fear he will never be able to return, Josiah.'

'I agree, Daniel,' said Dr Harker. 'How do I get the money to him.'

'With all due respect, I think this rather lies within my area of expertise—'

'No, Daniel,' interrupted Dr Harker. 'You have done enough and risked enough. You have already done far more than anyone had a right to expect. I will deliver the money.'

'Be reasonable, Josiah,' said Thornley. 'The risks I have taken, I have taken willingly. I thank you for your concern, but I really think—'

'I must insist,' said Dr Harker. 'My mind is made up on the matter. Besides, if Jamie is to leave these shores then I would like to see him one last time.'

'Very well,' said Thornley reluctantly. 'I must respect your wishes in this, I suppose, as you are providing the money—'

'Indeed. Now what is the plan?'

'The plan?' said Thornley, hesitating slightly. 'The plan – yes, of course. Jamie's escape will be effected two days from now, on Thursday evening,' he said. 'He will leave Newgate under cover of darkness and go straight to the rendezvous point. You will need to ride north that night, out of London on the Hampstead Road. You will pass a stables and blacksmith's forge on your left; about a mile after that there is a blasted oak beside the road near to a barn. That is where Jamie will be waiting.'

Tom inched away and tiptoed out of the front door, taking as much time as he dared to close it as silently as possible. He hurried through the courtyard and out into Fleet Street, his mind reeling. There could be no doubt now: Dr Harker was at the very least helping a member of the Jacobite cause. At worst he was a Jacobite himself.

The TOWER Menagerie

Tom saw Nathaniel Greaves in the distance as he walked towards the Stocks Market. He was still having great difficulty seeing this stranger as his father. Greaves had his back to Tom; he stood at the foot of the statue of Charles II, listening to a fiddler. Tom tapped him on the shoulder and he looked round and grinned, but turned back to the fiddler, clapping his hands to the tune. A small boy came up to them holding a battered pewter dish and Greaves tossed a few shining coins into it. The boy smiled and the fiddler shouted, 'Thank you, sir! You're a gentle-man, sir!'

'You're very generous,' said Tom as they walked away.

Greaves shrugged. 'I can afford to be,' he said. 'And I love a bit of music.' He took a lungful of London air and spread out his arms as if about to break into song. 'I'm very glad to have your company,' he went on. 'Very glad.'

'I'm glad you're glad,' said Tom.

'Have you thought any more about my offer?'

'Yes,' replied Tom. 'I have thought about it a lot.'

'And have you reached any decision?'

'No. No, I haven't.'

'Well, that's a relief!' said Greaves.

'How so?' asked Tom.

'I thought you'd turn me down flat,' said Greaves. Tom smiled. 'So,' his father continued, 'I thought we might go on a little excursion, you and me.'

'An excursion?' said Tom. 'Where?'

Greaves whistled and waved at the driver of a hackney carriage; it rumbled up the street and came to a halt beside them.

'Come on, Tom,' said Greaves. 'Get in.'

'Where to, friend?' asked the cab driver.

'The Tower!' Greaves shut the door behind them and the driver flicked the reins. The cab jerked forward, rattling down the cobbles towards the river.

'The Tower?' said Tom, the image of Lord Derwentwater's severed head making an unwelcome reappearance in his mind.

'Yeah,' said Greaves. 'I thought we might go to see the lions. That's if you want to.'

'Yes. Of course.' Tom hadn't been to the Menagerie for ages. The last time he had been was with Will. It was one of the few times that Tom had ever seen Will stand still or remain silent for any length of time. Tom had smiled at him as they stood in front of the animals and assumed it was a sense of wonder that had struck Will dumb, but when his friend turned, Tom saw tears in his eyes. They had left soon after and Will had barely spoken all the way back to Fleet Street. Tom never asked him what had upset him, and Will never mentioned it.

'And it's not just any old day down at the Menagerie,' said Greaves, searching his pockets. 'Look here!' He held out a card for Tom to read. It was an invitation to the Tower Menagerie to see the lions being washed in the moat. It had a crudely drawn illustration of a wide-eyed lion on it. 'What about that, then? That ought to be something to see, eh, Tom?'

Tom smiled and raised his eyebrows.

'What?' his father asked.

'It's a joke.'

'A joke?' said Greaves. 'What do you mean?'

'The lions being washed,' said Tom. 'It's a joke. It's April the first.'

'Well I'll be . . .' said Greaves.

'They do it every year. They only really catch foreigners now, because everyone in London is already in the know.'

Greaves shook his head and grinned. 'Foreigners, eh? Well, I suppose I am a foreigner now, in a way. What a chub! All Fools' Day. I must be getting old.' Then he laughed and threw the card out of the carriage window. 'So how come you ain't working for old Marlowe any more?' he asked.

'It's a long story,' said Tom.

'Long, or you just don't want to tell it?'

Tom smiled.

'And this Dr Harker fellow,' his father went on. 'You're his apprentice, are you?'

'Not exactly,' said Tom.

'Not exactly? Strikes me you either is or you ain't. And what trade is he teaching you anyway?'

'It's a bit late for you to take such a concern in my upbringing, don't you think?' said Tom. 'I believe you were once an engraver by trade.'

Greaves raised his hands in mock surrender. 'That's fair, Tom,' he admitted. 'I've got no right to poke and pry.'

'No,' said Tom. 'You haven't.' But he smiled. He wanted to remain angry at Greaves but he found himself liking him despite himself. 'I'm just finding it hard to make sense of all this. A few weeks ago I knew who I was and now I find I wasn't that person at all.'

'It ain't you that's changed, Tom,' said Greaves. 'And from what little I know there ain't no need for you to change neither. I got no right to take any credit for you – I wish I could – but from what I see you're a fine lad.'

'Tower!' shouted the driver as the carriage slowed down and stopped.

Greaves paid the fare and Tom took in the view. Though the clouds out to the east were almost black, the sun now shone where they stood, and lit up the battlements in front of them, and the White Tower beyond. They walked down towards the entrance, paid their money at the gate and walked across the moat to the Menagerie.

There were various animals there, but like most people Tom and his father made straight for the lions. When they got to the dens, Greaves wafted his hand in front of his nose.

'It stinks as bad as Fleet prison in here,' he said, and it was true that the smell of animal dung, damp straw and the offal that had recently been thrown into the dens was overpowering even by London standards. 'I'm sure these brutes were livelier the last time I saw them. But then, we've all got a bit older, I suppose.'

'They look sad,' said Tom, looking at one of the

lions stretched out on the floor, his eyes half closed. A fly landed on the lion's nose and crawled across it but the lion did not stir.

'Sad or not,' said Greaves with a smile, 'that flea-ridden bag of bones would happily rip you to pieces if you went in there, and that's for sure.' The lion slumped over and closed his eyes, dozing. 'Hmmm. Well, when he wakes up, maybe.' He tapped the bars but the lion did not move. 'It makes you think, though, doesn't it?'

'What does?' asked Tom.

'Well,' said his father, 'the old story that if one of the lions dies then the king will die. You've heard that, haven't you?'

'Yes. Of course.'

'Well then,' said Greaves, dropping his voice to a whisper as an elderly couple passed by. 'If they shot one of these lions they could solve this Jacobite non-sense at a stroke, couldn't they? All we'd have to do is wait and see whether it was George or the Pretender that followed suit. Though I have to confess, Tom, I couldn't care less either way.'

'Do you mind if we go?' asked Tom.

'Mind? Why would I mind?'

'I'm sorry,' said Tom. 'I've spoiled your excursion.'

Greaves smiled and put his hand on Tom's shoulder. 'Nonsense,' he said. 'I've got you for company now, haven't I? You're a sensitive lad, Tom.

To tell the truth, seeing all these bars is bringing back a few unpleasant memories.'

'Yes,' said Tom. 'I've been in Newgate myself.'

His father stared at him in amazement.

'As a visitor!' said Tom, laughing.

'Thank goodness for that!' said Greaves. 'I thought there was a criminal career that you'd forgotten to mention.'

Tom laughed again. 'No,' he said. 'It was last year, during my adventure with Dr Harker and Ocean . . . and the Mohawk Tonsahoten.'

'Ah yes . . . The famous Death and the Arrow murders,' said Greaves.

'You know about them?'

'Oh yes. I heard you was involved. The Boston papers even carried the story, you know. I was thinking I really ought to read Dr Harker's book. I dare say, though, he made it seem more exciting than it was.'

'No, no,' said Tom. 'It was really exciting. Terrifying sometimes too. Dr Harker is such an amazing man and you should see Ocean . . .' Tom trailed off.

'Yes?' prompted Greaves.

'Well,' said Tom, 'it was dangerous and frightening and everything, but I never felt so alive as in those days. I lost my best friend in Will and then along came Dr Harker and Ocean and they put their lives at risk to track down his killer. But now they . . .' He trailed off again.

'What is it, Tom?' asked his father.

'Well,' said Tom, 'it's not easy for me to talk to Ocean at the moment, what with him being at the Lamb and Lion . . .' Greaves nodded. 'And I always felt Dr Harker trusted me, but now it seems like he doesn't. He doesn't trust me at all.'

'About what?' said Greaves.

Tom shook his head. 'I shouldn't say.'

'Well, you can't complain about Dr Harker not trusting you' – Greaves laughed – 'and then make it plain you don't trust me!'

Tom smiled. 'You're right. You're right. It's about time I told someone. But it mustn't go any further.'

Greaves put his hand to his heart. 'I swear, Tom.'

So Tom told his father about the executions on Tower Hill and about Daniel Thornley and about the Jacobite rebel pulled from the Thames and about Thornley's beating. He told him about Monsieur Petit and how he was really a Scotsman called McGregor. He told him how he had listened to the plan to break him out of Newgate and help him flee the country with the help of £100. And all through the telling, Greaves listened in silence until Tom had finished and then he breathed a great sigh.

'Well, Tom,' he said, 'that's quite a weight to have been carrying round. I'm glad you felt able to tell me, but if you don't mind me saying, I think this Dr Harker of yours is mixed up in something dark. Just leave it be, Tom, that's my advice. Dr Harker clearly doesn't want your help or he'd ask for it. I know the doctor is a friend of yours, but you need to think of yourself here. This could end at Tyburn.'

'I know,' said Tom. 'I just . . . I don't know.'

'I don't see that there's anything you can do, Tom.'

'I know, I know,' said Tom. 'But I don't know if I can carry on working for Dr Harker with all this going on.' He turned to his father. 'You won't tell anyone that I told you this, will you?'

'Course not, Tom. I know how to keep a secret,' said Greaves. 'Come on, let's walk back. It's been a while since I roamed my home town.'

'Yes,' said Tom with a smile. 'I'd like that.'

And so they did, Greaves pointing out all the sights as if Tom had never seen them before. He moaned at the condition of London Bridge and said that they should knock it down and start again. 'Nonsuch House looks like it'll fall down on its own before much longer!'

When they passed the Monument, Greaves turned to Tom. 'The Great Fire was the best thing that ever happened to London, if you ask me,' he commented. 'It's just a shame it didn't burn the rest of the place down with it. There's too much history here, Tom. Everyone's got their heads on backwards when they should look forwards.'

Tom smiled and wondered if this outburst hadn't

got more to do with his father's wish to wipe away his own history.

However, when they got to St Paul's Cathedral, Greaves looked up and whistled. 'None of this was here when I left, Tom,' he said. 'And now look at it. What do you say we don't go and take ourselves up to the top of that dome?'

Tom's face fell as he remembered the last time he had been up there and how he had nearly been thrown from the top. Nothing would have induced him to climb it again. 'I've already done it,' he said. 'It's nothing special.'

'Well, if you say so,' said his father. 'Mind you, I—'

'The White Rider robs again!' shouted a thin voice nearby. A sickly looking newspaper boy was standing among a knot of customers who muttered and tutted loudly.

'That's the highwayman Dr Harker was so interested in,' said Tom. 'Look, he robbed a coach near Hampstead two nights ago.'

Greaves looked about him and then took out his watch. 'Highwayman, do you say?' he said a little nervously. 'Will you look at the time, Tom! I had no idea it was so late.'

'Is everything all right?'

'All right?' Greaves repeated. 'Yes . . . Yes . . . Of course, Tom. No . . . I've just got some business to attend to. No rest for the wicked, eh?'

'I've enjoyed the time we've spent together,' said Tom.

'So have I,' said his father.

'The White Rider! The White Rider!' shouted the newspaper boy.

'Look, Tom, I've got to go,' said Greaves, slapping Tom on the shoulder and walking away backwards. 'I'll be in touch!' he called, and was soon lost in the crowd.

JAMIE McGREGOR

Dr Harker had not managed to get a single word out of his assistant beyond 'Good Morning' or the occasional 'Yes, sir' or 'No, sir' since the morning began. Tom was aware of the doctor's frustration but felt it served him right, given that he had been as tight-lipped as an oyster himself these past weeks.

'How was your day out with Mr Greaves?' asked Dr Harker, more brightly than he felt. 'Or is that private?' he added with a smile.

Tom did not return it. 'It was very enjoyable, thank

you, sir,' he said primly. 'My father has asked me to sail with him when he leaves.'

'Has he indeed?' said Dr Harker, trying to sound casual. 'And what have you said in response?'

'I have told him that I will think about it.'

'Good Lord,' said Dr Harker. 'Surely you would not give up everything you have here?'

'He is my father, sir,' said Tom. 'And it is a chance for me to see the world. He sails for Africa and then America. I want to have some adventures of my own, sir.'

'Yes, Tom,' said Dr Harker. 'Of course you do, and you shall, I'm sure. But still, you hardly know the man . . .'

'With all respect, sir,' said Tom, 'I hardly know you either, if it comes to that, but I would have trusted you with my life.'

'Would have?' said Dr Harker. 'Say what's on your mind, Tom.'

Tom hesitated.

'We're alone, Tom,' the doctor reassured him. 'Sarah and Mrs Tibbs are in the kitchen and Daniel is asleep in his room.'

'Well, sir,' said Tom, 'I mean that you have made it clear that you do not trust me and—'

'What makes you think I don't trust you, Tom?' asked Dr Harker. 'Whatever you know, or think you know, this was never a matter of trust. Why, I trust you as much as I trust myself. Honestly I do.'

'Then why shut me out, sir?' said Tom. 'I've been of help to you before. Maybe I can be again.'

'You have been a great help, Tom,' said Dr Harker. 'We have been through a lot and I hold you very dear. But that is why I have tried to protect you.'

'You need not,' said Tom. 'I know already, and your secret is safe with me, sir.'

Dr Harker raised an eyebrow and squinted at Tom a little. 'What do you know, Tom? *Exactly?*'

'Well, sir,' said Tom, dropping his voice to a whisper and quickly looking about him. 'Mr Thornley is a Jacobite and you and he are aiding another rebel, a Scotsman named McGregor.'

Dr Harker's expression became very grave. 'Have you told anyone of this suspicion?'

'No,' said Tom a little nervously, for Dr Harker had the same hard look he had witnessed on the way to the theatre.

'Tom,' said the doctor, 'this is important. Very important. Have you mentioned this suspicion to anyone at all?'

'I . . . That is . . . I might have said something to my father,' said Tom.

'Which one?'

'Well, both, as a matter of fact,' Tom admitted. Dr Harker put both hands over his face. 'Mr Marlowe thought it very amusing.'

'Did he?' said Dr Harker. 'I wish I could say the same. Did I not make it clear how dangerous it would be to speculate about these matters, Tom?'

'But I overheard you and Mr Thornley—'

'So you have been spying on me, Tom?'

'I had not meant to,' said Tom, blushing. 'Honestly, sir, I—'

'Never mind,' said Dr Harker with a sigh. 'The damage is done. And what of Mr Greaves? Did he think it was funny?'

'He didn't say,' said Tom. 'I'm sorry, sir. I needed to confide in someone and I haven't managed to speak to Ocean since . . . and you were behaving . . .'

'Well?'

'Suspiciously,' said Tom.

Dr Harker closed his eyes and leaned on his clasped hands as if in prayer. 'I am sorry, Tom. You are absolutely right,' he said. 'I *have* been behaving suspiciously. But tell me, what gave us away as being Jacobites?'

'Well,' said Tom, 'there was Monsieur Petit for a start.'

'Yes?' said Dr Harker.

'He was no Frenchman. I heard him speaking with a Scottish accent before I entered the room.'

Dr Harker chuckled. 'It was a poor ruse, Tom, but you are a clever lad to have seen through it all the same.'

'Then there was the night after the theatre,' said Tom. 'You knew so much about the murdered Jacobite and about the dagger – the skin—'

'Skean-dhu,' said Dr Harker.

'And I forgot to mention Tower Hill,' said Tom, growing in confidence. 'I saw tears in your eyes, Doctor.'

'You did,' Dr Harker agreed, nodding. 'You did.'

'And Mr Thornley,' said Tom. 'I believe that you and he are conspiring to help a Jacobite rebel – this man called Jamie McGregor – to escape this country and flee to the Continent to join the Pretender.'

Dr Harker smiled. 'You are a remarkably intelligent young man,' he said. 'Really you are. And you are correct in every regard—'

'So it *is* true!' said Tom.

'Except that I am not a Jacobite,' the doctor added. 'And neither is Daniel Thornley. In fact, quite the reverse in Daniel's case – Daniel is a government agent . . . a Jacobite *hunter*, Tom.'

Tom looked baffled. 'But how? . . . I . . . I don't understand, sir.'

'You have heard me mention my late wife?' said Dr Harker.

'Yes, many times. But I don't see what—'

'Mary was Scottish, Tom. That is how I came to know something of the ways of that country, and some of the language too.'

'I still don't understand,' said Tom.

'The man you met in my study is a Jacobite, Tom, just as you guessed. He is a Scotsman and not a Frenchman, just as you discovered for yourself, though he has lived in France in recent years. However, he is also my late wife's brother. His name is Jamie McGregor. It is he whom I am trying to aid. Not for his cause, but for the debt I owe to Mary's memory and, well, because however misguided I might believe him to be, Jamie is a fine man, and I would not see him die a traitor's death. That was why you saw tears, Tom, on Tower Hill. It was a tragic event, it's true, and tears were not out of place, but I cried for what might become of Jamie and what Mary would have felt had she been alive to see.'

'But you risk a traitor's death yourself, sir,' said Tom, 'aiding a Jacobite.'

'That I do, Tom. And that is why I wanted you to be at some distance from me. There is a kind of Bedlam fever at work in the country and there will be more deaths before this thing is finished. People are seeing Jacobites in every darkened corner.'

Tom smiled. 'Like me, I suppose.'

'No, Tom,' said Dr Harker. 'You used the evidence you saw to draw a perfectly logical conclusion. You simply did not have all the facts.'

'But why is Mr Thornley helping you?' said Tom. 'I

know he is an old friend, but why would he risk his life for Jamie?'

'Ah,' said Dr Harker. 'To answer that we need to go back many, many years to when we were both children, growing up some miles north of here, in Stoke Newington. Our parents were great friends and Daniel and I became inseparable. We went to school together. My father was a military man in his younger days and it was his fervent wish that I should live that life, but he had to accept that my interests lay else-where, just as I have had to accept that my own son has no interest in anything but the navy. He did, how-ever, teach both Daniel and me to use a sword – something I have had cause to thank him for. Daniel and I would spend hours in combat with our wooden swords.' He smiled at the recollection. 'Then the McGregor family arrived, with young Jamie and his lovely sister Mary.'

'Your wife?' asked Tom.

'Yes. Though she was only a girl then. I fell in love with her on sight. And so did Daniel.'

'Did you fight over her?'

'No,' said Dr Harker. 'We loved each other too much. But something changed between us. We were drifting apart anyway. We both went away to university, but though we stayed in touch, something was happening to Daniel. He was becoming more and more politically minded and more and more ferociously anti-Catholic. He became involved in the rebellion of Monmouth in the West Country back in 'eighty-five. Do you know about that, Tom?'

'A little,' said Tom. 'Monmouth was the bas— the illegitimate son of Charles the Second, wasn't he? He was to be king instead of James the Second on account of James being Catholic. I know he was defeated and executed.'

'Yes, Tom,' said Dr Harker. 'We call all hangmen Jack Ketch now, and that is because the real Jack Ketch – the chief hangman at that time – was so hated. It was he who executed Monmouth. I was there when he was beheaded. *Butchered* would be a better word.

'Monmouth paid him six guineas and begged him to do a swift job, but to no avail. The first time he dropped the axe he hit the block and only nicked Monmouth. It took four more blows of the axe and a sharp knife to finish the job. Ketch was lucky to leave the scaffold alive, the crowd were so sickened by what they had seen.

'But no less shameful were the hundreds of hangings that took place throughout the West Country. So many men were killed. It was a shameful thing, Tom; a shameful thing. Let's hope that history is not about to repeat itself.'

'But what happened to Thornley?'

'Well, he managed to escape. He's a remarkable

man. Then, when James was deposed, he was recruited as a government agent.'

'And you married Mary?'

'Neither her parents nor mine wanted us to wed, but they could see that we were in love and had the goodness to put their prejudices to one side. Her parents had moved from Scotland to try and give their children a wider outlook on life, away from the provincial politics of their homeland. But Jamie always had a romantic attachment to Scotland's past. The Act of Union nine years ago was a great blow to him; to see the Scottish nation joined to England and swallowed up in this new nation of Britain. And then to see the Stuarts sidelined in favour of a German prince.'

'And what of Mr Thornley?' asked Tom.

'Daniel was devastated when Mary chose me,' Dr Harker told him. 'Though his pride would not allow him to show it. He attended the wedding. He wished us well. But it was plain to see that some part of him had died. He had taken to his new profession with the same zeal with which he had followed Monmouth. I have barely seen him since, until that day on Tower Hill.'

'How did your wife die, sir?' said Tom. 'If you don't mind me asking.'

'She was murdered, Tom.'

'Murdered?' said Tom. 'Why?'

'That's just it,' said Dr Harker. 'For no reason at all. She was the victim of street robbery and fought back. She was a proud woman and wasn't going to give up her purse without a struggle. She shouted for a constable and one of the thieves stabbed her.'

'I'm so sorry, sir,' said Tom.

'Thank you, Tom,' said Dr Harker. 'I do not talk about it and I try hard never to think of it.'

'That's why you were so keen to help,' Tom realized. 'When Will was murdered. Even though he was a thief himself.'

'Yes, Tom, I think it is. She meant the world to me. I was away on my travels when it happened and it was weeks before I even got the news. I missed the funeral, of course, and Mary's parents have never spoken to me since. I think they blame me for her death because I was not here to protect her. But not Jamie – he knew how Mary encouraged me in my work.'

'But what did Jamie want when he visited you?' said Tom.

'He came to give me this.' Dr Harker took a locket on a gold chain from his pocket and, after opening it, passed it to Tom.

'This is your wife, Dr Harker?' asked Tom, looking at the tiny painting.

'Yes, Tom,' said Dr Harker. 'That's my Mary.'

'She was very beautiful.'

'She was. She certainly was. Jamie risked his life to

bring that to me. Do you see why I have to help him, Tom?'

'Yes, Doctor,' said Tom. 'I do.'

'Jamie is in Newgate now. Daniel has bribed a turnkey to set him free and I am to furnish him with sufficient funds to leave the country and join his comrades.' Tom nodded. 'You realize that to give money to a known Jacobite would be a hanging offence at best,' said Dr Harker gravely.

'At best?' said Tom with a wry smile.

Dr Harker did not return it. 'At worst it might mean being drawn and quartered too. To have your innards ripped out while you're still alive, Tom. To be hacked up, boiled and spiked on Temple Bar.'

'So you refused?'

'No,' replied Dr Harker. 'Refusing Jamie would be like refusing Mary. I agreed to get him his money if it meant he might be safe. Everything is in place. I deliver it tomorrow.'

'Will you . . . ?' began Tom. 'Will you be all right, sir?'

Dr Harker smiled. 'I don't know, Tom,' he said. 'I hope so.'

Tom had never seen the doctor look so worried or try so hard to seem as if he were not.

'Now, Tom,' Dr Harker went on, 'I have to leave you for an hour or so. The Royal Society is holding a lunch for a visiting German scholar, and we are all keen to prove ourselves the more intelligent.' Tom smiled. 'Could you go through the contents of the small chest and get them ready for when I return?'

'Of course, sir,' said Tom. 'And thank you for confiding in me.'

Just as he was about to leave, Dr Harker turned back to Tom. 'Are you really thinking about going with Mr Greaves, Tom?' he asked.

'Yes . . . That is . . . I don't know,' mumbled Tom. 'I think I ought to at least think about it. I do want to see something of the world, sir. For myself, I mean.'

Dr Harker patted Tom on the shoulder and said farewell, leaving him alone in the study.

Tom heard the front door slam as Dr Harker left, went over to the wooden chest the doctor had indicated and opened the lid. A wonderful smell emerged, as if some exotic, tropical air were being released from its captivity. And inside the box there was a piece of cloth made up of thin, multi-coloured stripes. Tom lifted it to find a polished wooden figure of a black man, beautifully carved. He held it up and looked into its eyes.

Suddenly he was aware of a movement to his left. At first he thought he had imagined it because the room was so clearly empty, but no; the movement was outside the window. He crept over to see a man shinning down the drainpipe. He bolted out of the study, running down the stairs two at a time, out of the front door and down the steps and skidding round the corner, headlong into a person standing at the foot of the wall.

'Watch out, Tom!' he shouted. It was Nathaniel Greaves.

Tom stood staring at him. 'What were you doing? Were you trying to break into Dr Harker's study?' he shouted.

'What?' said Greaves indignantly. 'Have you lost your mind?'

'I saw you with my own eyes!'

'You did, did you?' said Greaves.

'Yes, I did,' said Tom. 'You said you'd changed.'

'Do you really think I was thieving?'

'Well, why else would you be up a drainpipe?' said Tom.

'I wasn't up no drainpipe, you goose!'

'Well, I don't see anybody else here!' Tom waved his arms, pointing around them.

'He wasn't likely to stick around, was he?' shouted Greaves. 'In any case, you cheeky sprat, I wasn't no burglar, I was a— Well, no matter – I wasn't no burglar.'

'I know what I saw,' said Tom.

'No you don't,' said Greaves. 'You know what you *think* you saw. It *wasn't* me! And I ain't standing here to listen to my own flesh and blood sing false witness, neither! You watch yourself, Tom. A man like that won't think twice about killing if he's cornered. You're in danger, Tom. Mark my words.'

'A man like what?' shouted Tom, but he shouted to an empty courtyard. Greaves had gone.

The White Rider

Dr Harker mounted his horse, patting him on the neck and smoothing down his mane. The horse snorted and shifted its weight, scraping a horseshoe across the cobbles. The doctor brought out the locket and opened it. He looked at Mary's face, sighed, closed it again and returned it to his pocket. Thornley, who was still recuperating at Dr Harker's house, stroked the horse's face and looked up at his friend.

'She would have been proud of you, Josiah,' said Thornley. 'You take care, do you hear? It doesn't feel right staying here and watching you go like this.'

'You have done enough, Daniel,' said Dr Harker. 'Wait here and . . . well, I shall see you when I return.'

'I shall be here. Everything will be fine, Josiah,' Thornley reassured him. 'I know it will.'

Dr Harker was about to set off when Tom came running into the courtyard. 'Good day, Mr Thornley. Dr Harker!' he gasped. 'I thought I might have missed you. I'm coming with you!'

'No, Tom,' said the doctor. 'I thank you – sincerely. But I cannot ask this of you.'

'You don't have to ask,' said Tom. 'I've made my mind up, sir. I'm coming with you. I'm your assistant, am I not?' Dr Harker smiled.

'You're a brave lad, Tom,' said Thornley, and he too smiled one of his customary broad smiles. 'Josiah has told me that he has confided in you. I'm sorry if I gave the impression that I did not trust you. My business is all about secrecy.'

'I understand,' said Tom. 'It's forgotten.'

'Splendid!'

'Very well, Tom,' said Dr Harker. 'To tell the truth I shall be glad of the company.'

The doctor hired a horse for Tom from a nearby stables and the pair set off along Fleet Street, heading west towards the Strand and the setting sun. They turned right and north onto Drury Lane, riding through the clamour of Covent Garden, as the usual throng headed for theatres, coffee houses and clubs, while hawkers and pickpockets did their best to relieve them of their purses.

The crowds began to thin as Tom and Dr Harker reached Tottenham Court Road, and in no time at all they had left the metropolis behind them and rode with open fields on either side, heading towards Hampstead and Highgate as dusk became darkness.

The night was clear and cold and an amber full moon was rising above them. Tom was a city boy through and through, and the featureless blackness all around them was alien and disturbing. An owl shrieked out like a strangled man and he gripped the reins as though his life depended on it. It seemed an age before Dr Harker pointed and said they were approaching their rendezvous point: a gnarled and broken oak that looked like a clutching hand. But there was no sign of McGregor.

To make matters worse, just as they were approaching the tree, Tom could see two riders coming towards them. The strangers stopped their horses and, though they were too far away to hear, Tom could tell by the movement of their heads that they were speaking to one another. After a few moments they kicked their horses on.

'Blast it!' said Dr Harker.

'What shall we do, sir?' asked Tom.

'Have your wits about you,' the doctor replied in a

whisper, staring ahead. 'Most likely they are fellow travellers and as nervous of us as we are of them.' Tom found it difficult to imagine how anyone could be as nervous as he now felt, but he tried hard not to show it. 'Jamie will stay hidden until they are gone, that is for sure.'

Gradually, the two riders came close enough for Tom to make them out a little more clearly. One was a rich-looking gentleman in a periwig and tricorn hat; the other a black man wearing a powdered tie-wig.

'Good evening,' said Dr Harker. 'How do you fare?'

'Well, thank you,' replied the gentleman. 'It is good to see a friendly face on such a lonely road.'

'That it is,' said Dr Harker, taking off his glove and offering his hand. 'May I introduce myself? I am Dr Harker of Fleet Street, London, and this is my assistant, Thomas Marlowe.'

'I am Henry Drayton,' said the gentleman. 'Once of Boston, Massachusetts.' He shook Dr Harker's hand without taking off his glove. Dr Harker put this down to different manners in the Colonies, but as he gripped Drayton's hand, he was struck by something odd about it. Tom felt it too when he in turn shook the hand.

Tom and Dr Harker looked at the black man at Drayton's side. Drayton followed their gaze and raised one eyebrow. 'Oh – this,' he said, as one might speak of a boot or a dog. 'This is my boy, Caliban.'

The 'boy' Caliban was, Tom thought, about twenty-five years old, though it was difficult to tell by moonlight. On mention of his name, Caliban looked up and nodded to Tom and Dr Harker.

'Good evening,' said Tom.

'Good eve—' began Caliban before being cut short by a vicious slap on the side of the head from his master.

Tom was shocked by the suddenness of this violence and his horse jittered, shaking at the bridle and twitching its legs nervously.

Drayton smiled at Dr Harker. 'You would not believe the money I had to pay for this dullard,' he said. 'It is getting harder and harder to buy a decent slave. This creature is worse than no help.' He hit his slave again, and this time it was Caliban's horse that jumped, lurching forward, almost throwing its rider off.

'Stop it!' cried Tom. 'Leave him alone!'

Caliban lost one foot from his stirrup and lurched towards Tom, who grabbed his arm to keep him from falling. Caliban clung to him and struggled back into the saddle.

'I see you have had no experience of slaves, young man,' said Drayton. As Caliban returned to his side, he raised his arm to strike him again, but quick as a flash, Dr Harker moved forward and grabbed his sleeve.

'What is the meaning of this!' he shouted. 'I cannot stop you from beating this man in an hour's time – would that I could – but if you strike him again in my presence, I will have to knock you down, sir!'

Drayton looked for an instant as if he were going to put this to the test, but he could clearly see that Dr Harker was a man of his word and thought better of it. He shrugged him off but lowered his hand to hold the reins.

'In Massachusetts, sir,' he told the doctor, 'this would not be countenanced. There a man is free to treat his slave in any way he likes.'

'You see no irony in the word "free" and the word "slave" appearing in the same sentence, then?' said Dr Harker. 'Have no fear, there are many places in England where you can exercise that freedom. But in this small place, for these few minutes, we will pretend that we are all men and all deserving of respect.'

Drayton snorted in derision and was about to say something when he stopped and squinted over Tom's shoulder. 'What the . . . ?'

Tom turned in his saddle and looked behind him down the road they had just travelled. In horror he saw another figure riding towards them – a tall man dressed in black. Under his hat, clearly visible in the moonlight, there was no face but a white skull. It was the White Rider.

Dr Harker and Tom turned their horses to face the

highwayman as he approached.

'Gentlemen, may I have your attention?' he called out in a strange, gruff voice. They all stared dumbstruck. 'Splendid, splendid,' he went on. 'I am the White Rider. I have four pistols and I am a very fine shot. Just give me what I want and none shall be harmed. Resist and all will die.'

Drayton laughed and turned incredulously to Caliban. 'What is this?' he shouted to the highwayman. 'What kind of fool joke is this?' He kicked his horse forward. 'You dare to—?'

The White Rider raised a pistol and shot Drayton as he rode forward.

Drayton fell back, still holding the reins, wheeling the horse round to face Tom, who now saw a fierce white glow burning in his chest, which took hold and sent up a plume of smoke to obscure his head as he finally fell from his horse to lie face down on the ground. The White Rider stared at the fallen Drayton in a kind of trance, but this was broken when the sound of hooves broke the silence.

Tom turned to see Caliban galloping away, back the way he had come. The White Rider drew another pistol from his waist and took aim, but there was little hope of hitting anyone at that distance and he turned back to Tom and Dr Harker.

'Very well, then,' he said. 'Now these interruptions are at an end, gentlemen, can we complete our business and be done, without any more foolishness? I have here a sack. Would you be so kind as to place all your valuables in it?'

The White Rider told Tom to ride forward; Tom turned to Dr Harker, who nodded. Tom urged his horse towards the highwayman. As he got closer, he could see that the skull was painted on over a real face, but his sense of dread did not diminish with that knowledge. He could now see eyes glinting in the black sockets but, demon or not, the highwayman had just killed a man in cold blood with little provocation. Tom took the sack that he was offered and rode back to Dr Harker.

'Quickly, gentlemen, if you please,' said the White Rider. 'And do not try to withhold anything from me. I can take the goods from your corpses if need be.'

Tom could see that Dr Harker knew there was no point in resisting: the doctor reached inside his coat for the bags of coins he had brought for McGregor.

'Splendid, splendid. Well, well,' said the White Rider, as he heard the coins jingling. 'It seems my luck is improving.'

Dr Harker put his watch in the sack and the locket McGregor had brought him with the portrait of Mary. He began to unbuckle his sword, but the White Rider put up his hand.

'No, no. You may keep your sword. These woods are full of rogues. And you, boy,' he said, turning to

Tom. 'What have you for the sack?'

Tom took his purse from his pocket and emptied the few coins it contained into the sack.

'Is that all?' said the White Rider. Tom did not reply. 'I said, is that all?'

'Yes,' said Tom.

The highwayman leaned forward and stared into Tom's eyes for what seemed like an age and then smiled. 'Splendid,' he said. 'Very well, then. Bring me the sack.'

Tom did as he was told and returned as quickly as possible to Dr Harker's side.

'The White Rider bids you adieu, gentlemen,' said the highwaymen. 'Go back to London.'

'But we have business here,' said Dr Harker.

'Not any more.'

'And what about this man?' said Dr Harker, pointing at Drayton's body. 'Are we to just leave him here like a dog?'

'Well,' said the White Rider, 'you have a choice. You can either leave him or join him.'

Dr Harker stared at the White Rider for a few seconds. 'Come on, Tom,' he said, urging his horse on.

Tom followed suit. Neither of them looked back.

They rode on in silence for half a mile until Dr Harker suddenly stopped his horse. Tom pulled on his reins and came to a halt beside him. To Tom's surprise, the doctor grabbed hold of the collar of Tom's coat and pulled him across so that his face was only inches away.

'Never do anything like that again, Tom,' said the doctor, angrier than Tom had ever seen him.

'I don't know what—' began Tom.

'Your watch, Tom. You could have got both of us killed for that damned watch.'

'My father gave me that watch!' shouted Tom. 'Mr Marlowe, I mean . . . my uncle!'

'And your uncle could have bought you a new one!' Dr Harker shouted back. 'I'm sure he would rather buy a watch than a coffin! That locket was very special to me too, Tom,' he said, finally letting Tom go and lowering his voice. 'I have so little to remember Mary by. I can never get that back.' He looked into Tom's eyes. 'Yet I gave it up gladly to preserve our lives, Tom. There are not many things worth dying for, lad. A watch is certainly not one of them.'

'I'm sorry, sir,' said Tom. 'I wasn't thinking.'

Dr Harker kicked his horse and moved off. Tom watched him ride away, still dazed by all that had just occurred, until the fear of the dark and the surrounding moors overcame him and he bolted after him.

Thornley was waiting for them when they returned and Dr Harker explained what had happened.

'Of all the accursed luck. And you saw no sign of Jamie?'

'None,' said Dr Harker. 'One can hardly blame him. I think he must have made his escape when the first riders approached.'

'That is a devil of a lot of money to lose,' said Thornley.

'The money does not matter!' Dr Harker pulled off a boot and threw it against the wall. 'It is Jamie who matters.'

'I will have to try and make contact with him.'

'It's too dangerous,' said Dr Harker.

'Let me worry about that,' said Thornley with a smile. 'Danger and I are old friends.'

'I cannot thank you enough for this, Daniel,' said Dr Harker. 'Do you really think you will be able to find him?'

'It is my job, after all,' said Thornley with a smile.

'But where will you start?'

'I don't know. But I will start now.' With that Thornley tipped his hat to them both and headed out of the courtyard.

'But it's the middle of the night!' shouted Dr Harker.

'The night I also count among my very closest friends!' he shouted over his shoulder.

A *freshly* DUG GRAVE

'Tom,' said Dr Harker a few days later, 'put down that pen. We have an appointment and we do not want to be late.'

'An appointment?' asked Tom, looking up from his writing. 'Who with?'

'Dr Cornelius,' said Dr Harker, grabbing his cane.

'Dr Cornelius? I don't understand, sir.'

Dr Harker banged his hand down on a pile of books, sending up a cloud of dust. 'I can do nothing more about Jamie. I am forced to leave that to Daniel.

But I am determined to find out more about this White Rider fellow, Tom,' he said. 'It is not simply the money, though heaven knows that is maddening enough given that it leaves poor Jamie without the funds to leave the country. No, Tom, if it were just the money I would mark it down to the crime-ridden age we live in and let go. I have to confess it is the theft of the locket that angers me so. Besides, I cannot sit back and do nothing while Daniel takes all the risks.'

'But what has Dr Cornelius to do with the White Rider?'

'He has the White Rider's victim, Tom,' said Dr Harker. 'The body of the man we saw murdered was sold to Surgeons' Hall. It is as good a place to start as any.'

Though Tom had been forced to revise his view of surgeons since he met Dr Cornelius during the Death and the Arrow murders, he was still not entirely comfortable visiting Surgeons' Hall. Dr Harker had been sent word that the body of Henry Drayton had been picked up by two enterprising farmers and sold to the surgeons.

Dr Cornelius was waiting on the steps, tall and thin and elegantly dressed as usual, leaning on his cane, his eyes half closed. He shook Tom and Dr Harker warmly by the hand and suggested that they all went across the road for a coffee.

'Now then,' said the doctor once they were all seated. 'What can I do for you, my good friends?' His long white fingers drummed on the tabletop. Tom noticed that there were small round stains on the fringe of the lace that was bunched at his throat and realized with a slight shiver that they were splashes of blood.

Dr Cornelius seemed to guess what Tom was looking at. 'My profession still fills you with horror, does it not, Tom? But this is the only way we can improve our knowledge of the human body, don't you agree? Dissection of the dead will help us heal the living.'

'Yes, sir . . . I mean, no, sir . . . I mean . . .'

Dr Cornelius laughed. 'There are few who do not find it odious, Tom,' he said. 'But one day it will be different. Or so I hope. Now what is it? Do you need my help?'

'You have the body of the man shot by the high-wayman they call the White Rider,' said Dr Harker.

'*Had*,' corrected Dr Cornelius.

'Had? Has he strolled off then?'

'No,' said Dr Cornelius with a withering smile. 'He was dead, sure enough. No, he was claimed.' He took a sip of coffee.

'Claimed?' said Tom. 'By who?'

'Well, I was not there myself,' said Dr Cornelius. 'A black manservant turned up with a rather large amount of money as a donation to our work in return for the body of his master. My colleague Dr Bennett dealt with it. I am afraid his interest in the contents of the servant's purse overwhelmed all other concerns. I am sorry I cannot be of more help. What interest do you have in this man, if you don't mind me asking?'

'It's complicated, Jonathan,' said Dr Harker, looking warily around. 'To be honest with you, we don't quite know what we're looking at yet. Until we do, it's best we say as little as possible.'

'Understood, Josiah,' said Dr Cornelius.

'Is there anything you can tell us about the body?' asked Dr Harker.

'Well,' said Dr Cornelius, 'I can tell you that he was shot, but I gather you know that already. I can also tell you he had a burn mark on his chest, though it was certainly the shot that killed him. There was a silver flask in his breast pocket and the bullet went clean through it. It seems to me there was some sort of explosive substance contained therein and the shot ignited it.'

'Extraordinary. But what about his hands? Was there something special about his hands?'

Dr Cornelius smiled. 'Yes, there was. He had a crippling burn there. It was old. It could have been an accident, but I feel sure he had been burned on the hand for theft some years ago.'

'That is why he has wearing gloves!' said Dr Harker. 'I knew there was something odd about his hand.'

'Yes,' said Tom. 'I noticed that too!'

'This business gets foggier and foggier, does it not, Tom?'

'It certainly does, sir,' said Tom.

'You seem to know more about this death than you are saying, Josiah,' said Dr Cornelius.

'Well, I have to confess that I am baffled,' said Dr Harker. 'Tom and I heard an account of a White Rider attack in which a man fell lifeless to the ground after being pointed at by this spectral highwayman. The witnesses say he glowed as if on fire before he dropped.'

'But this man was shot,' said Dr Cornelius.

'Yes. There is something strange about that, I grant you.'

'Perhaps the witnesses were mistaken,' suggested Dr Cornelius. 'Perhaps he always shoots them. Were the bodies of the previous victims examined?'

'No,' said Dr Harker. 'They were never found.'

'Never found,' Dr Cornelius repeated. 'Then we have no evidence either way. In any case, I am merely a humble surgeon' – he got to his feet – 'and I must get back to the hall. I have a dissection at two o'clock and the Prince of Wales is coming to watch. Dreadful bore, but there you have it.'

'Thank you for your time, Jonathan,' said Dr Harker. 'Are you sure there is no other help you can give us?'

Dr Cornelius took a last sip of coffee and looked

around. 'Listen,' he said, leaning forward and dropping his voice to a whisper. 'I should not really tell you this, but the body was taken to St Mary's Church. You may find something there.'

'Thank you again, Jonathan,' said Dr Harker.

'Good luck,' said Dr Cornelius.

As Tom and Dr Harker walked through the church-yard gate, the sexton was filling in a newly dug grave. A robin was ducking his beak into the pile of earth beside him and, after several goes, yanked out a long fat worm and flew off to a holly bush to eat it.

'Good afternoon, my man,' said Dr Harker.

'Uh-huh,' said the sexton, heaving another shovel full of clay into the grave.

'Anyone I might know?' Dr Harker nodded at the grave.

'Depends who you know,' said the sexton. 'It's thirsty work, this shovelling. Awful thirsty.'

Dr Harker tossed him a coin and the sexton caught it in mid air.

'Henry Drayton. Friend of yours?'

'Who paid for the coffin?' said Dr Harker.

The sexton wiped his brow. 'Hungry work, too,' he said.

The doctor tossed him another coin. 'Who paid?' he repeated.

'Black boy, he was. Says his master was this Drayton

fellow's great friend, though it's strange to say that the master weren't here in person for the ceremony.' The sexton put one of his filthy hands into his breeches pocket and pulled out a piece of folded paper. 'I'm to get the headstone carved as well. This is what he wants written on it. Read it, if you can.' The sexton passed it to Dr Harker, who read it and passed it to Tom.

' "As you from crimes would pardoned be," ' read Tom. ' "Let your indulgence set me free." '

'What kind of words is those for a Christian grave, I ask you?' said the sexton.

'They are the last lines of *The Tempest*,' said Dr Harker.

'Opera, is it?'

'No, it is certainly *not* an opera,' said Dr Harker crossly. 'Does no one remember William Shakespeare?'

'Anyway,' said the sexton with a shrug, 'he paid his money so I'll make sure it's done. His master's got plenty of money, I'll say that.'

'But I thought Drayton was his master?' said Tom.

The sexton shrugged again.

'And do you know this master's name?' asked Dr Harker.

''Fraid not, but the black fellow's in there now' – he gestured towards the church – 'with the vicar, though if you want my opinion they shouldn't let the likes of 'im in a . . .'

Tom and the doctor ignored the sexton's speech and strode off towards the church. Henry Drayton's black slave, Caliban, was just leaving and walked straight into Dr Harker.

'Now then,' said Dr Harker. 'Just the gentleman we've been looking for.'

The slave kicked out at the doctor with all his might and ran, vaulting over a tomb in the graveyard with Tom in pursuit. Caliban was fast. He sprinted towards a wall that seemed too high to climb, but he leaped onto a headstone and then to the wall, clambering over and jumping down. By the time Tom had run round through the churchyard gate, he was gone.

Dr Harker limped up behind him and they stared down the empty street. 'What the blazes is going on, Tom?' asked the doctor.

Tom could think of nothing to say.

'Why would this Caliban fellow show such loyalty to a man who used him so badly? And why is he running from us now? It doesn't make sense, Tom.'

Dr Harker suddenly slapped the hilt of his sword. 'Tom!' he said. 'You were right. I should have trusted you and Ocean from the start. We need someone with his knowledge of London's criminal fraternity. If there is anything to be learned about this White Rider fellow, Ocean's the man to find it.'

the BROKEN MAST

'**T**om!' said Mr Marlowe as his nephew walked into the Lamb and Lion printing house. 'I ... I wasn't expecting to see you.' Mr Marlowe's big hands flexed and relaxed like a nervous schoolboy's.

'I was looking for Ocean,' said Tom.

Mr Marlowe nodded, and wiped his hands on a cloth. 'I see.'

'Are you well?' Tom asked, instantly regretting the coldness of his last remark.

'Me?' said Mr Marlowe. 'I'm fine, Tom. Yes, yes. I'm fine. How about you?'

'I'm fine,' said Tom.

'Good, good. That's ... good. And how is Dr Harker?'

'He's well,' replied Tom. 'But he has a problem that Ocean may be able to help with.'

'Does he now?' said a voice behind Tom. It was Ocean.

'Ocean!' said Mr Marlowe, relieved at the distraction. 'Tom's here from Dr Harker's. He needs you on some business or other.' Then he muttered that he must get back to work, that pamphlets weren't going to print themselves, and disappeared from the room.

'He's a fine man, your father,' said Ocean.

'He's not my father,' corrected Tom.

'Sorry, Tom,' said Ocean. 'I wasn't thinking.'

'But you're right,' said Tom. 'He is a fine man.'

'I'm not one for getting involved in someone else's problems, Tom, but this is hard for him too, you know,' said Ocean.

Tom nodded. 'I know it,' he said.

Neither of them spoke for a while until Tom broke the silence to change the subject. 'Look, Ocean, I'm here because Dr Harker needs your help.'

'Then he has it, Tom,' said Ocean. 'What's the trouble?'

'I'll tell you what I can as we walk.'

★ ★ ★

A few days later, Sarah the maid knocked on the door to Dr Harker's study and showed Ocean in. Tom and the doctor shook his hand and then sat down, eager to hear his news.

'I've made some enquiries just like you asked, Dr Harker,' said Ocean.

'And?'

'Well,' said Ocean. 'The White Rider is a mystery. No one knows a thing. Not one single thing. It's like he really was a spectre.'

Tom looked at Dr Harker.

'He is no ghost, Tom,' said the doctor with a smile. 'Of that I am in no doubt. Did you really discover nothing useful at all?'

Ocean glanced quickly at Tom and then back to Dr Harker. 'Well, sir,' he said. 'I can't say, right now—'

'Can't say?' said Dr Harker, furrowing his brow. 'What do you mean?'

'I have an informant who knows something, but I need you to hear it from his own lips,' said Ocean.

'Why? What is it that you won't tell us yourself?' Then, seeing that Ocean would not be moved, the doctor sighed. 'Very well,' he said. 'Go and fetch him and we'll hear what he's got to say. This is urgent, Ocean.'

'I know that, sir,' said Ocean, glancing at Tom again. 'It's just that he can't come to us. We need to go to him.'

'I fail to see the problem, Ocean,' said Dr Harker. 'Take us to this informant of yours. Take us now, if you like. The sooner the better.'

'The problem is, sir,' said Ocean. 'This fellow of mine – this informant – he lives in the Wapping Mint. He's a convict, sir, and he won't come out for fear of Hitchin or some other thief-taker arresting him.'

Tom stared wide-eyed at Ocean. The Wapping Mint was the last of London's criminal 'sanctuaries', where thieves and cut-throats lived by their own rules.

'The Wapping Mint,' repeated Dr Harker nervously. 'I see your point, Ocean. But, nevertheless, if we must go there, then we must.'

'Very well, then. This is for you, Tom.' Ocean reached into a bag at his side and tossed him a cudgel. 'We need to go armed, gents. It will look odd if we don't, and in any case we might need some help. If anyone but the doctor and me comes near you, Tom, give them a tap on the hat rack with that. As for you, Doctor, I know you're a demon with that sword, but it's going to mark you out as a gentleman. Pistols would be better, if you have them.'

'I'll find something suitable,' said Dr Harker. He went upstairs and Ocean leaned towards Tom.

'This is dangerous country, Tom,' he said. 'All our lives are dangling now. Don't talk to anyone. Don't look at anyone. Just stick close by me and listen.'

Dr Harker returned and the three men stood in the hallway.

'We all ready then?' said Ocean.

'I think so,' Tom replied.

'Lead on, McDuff,' said Dr Harker.

Ocean stared at him. 'You won't be saying anything like that when we're at the Mint, will you, Doctor?' he asked.

'Well I . . . No, I suppose not.' The doctor looked a little crest-fallen. Tom smiled to himself.

'Thank God for that,' said Ocean.

The three friends took a carriage to the Tower, just as Tom had done with Greaves, but the area seemed very different now as dusk began to fall. Ocean led them down by the river beyond the Tower, where the water seemed to be so filled with ships that Tom felt he could have walked clear across the Thames, jumping from one to the next.

Lanterns were being lit and rowing boats were working their way among the ships, some to the north shore and some to the south. Sailors called out to one another and Tom could hear women giggling, and from a ship nearby he heard a mournful voice singing in a language he did not recognize. Everywhere there was the background rasp of hemp ropes, the rustle of canvas and the slap of the water against hulls.

'There!' said Ocean, pointing ahead of them. 'That's where we're meeting him.'

Tom peered into the gloom and saw a tavern among the jetties and warehouses. A fiddler was playing at the door and a sign saying THE BROKEN MAST hung above his head.

The tavern was clad in weatherboarding that was so rotten and distressed it looked as if it had been ripped from the hull of a sunken ship, and inside it was as dark as the hold of a cargo vessel, small candles dimly twinkling among the fog of pipe smoke. Ocean made straight for a table in the far corner where three men were sitting, huddled in conversation. As they approached, two of the men immediately stood up and walked away without a word.

Ocean beckoned Tom and Dr Harker to sit down. 'This is Smiling Jack,' he explained. 'He's an old friend of mine.'

'Pleased to meet you,' said Tom with more confidence than he felt. 'I'm—'

'I don't need to know your name,' said Smiling Jack. 'Ocean here has vouched for you and that's enough for me.'

Tom could see that it was not the man's cheerfulness that had won him the nickname. He had a scar which ran from the corner of his mouth, sloping upwards for several inches towards his ear. It gave the effect of a permanent smile, totally at odds with the grimness of his actual expression.

'Tell them what you told me,' said Ocean.

'Well,' began Smiling Jack, 'Ocean here tells me he knows of a cove what's been a King's Passenger and I remembered him straightway as a flash cove who got himself clapped up in the whit for working the rattling lay. He was in this very place only the other night. Never forget a face. Should have been scragged too, as it happens, but caught the ferry instead. Last time I saw him he was in his darbies down by the river. I was seeing off a cull of my acquaintance who'd been done for working the kid lay. Died on the journey, poor devil.'

'There,' said Ocean turning to Tom. 'What do you say to *that*?'

'Er . . . What did he say, Ocean?' said Tom.

Ocean and Smiling Jack laughed. 'He's talking about your father,' said Ocean. 'About Greaves.'

'What about him?'

'Weren't you listening?' said Ocean. 'Greaves worked the rattling lay.'

Tom still looked blank.

'He was a highwayman.'

'A highwayman?' said Tom, turning to Dr Harker.

'Might be an idea to keep your voices down, gents,' said Smiling Jack. 'There's many a man here who answers to that description, but few you would want to meet.'

'So you've brought me here to peach on my father!' shouted Tom.

'I'm peaching on no one!' hissed Ocean. 'I knew you'd never believe it coming from me.'

'So what if he was a highwayman?' said Tom. 'It doesn't have to mean anything.'

'No it don't,' agreed Ocean. 'But Dr Harker asked me to ask around, and this is what I found out.'

'Please,' said Smiling Jack nervously. 'Keep your peace—'

'What's going on here, Jack?' said a man behind Dr Harker.

The doctor turned round and inadvertently knocked the man's drink out of his hand. He stood up at once and said loudly, 'My good fellow, I really am most terribly sorry.'

The tavern went suddenly silent and all eyes turned towards Dr Harker.

'Oh no,' said Ocean under his breath.

'What have we here?' shouted a man with an eye patch at a nearby table. 'We seem to have a Justice of the Peace in the establishment!'

'Or maybe it's the Lord Mayor!' shouted another.

Dr Harker took a step towards them.

'What are you doing, Doctor?' hissed Ocean.

'Allow me to introduce myself!' shouted Dr Harker. 'They call me Gentleman Joss Harker.'

124

'Do they now!' shouted the first man, getting to his feet. 'And how come we ain't never heard of you?'

Four men pulled out pistols, cocked them and aimed them at Dr Harker. At the same time Ocean stood up, drew two pistols himself and pointed them at the man with the eye patch.

'You gonna shoot us all then, Ocean, with two pops?' said the man.

'I ain't aiming at all of you, Tyler,' said Ocean. 'They're your dogs. You whistle and they come to heel. Well, you better whistle fast, 'cause if one of them so much as sneezes, so help me, I'll blast you to fish bait.' The four men held their ground. Ocean held his. 'My fingers are getting twitchy!' he shouted.

'All right,' said Tyler. 'Calm down. We're all friends here. Garret, Rich, Preacher, Fuller – drop your shooters.'

Ocean didn't move.

'I thought you'd gone respectable on us,' said Tyler with a snigger.

Ocean ignored him. 'He's with me!' he shouted, shoving Dr Harker back to his seat. 'Anyone got a problem with that, then let's hear it.'

'We know you, Ocean,' shouted a man at the back. 'There's no cause for trouble!' There was a murmur of approval and Ocean relaxed and let his pistols drop.

'Yeah, but who is this mate of yours, Ocean?' shouted someone close by.

Suddenly Dr Harker was on his feet again. Ocean made a grab for him but it was too late.

'I have only recently arrived from Massachusetts,' said the doctor, 'where I gained some notoriety for working the rattling lay.'

Tom stared at Ocean, who closed his eyes and slowly shook his head.

'I ain't never seen a highwayman go about the town without his pops,' said a man nearby.

'Pops?' said Dr Harker. 'Pistols? Good Lord, no. Dreadful things. They make such an awful din.'

This statement was met by raucous laughter and Tom saw Ocean take up his pistols; his trigger-finger twitched.

'He don't like the din,' said a bearded man nearby. He was tipping his chair back against a wooden post. 'And how exactly would that work then? How do you get the attention of them as who you're going to tax, if you ain't got any cannons? Do you wave your handkerchief at them, then?'

Dr Harker suddenly reached into his coat pocket and hurled something towards the man. It happened too fast for Tom's eyes to follow, but he heard the thud and turned to see the tomahawk he had been admiring in the doctor's study, stuck through the man's hat, pinning it to the wooden post behind him. The room was silent. The man gingerly lowered his head. The hat stayed where it was.

The room erupted into laughter.

'You're all right!' said a huge man standing next to Dr Harker. He patted him on the back so hard he nearly knocked him over.

Tom looked at Ocean, who raised his eyebrows, shrugged and sat back down.

'He don't like the din!' shouted someone in a mock-aristocratic voice, and everyone laughed again.

'Now if you'll excuse me, gentlemen,' said Dr Harker. 'My friend Tom and I have some pressing business to discuss with Smiling Jack and Ocean Carter here.'

'Give the man his hatchet back,' said Tyler to the other man, who had pulled it from the post and was turning it over in his hand.

'Gladly.' The man raised it above his shoulder and hurled it at Dr Harker. Again Tom only saw the flash as it hurtled by, but the man's aim was not as good as the doctor's and when Tom turned he saw that the huge man who had slapped Dr Harker on the back had blood pouring from his ear. The tomahawk was stuck into the post behind him and had taken a piece of his ear with it as it passed by.

'It might be a good time to leave,' said Ocean, and he grabbed Tom and shoved him towards the door. Dr Harker pulled out the tomahawk and the giant bellowed like a bull and charged forward, knocking chairs, tables and customers flying. Tom, Dr Harker and Ocean made it through the door, as bottles and mugs rained down behind them.

'Gentleman Joss?' said Ocean, as they stood panting outside. Dr Harker blushed. Tom laughed. 'You are an amazing man, sir, and that's a fact.'

'I will take that as a compliment,' said Dr Harker.

'I'm surprised you let the man throw the tomahawk at Dr Harker,' said Tom to Ocean, excited now that the fear had gone from his stomach. 'Did you know he would miss?'

'No,' said Ocean. 'I knew the doctor wouldn't have thrown the thing if he didn't have a plan for when it came back.'

'A plan?' said Dr Harker.

'Yeah,' said Ocean. 'I figured you'd . . . I don't know . . . catch it.'

'Catch it?' The doctor chuckled. 'Oh dear me, no. You can't catch a tomahawk in mid air. Quite impossible.'

Ocean stared at him in disbelief. 'Gentleman Joss,' he repeated, shaking his head. He laughed and turned to Tom, but Tom was thinking of other things.

'Tom?' said Dr Harker.

'It's my father, isn't it?' he said. 'Greaves is the White Rider. All that stuff about changing his ways and taking me to America was all lies—'

'We don't know that, Tom. We don't know anything for sure.'

'Come on, Doctor,' said Tom. 'We know he was a highwayman in the old days. I saw him spying on your house and the White Rider was disguising his voice to hide his identity. It has to be him.'

'You saw him spying on my house?' asked Dr Harker. 'Why did you not say anything?'

'I don't know, Doctor,' said Tom. 'I could not bring myself to peach on my own father. I hoped there would be an explanation.'

'And there may yet be,' said Dr Harker.

Tom looked up at the night sky and then back to his friends. 'This is all my fault! I should never have told him anything. I should never have trusted him.'

'Don't get me wrong, Tom,' said Ocean. 'It was me who found all this out about Greaves, but there's things that don't make sense here. It don't smell right to me. There's something we ain't seeing in all this.'

'I think Ocean is right, Tom,' said Dr Harker. 'We need to find out more.'

'Why did he have to come back?' said Tom, looking out across the Thames.

Just then, a man suddenly crashed through the window next to them and lay groaning among the broken glass. He slowly got to his feet, dusted

LONDON BRIDGE

Tom was walking home towards Dr Harker's house one evening, stopping occasionally to try and scrape some cow dung from his boot heel, when he looked up to see Nathaniel Greaves standing on the pavement ahead.

'Tom!' shouted Greaves. 'I need to talk to you!'

'Well I don't need to talk to you!' Tom tried to walk past him but Greaves stood in his way. 'I've got ink here for Dr Harker. He's expecting me.'

'This is important, Tom.' Greaves grabbed hold of

his arms. 'You've got to listen!'

'I know you were a highwayman!' shouted Tom.

Greaves stared at him and let go. 'Look, Tom—' he began.

'Don't!' shouted Tom. 'I don't want to hear any more lies!'

'You've got it wrong, Tom. I'm here to see Dr Harker myself.'

'Dr Harker?' said Tom. 'What do you want with Dr Harker?'

Suddenly, over Greaves's shoulder Tom saw someone he recognized skulking beside the courtyard entrance and then moving away down Fleet Street towards the City. It was Caliban.

'I've got to go,' said Tom.

'Tom!' shouted Greaves. 'This can't wait.'

But Tom wasn't listening. He was too intent on not losing sight of Caliban as he moved through the crowd.

As he followed as close behind as he dared, Tom began to notice that Caliban would occasionally stop and skulk in a doorway or flatten himself against a wall or stand on tiptoe, peering down the street. Tom recognized these movements because they mirrored his own. Caliban was following someone. But who? Tom strained to see, but he could not see that far ahead.

The route they took was a meandering one: first

east, then north, then south, but all the while they were gradually heading down the river towards London Bridge. The crowds began to thicken as they neared the bridge. Dozens of hawkers and street traders lined the pavement to take advantage of the traffic passing through. An oyster girl with a freckled face and bright pink fingers winked at Tom and gave him a dimpled grin. He blushed and hurried on his way.

Tom struggled to keep Caliban in view as they started across the bridge – a street of shops, taverns and houses stretching across the river – but saw him stop outside a shop and, after a pause to glance around, go in.

A few seconds later, Tom reached the shop itself. It was old and dilapidated and was seemingly unoccupied. Over the door, hanging from a rusting tangle of curlicues, was a cracked and peeling painted wooden sign showing a golden parrot. Above the bow-fronted window the sign said: THOS. PARROT, GLOVE-MAKER.

A breeze was picking up and the sign creaked as it swayed to and fro. It was a melancholy sound, almost like a groan, and it filled Tom with an unnatural feeling of foreboding. But however sharp his sense of dread, curiosity was a powerful medicine.

The door creaked as forlornly as the sign, and would not open properly, forcing Tom to squeeze through into the pitch blackness of the interior. Panic surged up inside him as he realized that he had not the faintest idea who or what lurked in that darkness, but as his eyes adjusted to the gloom he could see that the room was empty. There was a faint light at the far end, seeping down a stairwell, and Tom edged his way towards it.

The stairs were bare and missing treads in several places. Woodworm and rot were fighting each other for the treads that remained and Tom took a deep breath every time he took a new step for fear that the whole staircase would collapse.

Slowly and gingerly he reached the first floor. The floorboards here were little better than on the stairs and were cracked and eaten away in places, showing the joists and occasionally glimpses of the floor below. From a room at the end of the hall came a noise; the noise of someone pacing the room.

Tom moved to follow the noise, but no sooner had he done so than an arm was clamped around his neck, a hand covered his mouth and a voice hissed in his ear, 'If you want to live, don't make a sound!' Tom's attacker edged him over to a corner at the top of the stairs and turned him round so that they were face to face.

'You!' said Tom. It was Caliban.

'Be still, if you want to live,' he whispered. Tom could see he held a cocked pistol in his other hand.

'Good advice!' said a voice behind them as a pistol

butt flashed through the air. A second later the slave was lying at Tom's feet and Thornley was standing over him.

'What on earth are you doing, Tom?' he said with his usual broad smile. 'Are you trying to get yourself killed?'

'Thank you, Mr Thornley,' said Tom, rubbing his throat. 'But wait! I heard someone pacing around in that far room.'

Thornley pulled a dagger from inside the collar of his coat. He put his finger to his mouth and indicated that Tom should stay where he was.

Thornley crept noiselessly along the corridor, waited for a moment outside the door that Tom had pointed to and then burst into the room. An ominous silence followed. As Tom was trying to decide what he ought to do next, Thornley called his name.

Tom walked towards the door and found Thornley in the centre of the room.

'Whoever was here has bolted.' Thornley pointed to an open window.

Tom walked over and looked out. Below, the filthy waters of the Thames gurgled through an unseen arch in the bridge.

'It is rather a drop,' said Thornley. 'And this river is a cesspool, but if your life depended on it . . .'

'But who do you think it was?' asked Tom.

'Hard to say.' Thornley had gone back to the landing and was now dragging the unconscious Caliban into the room by his feet. He took some strips of leather from his coat pocket and began tying the slave's wrists and ankles. 'Do you know this fellow?'

'He is the slave of the man killed by the White Rider,' said Tom.

'So he is,' said Thornley, looking at Caliban more intently. 'This just gets stranger and stranger, does it not?'

'He seemed to be following someone,' said Tom.

'And you have no idea who it could have been?' said Thornley.

'No, sir,' said Tom. 'He was too far ahead.'

'And did you tell anyone what you were doing, Tom?'

'No, sir,' said Tom. 'There was no time. I saw Caliban and thought it best to get after him as best I could.'

'Splendid, splendid,' said Thornley with a wide smile.

Something raised the hairs on the back of Tom's neck, but he had no idea what it was. His nerves seemed to be tingling and trying to warn him of something . . . but what? He heard the words, 'Splendid, splendid,' echoing in his ears. Then it came to him.

'*You* are the White Rider!'

15

THE Open WINDOW

'Me?' said Thornley nonchalantly. 'Why, Tom, I think I hear Bedlam calling. I was at Dr Harker's house, remember? How could I have left the house and returned without his nosy maid and cook seeing me?'

'Yes . . . Yes . . . Of course . . . It was *you* I saw, not my father, climbing down the drainpipe!' said Tom. 'It was you! You must have been climbing out of your room . . . You were practising . . . seeing if you could get out of the house unseen.'

'This is all pure fantasy, Tom,' said Thornley. 'And this is the thanks I get for saving your life just now!'

'You were here already — it was *you* in this room!' shouted Tom. 'Of course! You didn't follow *me*; Caliban was following *you*! You recognized him just now, when I said who he was. And how could you have recognized him? You could only have seen him if you were there that night as the White Rider.'

'I'm sorry, Tom,' said Thornley with a grin. 'You understand that I will have to kill you now, don't you?' His pistol lay on the floor between them. He could see Tom looking at it and his grin widened. 'Go on, Tom. Try to get it. Let's add some sport.'

'Leave the boy be!'

Tom and Thornley both turned to the sound of the voice. It was Nathaniel Greaves, holding a sword.

'Well, well,' said Thornley. 'Isn't this touching? The prodigal father come to save his son?'

'I won't take much persuading to run you through,' said Greaves.

'I dare say not,' said Thornley, looking at the pistol on the floor. 'The question is, will you reach me before I reach the pistol and blow your head off?'

'We don't ever need to find that out,' said a voice behind Greaves. 'Because have no doubt that I shall drop you before you take one pace forward.' It was Ocean, holding a pistol, with Dr Harker beside him.

'This is my fight, gentlemen,' said Dr Harker,

drawing his sword and pushing himself past Ocean and Greaves.

'But I don't have a sword, Josiah,' said Thornley. 'They tend to get in the way in my line of work, I find.'

'You are welcome to borrow mine, you rodent,' said Greaves.

Thornley smiled. 'I think not,' he said. 'You may hand me over to the authorities, if you wish. You know that they will take my word over yours. And besides, even if they believed you, I am too good an agent for them to lose. Either way I will take my chances.'

'They'd let a man like you walk free while petty thieves swing from the gallows!' said Ocean bitterly. 'I ought to kill you myself.'

'I realize these things must be difficult to under-stand for someone of your . . . limited intelligence,' sneered Thornley.

Ocean took aim and looked ready to pull the trigger.

'Ocean,' said Dr Harker. 'No.'

Ocean took a deep breath and lowered his pistol.

'How did you find me?' asked Thornley.

'Mr Greaves saw through you first,' said Dr Harker. 'He saw you climbing out of the house.'

'Yeah,' added Greaves. 'I knew I'd seen you before, and I was right. I'd seen you arguing with Noah

Fletcher down at the Three Crowns. I asked around and found out that you had run up some serious gambling debts and I heard too that your life was going to be forfeit unless you came up with the money in the next few days. They gave you a good hiding to show they meant business, didn't they?'

'But how did you find this place?' asked Thornley.

'You didn't think they were just going to let you walk away without keeping an eye on you?' said Greaves. 'They followed you, you chub. It was expensive, but in the end they told me where you were.'

'And you made the whole thing up about McGregor,' said Ocean. 'Jamie McGregor was in Newgate just like you said – I checked with Reverend Purney – but you never had any intention of getting him out.'

'Why couldn't you just have come to me and asked for the money? Do you think I would not have helped you as I was going to help Jamie?' said Dr Harker.

'I did not want your help, Josiah,' said Thornley. 'I did not want to exchange one debt for another.'

'There is no debt between friends,' said Dr Harker.

Thornley laughed bitterly. 'This is why I didn't come to you, Josiah. Always so gracious and magnanimous. Even when you took Mary from me—'

'I did not "take" Mary,' said Dr Harker. 'Mary chose to be my wife.'

'And now she is dead!'

'You blame me for Mary's death?' exclaimed Dr Harker.

'Of course I do! You left her here to fend for herself and she was murdered!'

'And what kind of life would she have had if she had married you?' shouted the doctor. 'Married to some murderous liar!'

'I am what I am because of you!' replied Thornley. 'If I had married Mary I would have been a different man!'

'How dare you blame Mary for what you've become,' said Dr Harker. 'You enjoy your work, Daniel. That is the truth of it. You like to kill.' Thornley smiled but made no response. 'But what I don't understand is why you didn't arrest McGregor earlier,' said Dr Harker. 'You knew he had contacted me, so you were clearly following him. Why did you let him move about freely?'

Thornley sighed. 'He was going to solve all my problems,' he said with a smile.

'How?'

'So he did not tell you then?' said Thornley.

'Did not tell me what?' asked Dr Harker.

'Jamie was in possession of a very valuable item.'

'Was?'

'He was searched on his entry to Newgate and nothing was found.'

'And what is it?' said Dr Harker. 'This valuable item?'

'Well,' said Thornley, 'these coves are damnably secretive. All I know is that it is priceless, and it must, perforce, be small enough to be easily carried and secreted.'

'Jewels?' suggested Dr Harker.

'My thoughts precisely, Josiah,' said Thornley. 'And not just any jewels. I believe they are jewels given by Queen Elizabeth to Mary Queen of Scots as a bribe to buy her good behaviour. It was a wasted gesture, of course, but these jewels seem to have been squirreled away back to Scotland after Mary's death. I believe that Jamie's family was given the task with looking after them.'

'I never thought you a person so concerned with material things,' said Dr Harker.

'Hah!' snorted Thornley. 'There speaks a wealthy man!'

'You are hardly a pauper, Daniel,' said Dr Harker.

'Ah, but I do so love to gamble, Josiah. I have gambled my money away and with it all my dreams of escaping this foul work and sailing away to foreign waters where none know me and I can be something more than the stinking creature the government has made me.'

'Your enthusiasm for cruelty is your own,' said Dr Harker.

'Perhaps, Josiah,' Thornley replied. 'Perhaps. In any event, had I found the Jacobite treasure then I could have paid my gambling debts and we would all have been spared this unpleasantness. But now I must say farewell.'

Thornley made his move. But instead of making for the pistol or the sword, with one swift movement he pulled a knife from his sleeve, grabbed Tom and put the blade to his ribs. Tom could feel the point straining at the fabric of his coat, as if one slight effort on Thornley's part would cause it to burst through and bite into his flesh.

'Very well then, gentlemen,' said Thornley with a smile. 'I hope you will understand that though I have no desire to harm the young lad here, I will kill him in a heartbeat and without a care or a moment's thought if any one of you takes a step in my direction. Very, very slowly, now; place all your weapons on the floor in front of you. Splendid, splendid. Now kick them towards me.' Ocean's pistol and the two swords skidded across the floorboards. 'Excellent. Now, if you would all be so good as to line up against that wall. That's it. Good. Well away from the door, Mr Carter. Good man.' Thornley edged Tom towards the door and his escape route down the stairs.

'And so I bid you farewell, my friends,' said

143

Thornley with a little bow, but just as the words left his mouth, the floorboard he stepped on gave way and made him stumble enough for Tom to throw himself free. For an instant there was stillness in the room as Thornley realized that his shield was gone and that the weapons now lay about equidistant between him and Dr Harker, Ocean and Greaves but out of reach of any of them.

He clearly decided that the odds were stacked against him: the doorway was blocked. He tipped his hat, turned and, quick as a snake, made for the other end of the room. Ocean hurled himself to the floor, grabbed his pistol, cocked it and fired, just as Thornley threw himself headlong through the window.

16

CALIBAN

Dr Harker and Ocean ran to the open window in time to see the splash Thornley had made when he hit the water. They waited for him to surface, but nothing appeared save for his black tricorn hat, which bobbed about on the surface like a duck.

'The tide's going out,' Ocean observed. 'Those currents are powerful strong.'

'Maybe so,' said Dr Harker. 'But then so is Daniel.'

'I'm so sorry,' said Tom to his father.

Greaves grinned. 'What for?' he asked.

'For thinking you were trying to steal from Dr Harker,' said Tom, a little embarrassed to even say the words. 'For thinking you were a rogue.'

'Yes,' said Dr Harker, walking over from the window. 'Your father had his suspicions about Thornley right from the start but feared that we would not believe him. He told us that he had tried to warn you about Thornley but you would not listen. We have a lot to thank him for. But what were you doing here, Tom?'

'I followed him,' said Tom, pointing to Caliban, who was just coming to.

'Please, sir,' the slave said with a groan. 'I beg you, sirs. Untie me. Caliban ain't done nobody no harm.'

'I think we'll keep you just like that until we find out what's going on here,' said Dr Harker.

'If it pleases you, sirs, then I will tell you all I know,' said Caliban, flinching as if from an invisible blow. 'If it pleases you, sirs.'

'Speak up then, man,' said Dr Harker. 'But could you do us all the favour of dropping the act? Whatever you are, you are certainly not the cringing fool you are pretending to be.'

After a small pause Caliban returned Dr Harker's smile and then sat more upright. His whole bearing changed in an instant, and Tom noticed how he seemed to have grown to become the biggest man in the room.

'What do you want to know?' he asked.

'Who you are, for a start,' said Dr Harker. 'Who you *really* are.'

'Who I really am . . . Well, that is an interesting question. I am an African, I suppose – though I have forgotten my language and my people . . . even my own name.'

'We thought you might be a little more specific,' said Greaves. 'You're a slave, aren't you? Well, whose?'

'*Was* a slave,' Caliban corrected, giving Greaves a withering look. '*Was* a slave. Now I am a free man.'

Greaves snorted. Caliban stared at him with cool intensity.

'You were born in Africa?' asked Greaves.

'I was. I was taken by men from the north and sold to white men on the coast. Then I was shipped to the Americas.'

'To Maryland or the Caribbean?'

'Maryland. I was not even aware that there were such things in this world as ships and had never seen an ocean. The journey was a waking nightmare, shut up in those stinking holds. I hoped each night that I might die before I woke, and cried each morning when I found that I had survived. Many did not. If we had been cattle they would have taken more care of us.'

Greaves shook his head and walked away to look out of the window.

'And what happened when you got to Maryland?' asked Dr Harker.

'I was sold,' Caliban told him with a cold smile. 'My teeth were checked and my eyes peered into and my body searched for any signs of illness, and I was sold, like a horse. Though not for as much money, naturally.'

'But you are educated.'

'Yes,' replied Caliban. 'My master was rich and learned and it amused him to pass on some of that learning to me, as you might teach a dog to do tricks. To entertain his friends he would ask me to recite poetry or do mathematics. How the ladies laughed and fluttered their fans.

'It was he who named me Caliban, though I had no idea then what the name signified, other than the master thought himself well pleased with the joke.'

Dr Harker saw the puzzled look on the faces around him. 'It is the name of a character in Shakespeare's *The Tempest*,' he explained. 'A creature who is enslaved by the magus, Prospero.'

'Yes,' said Caliban. 'And like Prospero, my master proved himself better than I thought and granted me my freedom on his deathbed. I was free again, though trapped now in a foreign land with no family and no hope of employment; nobody was going to *pay* someone like me.

'I quickly fell to crime and when I was caught by an innkeeper, he said if I would be his slave he would not fetch the sheriff. He chained my legs to stop me

148

from escaping and used me like a dog. I managed to escape and met up with Henry Drayton. We became a team, and a man cannot ever have had a finer friend. We worked our way up the coast to Boston, and then one day Henry slapped the table as we were counting our money and suggested that we should go to England.

'He had been an actor here in his younger days before going to the Americas to seek his fortune, only to be burned in the hand for stealing when the fortune never came. And so we came and plied our trade, surviving by our wits until that fateful night.'

'By your wits?' said Dr Harker. 'What was your trade exactly?'

Caliban smiled. 'We worked the kid lay.'

'The kid lay?' Tom asked.

'They were conmen,' explained Ocean.

Caliban nodded. 'I am near invisible to white people. If they notice me at all, they see a slave; a dullard, something less than the horse they ride. They would not credit me with the intelligence to steal.' He smiled. 'Which made the stealing that much more of a pleasure. I would play the lumbering slave to Henry's gentleman. It worked very well.'

'So that's why Drayton hit you,' said Tom. 'You spoke up when you were supposed to be his slave.'

'Yes,' said Caliban. 'I forgot myself for an instant. Henry was always quick like that. And you, sirs' – he looked at Tom and then at Dr Harker – 'you showed a rare kindness towards me. I thank you for that, ruse or not.'

'I did what any man should have done,' said Dr Harker.

'Hah! *Should*, maybe,' said Caliban. 'But few *would*. You are more rare than you realize. The last man who treated me so well was Henry Drayton. And now he is dead.' Caliban stared ahead as if Drayton was once more dying in front of him.

'I managed to get away in the confusion and returned later to retrieve Henry's body, but when I arrived, a farmer was already loading it into his cart and heading for London. I heard him say that he would sell it to the surgeons and I eventually made my way to Surgeons' Hall and redeemed it. Then, of course, we met again.'

'Why did you run,' said Tom, 'when we met you in St Mary's churchyard?'

'How could I have explained being there? It would have seemed odd, especially after you had witnessed his treatment of me,' said Caliban.

'Seeing you again and hearing of your enquiries about Henry had got me to thinking,' he went on. 'I had sworn revenge on Henry's killer, but of course, I had no idea who he might be then. I needed to try and discover what your interest in Henry really was, and if there was any link between you and the highwayman.'

'Why did you think there might be?' said Dr Harker.

'Well,' said Caliban, 'for one thing, the White Rider was disguising his voice.'

'Yes,' said Dr Harker with a smile. 'We noticed that too.'

'I thought to myself, well, he could be trying to sound more frightening, but if he was disguising his voice along with his face, then he could only be disguising it from you or the lad.'

'Why not from you?' said Tom. 'Could he not have been someone *you* knew?'

'I had never been to England before,' said Caliban. 'And it was years since Henry was here. It didn't seem likely.'

'But how did you find Thornley?' asked Dr Harker.

'Well,' said Caliban, 'I remembered that you told Henry that you lived in Fleet Street – on the night you met us on the Hampstead Road. It didn't take much to find you. I watched the house and noted the comings and goings. I watched and waited for some clue as to who Henry's killer might be.'

'And what did you learn from all your watching and waiting?' said Dr Harker.

'Not much at first,' replied Caliban. 'Everybody seemed to be acting so suspiciously. At first I thought it might be Mr Greaves there—'

'You weren't the only one, by all accounts,' said Greaves.

Tom felt himself blush and Dr Harker coughed nervously. 'And what made you decide it was Thornley?'

'Well, Greaves here and Thornley have similar builds, but it was something I heard Thornley say, even though he had disguised his voice that night—'

'*Splendid!*' said Tom.

Caliban smiled. '*Splendid, splendid,*' he said. 'It was something about the way he said it – I had heard him before when I was watching the house. Then I was sure. Well, almost sure . . .

'I followed Thornley to this lair,' he went on. 'But once here I could not do it. When it came to the doing of it, it took a strength I don't have to pull that trigger.'

'Maybe you ain't the killing kind,' said Ocean. 'No shame in that.'

'No,' added Dr Harker. 'No shame at all.'

'I was just leaving,' Caliban told them, 'when I heard Tom on the stairs. I was sure that if Thornley felt that Tom had uncovered his true nature then he would kill him and I had no wish to see another fellow die at his hands. I tried to warn Tom but it was too late.'

'I thank you for it,' said Tom.

'I thank you too,' added Greaves. 'I almost wish I hadn't sent for Under-marshal Hitchin.'

'The under-marshal?' hissed Caliban. 'You sent for the thief-taker?'

'Calm yourself,' said Greaves. 'He knows nothing about you.'

'He will find a black man with no master,' said Caliban. 'He can do what he likes!'

'I'm sorry. I sent word before I came here. I was sure it was Thornley we were dealing with. I thought we might need some help. He should be here any moment.'

Tom looked at Ocean and then at Dr Harker and he could see the same expression he knew he wore himself. Greaves had done nothing wrong in sending for Hitchin exactly. But the idea of giving anybody up into the charge of that odious man was hard to stomach. Suddenly there was a noise of men coming into the house.

'That'll be Hitchin,' said Greaves and went out onto the landing, with Dr Harker and Tom close behind.

Tom could see the top of Hitchin's hat as he climbed the stairs. The under-marshal grinned as he came up the last flight. 'Dr Harker,' he said. 'Master Marlowe. Mr Carter. We meet again. I'm glad to see that Mr Greaves has a little more sense of duty than—'

There was the sound of a scuffle from the room where they'd left Ocean and Caliban and then a crash. When they went in, Ocean was trying to get to his feet, but slipped back to the floor, holding a hand to his head, blood seeping out between the fingers.

'Ocean!' called Tom, running to help him.

Two of Hitchin's men ran to the window through which Thornley and now Caliban had jumped and looked down at the rippling surface of the river. 'He's gone, Mr Hitchin, sir. Good and gone.'

Hitchin thumped at the doorframe in fury, dislodging a sizeable piece of plasterwork from the wall. He stood there for a moment staring intently at the broken window, then his dead-eyed stare moved on to Dr Harker and Tom, who were helping Ocean to sit up, before he turned and led his motley guard out of the building.

The LAMB and LION

One day in May, Ocean arrived at Newgate with a delivery for the Reverend Purney to find the jail in uproar. There had been a mass breakout of Jacobite prisoners, and though many had been recaptured almost immediately, twelve had escaped, McGregor among them. The reverend loudly regaled The Quill with the story, telling how one particular Scottish giant had knocked him to the floor and would have killed him there and then – had the Almighty not interfered in the shape of a turnkey

155

with an iron bar.

Tom reflected on the news as he looked around the churchyard at St Bride's once again. Bluebells were growing at the base of Will's headstone. There was thunder in the air. It was growing darker, but the green of the grass and of the leaves on the trees was becoming more and more intense. The air was still and heavy and the atmosphere was dreamlike.

The cherub on Will's headstone smiled its crooked smile and Tom heard footsteps approaching behind him. It was his father.

'Tom,' said Greaves. 'I'm not disturbing you, I hope?'

'No,' Tom replied. 'I was just leaving. Goodbye, Will.'

'Dr Harker said I'd find you here,' said his father. 'Will was a friend of yours, I gather.'

'He was,' said Tom as they walked towards the gate. 'Look, I need to say I'm sorry.'

'Sorry? What can you have to be sorry for?'

'Sorry that I thought ill of you.'

Greaves grinned. 'You thought me a rogue, Tom. And who can blame you, for rogue I have certainly been, most of my life.'

'But you really have changed,' said Tom.

'I hope I have,' said Greaves. 'I needed to. And I could do with changing a little more. I have a temper I'm not proud of. But you have a temper yourself, I notice.'

Tom smiled sheepishly.

'The true rogue in all this was that snake, Thornley,' Greaves went on. 'I've met some fearsome men in my time, Tom, but . . .' He shook his head, half in wonder and half in disbelief.

'Yes,' agreed Tom.

'See here, Tom, the plain truth is that I am a very wealthy man,' said Greaves. 'Bellingham left me land when he died. I sold it for a hefty profit and bought a ship. Now I own three. Fortune shined on me and the thing that would finish it off is if you would join me, Tom.'

'I don't know,' said Tom.

'Come on,' said Greaves. 'Come to America with me, Tom. Come and make my business Greaves and Son. Let me try and make amends for all those years I deserted you. I know I can't make it all right, but I can try.'

'I have a life here,' said Tom. 'People here who depend on me.'

'Well, Dr Harker's a fine man. But he ain't your kin, boy. He has a son of his own, I've heard.'

'He does,' said Tom. 'But he relies on me, I know he does. And then there's my fath—' He blushed.

'Mr Marlowe can handle his own affairs,' said Greaves. 'Don't get me wrong, Tom. Old Marlowe has done a fine job with you – a better job than I would have done – but he don't need you like

I do. That Carter fellow seems able enough.'

'I just don't know if I could leave,' said Tom.

'Leave what? Leave this dunghill? Why not, lad? I'm offering you a chance to get away, and don't tell me that you haven't dreamed about it, because I can see it in your eyes whenever foreign lands are talked of. And I ain't suggesting transportation, lad. You can come back, you know.'

Tom smiled. 'I know. It's just . . .'

'Look,' said Greaves. 'It's a big step. A mighty leap. I know that. You hardly know me and what you do know ain't especially flattering. But if you come with me, Tom, I'll show you a different Greaves. And I'll show you the world too. Do you want to spend the rest of your days listening to tales of Dr Harker's adventures or do you want to have some of your own?'

'I'm sorry,' said Tom. 'I still need some time to think things through.'

'I'm sorry too,' said Greaves. 'Time's the one thing I can't give you, Tom. I've stayed in London far too long as it is. I take the coach to Bristol tonight. If the coach don't shed a wheel – or get interrupted by highwaymen – I should be there in a couple of days' time. My ship is waiting and the crew restless to sail. We're bound for Africa for our trade, and then America. Hear them names, Tom: Africa. America. Take the coach with me, and they won't be the stuff of dreams no more. Will you come, Tom? Will you, lad?'

Tom looked up at the sign of the Lamb and Lion as if he had never seen it before in his life. The strange face of the lion, so unlike the real lions he had seen at the Menagerie, seemed full of sadness as it looked down at him. That face, with its huge, limpid, human eyes, had frightened him as a child. The lamb resting in its paws seemed so small and vulnerable. It had never been clear to Tom whether the lion was guarding it or about to eat it. A flash of lightning lit up the sky as he and Dr Harker approached the printing house.

Dr Harker seemed to sense the conflicting emotions swimming around in Tom's mind and gently put his hand on Tom's shoulder.

'You have made the right decision, Tom,' he said.

'I know,' said Tom. 'I know it.' There was a distant rumble of thunder.

Dr Harker took two steps forward, turned the brass handle of the shop door and opened it with a smile. After a moment's hesitation, Tom entered. Ocean appeared in the doorway leading to the printing house, ink smeared across his forehead like a bruise.

'Tom,' he said with a smile. 'Dr Harker. Good to see you both.'

'And you, Ocean,' said Tom. 'Is he in?'

'Out the back, sorting out the yard. Keeping

himself busy, more like. Go on. He'll want to see you.'

Tom left Ocean and the doctor and walked through the printing house to the doorway through to the cobbled yard beyond. He stood and watched his uncle stacking empty barrels and smiled, remembering that he always did this at times of crisis. Then all of a sudden, Mr Marlowe saw Tom standing there and froze. He put down the barrel he was carrying.

'So,' he said. 'How are you, lad?'

'I'm well,' Tom replied. 'Though a little ashamed of myself for the way I spoke to you.'

'It's forgotten, Tom,' said Mr Marlowe. 'You had cause enough. I've wronged you. I know that.' Lightning flashed again and there was a loud burst of thunder above them.

'It's forgotten,' said Tom.

Mr Marlowe smiled. 'Greaves has asked you to go with him, I gather.'

'Yes,' said Tom. 'He has.'

'So. You have the chance to travel at last, like you've always wanted.'

'Yes.'

'And what of Dr Harker?' asked Mr Marlowe, picking up the barrel again.

'I have told him that I need to be with my *real* father,' said Tom.

'Fair enough,' said Mr Marlowe with a sigh. 'You can't—'

160

'And I told Mr Greaves the same thing,' said Tom.

For a moment Mr Marlowe did not seem to understand what Tom was saying, and he stood there with a puzzled expression on his face, until finally the meaning of Tom's words sank in and a look of uncontained joy flashed across his face like the sun bursting out from behind a dark cloud.

'Tom,' he said, tears welling in his eyes. 'I . . . I . . . don't know what to say.'

'I know, Father,' said Tom. 'I know.' And the two of them hugged as though Tom really had gone away to the Americas and had come back after many years.

'But you must not call me Father, Tom,' said Mr Marlowe, wiping the tears from his eyes. 'I reckon Greaves has earned the right to own that title. And I'm as proud to be your uncle.'

Tom nodded. Rain began to beat steadily against the window panes.

'But what about your travels?' asked Mr Marlowe eventually. 'What about America?'

'America can wait,' said Tom.

Another BODY IN
THE THAMES

When a body was washed up on the banks of
the Thames, Tom and Dr Harker once again
made a visit to Surgeons' Hall. Dr Cornelius told
them that the body had been in the water some time;
too long to identify it. But Dr Harker insisted that he
must see it for himself. Tom waited in the hallway and
he had never seen his friend look so grim as when he
emerged.

'The clothes are certainly Daniel's,' said Dr Harker.
He swallowed deeply. 'Much else it is impossible to say.'

Dr Cornelius reached into his pocket and pulled out a watch. He handed it to Dr Harker. 'They found this, Josiah,' he said. 'He was found by an honest man who handed it to the constable – who rather unusually was also honest. Do you recognize it?'

Dr Harker nodded. 'Yes. That is Daniel's watch. His father gave it to him when he left for university. I remember him receiving it. Despite everything I still feel sad.'

'You feel sad for the boy you knew,' said Tom.

Dr Harker smiled. 'Yes, Tom. And maybe for the boy I was.'

Dr Cornelius recognized that sentiment and shook Dr Harker's hand. 'If I can be of any more help, Josiah,' he said, 'you know where I am. I still owe you a thrashing at chess. Goodbye, Tom.'

'Goodbye, Dr Cornelius,' said Tom.

Tom and Dr Harker walked slowly back towards Fleet Street, taking the back lanes and alleyways to avoid the crush of shoppers and hawkers. In an otherwise deserted courtyard two red kites were squabbling over the remains of a discarded pie and took to the air in panic as the pair approached.

'You've made Mr Marlowe a very happy man,' said Dr Harker.

'And Mr Greaves a miserable one,' added Tom.

'Worse things have happened to him,' said Dr Harker. 'He seems to have a flair for falling on his feet.' Tom tried to force a smile. 'Mr Greaves is a slaver, isn't he, Tom?'

Tom stopped and stared at him. 'Yes, he is,' he replied. 'But how did you——?'

'It was a guess,' said Dr Harker. 'He promised to show you Africa and America and he seemed to know something of that business.'

'Yes,' explained Tom sadly. 'At first he spoke only of trade and cargo and I was on the verge of taking him up on his offer. Then, that day when he met me at Will's graveside, he finally told me what his "cargo" was. Then I just couldn't go. I couldn't do it. I don't know why.'

'Because you are a good man, Tom,' said Dr Harker. Tom had never been called a man before and he blushed a little. 'I'm proud to know you. May I shake your hand?'

'Of course, sir,' said Tom. 'Gladly.'

The two friends shook hands and then resumed their walk. Suddenly, they heard a familiar voice behind them:

'Gentlemen! What a pleasant coincidence.'

'Daniel Thornley!' said Dr Harker, grabbing the hilt of his sword. 'But . . . But how? I saw you dead . . . I saw your body!'

'Apparently not,' said Thornley with a grin. 'Come now, it was a simple enough matter to disguise that corpse. I was sad to lose my watch, but it was worth it. I would thank you to keep that sword sheathed, Josiah. I would hate to have to shoot you. But that won't stop me from doing so.'

'Your argument is with me, Daniel,' said Dr Harker. 'Let Tom go.'

'No!' Tom shouted. 'I'll not leave you, sir.'

Thornley laughed. 'Such loyalty you inspire, Josiah,' he said. 'It is as well that I am not sentimental.' The smile disappeared. 'I'm afraid I need more money, Josiah. All of it.'

'I thought your debts were paid.'

'Some, yes,' said Thornley. 'But a man like me runs up many debts, and not all of them can be paid so easily, and not all with money. I have a sudden desire to travel, Josiah, and there are those who want me to stay.'

'And not through friendship, I dare say,' said Dr Harker.

Thornley laughed again. 'Do you know, Josiah, I think you were the very last friend I ever had.'

'And how do you expect me to find money for you at this hour?'

'I am afraid that is *your* problem,' said Thornley, smiling. 'But I dare say that if I put a pistol to this lad's head, it is a problem you will quickly solve.' Thornley's attention was suddenly distracted by a drunk, who came tottering down the steps behind him and slumped in a doorway holding a keg of gin.

He turned back to Tom and Dr Harker, to find the doctor reaching for his sword again.

'Ah-ah-ah, Josiah,' he said, wagging his finger as if talking to a child. 'I'll take that.' He took Dr Harker's sword and threw it over the wall behind them. 'Don't play with me, Josiah, or you will see this lad killed and neither of us wants that.'

'I don't think you care who you kill!' said Dr Harker. 'What a monster you have become!'

The drunk groaned and muttered to himself.

'A monster? Listen to that,' said Thornley. 'I risk my life every day for the likes of that! For scum like that! I ask you, Josiah – is that right?'

Dr Harker did not reply. The drunk began to sing tunelessly to himself.

'I never intended to take money from you, Josiah, but as you know, I had run up debts with men who want them paid, and promptly. Had I found the jewel these Jacobite rogues were carrying, all this would have been avoided. I caught one of the rascals, but try as I might I could not persuade him to tell me where the item was. But I believe you met the man in question. After your visit to the opera.'

Tom realized that Thornley was talking about the Jacobite who was pulled out of the Thames. Thornley had killed him.

'McGregor was arrested before I could get to him and then the idiots at Newgate let him walk out. No doubt he is on the Continent with his friend James Stuart and I am left here with a problem. I am a marked man. These Scots take these things personally, as you know, Josiah. I have already had two attempts on my life. In short, I need to find employment in some foreign land, where my enterprising spirit will be appreciated. Russia perhaps. Those Muscovites appreciate a man with my abilities.'

'You have no sense of loyalty to your friends or to your country!' shouted Dr Harker. Thornley hit him round the side of the head with the pistol and he dropped to the floor.

'Dr Harker!' shouted Tom, coming to his aid. The doctor groaned and held his head.

'Get me the money that I need, Josiah, and I will go. Refuse and I will kill you and the boy.'

While Thornley had been talking, the drunk had risen to his feet and was shuffling towards him. 'Go away,' said Thornley without looking round, but with one deft movement, the drunk had a knife at Thornley's throat.

19

A Lock of Hair

'**D**rop the gun!' he hissed. Thornley hesitated for a second. The knife blade was pushed a little harder into his throat. The gun clattered to the cobbles. The man reached inside Thornley's collar and took out a knife, hurling it away down the alley. 'Turn round and face me.' Thornley turned and his attacker now placed the point of his knife at his chest.

'James McGregor,' said Thornley, smiling once more. 'I should have known. Those idiots in Newgate couldn't keep a dead cat caged for more than an hour.

Why they don't just shoot you people on sight, I will never know.'

'Be still!' said McGregor. 'With your left hand, and using your thumb and little finger, I want you to take out the knife you keep in your sleeve and then the one in your waistband.' Thornley smiled and did as he was asked.

'You killed Malcolm, you coward,' McGregor went on. 'He was scarcely older than the lad standing there. Killed him because he would not tell you about the treasure you sought to steal. What kind of man are you? You believe in nothing. You are hollow.'

'And what kind of man are you?' shouted Thornley. 'Maintaining friendship with the man who let your sister die in the street!'

McGregor threw Thornley's knives across the alley. 'I would rather Mary died knowing the few happy years she had with Josiah, than think of her with an animal like you.' He ripped a button off his coat and thrust it towards Thornley. 'Well, man? There it is, take it!'

Thornley laughed a dry laugh. 'What foolery is this? Kill me and be done with it.'

'Take it!' shouted McGregor, and Thornley picked up the button. 'You'll find the back will come away, if you prise with your fingers.'

Suddenly Thornley looked interested. He turned the button over and hurriedly fiddled with it until, sure enough, the back of the button flipped open like a locket. Thornley grinned and grabbed at the contents.

'But what is this?' he said suddenly. 'Is this some sort of joke? Does this pass for wit in the highlands?' He studied the contents of the button with an expression somewhere between bafflement and fury.

'It is no joke,' said McGregor. 'That is the treasure you have killed for. And treasure it is, too, and priceless. It is a lock of hair from a queen. The one you call Mary Queen of Scots.'

There was a look of utter disbelief on Thornley's face that lasted several seconds, before he raised his eyes to the night sky and began to laugh. It was a wild and humourless laughter and it ended only when McGregor leaned forward and shouted in his face.

'I'll tell you why Mary did not choose you, Daniel.' McGregor used Thornley's Christian name for the first time.

Thornley composed himself and his face became an expressionless mask. 'And why is that?' he asked.

'Because she was frightened of you! Aye, frightened of you! She saw you for the devil you are!'

Thornley suddenly lunged forward, yelling 'No!' at the top of his voice, grabbing McGregor's arm and forcing it up in the air, so that the knife now pointed to the sky, clamping his other hand round McGregor's throat. The force of the attack took the two men clear across the alley and McGregor slammed into the wall at the other side.

Thornley banged McGregor's hand repeatedly against the wall until he was forced to drop the knife. With his free hand, McGregor punched Thornley in the ribs and Thornley let go of his throat long enough for him to make a lunge for the knife.

As McGregor leaned forward to retrieve the knife, Thornley kicked him hard in the face and he collapsed semi-conscious on the cobbles. Thornley adjusted his coat and dusted himself down. McGregor tried to raise himself from the ground, but as he did so, Thornley kicked him again and McGregor rolled over onto his back.

'Stop!' shouted Tom.

Thornley looked round. Tom had picked up the pistol and was holding it in both hands, pointing it at Thornley, who smiled and kicked McGregor once more.

'Stop!' shouted Tom again. 'I will shoot! I will!'

Thornley turned to face him again and smiled at him as one might have smiled at a bothersome child. 'You will find that there is a lot more to pulling a trigger than moving your finger,' he said. 'You're a clever lad, Tom, but have you got the steel to look in my face and send me to the grave?'

Tom took aim again, but the pistol had begun to

feel heavy in his hands and he found it a struggle to stop them from shaking.

'Well, have you, Tom?' Thornley had begun to walk towards him, knife in hand. 'But maybe you're worried that you'll miss? Have you ever fired a pistol before, Tom? I don't suppose you have. And you've only one shot, of course. You don't want to waste it, do you? I'll make it easy for you. I'll come a little closer – how about that? Splendid, splen—'

McGregor leaped on Thornley from behind and knocked him to the ground. The two men rolled over and over across the cobbles, first one way and then the other, with neither appearing to gain the upper hand, until suddenly they came to a halt and for a moment lay motionless on the ground.

Then Thornley slowly got to his feet. Tom looked at McGregor and saw his white shirt dark and wet with blood. McGregor looked at the blood and put his hand to his stomach, searching for the wound. Thornley looked down at him and grinned; then he pulled a knife from his own chest and dropped lifeless to the ground.

'Put the pistol down, Tom,' said Dr Harker gently. He had finally come round and was sitting up. Tom stood in a kind of trance. 'Tom,' repeated the doctor. 'Put the pistol down.'

Tom watched McGregor get to his feet and walk over to look at Thornley's body, and came to his senses. He looked at the pistol in his hands and then at Dr Harker getting unsteadily to his feet. He let his hands drop and his friend put a hand on his shoulder.

They walked over to Thornley's body. McGregor was searching through his pockets.

'Here, Josiah,' he said, handing him the locket with the portrait of Mary. 'Keep better care of it this time.'

Dr Harker smiled fleetingly, but then stared down grimly at the body of Daniel Thornley. 'I cannot help feeling in some way responsible . . .' he began.

'No, Josiah,' said McGregor. 'You have nothing to reproach yourself with. Daniel Thornley was evil. Maybe he always was but we were children and could not see it. In any event, the man you loved died long ago.' Dr Harker nodded. 'We must away, Josiah,' urged McGregor. 'We cannot be found with his body.'

'I cannot just leave him here,' said Dr Harker. 'Like a dog in the gutter.'

'You will be hanged, Josiah, if you are connected with his death.'

'And what of you, Jamie?' said Dr Harker. 'How will you get to the Continent? I can get you some money if you give me a couple of days.'

'Thank you, no, Josiah,' said McGregor. 'France has had its fill of us, I think. No, I'm going home.'

'But what of James Stuart and your comrades in exile?'

'James Stuart!' McGregor closed his eyes as if in

pain. 'Och, he was in Scotland for forty-five days, Josiah! Forty-five days! He'll not come back. Brave men were willing to lay down their lives for him – *did* lay down their lives and *will* lay down their lives – but I'll not fight for him again. I would give my life gladly for my country, but I will not waste it. There'll be another time. Scotland is not done yet. Besides, my father has been ill and my mother needs me.'

'I'm sorry to hear that, Jamie,' said Dr Harker. 'I always liked your father. Though he never had much time for me, I seem to remember.'

'He liked you well enough, Josiah,' said McGregor with a smile. 'He was just too stubborn to show it. Stubbornness is a McGregor trait, as you may know.'

Dr Harker smiled and nodded. 'Goodbye, James,' he said, holding out his hand.

McGregor shook it and nodded to Tom. He turned and started to walk away. Something fluttered along the ground and came to rest on Tom's shoe. He bent down and picked it up. It was the lock of hair that Jamie McGregor had carried in his button. Tom ran after him, and he turned at the sound of the approaching footsteps. Tom held out the lock of hair and McGregor took it, squeezing it in his fist as if trying to gain strength from it. He managed to say a whispered thank you before turning and walking away once more.

'He still has to make it to Scotland,' said Tom as he walked back to Dr Harker.

'I think he will manage,' said the doctor. 'Now, Tom, I want you to fetch Dr Cornelius. Whatever Jamie says, I cannot leave Daniel here like this. We are not far from Jonathan's house. Do you remember the way?'

'Yes, sir,' said Tom. 'But what about you?'

'I'll be fine, Tom,' said Dr Harker. 'I will hide the body behind those steps and wait for you to return. Quickly now.'

Twenty minutes later, Dr Cornelius arrived driving a small cart, with Tom sitting next to him. They lifted Thornley's body into it and covered it with blankets.

'I cannot thank you enough,' said Dr Harker.

'Nonsense,' said Dr Cornelius. 'I shall take the body to Surgeons' Hall, Josiah. I suggest you and Tom get home before anything else happens. I will speak to you tomorrow.' He flicked the reins and the cart trundled off.

Dr Harker clapped Tom on the back. 'Come, Tom,' he said. 'We'd best be off as Dr Cornelius says.'

'Do you think that lock of hair really is from the head of Mary Queen of Scots, sir?' said Tom as they started to walk towards Fleet Street.

'Well, Tom,' said Dr Harker. 'When the Queen of Scots was executed, the axeman held up her head, just as we saw at Tower Hill, only to discover the hair that covered it was a wig. So' – he smiled – 'it may be a lock of the wig of Mary Queen of Scots.'

Tom shook his head at the idea that men might have died for the false hair of a long-dead queen.

'But you see, it does not matter, Tom,' said Dr Harker, 'Whether it was the hair from her head, the hair from her wig or the hair from a wolfhound. It is what men believe it to be that matters.'

20

Here lies the Body of

The Tempest

'Well, Will,' said Tom with a sigh, as he visited his friend's grave again. 'Here I am, a Londoner still. Maybe my father's offer of travel will be the last I get and I'll stay here all my days.' He sighed at the thought and looked across the graveyard to the rooftops and spires of the City, with the dome of St Paul's rising above them. 'Still,' he said, turning back to the carved cherub on Will's headstone, 'there are adventures enough to be had in this town, it seems.

'You're about the only one I can talk to about the things that have happened over the last weeks, Will,' said Tom. 'Dr Harker has forbidden me and Ocean to talk about it, for fear of what might happen to us all if anyone found out. It's as though it never happened, Will. But it did.

'Jamie McGregor managed to get back to his family, though not without difficulties. He worked his passage on a Newcastle-bound collier. In Newcastle he was about to board a ship to Edinburgh when he saw government men on the quayside and was forced to travel overland as best he could, sleeping out on the moors and sheltering in barns and outhouses.

'He must have told his parents about how Dr Harker had risked his own life trying to help him, because a few days ago the doctor received a letter from them saying they were sorry for the way they'd treated him and wished for a happier time in which the doctor "and his young assistant" might visit them in Scotland.' Tom smiled. 'I know it's not America, but it's better than nothing!' He chuckled to himself.

'And as for Thornley,' Tom went on. 'The day after he was killed, me and Dr Harker went to Surgeons' Hall. Dr Harker wanted to give him a decent burial but Dr Cornelius said it was too dangerous; that if someone found out whose body it was we would all be done for.

'Dr Harker agreed and Dr Cornelius said he

should leave it to him. He would deal with the body.' Tom shuddered and screwed up his face. 'It's best not to think of how old Cornelius will "deal" with the body, eh, Will?' And Tom tried, unsuccessfully, to put the subject out of his head. 'Still,' he added, 'it's no more than Thornley deserves, if you ask me.'

Dr Cornelius's caution was well founded. The public mood towards the Jacobites was still one of paranoia and hostility, and a few days later more Jacobites met their ends in London, drawn through the streets on hurdles. They were dragged behind horses, all along the cobbled streets, to Tyburn's Triple Tree, there to meet the most terrible of all deaths: the traitor's death. Crowds jeered from balconies and windows and spat and cheered from pavements while children laughed and frolicked behind the soldiers as if it were a parade. At Tyburn the men were hanged and taken down while still breathing to be hacked about and butchered with less mercy than the pigs at Smithfield to chants of 'God Save the King!'

That same night Tom and Dr Harker were at the theatre again, this time with Ocean for company. It had been Dr Harker's idea that they should go and see a performance of *The Tempest*, Shakespeare's story of the wizard Prospero and his daughter Miranda, of his spirit servant Ariel and his monstrous servant Caliban.

Tom was captivated by the magic of the play,

though he found it hard to keep up with what was going on. Ocean nodded off very near the start and began to snore, despite frequent nudges from Dr Harker. The actor playing the character Caliban wore a costume covered in scales and feathers and rags. He shambled about the stage and could not have seemed more different to the quick-witted other Caliban. Even so, Tom found himself sympathizing with this monster, who now found himself ruled over by Prospero in a land that had once been his by right.

When Prospero's daughter said, 'O wonder! How many goodly creatures are there here! How beauteous mankind is! O brave new world/ That has such people in't!' she was talking about the men who were shipwrecked on the island during the tempest, but Tom found himself thinking of all the people who had made the things he and Dr Harker were cataloguing. He found himself thinking of the events of the last weeks. He thought about Jamie McGregor and he thought about Thornley. He thought about his father, Nathaniel Greaves, and the grim cargo he carried. And he thought about Caliban the African, as Prospero was addressing the audience for the last time:

'And my ending is despair,
Unless I be relieved by prayer;

180

Which pierces so, that it assaults
Mercy itself, and frees all faults.
As you from crimes would pardoned be,
Let your indulgence set me free.'

Later that evening, the three friends stood outside the front door of Dr Harker's house. It was still warm and the sky looked like blue satin. Bats were hunting moths, swooping around the lantern over the door. No one seemed to want to instigate the parting. Ocean broke the spell finally by bidding Tom and the doctor good night and turning to leave.

As he did so, the sound of hooves grew like a clap of thunder, and into the courtyard came a horse and rider. Ocean reached for his pistol but Dr Harker grabbed his arm. The rider pulled his horse to a skidding halt on the cobbles and lifted his head. Tom looked on in horror. It was the White Rider!

The highwayman pulled on the reins and the horse reared up on its back legs and then clomped down again onto the cobbles. The White Rider lifted his hat and, holding it to his chest, made a slow bow to them, then he replaced his hat, turned and cantered out into the street and away.

'What's going on?' said Tom. 'How can that be? Thornley's dead. We saw him killed.'

'Are you sure, Tom?' asked Ocean. 'It wasn't

another trick? These people are slippery as eels.'

'No,' said Dr Harker. 'I have been so stupid, Tom. Thornley *is* dead. There is no doubt about that. Do you not see what this means?' He turned to face Tom and Ocean. 'It's obvious! There were *two* White Riders!'

'Two?' exclaimed Tom. 'But how?'

'Thornley only *pretended* to be the White Rider to steal from me. He could hardly have been expected to do all those other robberies. That was the real White Rider.'

'But then who the devil's the real one?' asked Ocean.

'Caliban!'

'Caliban?' said Tom and Ocean simultaneously.

'Do you not see?' said Dr Harker. 'Daniel Thornley's plan to dress as the White Rider and rob us would have worked perfectly had he not chanced upon the *real* White Rider that night. Henry Drayton and Caliban were a team, just as Caliban said, although I think that it was Caliban, rather than Drayton, who was the brains in the company.

'Drayton played the part of the victim in the robberies. They worked the kid lay, just as Caliban told us. They fooled the travellers in the stagecoaches into believing that the highwayman had supernatural powers. Drayton fired a blank charge at Caliban. Caliban pointed his finger, and while Drayton's back was turned to his audience he set off a flash, making it seem as if he had been hit by some invisible force. He then dropped the charge and fell, apparently life-less, to the ground. The terrified passengers would now be very co-operative. Once robbed, the coach drove off and Drayton could come back to life ready for their next adventure. It really is delightfully conceived.'

'Drayton had the charge in his pocket,' said Tom. 'That's why there was the explosion when Thornley shot him.'

'Yes,' said Dr Harker. 'That must have come as rather a shock to Daniel.'

'But can you really be sure of this, sir?' asked Ocean.

'Not of everything, of course,' said Dr Harker. 'But I am reasonably confident of my conclusions.'

'Well I'll be . . .' Ocean shook his head, turned away and chuckled to himself.

Dr Harker suddenly clapped his hands together. 'Of course!' he exclaimed. 'How stupid of me.'

'What is it, sir?' said Tom.

'"As you from crimes would pardoned be, Let your indulgence set me free," ' said Dr Harker.

'Dr Harker?'

'You let him go, didn't you?' said the doctor, turning to Ocean.

'Let him go? Let who go? What do you mean?'

'Caliban. I would have thought it plain enough,' said Dr Harker, laughing.

'Maybe you missed that bump on my head, Doctor,' said Ocean. 'But it was there sure enough.'

'I think you told him to hit you, Ocean,' said Dr Harker. 'After you'd untied him, of course. He hit you hard enough to leave a bruise but not to do you harm. You feigned the rest.'

'And why would I do a thing like that?' asked Ocean. 'Aiding a man like that. Why, that's a hanging offence in itself. Why would I do that for a slave? For a man I never met?'

'Because you did not want to see him hang,' said Dr Harker slowly. 'I know that sentiment myself, remember. You did not know he was the White Rider then, but you still had good reason to believe that as a black slave convicted of thievery, hanging would be his fate. For what it's worth, Ocean, I would not have seen him hang myself, White Rider or not.'

'Nor I,' added Tom.

'So we need speak no more about it, then, as we are all agreed that he was a man worth the saving,' said Dr Harker. 'Ocean's intervention will be our little secret.'

'Agreed,' said Tom.

'You certainly have an colourful imagination, Doctor,' said Ocean. 'It would make a good ending

184